Praise for Once *Upon a Time in Hell's Kitchen*

"Colin Broderick again sucks us into a world that doesn't let go."

Josh Brolin, author of
From Under The Truck & *Dune: Exposures*

Praise for Colin Broderick's Work

"Broderick writes with clarity and heart."
T.J. English, author of *The Westies*

"Colin Broderick has that magic touch that allows him to mix comedy and tragedy in just the right proportions."
Billy Collins

"Colin Broderick is in the front rank of Irish storytellers."
Malachy McCourt

"I have great admiration for the style and the tenacity and the sheer swerve of Colin Broderick's work."
Colum McCann

ONCE UPON A TIME IN
HELL'S
KITCHEN

COLIN BRODERICK

Author Photo courtesy of Patrick Glennon
Production by JW Manus

This book is dedicated to
the four people who matter more to me
than anything in the world:
Rachel, Erica, Samuel, and Bruce.

Part 1

1

Danny rubbed the scuffed knuckles of his fist and peered out the kitchen window down onto Tenth Avenue below. He watched Enzo Mazzella lean to unlock the steel shutter of the fruit stand across the way and send it rolling up into its rusty sock with a loud rattle. A flock of pigeons scattered, throwing winged shadows up over the tenement façade.

It was officially morning in Hell's Kitchen.

"Ya hurt your hand?" his mother said. He hadn't heard her enter the small galley kitchen behind him.

"It's nuttin', Ma."

"Think I can't see?"

Danny sipped his coffee and kept his back to her. He'd hear about the cut over his right eye later that night at dinner. She hated him fighting. But what could he do?

She shifted her weight on her cane and lifted the rosary beads hung from the nail next to the framed picture of a thatched cottage in the Irish countryside. That cottage and those rosary beads had been hanging there since as far back as Danny could remember. Almost thirty years in this damned apartment. He should've had

3

her out of here by now. He'd told her he would. Promised her. But it's not as easy getting out of The Kitchen as it is getting in.

"Come down to Mass with me," she said, without looking at him. His mother didn't live in Hell's Kitchen. Far as she was concerned, she lived in the parish of The Church of the Sacred Heart of Jesus. She'd been a part of this parish since she'd moved here from Donegal over fifty years ago.

"I can't. I gotta feed the birds."

"Birds can't wait forty-five minutes?"

"I gotta go to work, Ma. I gotta feed the birds then I gotta go to work."

"You're in such a big hurry, whaddya doin' moping by the window?"

"I ain't mopin' . . ." He stopped. She had a way of getting into him like nobody else. She could shank him with a few simple words. "You say a prayer for me while you're there."

"Blue in the face prayin' for you to grow some sense. Damn pigeons flew off with what little was left of that brain of yours, far as I can tell. Try to remember to lock this door when you leave."

She blessed herself out of the holy water font and pulled the apartment door behind her.

He'd started to bark back about locking the door, but he bit his tongue. Lock the door! What would they take? Who'd want it? A thirty-year-old couch. Couple of chairs you wouldn't waste the time to lift out of a dumpster. A small enamel-topped kitchen table. You could leave the damned door open, and the address stapled to a tree on the corner of Forty-second and Broadway and you still couldn't find somebody to take this trash away. Most valuable thing she had in this apartment was that damned picture of Ireland and her holy water font.

Lock the door, my ass.

*   *   *

Danny finished his coffee and rinsed the cup. The cool water felt good on his knuckles. It had been a tough fight. That kid didn't want to go down. He tried to put him away without hurting him too much. He really did. But the kid just wouldn't stay on the damned floor. He got tired holding him off. So, he did what he had to do. Dumb kid. Why'd he have to get back up?

Then he'd been awake half the night with a pain in his chest. What the hell was that? Couldn't be his heart. Couldn't be. He was too young. He held his hand to his chest. How would you know it's your heart? He'd heard it said you could tell. But he couldn't tell shit. His heart felt heavy this morning. Like it was cramped in there. But it had to be. Right! He'd been worked up. That kid had really come for him. Of course, his heart was beating heavily this morning. The crowd loved it. The blood. The broken teeth on the floor. That's what they'd come for, Logan and the crew. Well, they got it. And plenty of it. And he got the purse. Two hundred bucks. It wasn't going to get him out of the hole, but it was something. It would make a dent in the back rent, the food bill for the birds over at Morty's, and Ma's blood medication. Wha'd he care if the kid got hurt? He didn't drag him into the ring. Dumb fucking kid.

Danny locked the door and made his way up the last flight of stairs to the roof. Soon as he stepped out onto the roof he felt better. His head cleared. He could hear his birds calling out to him before he reached the coop. They were the only thing he knew could fix him like that. He unlatched the door and stepped inside.

"Let's go, sleepy heads." The birds rose about him in a great symphony of flapping wings, coos, and excited chatter. He held out his hands to feel the tips of their wings brushing past him.

"Yes. I'm happy to see you, too. Come on, everybody up, let's go, let's go." He nudged Dorothy and Rubin, and Rocky, and Charley. He had names for them all. "Come on, let's go, can't lay in bed all day. You know the rules, no food 'til everybody gets out and gets some exercise. You too, Bluey."

He reached to pick up Bluey, but she wriggled away from him. "Whassamatta wit you this morning?" He noticed Henry, standing tall, strutting back and forth, on a nearby ledge. He lifted Bluey gently. Under her sat an egg. "Ah, look at that. You do this, Henry?" Henry rocked his head from side to side. "You're proud of yourself, huh." He set Bluey back on the egg and stroked her softly along her back. "Let me get you a spot sorted all out on your own. You like that? That alright with you, Henry? She can't be in here with all this racket. I'll make you a nice little nest."

"Who you talking to in there?"

Hearing the voice so close behind him, Danny jumped. He spun to see Logan Coyle filling the door of the coop. Terry Flannery wasn't five feet behind him.

"Logan, whaddya doing' up here?"

"Who you talking to in there? You talking to the birds?"

"Yeah. I talk to them some."

"Hey, Terry, you hear that, he's in here talking to the birds."

Terry fished a pack of smokes out of the pocket of his jacket.

"Danny Boy McCoy, bird man of Hell's Kitchen." Logan laughed.

Danny moved away from Bluey. He didn't want her upset. He could tell Logan made her uneasy the way she shifted her body on the egg, as if she could sense the danger nearby.

Logan stepped aside to let Danny out past him.

"Jeez, how the hell you stand the smell in there?"

"It ain't so bad."

6

"Ain't bad! I think maybe you got your nose broke one too many times, Danny. Place smells like a fucken sewer. Whaddya see in these damn things?"

"I like 'em."

"What's to like!"

"I like to see 'em fly."

"So whaddya got 'em cooped up in here for then?"

"They fly. I let 'em out."

"Oh yeah. So, what's the angle?"

"Whaddya mean?"

"I mean what's the hustle? How you make money offa these things?"

"It ain't a hustle. I just like 'em, is all."

"Right."

"It's not a hustle."

"I don't get it."

"I just like 'em. I come up here, I see the birds, I feel better, I guess. It's peaceful."

"Peaceful, huh!"

"Yeah. It's just, ya know, it's nice."

Logan was still standing in the door of the coop staring in. He nodded to Bluey. "What's this one's problem. He sick or some shit?"

"That's Bluey, she's got an egg."

"Bluey? You got names for 'em, huh!"

"Yeah. Hey, Terry . . . I bum one of those?" Danny said, nodding to the pack Terry had pulled from his jacket pocket.

Terry handed him a smoke and lit them both.

"You got names for all these birds?" Logan went on.

"Yeah."

"You telling me you know every single bird by name?"

7

"Yeah."

"How many?

"I got a hundred and eighty-six right now."

"A hundred and eighty-six birds! And you named every single one of them!"

"Sure. You got a name."

"Yeah, I know I got a name, Danny, but that's 'cause I'm not a goddamn pigeon. What you call this one?" Logan said, pointing to a bird perched on the ledge above the door.

"That's Barney."

"Barney." Logan laughed. "And what about this one?" he asked, pointing at the other bird strutting around in the coop.

"That's Henry. Bluey's partner."

"No shit!"

"Hey, Henry, you been banging Bluey in here. Looks like you wore her out."

"She don't like that," Danny said, softly.

"Who don't like what?" Logan snapped. "The pigeon? You telling me the pigeons don't like me bustin' their balls?"

Danny knew he'd said too much. "I mean, she's just nervous is all, she's a nervous bird."

"You hear that, Terry . . . she's a nervous bird." Logan laughed. "Maybe you should get her to a therapist. Jesus Christ. Nervous bird! You're really are a piece of work, Danny."

"That was some fight last night, Danny," Terry said. "You made some mess of that kid's face. Right, Logan. Gave him some beating."

"Yeah. Turned him into mince meat." Logan nodded, stepping away from the coop. "Made a bundle off that dumb spic. Didn't we, Terry?"

Terry didn't respond. That was Terry. Terry had always been

like that, ever since they were kids in the streets. He didn't say much. Always looked like he had something eating away at him. He was worse after he got back from 'Nam. He'd come back with a hair-trigger temper that left everyone in the neighborhood wary of crossing his path. He wasn't home a year 'til they sent him to some nuthouse upstate 'cause he shot some black guy outside of the Shamrock bar over on Seventh Avenue. Three people he'd murdered since he'd got back to The Kitchen. Lawyers said it wasn't Terry's fault. He wasn't right in the head no more. Said he got the nightmares from serving his country. Guy was a goddamned Green Beret, for chrissakes. So they dosed him with some Thorazine and kicked him back out on the street again.

Danny'd heard whispers about how they'd messed up his dick over there in 'Nam. A handful of grunts put him on an operating table one night when he was passed out drunk and tried to circumcise him as a joke. Only they screwed it up and butchered his dick and Terry hadn't been right in the head since. Danny couldn't blame him.

"We gotta get you set up in another fight again soon," Logan said, ducking and diving, jabbing a few mock punches Danny's way.

"Naw, I'm done."

"Whaddya mean you're done?"

"I don't wanna fight no more."

"Yeah, right," Logan said, slapping him on the shoulder. "You ain't done."

"I'm done, Logan."

"That's what you always say. That's alright, you don't have to worry about it right now. You're still sore from last night. Relax. Forget it," Logan said, dismissing Danny. He moved to the edge of the roof, and peered over the parapet, down at the avenue. "You got some view from up here, huh."

"Yeah, I see everything from up here."

"I'm sure you do." Logan sneered. "You peeking into bedroom windows from up here at night, Danny?"

"I didn't peek in nobody's windows."

"Jesus Christ, would you fucken relax, I'm bustin' your balls, for chrissakes. Man, look at that . . . you see Mannion's place from up here. You see this, Terry?"

Terry and Danny joined Logan to peer over the parapet.

Logan turned cold-eyed staring down at Mannion's Tavern sitting on the northwest corner of Forty-fifth and Tenth. Neither Terry or Danny interrupted him. They both knew Logan hated Pat Mannion ever since Mannion had kidnapped his father years earlier.

Logan was just a boy when Mannion's men had grabbed his old man and dragged him to a basement in a local tenement and tied him to a chair. Mannion had slapped him around, pistol whipped him, humiliated him, demanded he get his wife, Logan's mother, to pay a ransom for his release. Logan never got over it. His old man was as straight as they get in The Kitchen. An accountant. Lived by the book. Never hurt nobody. He didn't deserve it. Tied to a chair in a puddle of his own piss. It wasn't the kind of thing a boy was likely to forget. 'Specially a boy like Logan.

Logan Coyle didn't forget shit.

"Just about see your place, too," Danny said, leaning out over the parapet and moving their attention south.

Logan and Terry turned and gazed down Tenth Avenue. Sure enough, you could just about see the front of Logan's place, The Wolf, not two blocks south of Mannion's Tavern on the northeast corner of Forty-third.

"No shit. You see the whole goddamn world from up here, Danny," Logan said, staring back and forth along the stretch of Tenth Avenue between his own place and Mannion's.

Logan was right. Far as Danny was concerned, this damned neighborhood was the world. Hell's Kitchen covered a ten-block radius from the roof where they stood. From Thirty-fourth Street to the south, up to Fifty-seventh to the north. From the west side of Broadway to the piers along the Hudson River.

"I need you to come with us," Logan said to Danny.

"I gotta go to work."

"Well, you're gonna be late."

"I can't . . ."

"What are you gonna do, bust my balls? I ask you to do one thing. You gonna make me beg. I need you for an hour. One hour. Who takes care of you when you need it, huh! What are you into me for now, three fifty?"

"I'll pay you, Logan."

"Pay me! You haven't even kicked up the vig for three weeks, Danny. You hear me bustin' your balls! I ask you what you're gonna do with last night's purse? No. 'Cause we're friends. Right!"

"You're right. I'm sorry, Logan." Logan hadn't actually given him the purse for last night's fight yet. Whatever he had lined up for Danny this morning was going to be figured into whether he'd see any of it at all.

"Tell you what I'm gonna do, 'cause we're friends, I'm gonna forget the vig you owe me. It's gone. Forget it. Not the principle mind you . . . you still owe me the three fifty." Logan emphasized, holding up a finger. "Just the vig. Gone. Okay!"

"Okay. Thanks, Logan."

"We just gotta go do this one thing. It'll take an hour, tops."

"Sure, Logan." What was he gonna do! He was in deep. Three

fifty to Logan. The back rent. The bird feed bill. He'd just taken another buck fifty from Murph the Mule at five points the week before. There was no choice. He had to go with Logan. Logan was holding last night's purse. If he was gonna eat he had to go.

"Let's go," Logan said, heading for the stairs. Terry and Danny followed him.

"Don't you gotta put the birds away?" Terry asked, as they reached the door.

"They don't need me to tell them how to get home," said Danny. "I ain't holdin' 'em here."

"You ain't afraid they'll fly away?" Terry asked, holding the door for him.

"Naw," said Danny. "They don't know how to get out of The Kitchen any more than we do."

2

Terry and Danny stood behind Logan as he knocked on the third-floor apartment door. Danny didn't need to ask whose door it was. He'd been over here enough to know this was Tommy Ryan's place. He'd gone to Sacred Heart with Tommy and his older sister Tina. They weren't the kind of friends went out for drinks or nothing like that, but he knew who he was. Tommy worked as a carpenter, followed his old man into the trade. Unfortunately, he'd also followed him into every gin mill and poker game on the West Side. Tommy Ryan was a lush and a degenerate gambler.

Danny didn't need Logan to paint him a picture about what was up. If Logan was banging Tommy Ryan's door at nine o'clock on a Saturday morning it was 'cause Tommy owed him money.

Everybody in the neighborhood seemed to owe Logan these days.

"Open up, Tommy, I know you're in there," Logan said. "Don't make me have to come back here to see you."

The door opened.

"Sorry, Logan. I was sleeping."

"Sure you were," Logan said, squeezing past him into the apartment.

13

Tommy stood aside to let them in. He was barefoot and bare-chested, wearing a pair of grimy jeans.

"Hey, Terry," Tommy said, as Terry walked in past him. "Hey, Danny. Great fight last night. You damn near fucken killed that kid, huh!"

"Yeah," Danny said, keeping his head down as he passed Tommy in the doorway. He didn't want to appear too friendly. He knew Logan didn't drag him all the way over here to shoot the breeze.

"Jesus Christ, Tommy, it fucken stinks in here. Open a fucken window or something, for chrissakes," Logan said, standing in the middle of the small cluttered living room.

"Yeah, sure, sorry, let me open a window. Listen, Logan—"

"No. Just shut the fuck up," Logan snapped. "Sit down."

Tommy did what he was told. He moved around the littered coffee table and sat on the filthy futon couch with his elbows resting on his knees.

The place was a pigsty. It really did stink. There wasn't a clean surface in the whole place. Danny noticed Tommy's leather tool belt lying in the middle of the coffee table surrounded by empty beer bottles, cigarette butts, and half-empty Chinese food containers. He saw Logan notice it, too. Logan reached down and slipped the claw hammer from the loop in the tool belt and held it up in front of his face, inspecting it as he spoke.

"How's work going these days, Tommy?"

"Not bad. You know. A week here, a week there."

"And the horses?"

"Logan . . ."

"Shut the fuck up, Tommy."

Tommy stopped again. He sighed heavily. Logan was pissed. And all three of them in that room knew Logan Coyle was not somebody you wanted holding a claw hammer in his hand while he was pissed at you.

Ever since Logan had gotten back from his most recent bid in Sing Sing on a murder rap, he'd been hellbent on ripping the neighborhood from Mannion's grip. Logan was on a mission. And nothing was going to stand in his way.

Pat Mannion had run Hell's Kitchen since Hughie Mulligan had handed the rackets down to him on a greasy platter, but as far as Logan was concerned, Mannion's time was up. Far as Logan was concerned, Mannion was a fucken dinosaur. Mannion was known around the parish as a "gentleman gangster." Everybody liked Pat Mannion. Hell, even Danny's mother liked the guy. She'd mention seeing him at Sunday Mass with Elaine and the kids. How he always smiled and said hello. But Danny, and every guy in the street, knew that behind Mannion's polished veneer lay the stone-cold heart of a killer. The neighborhood had been on edge lately. It felt that at any minute the tension between Mannion and Coyle might erupt and tear The Kitchen in two, turn the sidewalks red with blood.

"You know what happens when word gets out on the street that you can borrow money from Logan Coyle and you can get away with not paying him back?"

"I'm sorry, Logan. I'll sort you out. I promise. I'll get it for you today."

"Too late, Tommy."

Logan nodded to Danny and Terry. The two men knew instinctively what he wanted them to do. Terry sprang across the table and wrapped his arm around Tommy's neck, holding him in a headlock.

Danny was slower to move. He didn't wanna do this.

"Put his hand on the table," Logan barked.

"No, Logan, please . . ." Tommy started.

"Shut him up, Terry," Logan snapped.

Terry clamped a hand over Tommy's mouth. Danny grabbed Tommy's left hand and pinned it to the table. Logan reached into the tool belt and pulled out a shiny three-inch nail. Tommy struggled, but Terry and Danny had him pinned good.

Logan put the tip of the nail on the back of Tommy's hand and drove it straight through into the wooden table with an ugly crunch. Logan hit it twice more to make sure the nail was well and truly caught in the solid oak top. Then he nodded at Terry and Danny to let him go.

Tommy cried out in pain.

Logan slapped him hard in the face.

"Shut the fuck up, pussy. Suck it up. This is what happens when you think you can fuck Logan Coyle. Next time I'll drive that nail into your fucken head. You hear me?"

Danny turned away as Tommy nodded through muffled sobs.

"Here," Logan said, tossing the claw hammer on the coffee table. "You can take that out once we leave. I wanna see you down The Wolf with my money no later than Friday afternoon."

Tommy continued to sob and moan, staring at the nail pinning his hand to the table. A trickle of blood began to form a pool on the oak top.

"You hear me?" Logan said, grabbing a handful of Tommy's hair and turning Tommy's face toward him so Tommy was forced to peer up into Logan Coyle's steely blue eyes. "Don't ever try to fuck me again."

Logan straightened himself, and turned to Danny. "Go clean up, Danny. You got blood on your face."

Danny instinctively wiped his hand across his face. A red streak of Tommy's blood stained his palm. He stepped into the cluttered kitchen and rinsed his face and hands quickly in the overflowing sink, then, not seeing anything clean enough to trust in Tommy's kitchen, he wiped his face dry with his t-shirt.

"Come on," Logan said. "Let's go."

Danny glanced at Tommy as he passed back through the living room. Tommy had lifted the claw hammer in his right hand and was staring down at the impossibility of his bloody hand nailed to the table. He was in for a whole lot more pain before he would be able to wrestle that nail out of the oak, and out of his hand.

Tommy raised his hand with the hammer toward Danny and pleaded, "Please, Danny. Take it out."

Danny spotted a half-full bottle of Jack Daniels on the cluttered dresser by the door. He grabbed it and shoved it at Tommy.

"Pour some of that on it and drink the rest before you pull," he whispered. Then he put his head down and hurried on out into the hallway after Logan.

3

Danny stepped through the door of The Ward. The smell hit him at the door as it always did: stale sweat, moldy leather, determination, cheap musk, and hope. The Ward was the oldest boxing club in Hell's Kitchen. Owned by local boxing legend Paddy "Cockeye" Ward.

Paddy was a former Golden Gloves champion whose professional career had been cut short after he'd been shot in the back by a stray bullet in a pizza joint one night over on Ninth Avenue. The bullet, intended for Luca Moretti who was handing Paddy a slice of Sicilian as the gunman fired, had lodged in Paddy's neck, just to the left of his spine. It was a testament to what a tough bastard he was that he'd survived at all. But the doctors said the bullet was too close to the spinal cord to risk removing it. So, there it stayed for the past twenty years. A hard lump the size of a knuckle had knocked Paddy's head forever slightly cocked to the right-hand side and earned him a lifetime of free pizza from an eternally grateful Luca Moretti, and the moniker, Cockeye Ward.

About a year after the shooting, he'd opened The Ward on the second floor, above McCauley's Auto Repair, on the northwest corner of Thirty-eighth and Eleventh Avenue. Cockeye wanted it to be a safe place for local kids to come in off the streets. He'd never fight a champion fight again, but maybe he'd be able train one up from the neighborhood. Keep a few of them out of trouble while he was at it.

Danny tried to duck past Cockeye's office, but Cockeye was on the other side of the room, leaning against the ropes, staring right at him when he came in.

"Whad're you, working half days now?" Cockeye yelled. Two young local boxers Danny recognized were sparring in the ring.

"Sorry, Boss." Danny always called Cockeye "Boss." Out of respect. He'd been coming into this gym since the first year it opened when he was just thirteen years old. He didn't have no money to train back then so Cockeye put him to work cleaning the toilets, sweeping floors, and running for coffee and sandwiches for whoever needed it. Cockeye saw something in Danny that he couldn't see in himself. Trained him up for the Golden Gloves. Made it all the way to the finals. Cockeye never saw it as a loss like Danny did. Far as the whole neighborhood was concerned, Danny Boy was The Champ. Their champ.

"Jesus Christ, what happened you?" Cockeye said, noticing the fresh cuts and bruises on Danny's face.

Danny put his head down and hurried on back to the locker room. He hadn't told Cockeye about last night's fight at the pier. Far as Cockeye was concerned, the bareknuckle fights were for losers and scumbags.

Danny hadn't even pulled open the door to his locker when he heard Cockeye's voice behind him.

"Turn around."

"It's nothing."

"Turn around."

Danny turned his bruised face to Cockeye.

"Ah, Jesus Christ, kid. Who set it up?"

"I needed the money."

"Who?"

"Coyle."

"That fucken scumbag. Didn't I tell you, stay away from that guy. He's no good."

"Logan's not so bad."

"He's a degenerate. A thug. Him and his whole crew."

Cockeye stepped forward and pulled up Danny's t-shirt, revealing the badly bruised ribs.

"Who'd they put you in with?"

"Some kid from the Heights."

"Who?"

"Gonzalez."

"Hector?"

"Yeah."

"And?"

"I put him down."

"You proud of yourself? You feel like a big man now?"

"Sorry, Boss."

"Get outta here."

"I'm sorry."

"I don't give a shit. Get outta here. I don't want to see your fucken face back here 'til those bruises are gone. Ya hear me! Go. Get outta my sight."

Danny pulled his shirt back down over his battered ribcage as he pushed past him for the door.

"You needed a few bucks, why didn't you come to me?" Cockeye said, almost in a whisper, stopping Danny in his tracks.

"I didn't wanna put you out."

The two men lingered for a moment. Danny stared at the floor. Cockeye behind him, shaking his head, in silence.

"Be back here tomorrow. Ten o'clock. And don't be fucken late."

"You got it, Boss. I'll be here."

Danny was on his way out of the gym when one of the kids who'd been sparring slipped out of the ring and approached him, holding out his gloves.

"Hey, Danny . . . you think you could sign these for me, please."

Danny was always shocked that someone would want his name scrawled on something.

It had been eight years since he'd fought the Golden Gloves. He hadn't won a real fight since. But people remembered. They treated him like a hero of sorts. A kid from the West Side who'd beaten the odds. A kid like them. To many young hopefuls in The Kitchen he would always be the champ: Danny Boy McCoy. The kid who boxed his way to the top.

Except he hadn't.

He was still here.

He glanced around, and found a marker sitting on an old dresser by the door, and scrawled, "Danny Boy McCoy," across both gloves. The kid was beaming. Like he'd just crossed paths with Kennedy. A couple of other young boxers, now emboldened, seeing him with the marker in his hand, rushed up with their own gloves, and he wound up signing five or six pairs in the same fashion.

As he signed the last one, he looked up to see Cockeye, leaning in the office door, his arms folded, regarding the situation with a sad smile.

Danny met his eyes. Cockeye turned and disappeared into his office, closing the door behind him.

4

As Danny made his way back to Tenth Avenue across Forty-fourth Street he felt that pang in his chest again. He stopped and held his hand to his heart. He was short of breath. The world blurred and before he could reach to steady himself against a wall he blacked out.

When he came to, a girl was leaning over him. For a moment he wasn't sure where he was or what had happened.

"Hey, mista," she was saying, tapping his shoulder. "You okay?" The girl's face was hidden in a curtain of blonde hair. "Mista. Can you hear me? You alright?" The sunlight behind her made it impossible to see her features.

"Yeah, I'm good," Danny mumbled, though in truth he wasn't sure what the hell had just happened, or where he was.

"You passed out."

Danny pushed himself up.

"Wow, take it easy," she said, a hand resting on his shoulder. "Not so fast there, buster. Just sit for a minute."

Danny shifted himself around so that his back was against the wall. He was seated on the sidewalk about halfway down the block. The girl was hunkered in front of him. He could see her now. She was maybe twenty-five, with shoulder-length dirty-blonde wavy hair, and wearing red lipstick, a short black leather skirt, and fishnet stockings. She was chewing gum and when her face brightened into a smile, faint wrinkles appeared in the corners of her eyes, and he noticed a thin line of freckles speckled along the tops of her cheeks.

"I'm Trixie," she offered, in a voice that had broken glass in it.

"Danny."

"Danny fell," she said, with a chuckle, exaggeratedly chewing her gum, her elbows propped on her knees. "How you feeling, Danny?"

"I'm okay. What happened?"

"You was walkin' along, next thing, boom, you just flopped over. Like a fish. Lucky ya didn't whack ya head." She reached out and touched his face, traced the line of the dark bruise under his right eye. He was tempted to tell her she was the first girl to have touched him in a long, long time. "Looks like you took a beating somewhere else."

"I was in a fight."

"Oh yeah! How's the other guy look?"

"Not too good."

"Good." There was that smile again. "You ready to stand up, cowboy?"

"Yeah, I think so," Danny said, bracing himself to stand. She stood and reached a hand down to hoist him up. He took it.

When he was on his feet he was looking down at her. She couldn't have been more than five feet three in heels.

For a moment they just stood there. Her staring up. Him staring down. Her waiting for him to say something. Him waiting for her to say something. She smiled as she took in the full scope of him up on his feet. He was a big man, Danny. Not handsome, but brutishly powerful, with a flat boxer's nose, and heavy-lidded eyes that gave the impression he was forever brooding. He had a broad chest and thick muscular arms that hung by his sides as if weighed down by two enormous hands like forging anvils.

"Serial killer, or teddy bear?" she asked, squinting her eyes at him. "I'm gonna go with teddy bear."

She turned her head to the right just then, as if something had caught her eye, and her expression shifted. He turned, too, and watched a black Cadillac roll slowly past them and come to a stop not twenty feet away.

"That's my ride," she said, nodding to the car. "I gotta run."

"Okay," he said.

"You gonna be able to find your way home without fallin' on your face again?" There was that smile again.

"Yeah. I'll get home."

She backed away from him toward the Cadillac, keeping him in her gaze, "You live around here?"

"Yeah, over on Tenth."

"So maybe I'll see you around."

"Yeah . . . I'll see you around," he called.

Whoever was inside opened the rear door for her and she slipped inside. The car idled for a moment then pulled out slowly and moved off down the block.

5

When Danny entered The Wolf a few hours later to see Logan about collecting the purse from the previous night's fight, Mack Cantor was behind the stick.

"Look who it is!" Mack yelled, swinging a dirty rag around over his head. "Look guys, it's The Champ."

An enthusiastic cheer went up from the familiar crew of locals. Danny recognized most of these mutts at a glance. A row of narrowback dominoes seated the length of the bar. Every last one of them had been down at the pier for the fight the previous night. They raised their bottles to Danny in salute.

Danny's win was a fine excuse to stay lit for a day or two. Not that this crew needed an excuse to stay lit. Most of these guys hadn't sobered for more than a few hours at a time since high school.

Since Logan had become owner of The Wolf, the place had become the go-to gathering spot for the neighborhood misfits: the gamblers, the thieves, the drunks, the kids who couldn't see themselves ever being able to hold down a nine-to-five job. These were Irish-Americans for the most part, second or third generation. Many of them had a direct line of heritage back to the famine.

There were guys in this bar whose great-great-grandfathers had stepped off famine ships on the West Side of Manhattan and didn't make it more than twenty blocks farther the rest of their lives. Danny's mother once said that at the heart of Hell's Kitchen was a rotting black spud.

"What're you having, Danny?" asked Knuckles. "First one's on me."

"Naw, I'll get it," insisted Cheddar, fumbling in his pocket and fishing out a ball of crumpled bills.

Danny'd seen Stevie Knuckles and Timmy, who everyone knew as Cheddar, down at the pier just before the fight began. They'd been front and center, yelling him on.

It was rare to enter The Wolf and see either one of these clowns without the other. Knuckles and Cheddar had grown up together. They were inseparable. Danny had known them from as far back as he could remember. The three of them had taken their first holy communion together at Sacred Heart, played hockey together just up the street at Hell's Kitchen Park and gotten drunk together, for the very first time, on a bottle of Father Connolly's altar wine they'd swiped from the sacristy.

"I ain't stayin'," said Danny.

"The hell you ain't," snapped Mack. "Sit down."

"I just gotta see Logan."

"Logan's gone," said Mack. Mack was older than the rest of this crew. He was new to The Wolf. Up until recently Mack Cantor was considered one of Pat Mannion's top guys. For years, he'd been a bartender up the street at Mannion's Tavern. The fact that he was in here now, behind Logan's bar, was another sign of the lengths Logan Coyle was willing to go to undermine Pat Mannion's standing in the neighborhood.

Mack was something of a legend in the neighborhood. He'd

done serious time up in Attica. He'd even taken part in the legendary Attica riot just a few years earlier. A story he loved to retell in The Wolf to anyone with an ear to listen. But Mack's real notoriety was related to the skills he had picked up when he worked in the kitchen at Attica as a butcher.

Danny'd heard the rumors same as everybody else. It was whispered that Mack had whacked some junkie who owed him money, hacked him up into little pieces, and tossed him in the East River. It was also rumored that he'd made a few people disappear for Mannion over the years.

Rumors.

Danny'd heard Mack referred to as The Butcher. But he took the stories he heard in the bars around Hell's Kitchen with a grain of salt. You heard a story in The Kitchen, you could whack it in half and believe about half of what was left. The Mack Cantor he knew was, for the most part, a likable guy. He was tall, with thick dark hair, square-jawed and handsome. He had a certain old-world swagger about him, like if John Wayne had grown up on Tenth Avenue.

Mack was another one he'd heard dropping remarks about how Mannion's time running the neighborhood was up. Mannion was old-school. The kind of guy handed turkeys out of the back of a truck at Christmastime. But the day of the gentleman gangster was over and done with. There was a new breed of gangster on the West Side and they didn't give a flying fuck about the old way of doing things.

In Danny's lifetime he'd witnessed Forty-second Street transform into the dark artery of American desire that it had become. Peep shows, dealers, hookers, pimps, hustlers and Johns. It had started as an itch, to scratch the polished veneer of the 1950s, and now it was spreading through the neighborhood like a cancer.

Then came the smack.

Heroin was changing the game for everybody.

"I'll have a coke," Danny said.

"The fuck you will," snapped Mack. "You'll have a beer or a shot same as everybody else. You can drink that other shit when you're up there chatting to your birds . . . but not in here, pal. We don't serve coke in this bar . . . not unless there's vodka in it. Isn't that right, boys?"

That got a good laugh.

"Fuck it then," said Danny, knowing it was useless to argue. "Give me a Jameson."

"There you go," shouted Cheddar, raising his bottle in a toast.

"To the champ," added Knuckles.

"Don't you guys ever go to work?" Danny asked, busting their balls. Nobody really worked in The Kitchen anymore, far as he could see.

"Fuck you talking about? We work," Knuckles snapped, defensively.

"Doing what?"

"Security, over at The Garden," said Cheddar.

"Rangers played Boston coupla a nights ago," added Knuckles. "Where'n the hell was you?"

"Home," said Danny, sipping his Jameson. "Good game?"

"How the fuck would I know!" Knuckles snapped.

" 'Cause you were there."

"Wha' do I give a shit who won. We were working security detail. Logan got us in for the night."

"You didn't see the game?"

"Naw, man, but we made a fucking killing."

"How?"

"Middle of the game we went through the locker room. Checked all their bags. Wallets. You know how much cash these mother-fuckers are carrying around in their back pocket?"

"You went through their lockers?" Danny asked, seeing a thin smile crack on Knuckles' lips. Knuckles wanted to tell him the story. Knuckles loved to tell every detail of a scam. He lived for this shit. Danny egged him on because that's how these conversations went. "Wha'd you do?"

"Listen, we didn't clean 'em out or nuthin'. We just waited to the game's on, see. Then me and Cheddar, we go back there to the locker rooms, real casual like, like we're keeping an eye on things, you know what I mean? Cheddar stands by the door, I go in and pull open a few lockers. Take a peek in their wallets. Pull a twenty here, a fifty there. Depending. You know! Nothing nobody's gonna call the cops about. Whadda they know! They come in after the game, they get showered, snap a few towels at each others balls, act like a bunch of jerkoffs, next thing, they're getting ready, pull their pants on, open their wallet, oh, look at that, still full of cash. Who's gonna count? So it's short a couple of twenties! They figure they dropped it somewhere along the way. Tipped the driver more than they should. It's nuttin'. Small change to these fagollas. Fuck 'em."

"How much?" Danny asked. Not really quite listening to what he was saying. He'd heard this story before a million times in The Wolf. Not this particular one, but stories like it. These guys were up to every hustle in the book. One day it was a truckful of cheap smokes, the next it was a rack of suits they'd jacked from a loading dock in the garment district. One scam more ingenious than the next. It never stopped.

"I dunno," Knuckles said. "How much we get, Cheddar?"

"Off the Rangers?" whispered Cheddar, glancing around like he was afraid the place was wired. "Maybe three hundred bucks."

29

"Three hundred?" Danny asked, acting surprised. Like he gave a shit.

"That's just the Rangers," Knuckles went on. "We were maybe a little worse on Boston."

"You went through Boston's lockers, too?"

"We're security. We can go wherever the fuck we like. Who's gonna stop us? *We're* the fucken security."

"Fuck Boston," added Cheddar.

"Boston can lick my fucken balls." Knuckles laughed, grabbing his crotch for effect.

Danny nodded to Mack for another one. It was easy to keep going after the first. The alcohol softened the pain from the battering his body had taken the night before, eased the worry over his mother's deteriorating health, his own recent chest pains, the debt he had accrued over the past couple of years, not to mention, Cockeye's disappointment in him at the gym earlier that day.

The first glass of whiskey burned in his heart like a campfire and it was good to be in the bar, laughing and trading stories with his childhood friends. Dinner could wait. His mother could wait. The birds could wait. He'd have another one. And another.

By nine o'clock he was ordering rounds for the bar. He'd borrowed a twenty from Mack to send out for a pie from Moretti's. And then at some point he noticed Benny Black, or as everyone knew him, "Blackie," was behind the bar, pulling the pints, though he couldn't remember exactly when Mack had ended his shift and Blackie had taken over.

The night fragmented into a series of hazy snapshots. Knuckles was at the jukebox, playing "Rhinestone Cowboy" for the fiftieth time. Another round of shots. Laughter. Then, at some point, Danny, Cheddar, and Knuckles had locked arms and were singing along at the top of their lungs to the song . . .

30

That's when the first shots rang out.

At first it sounded like a firecracker had gone off outside. Then it came again. *Rat a tat tat.*

"That's a fucken machine gun," Blackie said, tossing his rag in the well, and leaping the bar in a single bound. There was a mad scramble for the door to see who was causing all the excitement. The shooting was coming from right outside.

Danny's reflexes kicked in and he was one of the first out the door, scanning the avenue for the source of the gunfire which had come in five or six powerful bursts echoing off the tenement walls. Yelling could be heard from down the block, then Knuckles pointed up.

"There."

They all looked up to see a couple of dark figures ducking behind the parapet of a building up the middle of the block, about halfway between The Wolf and Mannion's Tavern.

Danny's building.

There was one last burst of gunfire and the two figures retreated into darkness.

Danny ran toward his building. A few frightened pedestrians were on their feet running for cover, shielding their heads with raised arms. As he reached the building door he noticed three men come up from behind a bullet riddled car just across the street. He only recognized one of them at a glance: Pat Mannion. Mannion recognized Danny, too. Glared right at him, then, as if trying to piece it all together, he glanced up, to the roof of Danny's building, and back again to Danny.

Whoever had been on Danny's roof had just tried to assassinate Pat Mannion. Danny had a pretty good idea who it could be. He was pretty sure Mannion did, too.

6

"You and your friends happy with yourselves now!" Danny's mother growled in a low whisper as he entered the kitchen the following morning. She was already seated at the small table, dressed as always for morning Mass, nursing the thin china cup with her tea. Her back straight, her gaze fixed upon him as he moved to lift a cup off the rack. "Shoot a man going about his business. Is that how your friends do things now in the neighborhood? Is that what it's come to?"

"Ma, I don't know nuthin'."

"Course ye don't," she spat. "Nobody saw nuthin'. Right! 'I didn't see nuthin', officer.' 'I never heard a thing, officer.' You take me for a damn fool? You think I didn't spend fifty years of my life walking up and down these self-same streets? Don't you stand there and treat me like I fell off a boat onto the pier yesterday, Danny McCoy."

Danny took a cup and tried to keep his hand steady as he poured himself a cup of hot tea from the pot. He was not equipped for this level of interrogation just yet. His head felt like somebody'd taken a bat to it.

His mother sighed deeply, as if to compose herself, as if to begin again.

"When Bridie McCaffrey's husband died and left that poor woman with not a pot to piss in or a window to throw it out, and four young children to drag up all on her lonesome, who gave her an apartment to raise them in? Who gave her a job cleaning floors, and a few shillins in her pocket at the end of the week to make sure there was food on the table for them? Pat Mannion. That's who. When the roof of the rectory needed fixed and there wasn't enough in the basket to launder the vestments, who sent the carpenters free of charge? Pat Mannion did. When half this neighborhood couldn't afford to put a slice of ham or a crust on the table for Thanksgiving, who stood on that corner down there, year after year after year, handing out free turkeys out of the back of a truck? Pat Mannion did. And don't you try and stand there and tell me you didn't sit at this very same table and eat it yourself, for ya did, and you were grateful for it, like the rest of us. What did this other—" and here she seemed to struggle for a word bitter enough to relay her complete contempt for Logan Coyle, "—tramp, do? What?"

"I—"

"I'll tell you what he did!" his mother said, standing to face Danny now in the cramped kitchen. "He did nothing. Nothing. He took and he took and he took and he went off to live in a big house in New Jersey. New Jersey!" She spat, shaking her head as if unable to process the absolute treachery of somebody who'd consider moving to the other side of the Hudson. "And he's still taking . . ."

"Ma—"

"No. Just you listen to me for once. Listen to this one thing if you never hear another word comes out of my mouth: Logan Coyle is a crook. A lowlife. He's a user and a snake. He's no better than a goddamned guinea. Mark my words, he's going to bring this neighborhood to its knees. He's not man enough to call himself an Irishman. He doesn't have the decency in him. And if I hear one whisper that you're working for him . . . my son . . . my boy . . . by God I'll do time for your hide . . . you hear me . . . I'll take you out with my own bare hands."

It wasn't the first time she'd off-handedly told him she'd string him up, but it was the first time he believed her. He said nothing. Her words ping-ponged about in his head with the events of last night like a faulty pinball machine.

For a moment longer she stood as if the outburst had glued her frozen in time. Then she blinked and began to take deep belly-filling gasps of air. And she nodded her head as if in agreement with her own righteousness.

"With my own bare hands," she repeated.

Then she lifted the rosary beads off the nail. Dipped the tip of her finger into the consecrated well and scored the cross on her forehead, chest, and shoulders as if to seal her murderous covenant with God.

7

Danny could sense the fear in his birds when he opened the door to the coop. He stepped inside and they snapped their wings about him, lighting on his shoulders, on his head, on his outstretched arms in a frenzied attempt to express their concern.

"I'm sorry," he said. "I know. I know. It's okay now. It's over. It won't happen again. I promise."

He'd sat awake most of the previous night in his darkened kitchen, expecting the cops to show up at his door about the shooting on the roof. But no one came.

An hour after he'd been home he watched a man he didn't recognize open the door of the bullet-riddled Impala across the street, wrestle with the steering column, and within thirty seconds had it hot-wired. The driver casually pulled out and drove off down Tenth Avenue. One of Mannion's men no doubt, directed to clean up the mess.

It's possible, because no one had been hit, that the cops didn't care enough to waste time, or ball sweat, trudging up and down tenement stairs at midnight knocking on doors for answers they knew they wouldn't get. It was also possible that the cops who patrolled the area were told to stay away by Mannion himself. It was well known Mannion had a few local cops on the payroll. But it was even more likely that the cops didn't even know it had happened. Nobody in The Kitchen called the cops. Ever. The Irish policed themselves. If you knew what was good for you, you kept your mouth shut, and your nose out of anything that didn't concern you directly.

But it was obvious to Danny that everyone in The Kitchen knew what had happened by breakfast time that morning. His mother had confirmed as much. Logan Coyle had taken a shot at Pat Mannion and he'd missed. That meant blood was coming. Mannion would retaliate. He'd have to. He didn't have a choice. That's just how things operated on the street. If Mannion didn't retaliate, he'd lose credibility. And if he lost credibility, he'd lose control. And if he lost control, he and his family were in danger. Mannion had been around too long to let that happen.

Danny took the flag down off its hook and flagged the birds for an hour. They circled about his head, following the pole as he led them to and fro in a wide graceful arc. He smiled as one of his tumblers flipped backward and dropped and twisted in a death spiral for almost twenty feet, miraculously righting herself no more than a foot off the tarmacadam rooftop and then swooping suddenly upwards again to join the rest in a playful dance.

Most people collected birds for sport, for racing, or breeding. Danny didn't give a damn about any of that. Danny's birds were family. He took in every stray bird that needed a home. There were rock pigeons, tumblers, white-tips, and bandtails. He didn't care. They were all equally beautiful to him. There were birds here he'd found sick in the street and nursed back to health. Birds brought to him by neighbors who'd found them injured or ill on their fire escapes and didn't know what else to do with them. There were a handful of birds in his flock that had been gifted by other pigeon owners that he knew from the Bronx, Queens and Brooklyn. Birds that didn't fit whatever standard they were trying to keep in their coops. If a bird wanted to fly away he let them fly. None did. Danny's birds stayed 'cause they liked Danny. And he loved them. It was that simple.

He spent extra time with them this morning. He sat quietly for an extra hour, tossing them small handfuls of seed, listening to their chatter, watching them dance and play and peck. If one needed to be held he held her. When he sat alone like this they would come to him to feel the soft touch of his fingers on their wings or their heads. They would lean in to him. Sit on his shoulders. Cock their heads and stare up at him as if to say, "Hey! You alright there, pal?"

"Yeah, I'm alright," he'd reply. "I'm good. Thanks for asking."

This was the only place he could truly settle his thoughts. Feel at peace. Try to figure things out. With his birds. There was nobody to judge him one way or the other up here. The birds didn't judge. The birds just let him be.

He lifted an old bandtail named Wilbur and nursed him in his lap. Wilbur had been with him longer than any other bird in the pack. Almost nine years now. Wilbur knew him. Wilbur would come to him like this when he had a lot weighing on him. Like he understood. Like he was listening. Like this old busted bird could feel the very weight of his soul.

Danny knew he had to get out of The Kitchen. He'd known it for years. But it was time. The Kitchen of his childhood was over. The signs were everywhere. Used to be you could walk these streets and have some sense of security. Some sense that you were living in an actual neighborhood. Sure there were plenty of people you didn't know walking around, but still, you knew their faces for the most part, or their families.

This used to be a neighborhood. A crew of guys showed up causing trouble, you knew they wasn't from around here. They got their heads cracked and they didn't come back down here no more. But that was over now.

Not that there wasn't trouble before, there'd always been trouble, but it felt contained. Local. But the heroin and the peep shows had changed all of that. Used to be that stuff was only over on the Deuce. That was the dark spine of the thing. Forty-second Street. But lately the peep shows were creeping farther west and up Ninth and Tenth Avenues like the demonic tentacles of some primeval beast taking form. Hustlers and Johns were drifting deeper into the neighborhood. And with them, following the money, came the rackets, the mob, the Italians. Mannion had been pushing back against all that. Many in the neighborhood considered him the human dam that stood singlehandedly against a flood of chaos that threatened to sweep what was left of the old Irish neighborhood right off the end of the piers into the Hudson.

Danny knew if he didn't get his mother out soon it was going to be too late. Maybe too late for them both.

Logan Coyle had probably started a war with last night's shooting. What was left of any sense of order was about to be obliterated. Coyle had tipped the applecart into the middle of Tenth Avenue. Danny had a gut feeling that the coming transition was going to be brutal. Many wouldn't survive to see the new dawn.

Danny's mother's health was fading fast, too. He could see her leaning more and more on the cane. Soon she was going to be a prisoner in either the apartment or, God forbid, some old-people's home. There was just no way she was going to be able to navigate those five flights of stairs for much longer. It was already a struggle for her. Three flights and she had to sit for a breather, letting the other tenants pass her by. He had to get her out. She was all he had. He was all she had. He was her only remaining family. It was on him, damn it.

He threw the birds another handful of seed. He liked to mix crushed peanuts in there. They liked that. They rooted them out with their beaks, like children checking for special treats in the bottom of a Halloween bag.

For a couple of years now he'd been thinking about a little place up in the country, somewhere upstate. His buddy Liam Kelly from down the block had gone out to the big music festival up there a few years ago and had loved the area so much he'd decided to stay.

Danny'd bumped into him at Paddy Brennans' funeral a few months back and Liam had told him all about where he was living now. "A little cottage, right on the outskirts of the village, with a creek, and some chickens. You could build a coop for your birds. Take them with you. You could get out, Danny. You done your time," he'd said, like The Kitchen was the penitentiary. "Take your ma, make a go of it, 'fore it's too late." He looked good too. Like he was more relaxed. You could see it in him. In his eyes. The country.

Danny figured if he could put a few grand together he'd have enough for a downpayment on a little place out there, with an acre or two of land. He could buy an old van, use that to take his mother and any of her dusty old furniture she wanted to bring along, and then he could come back and take the birds, the coops, and all the rest of it up there with him. He could do it. The way he figured it, a few runs he'd have everything they needed moved up there. Maybe get himself a little job. Liam said he'd help him get set up, knew some local contractors, could easily get him a job on a crew swinging a hammer. He said the money wasn't great, but you didn't need a whole lot to live on out there.

"I'm going to do it," he said aloud to his birds. "I'm gonna get us out of here. Who wants to move to the country?"

8

Danny didn't notice the light gray Ford Crown Victoria inching slowly up behind him as he walked the stretch between Tenth and Eleventh Avenues on Forty-seventh Street, until it was right alongside him.

A guy in a suit with broad shoulders stepped quickly out of the front of the car, blocking his path with a snub-nosed revolver.

"Get in." It was the man they called The Greek. One of Mannion's top guys.

Danny took a beat to assess the situation. The gun was leveled at his torso. If he made a move to run, The Greek was gonna put one in him. No question. The Greek casually opened the rear door and motioned with the barrel of the gun without taking his eyes off Danny for a second.

Danny glanced into the backseat of the Ford and there was Pat Mannion. Stone faced.

"Get in the car, Danny."

Danny got in. The Greek closed the door and got back in the front passenger side, casually slipping the gun into a chest holster under his jacket. Danny recognized the guy driving the car right away as Tommy Dillon. Another one of Mannion's heavy hitters.

40

Dillon, The Greek, Mack Cantor, and Benny Black had all worked together for Mannion for a time. Most of those guys worked for whoever could pay their rent that particular month. Apparently Mannion wasn't paying them enough lately. He was seeing more and more of Mack and Blackie down at The Wolf. They were taking bartending shifts with Coyle to survive between jobs. They hadda eat. But not Dillon. Or The Greek. You weren't going to see these two guys down at The Wolf looking for a shift. These guys were Mannion's right-hand men. Loyal all the way. In fact, now that he saw him, Danny realized it was probably Tommy Dillon he'd watched move the Impala the night before. Same broad shoulders. Same somber demeanor.

Tommy eyed Danny in the rearview mirror until he was good and sure Danny knew that he was watching him and that he better not fuck around. Then he pulled out and continued driving, on toward the river.

"How you been, Danny?" Mannion began. Danny knew Mannion. And he knew Mannion knew him. Not that they'd ever had a conversation, but Mannion knew his mother from way back. They weren't friends but he'd say hello to her if he saw her on the street or at Mass, same as he would with any of the older women in the neighborhood. Mannion had also been at one or two of his fights along the way. It was rumored he'd been a half decent boxer himself in his day and he still followed the sport diligently. But Danny hadn't seen him at any of the fights Coyle had organized down on the pier. That wasn't Mannion's style. Mannion wouldn't do anything publicly to tarnish his reputation as a stand-up guy in the neighborhood. What he did out of the watchful gaze of grandmothers and priests was a whole other matter. Mannion hadn't been able to keep control over the entire neighborhood rackets since Hughie Mulligan stepped aside by saying a few decades of the rosary.

"I'm good, Mr. Mannion."

"Pat. Call me Pat."

Mannion gave him a moment. But Danny decided the less he said right now the better it would be for him in the long run.

"How's your mother holding up? She alright?" Mannion asked.

"Yeah, she's good."

"Good woman, your mother. I see her on occasion over at morning Mass."

Danny nodded and stared off out the window. He knew Mannion hadn't picked him up to chat about his mother. That wasn't the kind of conversation you needed a gun for. Mannion was setting the table. He'd get to the main course in good time.

"Heard you were fighting over here a couple of nights ago." The car was passing under the rusted husk of Miller Highway and on to the abandoned pier. "You should stay away from those bums. Let me help you. Set up a real fight."

Danny continued to say nothing. Mannion was still going through the motions.

The car pulled about halfway down the abandoned pier and stopped in the shade of a dilapidated warehouse.

Danny watched a small red tugboat in the middle of the Hudson pushing a barge piled with garbage. A flock of seagulls fluttered around the refuse, screeching and whistling. The birds were the only sign of life down here this time of morning.

"Whaddya know about last night, Danny?"

There it was. The main course. Mannion's voice dropped an octave. The small talk was over.

"I don't know nuthin'."

"Who was up on the roof?"

Danny kept his mouth shut. They both knew who was up on the roof. Mannion just wanted somebody to say it out loud.

"I swear, Pat. I don't know nuthin'. I was in The Wolf when it happened. You can ask anybody."

"Who was with you?"

"Benny Black was doing bar. Stevie Burke, Timmy Keenan, they was all there."

"Was Coyle there?"

Danny clammed up again.

"What about that other nut, Terry Flannery, was he in there?"

Danny looked down at his knees.

Mannion nodded to The Greek. The Greek spun around and grabbed Danny's right hand and pinned it against the side of the headrest while Tommy Dillon produced a pair of pruning sheers and locked them around the base of Danny's thumb.

"Who was on the roof, Danny?"

"It was dark. We couldn't see."

"Who couldn't you see?"

"I don't know."

"You ever see a four fingered boxer, Danny?"

"I swear."

"Who?" Mannion yelled, sending a spray of spit into his face.

"I swear on my mother's life. I didn't see their faces."

Mannion grabbed a handful of Danny's hair, and held him tight as he leaned in close to his face.

"Gonna ask you one last time, Danny. Was it Logan Coyle and Terry Flannery took a shot at me from your roof last night?"

"I don't know, Pat. Honest I don't."

Mannion stared deep into Danny's eyes. Looking for the slightest hint that Danny was holding out on him. Then he released him. He nodded, and Dillon and The Greek released him, too. Danny folded his arms across his chest and reflexively tucked his fingers under his arms.

43

"Whose side you on, Danny?"

"I ain't on nobody's side."

"Everybody's gonna be on somebody's side of this thing, sooner or later."

"I don't want no trouble. I don't bother nobody."

"How much you owe Coyle?" Mannion asked.

Danny said nothing. Mannion was fishing. It was well known that Coyle had started his own shylock operation out of The Wolf.

"Coyle thinks he's gonna start operating his own shy without kicking up he's got another thing coming. This is Hyman Goldstein's turf. You know who Hyman Goldstein is?"

Danny said nothing. He knew who Goldstein was. Maybe not *knew him*, but he'd heard about him plenty.

"You know who Hyman Goldstein works for, right?"

Danny shook his head.

"Goldstein's with the Fallacis. You know who the Fallacis are, Danny?"

Yeah. He knew.

"Hyman operates for the Fallacis and I look out for Hyman in The Kitchen. You understand? Anybody else we see operating in The Kitchen is going to pay. And it won't be in dollar bills. You get it? Coyle thinks he's some kind of a big operator all of a sudden! You know what the Italians do when you can't pay your debts, Danny?" Mannion paused, leaving another window open for Danny to step into the conversation. "They cut your dick off and they shove it in your mouth. That's what they'll do. Then they come for your mother."

Danny turned his head and stared off out the window. A rat darted out of a pile of discarded car tires and ran back in again.

"Let me help you, Danny," Mannion said, resting a hand on Danny's shoulder.

"I don't want no trouble, Pat. Not from you, not from Logan. I don't want no trouble from nobody."

"Well, it's too late for all that now, Danny, isn't it? You're in it already, same as the rest of us. You just gotta ask yourself: Whose trouble you fear the most?"

Mannion released Danny's shoulder and nodded to The Greek.

The Greek got out and opened Danny's rear door. Danny got out.

"You know where to find me, Danny," Mannion said.

Then The Greek closed the back door, and got back in the car.

Danny watched the car turn and slowly drive back toward the neighborhood the way they had come.

A foghorn bellowed in the harbor. A seagull cried and took flight. He rubbed a cut on his thumb where the shears had nicked the skin.

He had to get his mother out of Hell's Kitchen before it was too late.

9

Danny was slugging the heavy bag for about twenty minutes without a breather. Sweat dripped off the end of his nose and ran down his chest, soaking the waistband of his shorts.

"Who got under your skin this morning?" Cockeye had stepped up quietly behind him.

Danny stopped, and let his arms hang loose by his sides. His shoulders burned.

It felt good to burn.

"You don't wanna talk about it. Fine," Cockeye said dismissively, turning to walk away. "Go ahead. Kill the bag."

"I need something," Danny mumbled. Cockeye stopped about five feet away and turned to him.

"Name it."

"I need a shot."

"Danny . . ."

"Something big."

"How much debt you in?"

"I need a big fight."

"You need a fight or you need money?"

"I need this."

46

"You haven't had a fight in two years."

"I fought two nights ago."

"Fight! You call that a fight? Couple o' dumb lugs sluggin' each other half to death in a shed down the pier. That's not a fight. It's a barroom brawl."

"Least I got paid."

"Oh yeah, what they give you?"

Danny hung his head. Logan still hadn't given him a dime of the purse.

"How much?"

"Two."

"Jesus fucken Christ, Danny . . . you risk getting your face smashed to a pulp to entertain a bunch o' crooks for a lousy two hundred bucks. What are you, a goddamn circus clown?" Now Cockeye hung his head.

"What do you want from me?"

"I want you to wake up, kid. I want you to use your goddamn head."

"Whaddya think I'm doin' . . . ya think I still wanna still be in here sweepin' floors for you in ten years—"

"What's wrong with sweepin' floors? Least it's honest."

"It's not enough."

"Enough for what?"

"I gotta get Ma out of here."

"She don't like The Kitchen no more?"

"She can't walk up the stairs."

"So get an apartment on the ground floor."

"I can't even pay the rent on the one we got."

"Where you gonna go?"

"I don't know."

"What, is Coyle gonna take you out to New Jersey with him?"

"Upstate maybe. The country."

"The country." Cockeye was shaking his head now.

"Yeah."

"Whaddya gonna do up there, raise chickens, grow carrots? You gonna start a farm, Danny?"

"Maybe. I dunno. I gotta get her out."

"So go, get her out then."

"How?" Danny took a step toward Cockeye. His fists were balled. His arm and chest muscles coiled, tight as springs. He was yelling now. "I'm tellin' you, I don't got no money to go nowhere."

"So get another job," Cockeye yelled back, taking a quick step forward so the two men were face to face. Danny was a good head taller than Cockeye but Cockeye was still as fast and dangerous as a viper spittin' rusty nails when his fuse was lit.

"I need a fight," Danny repeated, standing his ground.

"You're not good enough for a real fight no more."

"I can get in shape again."

"You don't have the discipline. I throw you in the ring with a real fighter right now he'd tear you apart."

"I need a fight—" Danny yelled and then stopped. It was useless. Cockeye knew him better than anybody. Cockeye knew he wasn't ready for a big fight. And deep down Danny knew he was right.

He shoved past Cockeye and stormed out of the gym, flinging his gloves into a corner as he went.

10

First person Danny saw sitting at the end of the bar when he entered The Sunbrite Salon was Tommy Ryan, one hand bandaged, the other nursing a glass of whiskey. Tommy glanced to the door and seeing Danny enter, he quickly tipped the remaining whiskey down his throat and rose to leave.

He kept his head down as he hurried out the door.

"Hey Tommy—" Danny started, but Tommy ignored him, and went on out. Danny didn't blame him. Somebody held his hand on a coffee table to be nailed, he wouldn't want to see much of them either.

Danny'd come up to The Sunbrite, hoping to avoid seeing any of the crew from The Wolf. He should have known better.

Halfway down the bar sat Knuckles and Cheddar, waving for him to join them on a stool. "Rhinestone Cowboy" was playing on the jukebox. A good sign they were already half in the bag. Everywhere you ran into these two lately you had to put up with hearing that damn song on repeat about twenty times in a row.

"Tommy Ryan didn't look none to happy to see you." Knuckles grinned as Danny pulled up on a stool next to them.

49

"Maybe he's pissed he's only got one good hand to jack off with now," added Cheddar.

"Yeah, Danny, how's the poor guy s'posed to cup his balls and jack off at the same time. Thas a goddamn shame, that's what that is," Knuckles went on.

They were on a roll, but Danny wasn't laughing. If these two clowns knew he was in the room with Logan Coyle when Tommy Ryan had his hand nailed to a coffee table, then half the neighborhood knew by now. Of course, that's exactly how Logan would want it. He wanted it known that if you tried to stiff Logan Coyle, look forward to a world of pain.

Danny ordered a beer and had the barkeep back the other two up. The bartender dealt up a couple of coasters on the bar as markers and made change.

Danny was taking a swig out of the bottle when he saw that girl again. Trixie. She was seated at one of the booths in back with some guy he didn't recognize. She looked like she was having a good time. Laughing at whatever this guy was saying to her just then. Seeing her easy smile, Danny felt a sharp pang of jealousy. She glanced over just then and caught him staring at her. He waved awkwardly and she waved back with a bright smile then turned her attention back to her friend.

"You know that piece of ass?" Knuckles said, eyeing Trixie's bare thighs under the table.

"Wow," added Cheddar, "she's a good looking girl, Danny."

"Guys," Danny said, "leave it."

"Fuck you. Leave it?" snapped Knuckles, who looked like he was on a lot more than booze. His eyes, wide as saucers, were practically doing cartwheels back and forth across the bridge of his nose. "Who is she?"

"Some girl."

50

"Any sisters?" Knuckles sneered.

"Hey, Knuckles," Cheddar said, nudging Knuckles in an attempt to steer him away from leering at Trixie. "Tell Danny 'bout last night?"

"What about last night?"

"The story. You were just telling me! We were down the theatre."

"Oh yeah, yeah." Knuckles nodded. "So get this, Mack got us in as ushers on one of those big Broadway shows over on Forty-fifth. What the fuck was that show?" Knuckles asked, turning to Cheddar, snapping his fingers to jog his memory.

"I dunno," Cheddar said, with a frown. "Some choir shit."

"Chorus something . . ." Knuckles said, digging around in his drug addled brain.

"*Chorus Line*," Cheddar said, raising his hand with the answer, like he was back in grade school.

"Yeah, that's it," continued Knuckles. "*Chorus Line.* Here we are, we're all dressed up in these little fucken purple costumes they put you in, white shirt, the little dickie bow, the whole bit, and we're handing out these playbills, showing these jackoffs to their seats, like we give a fuck, and here comes this piece of ass, I mean this chick, am I right, Cheddar?"

"No, he's right. She was beautiful."

"I mean this chick was built. And I'm like, 'Just follow me, love.' And I take her down to her seat. And I'm playin' it real sweet, like butter don't melt in my mouth, right, asking her where she's from. And she's like, 'Oh, Am from Tennessee', or some shit, and, get this, she's in town for two nights to see the show. Alone. And I'm like 'Aw, isn't that wonderful. Isn't that nice. Good for you, sweetheart.' So during intermission I come back up and I whisper in her ear, 'Hey listen, you have a favorite actor in the show?' And she tells me some friggin name, seriously I can't even remember what she said, and I'm like, 'Oh my God, he's like my best friend.' 'You know him?' she squeals. And her eyes almost pop out of her fucken head. Like, she can't fucken believe it, right! 'Do I know him!' I say, acting like I'm offended, 'Wasn't he only just sleeping on my couch last night.' 'Listen,' I say, 'give me that playbill, Sweets, 'n' I'll run backstage and have him sign it for you.' Well she can't believe this shit. Right! She's like, 'Really! Really! You'd do that for me?' 'Sure, sweetheart. Sure. It's no problem.' So I take her fucken playbill and I run it out into the lobby, scribble a signature on it, she don't know shit, right, what she gonna compare it to? It's a scrawl. I bring it back, and I give it to her, and this chick, I mean, she flips. Flips. She's practically screaming. I'm like 'Hey, you wanna meet him after the show? We're goin' out for drinks. You should come along.' 'You mean it. Really?' Danny, this girl, I mean, am I right, Cheddar?"

"No, he's right, she was beautiful."

"So I take her over to Rudy's, and all along I'm telling her, 'Oh they should be along any minute now, love, and I'm feeding her fucken Jack Daniels for two hours' . . ."

There's a pause in the story. Danny had barely been listening. He doesn't care. He's heard this story, or one just like it, every single time he's met these clowns for the last ten years.

Danny was focused on Trixie. He really didn't like that she was back there giggling with some guy. Well dressed guy, at that. Nice hair. Khaki pants. Expensive boots. A shirt that cost more than four bucks. Every time she laughed at one of this jackoff's jokes it was like someone gave his heart a kick. He realized Knuckles had stopped talking and was staring off blankly into space.

"So you got laid?" Danny said, nudging the story along to its logical conclusion.

"Naw." He shook his head.

"You didn't get laid?"

"Naw. She got sick."

"Sick?"

"Yeah. She threw up. I think the whiskey was too much for her. She was cute though. Real sweet. Funny too." He seemed suddenly sad about it all.

"You get her phone number?" Danny asked, feeling maybe Knuckles had really connected with this girl.

"Phone number! What the fuck am I gonna do with her phone number? What? I'm gonna call her down in Tennessee!" Knuckles snapped, roaring back into the conversation again. "Man. I'll tell ya. We need to get some real work soon. These random shifts ain't cuttin' it no more, Danny. Half thinkin' about goin' up to the Tavern to see Mannion 'bout a fucken job down the piers."

It was well known that Pat Mannion had his hand in all the local unions. Stagehands. Dock workers. Ticket collectors. Movie props. You name it. It had all been handed down to him from Hughie Mulligan. It was well known Mannion's crew were collecting no-show checks from any number of businesses around the neighborhood, under the guise of protection, of course. Pay or suffer.

Mack was still lifting a weekly check for a no-show security man job over at The Garden. He was still connected to that whole world which was how he was able to get Cheddar and Knuckles occasional shifts here and there. But that wasn't enough for these two. These two wanted a guaranteed weekly paycheck for doing nothing at all. Far these two were concerned, work was for suckers. For guys not sharp enough to beat the game.

Danny noticed Trixie get up to leave with her friend and he turned his body away from her toward the bar, hoping she'd keep walking. He didn't want her to stop with him. Not now, not with Knuckles out of his mind like this.

"Hey." He heard her voice behind him. That same soft rasp. He had to turn. Her friend kept walking toward the door. Maybe she'd told him to go on and wait for her outside. "Danny fell. Right?"

"Trixie."

She smiled, pleased that he'd remembered her name.

"You make it home okay?" she asked.

"I'm good, yeah. Good."

For a moment they did that thing again. Her staring at him. Him staring at her.

"Jesus Christ, get a fucken room already." Knuckles laughed.

Trixie didn't flinch. Her eyes never left Danny's.

"I'll see you around," she said with a smile.

Danny nodded, and Trixie went on down the bar.

Knuckles leaned way back on his stool to watch her ass as she walked away. He raised his eyebrows at Danny and nodded his head in a sick sneer. Danny knew he was goading him. But he bit his tongue. Let it go.

Knuckles got up and slapped Danny's shoulder, "Now that's some serious fucken trouble right there, my friend." Then, with a chuckle, he went off to the bathroom in the back.

"She seems nice, Danny," Cheddar said, once Knuckles was gone. Danny smiled at his old pal. Cheddar had heart. He'd always had heart. More heart than any of them. Maybe too much heart for his own damn good.

Danny nodded. "Yeah, I think she might be."

"Be nice to find a nice girl," Cheddar said, almost in a whisper. "You know. Somebody to go home to at night."

Danny saw Knuckles emerge from the bathroom in the rear,

sniffing, rubbing his nose with the back of his hand. Whatever he was on, he'd just had some more of it.

"Yeah," Danny said. "That'd be nice." Then he stood up, before Knuckles had reached his stool, drained the last of his drink in a swallow, and set the glass down on what was left of his change.

"Where you goin'?" Knuckles said, grabbing Danny by the arm.

"Home," Danny said, pulling his arm away rougher than he'd intended.

"Come on. Stay for one more," Cheddar pleaded.

"Naw, I got to go. Ma's cookin' dinner. I told her I'd be there."

"Danny! I was only bustin' your balls, pal." Knuckles sniffed. "Danny!"

But Danny didn't turn back.

11

Danny stopped by Mazella's Fruit Market to grab a few fresh oranges for his mother. A peace offering. He had to make some effort to slow things down. He had to remember that this was not the time to lose control. She needed him now more than ever. This was not the time to fall apart.

Lately it had started to feel like the world was going to spin off its axis. He needed it to stop, or just slow down enough, for him to catch his breath. He tried to remember the last day he hadn't had a drink. The last night he'd stayed home, just ate dinner and watched TV with his ma.

Up until a just few months ago he was running three mornings a week. Skipping rope. Hitting the bag. He couldn't remember exactly when that had all stopped, but it had. A hangover here, a hangover there. Pretty soon he was either coming off a hangover or looking forward to the next one. It was a miracle he was still able to beat that kid down at the pier a few nights ago. He had to get off the merry-go-round. Get back in shape. Stop throwing money away in the local bars. Every week it seemed he was spending more money than he was earning. Five weeks in a row, he'd borrowed more than he'd earned. A twenty here. A fifty there. The vig had piled up over the course of a month and he was making no real attempt to right the ship. It was madness. And yet . . . and yet . . .

"How's my favorite lady?" Enzo Mazzella called out to him from the back of the store when he saw Danny rummaging through the few oranges left on the stand.

"She's getting by." Danny smiled. Enzo always had a smile. Every old lady in the neighborhood was his favorite old lady. And he meant it, too. He loved them all. Like sisters. Knew every name for a twenty-block radius.

"Tell her I said I'm upset she don't come in to see me no more."

"Her leg," Danny said, patting his own leg, as he made excuses for his mother.

"What leg? I see her go by the store on her way to Mass like she's headed for the Triple Crown at Belmont. You ask her; what I gotta do, start selling holy water in here?"

Danny laughed. "I'll tell her to come see you."

"You do that. You're a good boy, Danny. Here, what are you doing. Put those down," Enzo said, snapping the oranges out of Danny's hands and putting them back in the box. "You want to poison your mother! You don't love her no more! You bring her bruised fruit like this. I got a fresh box in the back. Just came in. Let me put a few in a bag for her."

Danny followed Enzo into the store. He nodded to Maria and to her daughter, Gabriela, who'd worked here from as far back as he could remember.

"Mr. Danny. Why you no come see us no more?" Maria teased.

"Maria. Nice to see you." Then, to her daughter. "Gabriela."

Gabriela had grown. He'd known her since she was knee-high. He'd never seen a sweeter kid. She smiled at him and put her head down again. She was no kid anymore. She must be all of twenty years old now, he figured. Maybe twenty-two. When did she become a woman? Maria, seeing her daughter blush, teased Danny: "She like you."

"Ma," Gabriela scolded. Her cheeks turned a deep red.

"See. Look how red she gets."

"It's nice to see you, Gabriela," Danny repeated, and went on back to join Enzo.

"Now look at these," Enzo was saying, leaning to rip open a fresh box of oranges and handing one out to Danny. "Smell that."

Danny put the orange to his nose.

"You smell how sweet that is? You take a bag of these home to your mother, you put a smile on her face, trust me. You tell her I said, eat two of these a day, better than any rosary."

Danny smiled. Enzo's energy permeated out of this store. One of the last bastions of hope in a crumbling empire.

"You tell her, I'll bet this orange against her all her rosary beads and her prescriptions, any day of the week."

Enzo spun the top of the paper bag in a flourish and shoved it in Danny's arms.

Danny started to dig for his wallet but Enzo clamped his arm. "Not today, Danny Boy."

"Enzo . . ."

"Cash register's all full. Couldn't squeeze another dime in there if you tried. Am I right, Maria?"

"Oh it's full, alright. But try getting him to take a dime out of it," she teased.

"Hey. Don't you start. She kids." They were like an old married couple, Maria and Enzo, bound together in a sea of fresh produce.

"I kid." Maria smiled.

"Thanks, Enzo," Danny said, moving toward the door.

58

"Don't worry. Next time I charge you double." Now Enzo laughed. A big belly laugh. Maria laughed, too.

"He will, too," she added.

Gabriela lifted her head and held Danny's eye for a solid beat as he passed by her toward the door. She seemed to lift her chest just then, and draw her shoulders back just a trace, to show she was not afraid of him, or of his gaze. Her cheeks were still flushed in a rosy hue and there was great bravery in the way she held her jaw firm, as if demanding that he consider her in all her beauty.

Standing there among the fruit stands, her eyes shone as pure and bright as any warrior angel.

Something stopped him then. Maybe it was loneliness. Maybe fear. Maybe the pure, unbridled magnetism of her proposal. All the rightness in her.

"I would like to take you out," he said clearly. As if another voice in him had spoken.

"When?" she said, without yielding even the slightest hint of her assuredness.

"Monday," he said. Knowing that he had committed to something momentous here. Something that could not be undone. Marie turned and busied herself sorting a crate of sprouts. Enzo stood watching as if not quite sure of what his role was in all of this. How he should react. In a way, he was like a father to Gabriela. She'd been in this store with her mother her entire life. That had to be more of a father than most had. It was a helluva lot more than Danny had ever known, that's for sure.

"I can be ready at six," Gabriela said.

"Six," Danny repeated. "I will meet you at your building, at six . . . Friday."

Gabriela smiled just then. But it wasn't just a smile. It was an admission of her heart to him.

12

When he opened the door to his apartment he knew his mother had calmed down since this morning's tirade. He was greeted by the sound of the Clancy Brothers and the warm aroma of what he recognized immediately as her famous shepherd's pie. It had been his favorite meal since he was a boy. He'd had her explain the recipe to him many times over the years, but he'd finally come to accept that the shepherd's pie she cooked for him could not be replicated.

She handpicked every ingredient. If the butcher handed her minced meat that didn't make the cut, she waved him off and went elsewhere. Same for the carrots, peas, and onions. She handpicked those, too, down at Mazella's. Then there was the gravy, a mix of spices and ketchup and God knows what else in there, a dash of this, a sprinkle of that, as she worked. It's possible she didn't fully know herself what it took. A layer of mashed potatoes, with a hint of butter, milk and pepper. The whole thing grilled under a crisping brown blanket of grated Irish cheddar cheese.

Maybe he hadn't the patience to make a decent shepherd's pie like she did. Maybe those things weren't meant to be replicated.

Maybe you had to birth a dish of your own, when you were good and ready. This dish was his mother's. So let it be.

He knew well this was not something she just threw together. This was a meal she would spend an entire afternoon preparing for him. This was what she cooked for him when she wanted to say, "I'm sorry. You are my son. And I love you." This was language. Her language.

This was a dish from another time, another place, in it were hints of, not just his own childhood, but of hers also. In it were memories of her own mother, long gone; her father, hungry after a day out on the farm . . . and back beyond that, too. A stew of love, and loss, and heartache, and distance. It had all of Ireland in it, and the Atlantic, too.

"Enzo sent you oranges," he said, handing her the bag.

She opened the bag and smelled them and she smiled.

He sat at the small enamel-topped table where she had placed her cassette recorder and her small collection of cassette tapes. He couldn't remember the last time he'd seen them off the shelf above the sink. Years maybe. Tommy Makem was singing "Carrickfergus." She had the window open to let the heat out, and the afternoon traffic hummed along outside on Tenth Avenue at an easy pace.

It was late summer. Rush hour was over. The commuters had gone home to New Jersey, Westchester, Connecticut, and Long Island, or wherever it was people went. Hell's Kitchen was just a village again. A small Irish village in a sea of other little villages: The Upper West Side. The Upper East. Washington Heights. Harlem. Morningside Heights. Sugar Hill. Midtown East. The Village. Little Italy and Chinatown. A handful of migrant villages struggling to retain some sense of identity in an ever shifting flood of newcomers.

"Leave them jeans on the back of the chair tonight and I'll put a stitch in them for you," she said, glancing at his exposed knee as she set a glass of milk before him on the table.

"I don't mind."

"I do. You think I want the whole neighborhood thinking I let you out the door looking like that. I didn't raise no bum."

"I'll leave them on the chair."

"Good," she said, sliding a steaming plate of shepherd's pie before him. "Mind, that's hot." She let her hand rest on his shoulder for just for a beat. Gave it the slightest squeeze. He reached up and put his hand on top of hers. There it was. He let go. She let go, and went back to the stove to serve herself a plate.

"They found a lump," she said, once she was sitting across from him, a forkful of shepherd's pie raised to her mouth, casually, as if this was no news at all.

"Found what?"

"At the doctors."

"When were you at the doctor?"

"Stopped in after Mass this morning. Pass me that salt there off the counter."

"Where . . . where is the lump?"

"Probably nothing."

"Ma, where did they find it?"

She patted her chest lightly, high above her breast as she gazed off out the window.

"They're gonna run some tests."

"What did he say?"

"What's to say? It's nothing. Old age. Eat your dinner 'fore it gets cold."

"Ma."

"I'll let you know when I know. I'm grand. I've survived a lot worse than lumps, I can tell you. Eat your dinner."

So he'd been wrong about the meal. It was more than an apology, it was this she needed to tell him. It meant it was serious. It meant she was scared. He had to get her out. Away from all the stress. The chaos.

"Did I tell you I met Liam Kelly?" he said.

"Eileen's boy?"

"Yeah. Met him that day I went down to Paddy Collin's funeral. He's moved out of the neighborhood."

"Where?"

"Upstate. Living outside of Woodstock."

"He left his mother!"

"No, Ma, *they* moved out there."

"Eileen left the neighborhood?"

"Yeah. They got a little place out there."

"To do what?"

"You know, live."

"Kitchen wasn't good enough for them?"

"Ma, they got a nice little house. Some property. He says it's great. People are nice. Says it's real quiet. I was thinking—"

She put her fork down, patted her lips with a napkin and eyed him with some concern.

"—it might be nice . . ." he continued.

"What might be nice?"

"Little place out there? You know, a little house. A garden."

"What did you do?"

"Ma."

"I knew it. Minute I saw you hanging out 'round with that damned Coyle crew . . ."

"Ma . . ."

"What did they get you involved in?

"Nothing. Ma. I'm not involved in nuthin'. Nuthin'. I swear. I just thought it might be nice . . . Jesus Christ . . ."

"Don't you use the Lord's name in vain at this table."

"I'm sorry, Ma. I just thought, maybe, you know, we'd think about it. Get out. Away from all this, you know. The neighborhood's changin'."

She sighed deeply and dipped her fork into her food.

"Might be nice to have a little piece of land to call our own." He knew she'd like that, *our own.*

She went quiet for a moment. Maybe she was picturing it. The old farm. Childhood. A flicker of something seemed to pass through her eyes, the ghost-laughter of memory.

"What do I know about gardening?" she said, coming back to him now, almost in a whisper.

"Well you don't need to know nothin'. It's just . . . you know . . . it'd be quiet. Nice. Eileen would be nearby. You always liked Eileen."

"She wasn't the worst of them."

"Wouldn't be any stairs. You could have a bigger kitchen. Look out your window, see some grass, trees . . . Liam says you gotta see the leaves change up there in the fall. Says you can't believe the colors, like it's a painting. Says he never seen his ma happier."

"What would we do? Sure we can't afford a house in the country."

She was right. They couldn't. He couldn't. Yet.

"But if we could?"

"Cost a bloody fortune," she said. "Alright for some people."

And there it was. She'd move. She'd move if he could make it happen.

64

He smiled at her.

"Let me get you another plate," she said, standing now with some authority, taking his plate back to the stove. "Gotta keep you strong."

13

He needed a fight. A big fight. It was the only way. He had to knock the drinking on the head. Get in shape. Start running again. The purse wouldn't be enough. But he'd bet on himself. Maybe get Cheddar to do it for him so nobody would know how much he was in for. He could trust Cheddar. He'd borrow big a couple of weeks out from the fight. Get Cheddar to put the money down with five or six different bookies in the neighborhood. Give him a few bucks for himself, make it worth his while.

If he did this right, he'd have Ma out of The Kitchen and up in Woodstock in time to watch the leaves change. They could rent a little apartment out there to start off. 'Til they got to know their way around. He'd want to take his time, get to know the place right, meet a few of the locals, get the lay of the land, before they bought a little place of their own.

It had to be just right for Ma. He'd know it the minute he saw it.

He could see it now. It wasn't a big place. It had a dirt lane running in to it through some tall trees. Nothing too showy. But real nice. Like something you'd see in one of them fancy magazines. One floor, so Ma didn't have to climb the stairs no more. It would have four bedrooms. Big one for him and an even bigger one for

Ma. They'd use the two smaller ones for guests, old friends they'd invite out from the neighborhood. And there'd be a long back garden, green as a Donegal meadow, all the way to a river. And at night she'd leave her window open to catch the breeze and she'd be able to hear the river running there, on their property, and then in the summer she'd sit down there with her feet in the water to cool off.

That's how it would be.

He'd build the new coops out there too. And a little shed. Place to store the feed and the gardening tools.

Maybe Gabriela is there, too. They'd have Enzo and Maria out to visit, of course. They'd lay it on real big when they'd visit. "That's a nice swing set," Maria will say, as Danny's casually turning some fat steaks on the grill. "You'll have to make some babies to enjoy it."

And he and Gabriela will smile at one another just then, and Maria will scream, "What! You're pregnant?" And that'll be how they announce that they're having a baby.

It was all so doable. It was clear to him now. He could see it.

There was only one way to get a fight like that organized that quickly. It had to be through Logan. It would have to be bare-knuckle. It would have to be down at the piers. It was the only way. He had to use what he had. Ma had that lump. Maybe it was nuthin'. But maybe it wasn't nuthin'. Either way. It was time. He had to make this happen now.

First thing he needed was the fight.

14

When he stopped into The Wolf around lunchtime the next day he saw Logan sequestered in one of the booths in back, having an intense conversation with a pudgy, bespectacled guy, about sixty. It didn't look like the kind of conversation Logan would appreciate Danny sticking his nose into.

Danny pulled out a stool at the end of the bar nearest the door and nodded to Mack who was about halfway down the bar chatting with a couple of the locals, Walter Hughes and Tony McElroy.

The two men nodded hello to Danny, and went back to whatever they were chatting about.

Mack sauntered up to Danny, tossing a bar rag over his shoulder. "Hair of the dog?"

"Gotta see Logan."

"You don't wanna get in the middle of that conversation," Mack said, almost in a whisper. "You wanna coke while you wait?"

"Sure."

"You know who that is?" Mack asked him, as he set the bottle on the bar to sweat.

Danny studied the guy again. "I might have seen him go into Mannion's place?"

"Exactly. That's Hyman Goldstein."

Danny took a sip of his coke.

"Biggest loan shark on the east coast," Mack continued. "That motherfucker's got millions on the street."

"He don't look like he's got a penny to his name."

"That's one serious fucking operator right there, my friend. Only guy I know can walk this neighborhood with pockets of cash without a care in the world."

"How hasn't he been hit?"

"You hit this guy, look forward to seeing your family hanging on meat hooks in some warehouse on the Brooklyn docks with Fat Joe's people going to work on them with a blowtorch."

"He's connected?" Danny was fishing for confirmation of what Mannion had told him.

"He's with Joe Fallaci. You see that motherfucker walking down Tenth Avenue, take my advice, pal, you cross the street to the other side so you don't accidentally bump into him in passing."

"What's he doing in here?"

"Good question. Mannion's been his main connect in this neighborhood for as long as I can remember. I've seen him in and out of the Tavern plenty when I work there. Logan's got his big toe in the shark-tank with this motherfucker."

Danny motioned with his eyes that they should drop it. Goldstein and Logan were sliding out of the booth in the back. Logan shook Goldstein's hand solemnly. The two men nodded and Goldstein went out past Mack and Danny without so much as a sideways glance as he put a fat stubby cigar in his beak and lit it.

"What the hell brings you in here so early?" called Logan, with outstretched arms as he came strutting down the bar toward Danny.

"Hey, Logan. How you doing?"

"I'm fucken great, Danny Boy. Couldn't be better." It wasn't often you saw Logan in such high spirits. Whatever he'd been yapping about to Goldstein had sure put him in a good mood.

Seeing Danny playing awkwardly with the coke bottle he held in his hands Logan nodded to Mack to give them some space. Mack gave the bar a rap with his knuckles, winked at Danny, and went off down the bar to shoot the breeze with McElroy and Hughes.

"What is it, Danny?"

"Nuthin'. I'm good."

"The fuck you are. What's goin' on?"

"It's Ma . . ."

"What happened? She okay?"

"Yeah . . . she's just got some health stuff, you know."

"Like what. Nothing serious?"

"Naw, she's gettin' old, you know. I gotta take care of her better."

"Whaddya mean? I don't know a guy in this whole neighborhood takes better care his mother than you do, Danny."

"She's got bills, you know, her leg's gettin' worse, the stairs . . ."

"Whaddya need, Danny?" Logan said, resting his hand on Danny's shoulder. "Say it."

"I need a fight. A big one. I need to get paid, Logan."

Logan was nodding.

"You're a good kid, Danny." Logan pulled a wad of bills out of his back pocket and peeled off a few hundred in twenties and handed it to Danny.

"Logan . . ."

"You put that in your pocket, Danny. That's from the fight, and there's a little extra in there to help with your ma. I don't want you worrying no more. You're one of us, for Chrissakes. I want you to listen to me." He tightened his grip on Danny's shoulder, forcing Danny to look up into his clear blue eyes. "There's some big changes coming to this neighborhood soon. I mean real big. This thing happens, none of us got to worry no more, you hear me?"

"What thing happens?"

Logan paused, taking a breath as if deciding if he was ready to share this sort of information.

"You know the Coliseum?

"Sure, the convention center, up on Columbus."

"Exactly . . . fucken guineas musta figured since it was on Columbus Circle they owned the fucken joint."

"I thought Jim Sullivan ran that place?"

"Yeah, for the fucken guineas . . . Fat Joe and the Fallacis. Well they're gonna tear it down, Danny, and guess where they're building the new one?"

Danny shook his head.

"Right here. In Hell's Kitchen."

"Where?"

"You know the old rail yard over on Thirty-ninth?"

"Sure. Behind The Ward."

Logan was nodding. "They're gonna build a brand new convention center right here in Hell's Kitchen. You know what this means, Danny?"

Danny wasn't quite sure what it meant but he could see Logan could see it. The vision was bright as day in his clear blue eyes.

"I'm talking millions . . . hundreds of millions in construction . . . right here, in our neighborhood. The jobs. The vendors. The unions. I mean, you're gonna have one of the biggest construction projects this city's ever seen happening a coupla blocks from where we're standing right now. Forget the concrete and steel, every single guy working on that job is gonna need to buy breakfast, lunch, booze . . . they're gonna need to borrow money, get laid. And we, Danny my boy, are gonna own a slice of every single dollar they drop. Every delivery truck. Every hangover. Every fucken blowjob. We get paid. That's what I'm talking about. And that's just the construction. You see what I'm sayin'? Once that place gets up and running we control the entire thing, the union jobs, the vendors, the parking . . . we get our people in there. We run the whole fucken thing."

"What about Fat Joe?"

"Fuck Fat Joe. He can keep the old one."

"I thought they were tearing it down."

"He can keep the rubble."

"What about Mannion?" Danny asked, regretting it the minute the words left his mouth.

"Fuck Mannion," Logan spat. "He's out. The Italians are out. They're all out. This new one's mine, Danny."

Danny noticed he said, "mine." He didn't say, "ours."

"Give me a week or so," Logan said, shifting tone. "I'm gonna make a few calls. Let's get you a decent fight. I'll find you somethin'. You ready? You stayin' in shape?"

"I'm ready."

"You were fucken born ready, Danny." Logan laughed, slapping his shoulder. "Am I right?"

Danny wasn't sure anybody was gonna be ready for the future Logan had planned.

15

He'd been leaning against the wall of her building on Forty-eighth Street with his arms folded, hoping none of the crew from The Wolf sauntered by, when she stepped in front of him clutching her purse in both her hands.

She caught him completely off guard. Danny was taken aback. He'd never seen her outside of the fruit store before. Never seen her out of work clothes. She stood directly in front of him and tipped her face up to him and smiled as if presenting herself for inspection.

She wore a form-fitting sunflower yellow dress that sat off her shoulders, and her long silky dark hair shone like Christmas in the evening light. For a moment he felt his chest tighten and felt sure that he might pass out again. Only this time, it was different. The fear quickly subsided and he shook his head and said, "Wow."

She put her hand to her mouth and giggled.

"I'm sorry," he said. "Hi, Gabriela."

"Hi, Danny." She smiled.

"You look . . . I've never seen you outside of the store."

"So how do I look?" she said. Smiled up at him with that same brave face he'd seen in the store a few days earlier.

73

"Beautiful."

"Thank you, Danny."

He felt like an idiot. Here she was, dressed like a princess, and he was wearing the same white t-shirt and jeans he'd been wearing all day. At least his mother had taken the time to stitch the knees over the weekend so he didn't look like a complete bum. The thought had never occurred to him that she would have gone to so much trouble to dress up for a date with him.

In truth he had no experience with dating at all. The few times he had been with a girl he'd been drinking. Over the years, he'd woken up in his fair share of strange beds, hungover and uncertain. But there'd only been one or two girls that he'd fallen into any sort of drunken routine with at all. He'd never had what might be considered a real relationship. He'd never once taken a girl out to dinner. Never once had a conversation with a girl about how they might feel about one another. God forbid. It just wasn't the way things were done in The Kitchen.

The guys and girls Danny knew drank in bars. Most of them had known each other since they were kids. They went home with one another out of drunken convenience. And sometimes by accident. If something more routine developed out of that mess, usually it was because one, or both of them, began to get jealous that the other might go off with somebody else. Jealousy was the only real emotion he'd seen expressed openly when it came to relationships in The Kitchen. But Danny'd seen many solid relationships flower out of a barroom brawl. A guy might see a girl he was home with a couple of nights earlier chatting to some other punk, and, boom, "That's my girl you're talkin' to, asshole."

Even Coyle wasn't immune to the Wild West way of doing things in the neighborhood. His wife Kate had been Benny Black's girl for years. Once Blackie had started bartending for him at The

Wolf, Logan started to see Kate more and more about the place. She was a tough, no-nonsense, neighborhood girl. She liked to have a drink. She was short and stocky and hard as an oak plank. Logan eventually went to Blackie and asked him if he'd mind stepping aside. Blackie said, "Have at it." That was how romance was handled among the men Danny knew: "Have at it."

"Should we walk?" Gabriela said, seeing Danny had no real clue what to do next.

"Yeah. Sure. You wanna go for a drink or somethin'?"

Gabriela smiled but she did not reply. He tried again.

"Or a movie?"

"Sure. That would be nice."

"Okay," he said, having no idea what was even playing. The last time he'd been to a movie theatre was with Cheddar a few years back. They'd gone to see some Bruce Lee movie over on the Deuce. He and Cheddar had thrown kung fu kicks, and karate chops at one another all the way home. It was the last time he remembered a night out with one of his pals that didn't involve getting loaded.

Danny took her to see a movie called *Jaws* that was playing at the Victoria in Times Square. She squealed and buried her face in his arm when the shark grabbed the girl in the opening act. And afterward, she insisted on taking him for a burger and fries at the Market Diner over on Eleventh Avenue.

"My treat," she said, as they strolled back across Forty-seventh.

"You had a fight," she said, as they sat across from one another in a booth by the window over burgers and vanilla milkshakes.

He nodded.

"Does it hurt?" she said, touching her own face where his eye was still healing.

"Naw."

"Can you tell me about it?"

"What do you wanna know?"

"I don't know. Who did you fight?"

"A guy from Washington Heights."

"Was he any good?"

"Naw."

"Are you?"

He shrugged.

"You beat him?"

"Yeah, I beat him."

"How does that feel?"

He shook his head and looked off out the window.

"So why do you do it?"

"I dunno. 'Cause I'm good at it, I suppose. 'Cause I been doing it as long as I can remember. What about you?"

"I don't fight." She smiled. "Maybe you could teach me."

"No. What do you do when you're not in the store?"

"I go to school."

"School?"

"I take night classes."

"In what?"

"I'm going to be a lawyer."

"Really? Why a lawyer?"

"My father."

"Your father was a lawyer."

"No." And here, she paused. She seemed to draw far into herself before she spoke again. "He was killed when I was five."

"Where?"

"In Queens. He worked in a deli, took care of deliveries, maintenance. A guy from the neighborhood comes in one day, pulls a gun to rob the place, my father tries to stop him . . ." She closed her eyes for a moment and breathed deeply. "Everybody knew who did it. We knew. The cops knew. The store owner knew. He was a local kid. A junkie. His older brother was a detective. The kid had used his gun. So they brushed it under the carpet. We couldn't get the store owner to testify. Cops had him scared to death. And, you know, my father was Peruvian. He was illegal. He didn't have any papers. So . . . it's not like he really mattered. Kid walked free. Probably still walking around the neighborhood."

"So you got out."

"My mother knew a couple of women over here. Enzo gave her a job . . ."

"And now you're gonna put the bad guys away."

"I'm going to try to do something."

"You're gonna be real busy around here."

She smiled.

"Is it true you keep birds?"

"Pigeons."

"How many do you have?"

"A couple of hundred."

Her eyes widened. "A couple of hundred! Can I see?"

"You want to see my birds?"

"Can I?" she asked, excitedly.

He'd never taken a girl to the roof of his building to show his birds. He felt strangely protective. He didn't want her up there. Yet. It felt too . . . revealing.

"I have a better idea," he said.

It was well past nine when he walked Gabriela into The Ward. Cockeye was leaning on the ropes coaching a couple of boxers in the ring. Some guy was rattling the speed bag like it had slapped his mother. Another guy jumped rope. A few others were on the weights.

"Watch that left. Watch that left," Cockeye yelled. "What are you doing?" he snapped, jumping into the ring and grabbing the young boxer's fists. "Hold them up. Like this. Don't leave yourself open."

Cockeye stayed in the ring next to the kid to show him; he threw a few jabs and begun to dance. "Like this. Bam. Bam. Bam. See. Watch the feet. See what he's doing? He's dancing around you. You gotta move. Keep yourself covered. Get out of the way of that left. Look for the opening." He threw a fast jab at the kid in front of him, almost connecting with his jaw. "See. Right there. When you see that opening, hit him with the right. Go again."

He'd been so immersed he hadn't noticed Danny and Gabriela until he slipped out through the ropes again and they were standing right next to him.

"Danny! Who is this lovely lady?"

"Gabriela," she said, extending her hand and smiling.

"Well hello, Gabriela," Cockeye said, smiling back. "What the hell are you doing with this bum?"

Gabriela laughed.

"He tell you he was a boxer?"

"I guessed."

"He tell you I taught him everything he knows?"

"No, actually, he didn't tell me that part."

"Well I tried. Sometimes I don't think he listens too good."

"I believe it." She smiled. Danny could tell they were connecting. Cockeye was a no-nonsense guy. And he could tell right away that he saw Gabriela was a no-nonsense girl.

"You like this clown?" Cockeye asked her with sincerity in his voice.

"He's alright."

"Well I'm gonna ask you to do me a favor," he said, taking her two hands in his and leveling her in his gaze. "I want you to tell him to stop dancing with the devil."

Danny sighed heavily. Gabriela glanced at Danny. She wasn't smiling now. She turned back to Cockeye.

"I'll look out for him."

"Good. You do that. Nice to meet you, Gabriela. Now you'll have to excuse me, I gotta get back to this, before these two hurt themselves."

"Nice to meet you, Mr. Ward."

As they left the club, down the stairs, and into the street, it occurred to Danny that if what Logan said was true, and they really were gonna build the new convention center west of Eleventh Avenue, this building would be the first to go. Everything Cockeye had built for the last twenty years would be razed to the ground. There's no way he'd be able to afford another gym in the neighborhood once this was gone. The Ward would cease to exist.

"What did he mean, 'dance with the devil'?" Gabriela asked him.

"He's crazy," Danny said. "You know how many times he's been punched in the head?"

"He didn't seem crazy to me," she said.

"Trust me, he says these things . . . I don't even know what the hell he's talking about half the time."

"What about you? How long you been getting punched in the head? You sure he's the crazy one?" she asked.

"It's different."

"How's it different?"

"I started off with a lot more brain cells to begin with."

She smiled again. But it was a sad smile. Danny caught the first glimmer of uncertainty in her eyes.

16

He was on the roof, tending to a sick bird, when Cheddar came to him with the news of the fight.

"Wow, I haven't been up here in years," Cheddar said, looking around at the birds in their coops.

"How'd you know I was here?" Danny asked, a little surprised to see his old pal on the roof.

"Logan told me you'd probably be up here with your birds. He wanted me to tell you he's got a fight organized for you."

"When?"

"Next Saturday?"

"In ten days! Is he crazy?"

"I dunno, man, he just told me to come tell you. Some Irish guy from the Bronx."

"Who?"

"He didn't give me a name. Said the guy was from the other side. Only been here a few weeks, needs the action."

"A bareknuckle guy from the old country?"

"That's what he said."

"Damn it," Danny said, holding an old bandtail named Rooster in his lap.

"What's the matter? You not in shape?"

"I thought . . . I just thought have time to train. Wha'd he say about this guy?"

"Nothing," Cheddar said, watching as Danny held open Rooster's beak and administered a shot of pink liquid down its gullet with a clear syringe. "Said the guy was a Mick. Off the boat. Stayin' up in the Bronx. Needed a real fight to get in the action over here. Don't worry about it. Look at you, for chrissakes? You're the fucken champ, Danny. You'll take him apart, easy. Fucken guy . . . what does he know . . . fucken sheep-shagger."

Cheddar followed Danny into the coop and watched Danny set Rooster back on his nest.

"Who's this little guy?" Cheddar said, bent over, peering in at Bluey on her nest.

"That's Bluey. She's nesting."

"How long?" Cheddar had always been the one guy Danny didn't mind coming to the roof. Cheddar had gold in him. You could tell the way the birds took to him. They'd come right up and sit on his shoulder. There was nothing to fear in Cheddar. The birds knew.

"Any day now. She's been on there for about a week and a half."

"Let me guess," he said pointing to Henry. "You the dad?"

"Yup. That's Henry."

"Hey, Henry. Looks like you're gonna be a dad real soon, pal. Good for you, man. Don't worry, I ain't gonna touch your girl. I'm just lookin'. Man, it's good to see you still doin' this, Danny. How long's it been up here?"

"Since we was kids."

"Goddamn bird coop's the only decent thing left in this neighborhood. How's your ma?"

"She's good," Danny said, and then corrected himself. "She ain't good."

"Whassamatta wit her?"

"I dunno. Somethin'. She's seeing the doctors and stuff. She can't even get up the stairs. I gotta get her out."

"Out?"

"I gotta get her outta the neighborhood. You know. Outta the city."

Cheddar had taken a seat on a wooden crate next to the parapet. He pulled a half-smoked crumpled joint out of his pocket and lit it. "Where would you go?"

"I was thinking upstate."

"The country?"

"Yeah. 'Member Father Connolly took us up there that one time when he tried to start the hurling team." Danny laughed.

"And we lasted ten minutes 'til we started beating on them fucken hillbillies with them sticks."

"Those were some tough Micks. Where was that?"

"Westchester somewhere. Over the bridge . . ."

"Rockland?"

"Yeah. Thas it. Last time he ever tried to take us crew out of the neighborhood. Think that was the last time I was out that way 'cept when I took the train up to visit some of the boys at Sing Sing couple a times," Cheddar said, and his mind seemed to drift a little with the smoke. Danny noticed his hands shaking as he pulled on the joint. "Nice out there," Cheddar said. Remembering.

"Yeah. Was nice," Danny said. "Met Liam Kelly few weeks ago. He's out there now."

"Rockland?"

"Woodstock."

"That the place where all the hippies are?"

"Says it's real nice. Him and his ma and his sister Maureen got a little house up there."

"Get the fuck!"

"Yeah. Garden. Trees. Says it's easy livin'. Got me thinking, maybe I take Ma up there."

"To Woodstock?"

"Yeah. Why not. Get away from all this. You know!"

"I don't know nobody in the country."

"You know Liam. You'd know me."

"I don't got that kind of money. How you supposed to buy a house, for chrissakes? Can barely afford to pay my bar tab."

Danny came over and turned a crate on its edge and sat next to Cheddar overlooking the parapet. Cheddar offered him a hit off the joint. Danny shook his head.

"Makes me stupid."

"Yeah, me too." Cheddar laughed. He looked small again. Like the boy Danny'd gone to school with.

"I got an idea," Danny said.

"Oh oh, here we go."

"Naw, it's legit. Sort of." Danny could see Cheddar was interested. The idea of a little place in the country out of the neighborhood was dancing around in his eyes. "I got this fight coming up, right?"

"Yeah."

"This don't go no further than me and you right," Danny said, leveling eyes with his old pal for assurance.

"Cross my heart and hope to die, Danny."

"What if I were to hurt my wrist over the next few days."

"Don't sound like a real smart way to win a fight, Danny."

"What if it wasn't hurt, but everybody thought it was hurt."

"How?"

83

"I show up in The Wolf with my wrist wrapped, say I sprained it training over at The Ward. Let everybody see me with it around the neighborhood. You know how everybody talks. Everybody starts betting for me to lose the fight right. The odds go against me. But we bet to win."

"I dunno, Danny, I don't got a whole lot of money to make a bet like that worth while."

"I go to the street for the money."

"How much?"

"Few grand."

"Who's gonna give you that kind of money?"

"I think I can get it," Danny said. "If I can get my hands on it, can you place the bets?"

He could see Cheddar running it through in his mind.

"A few hundred here, a few hundred there. You bet on me to win. Nobody'd suspect a thing. Anybody says, 'Why you betting on a loser with a bad wrist?' You say, 'We're old friends, and that's what friends do.' Who's gonna argue with that? Everybody knows we go back all the way."

"Then you kill the guy in the ring."

"I take that donkey apart."

Cheddar grinned, a wide foolish childish grin and he chuckled. "Man, it's good, Danny. You sure you can take this guy?"

"Trust me, they throw King Kong in there with me I'm ready to put that bear on the mat."

"How much you think you can get your hands on?"

"You in?"

"Maybe. How's this work out for me?"

"You want out of the neighborhood?" Danny asked him.

Cheddar nodded.

"You do this thing, I'll get you out. I take the money, buy a little van, and get a house sorted out there. Maybe I rent one for a little while, or maybe I buy, I dunno, depends on how things go. Liam says he'll help us get somethin' real cheap. I get Ma out, get her moved into the house, then I come back for you and your ma. You guys stay with us 'til we get you your own place sorted. Whaddya think? We get out and we get our families out. We leave this whole mess behind us."

"How'd I know you won't just get out there 'n' leave me hanging?" Cheddar said sheepishly, like he'd been left hanging his whole damn life.

"'Cause I give you my word," Danny said, and the two old friends looked each other in the eye, and they knew that was about as good as any contract was liable to get in this lifetime.

Cheddar extended his shaking hand. Danny took it.

"You takin' the birds?"

"Course I'm takin the birds."

"We can do this," Cheddar said, nodding his head excitedly. "Right!"

"We are doing' it."

Cheddar smiled a big foolish rubbery stoned smile. The way he looked right now, Danny thought, he could be ten years old again.

17

Lunchtime the following day Danny stepped into the Palm Lounge up on Broadway and Seventy-sixth Street. Hyman Goldstein's joint. The place he conducted much of his loan sharking business. Danny had never been to the place before, but he knew plenty from the neighborhood who had, and he'd been told this was how you went about asking Goldstein for a loan.

It was dark inside. The place smelled like last night's stale beer and cigarette smoke. A radio was playing 1010 WINS. Once his eyes adjusted to the dim light he noticed a thick-shouldered man in a white shirt was leaning on the end of the bar staring at him.

"Can I help you, pal?"

"I'm here to see Hyman Goldstein."

"He know you're coming?"

"No. I was told I could find him here?"

"Who told you?"

"Terry Flannery," Danny lied. He knew the bartender would recognize Flannery's name. It's possible the bartender might even recognize him. It always amazed Danny at how many people recognized him as "that boxer" outside of the neighborhood.

The bartender sized him up for a beat or two.

"What's your name?"

"Danny McCoy."

The bartender nodded.

"Let me see if he's here."

The bartender, without lifting his palms off the bar, turned his head and nodded to another man down the other end of the bar. The man peered at Danny for a moment then he got up and went farther back into the club. In a minute, he was back again. He nodded to the bartender, got back on his stool, and went back to reading his newspaper.

"Alright. Down the back. First door on the left. Make sure you knock."

The other man didn't so much as glance at Danny as he passed him by.

Danny went back and knocked the door.

"Come in."

Danny stepped into a small office. A room not much wider than the six-foot desk where Hyman Goldstein sat facing him with his back against the wall.

"Come in. Sit," Goldstein said, peering up at him through thick glasses.

Danny sat.

"Who'd you say you were?"

"Danny McCoy."

"The boxer?"

Danny nodded.

"Heard you got some bottle. What are you doing these days?"

"I'm training some . . ."

"Fight?"

"Yeah, I . . . it's a bareknuckle thing . . ."

Goldstein was shaking his head.

"Must hurt like hell, no?" he said leaning back, knitting his fingers across his belly.

"It's no fun getting hit no matter how you're gettin' it." Danny smiled. He'd been nervous about walking in here, but he was beginning to relax a little. Goldstein seemed like a decent enough sort at a glance. Like an accountant more than a gangster.

"But without the gloves?" Goldstein went on, frowning, "The knuckles, on your face like that!"

"Sure. It hurts. But when a guy's hitting you with his knuckles he's also afraid of breaking his own hand on your head ... see ... so maybe he's not hitting you as hard as if he had a glove on there ... you know what I mean? It's gonna look bad for a day or two, but you heal up pretty quick after a fight like that. A guy hits you with a glove, maybe that's worse."

"How so?" Goldstein said, and he leaned forward with his arms down on the desk.

"Well, you figure he's got padding now ... his fist is wrapped up real tight in there, his wrist is locked in, he ain't worried about busting his knuckles no more, he's gonna hit you with everything he's got, his whole weight, bam." Danny jabbed a fast right. "When that thing hits your head, your whole brain explodes ... knocks your brain around inside your head. Maybe you don't look so bad on the outside—like if you were bareknuckle—but on the inside, it hurts, for days ... weeks maybe. You can't think straight. Everything gets real dull, foggy, like your brain got bruised, you know?"

"Why would you do such a thing to yourself?" Goldstein asked. He looked genuinely heartbroken at the thought of it all.

"Why do you do what you do?" Danny asked.

Goldstein leaned back again, and chuckled, taking his glasses off and rubbing his forehead with his palm. "Why, indeed! Why, indeed! I've been asking myself that same question a lot lately. I guess—" he put his glasses back on, "—we are destined. Here you are. And here I am. Maybe we didn't plan on being here. But somehow we both made a bunch of little decisions along the way that brought us right here. Maybe we never had a choice in the matter. Maybe, no matter what we did, even if we got to go back and make fifty different decisions in the run-up, the universe would still have spat us out right here at this table, sitting across from one another . . . despite everything."

"God's plan."

"You believe in God?" Goldstein asked him.

"My ma does," said Danny. "I'm hoping that's enough for both of us."

Goldstein nodded, and they sat like that for a moment, regarding one another in silence, before he spoke again. "What can I do you for you today, Danny?"

"I need some money."

"How much?"

"Three grand?" Danny said. He'd been planning on asking for two but it came out as three. Maybe it was the conversation they'd just had. Maybe he felt like he could ask for that now without getting tossed out of the man's office.

"Three thousand dollars?" Goldstein said, picking up a pen and tapping the nib on a notepad on his desk. "May I ask why you'd need so much money, and how you'd plan to pay it back? The vig alone . . . I mean . . ." He upturned his right hand.

"My mother is sick."

"Ah. I'm sorry to hear that. What is it?"

Danny touched his hand to his chest. Goldstein nodded. "I've had my own troubles of late in that regard."

"Cancer?"

"The heart," Goldstein said, tapping his own chest.

"You gonna be okay?"

"They opened me up and cleaned the pipes. They think they have it fixed for now. But I don't know . . . I feel the devil's breath on my neck lately."

"I've got to get her the right help."

"She don't have insurance?"

Danny shook his head. He didn't want to get into specifics. He certainly didn't want Goldstein to know what he really wanted the money for. Goldstein seemed like a decent guy but he was pretty sure he wouldn't take kindly to the idea of Danny dumping the entire three grand on a boxing match. His own boxing match.

"You sure you want to take this sort of money from us?" Goldstein said. He didn't need to spell out who the "us" was. Danny knew that if he fell short on payments it wouldn't be Goldstein at his door with his little black book. It would be one of the goons he'd seen out front with a blackjack. Or worse.

"I can pay you back."

"Okay. I'll tell you what I'll do, Danny, 'cause I think you're a good kid. Usually a loan of this size I charge four or five percent vig, but I'm only going to charge you two. You think you can come up with sixty bucks a week?"

"Yes."

"Good. You bring your payment up here every week. No later than Friday noon. You hand it to Lou at the bar. He'll take care of you from here out. You take my advice, you try to get out from under this fast. This ain't like losing a fight, Danny. Don't let the vig get away on you. You let this thing away on you, you won't be able to punch your way out of this one. You hear what I'm saying. These people won't offer you a fair fight to sort this out, gloves or no gloves."

Danny nodded.

"Okay," Goldstein said, opening the small black book on his desk. "Danny McCoy. Three grand at two percent. There it is. It's officially in the book. And the only way that gets taken out of that book is if you pay it back . . . or . . ." and here, he leaned to open his desk drawer, retrieved three neat stacks of bills bound in elastic bands, and slid them across the table to Danny. "—something terrible should happen to you."

"Thank you, Mr. Goldstein."

"You're welcome," Goldstein said, standing to offer Danny his hand, to indicate they were done. "And you take good care of your mother. Maybe that's the only real vig God demands of any of us . . . an act of kindness here and there. Maybe that's what keeps the scales tipped in the right direction."

Danny nodded. He took the three bundles and slipped them into the pocket of his ripped jeans and made his way back out through the dark bar.

"I'll see you Friday," he said to Lou who was wiping the end of the bar with a rag.

Lou glanced at him coldly and went right on wiping the bar.

18

"The fuck happened your wrist?" asked Mack when he ran into Danny on the avenue on his way to start his shift at The Wolf.

"It's nothing." Danny shrugged. "Probably just sprained."

"How?"

"I dunno. I was working the heavy bag . . . I just . . . it went over on me."

"You gonna be okay to fight next Saturday?"

"I should be okay," Danny said, glancing at the wrist he'd bandaged not an hour earlier over at The Ward. He regretted starting this whole endeavor. He was tempted to go find Cheddar. Call the whole thing off. His wrist actually did hurt now as he held it, as if the lie had twisted his tendons.

Mack was shaking his head with a look of real concern. "It's only a week away, Danny. This fucken Mick is no joke."

"You've seen him fight?" Danny asked. He didn't know the first thing about this Irish guy he was supposed to fight.

"Yeah, I saw him."

"Where? I thought he was just off the boat."

"The Bronx. Few weeks ago. First week he was here. This guy's a fucken animal, Danny."

"Big?"

"Logan didn't tell you nuthin' about him?"

"Naw."

"Guy's like a wild bull. Wide as he is tall. No fucken neck—I mean, no fucken neck—at all," Mack said, puffing himself out, and pulling his shoulders up around his ears to demonstrate. "Arms like fucken tree trunks."

"Was he fast? Can he fight?"

"He was in with this black kid from Brooklyn . . . what was his name . . . Darius some shit or other . . . I mean, I saw this kid come in the ring first . . . big guy . . . I'm thinking, okay this jungle-bunny's fucken built, right. This is all over. Then this fucken Paddy gets in there and he just takes him apart like a rag doll. I mean they had to actually jump the ropes and drag this savage motherfucker off this guy before he turned that poor kid's face into pulp. I mean, he's just a goddamned . . ." And here Mack seemed to struggle for the word. "An animal, he's just an absolute fucken animal, Danny."

"Did you tell Logan about this fight?" Danny asked.

"Whaddya mean, tell him! Logan was right there with me."

"Logan saw this guy fight?"

"That's where he met him. Took him out for drinks up in the Liffey bar in Kingsbridge afterwards. Motherfucker drinks like he fights." Mack laughed, glancing at his watch. "Listen, I gotta hop, my shift is starting. You better get that wrist sorted before Saturday, Danny, or we'll have Paddy Brennan in the ring measuring you for a pine box to get you home."

So Logan knew, Danny thought, as he watched Mack race away down Tenth toward The Wolf. He knew and he didn't say a goddamned thing to him about this guy being an animal. Danny felt a surge of alarm. He needed to find Cheddar and get the three

93

grand back again. Call this whole thing off before it was too late. He could get to Logan. Tell him he really did hurt his wrist and he needed to reschedule. That would get him out of it.

On the other hand, Mack had really bought the damaged wrist story. There was a good chance he was already down The Wolf right now telling anyone who would listen that Danny was fucked. It would all work to drive up the odds against him. No. He had to roll with it. This was how he had planned it. Only better. Because Mack and Logan had actually seen the guy fight. They already thought Danny was beat, even without the sprained wrist.

All he had to do was beat this Irishman. He was still standing there thinking about it when he heard his name.

"Danny!"

"Gabriela." He hadn't seen her walk up. She was standing directly in front of him. He hadn't seen her since they'd been out to the movies together over a week ago. He'd been avoiding her, truth be told. She was too good for him. Too . . . decent. He hadn't even tried to kiss her goodnight when he'd walked her home after they'd left The Ward. It felt wrong. He wasn't worthy of her beauty, or of her purity.

"You hurt yourself?" she asked, reaching out to touch his bandaged wrist with the tip of her finger.

"It's nuthin'."

"If it's nothing why do you have a bandage on it?"

"I twisted it." And there it was. The first lie. He shook his head and looked off down the avenue. Damn you, Danny.

"You hurt it fighting?"

"Don't ask me no more questions about it. It's nuthin'." The words come out much harsher than he'd intended.

"I'm sorry," she said, her cheeks flushing. "I didn't mean to . . ." She let it trail off. Her eyes suddenly glassy.

"Ah, Jesus Christ . . . I'm sorry. I just got a lot on my mind right now. It's not you . . ."

"What is it? Can I help?"

Danny reached for her hand and took it in his. He was breathing deeply. His chest hurt. He closed his eyes and tried to slow his heart. He couldn't pass out again. Not now. Not in front of this girl. He really needed to go see a doctor about this thing.

"I'm stronger than you think I am, Danny," she said, taking a step toward him, slipping her arms around him, resting her face gently on his chest.

Every muscle in his body seemed to soften as she pulled him to her. "Shhhh," she said. As if she could hear the noise spinning around in his head. "Shhhh." He lifted his arms to her waist and pulled her into him, letting his cheek rest on the top of her head. She smelled of lemon and peach and answered prayers and her breathing took up with his and they lost something of themselves to the other. Handed it over, wordlessly, like an offering, a commitment. A vow.

"I've got this thing to do," he said, softly.

"A fight?"

"Yeah, that's part of it," he said, and she lifted her face to him then, and in her brown eyes were written the soft contours of her heart. "I gotta do this one thing. Then I'll come for you. Okay!"

"Okay, Danny."

He leaned down and kissed her, and she opened her mouth to him.

She was soft, and warm, and right. He gripped her tightly and pulled her to him, her tongue went to his and for a moment he almost lost himself entirely. He stopped. Pulled back. Braced himself with his hands on her shoulders. His breathing was heavy. "Not yet," he said.

She searched his eyes for reassurance, and found it there.

"Okay," she said. "Then I'll wait for you." Then she released him, took a step back, smiled, and went off again toward Mazella's.

He stood there with his back to the wall watching her walk away, feeling for the first time in his life that he'd handed some part of himself to another human.

There was only one way to feel complete again. It would be in her arms.

19

It took Cheddar about a week to come back with the news that the entire three grand had been placed in increments of a few hundred dollars a pop all over the West Side.

Cheddar found him on the roof of his building where Danny'd been practically living for the past week. He'd been staying away from The Wolf and The Sunbrite, but he made sure he was seen plenty around the neighborhood with his wrist wrapped. He was still making his shift over at The Ward, but he played up his injury there, too. He stayed out of the ring and off the bag while he was there. Busied himself, cleaning floors, and even repainted the locker rooms and bathrooms, making sure to hold the brush in his unbandaged hand.

He didn't want word getting around that he was in training, nothing that would turn the odds in his favor, and he definitely didn't want Cockeye to know he was getting ready for another bareknuckle fight for Logan Coyle down at the pier.

Cockeye had asked him about the wrist. Danny told him what he told everyone else, he'd sprained it. Meanwhile, he'd hung a new heavy bag on the roof, right by the coop. He was on that thing every day. He was skipping rope and running five to ten miles a day.

To make sure he wasn't seen on his runs, he'd walk out of the neighborhood before first light every morning and head east. Once he hit Second Avenue, he turned north, pulled his hood up over his head and set off at a trot, making a right across Fifty-ninth, over the Queensboro Bridge and on out through Woodside, all the way out as far as Shea Stadium, before doubling back for The Kitchen.

He'd forgotten how good it felt to be up and out that early, pushing through the discomfort and pain into that sweet sea of bliss, then crossing back over the bridge, the first light coming up over Manhattan, illuminating the troubled magnificence of the entire island, and everything it represented, all its bloody history, the possibilities, and the progress . . . the fear, tragedy, and hope. The only home he'd ever known. And here he was, putting everything he had on the line to get away from it.

"Not gonna lie, Danny," Cheddar said. "Nobody thinks you can take this guy."

"Whadda you think?"

"I think if you don't, you're in some serious shit." Cheddar laughed, uneasily. "Thas a lotta dough on the line, Danny. This donkey gets one clean shot at you . . ."

"Hey. Cheddar. I got this."

"Sure. Yeah. Sorry, Danny. I just . . . I worry, you know."

Danny watched Cheddar's hands shaking as he lit a smoke.

"You okay, man?"

"I'm good, yeah. Just hungover as shit, man. Taking these fucken goofballs last few days. Got 'em off Blackie. Fucken things are brutal. You want one," he said, reaching in his pocket. "I got a couple left . . ."

"No, I don't want a fucken goofball. It's ten o'clock in the morning. You crazy! When was the last time you sobered up for a couple of days?"

"Oh, so you haven't had a drink for a week and now you're mister fucken clean, huh!"

"Naw . . . forget it," Danny said. "I just don't want you to lose it on me. We're real close to gettin' outta here. I just want you to be okay."

"I'm sorry, man. You're right. I have been losing it lately, you know." Cheddar reached behind him and pulled a pistol from the waistband of his pants.

"What the fuck you doing' with a gun?"

"Had it for a while. Bought it off McElroy. Gave it to me for twenty bucks."

"What the fuck you need a gun for?"

"Everybody's got one. Blackie, Knuckles, Coyle, Mack, Flannery. You think I wanna be the only clown without one when the shit goes down?"

"What shit?"

"Man, this whole neighborhood's 'bout to blow. We gotta protect our shit you know."

"From who?"

"Fucken guineas, man."

"What guineas?"

"I dunno, Fat Tony, Skinny Sal, the fucken wops, man. Way Logan sees it, they're gonna come in here and take over the whole goddamn Kitchen once they start on that new convention center over here. You gotta be ready, man, war's comin', you watch."

"Well we're not gonna need guns where we're goin' . . . less you see a bear tryna climb in your bedroom window."

Cheddar laughed at that.

"You think they got bears out there?"

"Sure they got bears."

"Man, that would be some wild shit, right." He held up the gun. "Bam, bam, bam, take that Yogi."

Danny laughed. "That would be funny, alright." He watched Cheddar rise and stick the gun back in his waistband as he moved toward the coop.

"Hey, can you give me a little bit of seed so I can feed the birds a little bit?"

"Sure," Danny said, relieved to see him put the gun away. "They'd like that." He opened the door to the coop to let Cheddar inside.

"Hey," Cheddar called excitedly. "She's got a baby."

"What?"

"Look! It's a little baby bird."

Danny joined him in the coop, and looked over his shoulder at the tiny bird wrestling in the nest.

"Look at that! Good girl, Bluey," Danny said, as the two men hovered over the scene. Bluey paced nervously as her furry little squab struggled to stand upright in the nest. Henry strutted back and forth, proud as punch.

"Congratulations, Bluey," said Cheddar. "Look at this little guy. Looks like you got a real fighter on your hands here. Whatcha gonna call it?"

"Let's call him Cheddar," Danny said.

"Cheddar!"

"Sure. Yeah. You saw him first."

"Really!"

"Yeah."

"Naw, really! You gonna name him Cheddar?"

"Yeah. I'm gonna name him Cheddar."

"Hey, little Cheddar. I'm big Cheddar. It's nice to meet you,"

Cheddar said, visibly moved by the gesture. Danny stepped out of the coop to get Cheddar a small can of feed for the birds.

"Hey, you find Tommy Ryan?" Danny called, suddenly remembering that he'd told Cheddar to go find Tommy and give him what he needed to pay off his debt to Logan. He'd felt real bad ever since he'd helped hold Tommy so Logan could nail his hand to the coffee table. He'd always liked Tommy. It wasn't right.

"Man, you didn't hear?" Cheddar said, turning to him.

"Hear what?"

"Tommy's dead."

"Whaddya mean he's dead?" Danny said, frozen in his tracks, holding the tin can.

"Fucken guy took a nose dive off the roof of his building last night."

"No!"

"Landed in the middle of Tenth Avenue. Boom."

"Ah, Jesus Christ. Anybody see it happen?" Danny's thoughts immediately went to Logan.

Cheddar shook his head. "Not until he was on the ground."

"Ah man. No. What the fuck!"

"Yeah, too bad, right! Always liked Tommy. But he was fucked up too, you know. He was into everybody. Who knows how much he was in the hole for. Hey, least he's out now, right!"

"Whaddya mean, out!"

"He's out," Cheddar said, taking a deep draw on his smoke and turning back to the birds. "He's outta The Kitchen."

20

"Cancer," his mother said without looking up at him when he came in. She was seated at the small kitchen table, smoking a cigarette and drinking a glass of whiskey, a routine she usually reserved for funerals, weddings, and papal inaugurations.

"Ah, Jesus. Ma."

"I told you," she snapped. "Don't ever use the Lord's name in vain in this house."

"You sure?"

"Whaddya mean, am I sure! Don't be gettin' all worked up on me now. It's nuthin'. They'll take it off and that'll be the end of it."

"They're gonna operate?"

"Said the best way to go was get rid of them both," she said indicating her breasts with a wave of her hand across her chest. "That way you're done and dusted."

"Ma!"

"What! Like I need them! Shoulda chopped them off fifty years ago. Far better off without them, believe you me."

Danny slumped in the chair across from her at the table. He was stunned by the news. It hit him like a sledgehammer. Harder than any punch he'd ever received. Sure she'd been struggling of late, but he'd always figured she'd bounce back once he got her out of The Kitchen. Maybe it was foolish optimism but he'd pictured her tossing away the cane once she got out to Woodstock and started breathing that clean mountain air. Maybe it could still be like that. Maybe the docs were right. Slice them off. Get it over and done with.

"Get your clean shirt on," she said, stubbing her smoke out in the ashtray.

"For what?"

"Tommy Ryan's wake. That poor woman . . ." She let it trail off. She didn't need to explain it to Danny. He understood. The mothers of Hell's Kitchen carried a burden and a bond that was beyond language.

When they entered the McManus Funeral Home on Forty-seventh an hour later, the first person he spotted was Logan Coyle.

Coyle and his wife Kate stood somberly at the casket, paying their respects. Logan was wearing a black suit and a crisp white shirt. Danny watched Logan bless himself and then reached out to touch Tommy's clasped hands. The same hand he'd nailed to a coffee table not weeks earlier.

Danny was pretty sure everyone in this room knew Tommy was indebted to Logan and that it was possible Logan was somehow connected to him going off the roof of that building. But this was how things were in The Kitchen. Just because you knew a thing didn't mean you said it. In The Kitchen you learned early to keep your mouth shut. Even if the man responsible for your son's death was standing right in front of you shaking your hand and telling you he was sorry for your loss.

As Logan and Kate passed by Danny and his mother, they stopped.

"Hi, Missus McCoy," Logan said, taking her hand. "I feel like I never see you around the neighborhood no more."

"Isn't that a heartbreaker," his mother replied, stone-faced, turning away.

"Well, it's lovely to see you," Logan said, ignoring the brushoff with a smile before placing a hand on Danny's shoulder. "How's that wrist holding up?"

Danny shook his head to indicate that it wasn't good. This seemed to please Logan.

"See you tomorrow night, champ," he said, patting Danny on the shoulder before moving along.

"What's on tomorrow night," his mother whispered as she watched Logan and Kate make their way toward the door.

"Nothing," Danny said. "Probably expecting to see me up at the club to toast Tommy with the rest of the crew."

His mother turned from him and sighed as she shook her head.

Danny watched Pat Mannion enter the back of the room just then with his wife Elaine. Elaine was as beautiful as ever. She was all class.

Mannion and Logan practically bumped into one another in the doorway. Mannion stopped cold. Danny watched as Mannion leaned in and whispered something in Logan's ear. Logan seemed to sneer back at him before continuing out the door without a word of response. Mannion watched him go, stone-faced, 'til Elaine gave his hand a subtle tug and they moved on, joining the line of mourners to pay their respects for another son of Hell's Kitchen.

Death was big business in Hell's Kitchen.

21

Danny entered the makeshift ring just under a hundred and seventy-five pounds. His body felt lean and tight and fast. A cheer went up in the packed warehouse. A quick scan of the crowd revealed a sea of familiar faces and many that weren't familiar at all. Logan had really packed them in for this one. The air was hot, and thick with smoke. Beer bottles were being held aloft. A few of the boys were singing "Danny Boy." Someone yelled, "Take him apart, Danny." And then another roar went up and Danny shuddered as he witnessed the beast who'd entered the ring and stood directly across from him.

The Irishman was a bull. He was much shorter than Danny, but he was as wide and thick as a Buick. His head sat atop his meaty shoulders like a boulder that had landed there from a great height. His fists hung by his sides like a pair of concrete blocks. There was no motion in him. Just the two black eyes that lay under the great hood of his brow fixated on Danny in a cold murderous gaze.

Danny glanced ringside, and caught Logan's eye. Logan gave him the thumbs-up and clapped. "Come on, Danny Boy," he heard him yell. But Danny knew in his heart that no one in this room thought he'd get out of this ring in one piece. This was why Cheddar had managed to get such great odds for him to win. The bookies had him down as a dead man.

Declan O'Sullivan, the referee, was in the ring now, quieting the crowd. Declan was old-school. An Irishman from the other side. He was known to be a fair man in the ring. A man of great power. A man who could put himself between two enraged boxers, if need be, to save a man's life.

"Quiet," he yelled to the crowd. "Men. Would youse shut up a minute. Boys . . . shut the fuck up."

Once he had the room quieted, he motioned for Danny and the beast to join him in the center of the ring. When he had them right next to him, he laid down the rules.

"Listen to me now, lads. There'll be no biting. No head-butting. And no kicking. And I don't want to see any punching below the belt. And no hanging onto one another. Do you hear me? I want a fair fight. We'll have a good fight and we'll all go home."

Neither man spoke.

They continued to stare at one another.

They knew the rules.

"The fight continues until one man is unconscious or one of you says, Stop. You got it? Good. Now, let's have a fair fight and may the best man win. You ready? Wait for my hand . . ."

He raised his hand and watched the two men take a step back from one another.

Danny thought of his mother. Gabriela. His birds. Of Cheddar, and of Tommy Ryan taking a swan dive off the roof of his building. There was one sure way out of this neighborhood and that was to go straight through this beast of an Irishman.

Declan dropped his hand and the two men slammed into one another. Danny felt the familiar explosion of pain as the Irishman caught him with a solid right hook to the side of his head. For a split second everything went white. The beast was much faster than he appeared, and now he was pressing into Danny with a relentless flurry of solid body blows. Danny was struggling to defend himself. The sheer power of the beast had thrown him off guard. He had to push back, to find an opening, to get a solid shot at this animal, enough to slow him down a little just so he could catch his breath. The beast dropped his left for just a flash to throw everything he had into a solid fight-ending blow to Danny's ribs. Danny took the opening with his right and caught him square on the cheek bone just beneath the left eye. It was like hitting the front end of an oncoming steam train. But he could feel that he'd connected, and the beast was knocked momentarily off balance.

Danny took advantage of his shock and caught him immediately with a left that would have broken another man's jaw. The beast's eyes went wide with the shock of it. Danny took the pause to step back and find his feet beneath him.

He inhaled deeply for the first time since the assault had begun.

The right he'd taken had winded him and he was pretty sure a couple of his ribs were broken. He had to end this thing fast or this animal would turn him to a pulpy mess.

The beast had regained his footing and came at him again with a renewed vengeance, like a pit bull that had broken free of its tether. Danny braced himself, and went at him like he was a wall he had to fell with his fists. The adrenaline had kicked in and he was above and beyond all pain for now. His fists sailed down on the beast with meticulous brutality. The beast thundered away with an explosion of savagery. He caught Danny with another inhuman blow to the lower ribs and Danny almost buckled. The beast, sensing blood, was on him in a whirlwind of fists. *Bam. Bam. Bam.*

107

Danny felt his balance start to go. The beast was on his head. His face. His ribs. A hurricane of arms. There was no logic or skill to any of it. Nothing but pure brute force and rage. Danny pulled his arms in tight and braced himself for the end . . . and then . . . out of somewhere came the miracle clarity of survival . . . and his right fist was traveling up from below as if it had exploded from the very center of the Earth, an inverse lightning bolt, he could see it in slow motion as if it were apart from him, a ghost appendage, finding its way through the windmill of arms and it hit the beast on the lower left side of his jaw like a battering ram slamming into an oak door. The beast's head snapped with such force that it almost spun off his shoulders. His entire body lifted and seemed to levitate for just an instant, and then, his whole body sailed straight back and up. Danny watched as his opponent fell, silent as snow, and crashed to the ground before him, splayed out on the floor like a discarded child's doll.

It was over.

The room erupted in screams and yells. It all came suddenly into focus. He glanced to the audience. They were torn between elation and rage. The shock of his triumph and their own financial failure was beginning to register on their faces. No one had expected Danny to win. Their wagered money was before them, every wasted cent, motionless on the floor.

He caught Logan's face again in the front row. Danny could read the magnitude of the loss on his face. He could see also in that instant, a sense of the confusion on his face, Danny's wrist was supposed to have been damaged. The beast's win was a guaranteed certainty. This had been a sure bet.

How could this have happened?

Did you fucking lie to us about your wrist?

The twin questions were written in Logan's eye's like a pair of hand grenades that had lost their pins.

Danny closed his eyes and inhaled deeply.

He'd beaten the beast.

He'd taken a shot at everyone who didn't believe he could do it. He could finally afford to get his mother out of Hell's Kitchen.

22

He was twenty feet from the door of The Wolf the following morning when he saw Terry Flannery emerge from the bar, lighting a smoke. Flannery appeared ashen-faced and disoriented by the morning light. He raised his hand to shade his eyes against the glare of the sun and noticed Danny a few feet away.

"Danny. Hey man. How you doin?" Flannery said, somberly, shaking his head. "Still can't fucken believe it?"

"Can't believe what?" Danny asked, confused.

"Cheddar."

"Cheddar what?"

"You haven't heard?"

"Heard what?"

"Cheddar."

"What about Cheddar?"

"He's dead, man."

"What?"

"He's gone."

"What?"

"You didn't know?"

"What do you mean he's dead? He was at the fight . . ."

"He's gone, man."

"I don't get it."

"Knuckles shot him."

Danny's head was still dull and pounding from the fight. His rib cage ached with every breath. He'd gone directly home after the fight. He'd sat on his roof with the birds for half an hour or so and then gone to bed. It was what he always did after a fight. When a fight ended he wanted to be alone, in the dark, with his pain.

"What do you mean, Knuckles shot him?"

Logan came out of the bar just then, Mack behind him.

"Jesus Christ, this fucken kid, you know the goddamned heat he's gonna bring down on the neighborhood," Logan was saying.

"That cocksucker is dead," Mack spat. "I'm gonna fucken strangle him with my bare hands."

"Danny didn't know," Terry said.

"You didn't know Cheddar was gone?" Logan asked.

Danny just shook his head. He couldn't process what was happening. His head was still pounding from the fight. None of this made sense.

"Ah Jesus Christ. Look at this, there's another one," Logan said, nodding at the blue-and-white rolling slowly by the front of the bar. The two cops eyeing Logan, Flannery, Mack, and Danny, as they passed.

"What the fuck do you want?" Mack yelled at them, throwing his arms up.

"Hey, Mack, Mack," Logan said, placing his hands on Mack's shoulders. "Take it easy, pal."

"Fuck 'em. What're they gonna do, arrest me?" Mack's eyes were bloodshot and swollen like he'd been crying. He was in a rage. Cheddar had been one of the few people he really cared about. It was well known that Mack thought of Cheddar like a little brother.

111

"Cheddar's dead?" Danny asked again.

"Yeah, this fucken nut job, Knuckles, put two in his skull," Logan spat.

"Stupid fucking prick," Mack said, and then he turned and walked away as he began to sob.

"Mack!" Logan called after him. "Mack." But Mack kept walking.

"I don't get it," Danny said.

"They were in here last night after the fight," Terry explained. "Cheddar was out of his mind on some shit. He and Knuckles were fucking around busting each other's balls, next thing you know Cheddar pulls out a gun and points it at Knuckles. He's fucking around, you know! Being an asshole. Thinks he's being funny. Blackie's behind the bar, he jumps out and grabs Cheddar. Throws him out on the street. Tells him to go home, you know, sleep it off, but Cheddar, he wouldn't leave it alone—he just keeps coming back. Blackie throws him out again. Cheddar comes back again. He's out of his mind, you know. Stoned. So Blackie comes out of the bar and gives him a beating, sends him off up the block, thinks that's the end of it. Then Knuckles, he gets it in his fucken head that he's been disrespected and he needs to go do something about it, so he follows Cheddar up the block, finds him in front of his building and bam . . ."

"Shoots him right in the fucking face. You believe that shit?" Logan added, shaking his head. "How long those two clowns known each other."

"Their whole lives," Danny managed to say. "We've known each other since we were kids."

"Ah, I'm sorry, Danny," Logan said.

"Where's Knuckles?" asked Danny.

"Hiding out, up in Blackie's apartment," Terry said.

"Get this shit," Logan says. "Blackie comes in his apartment last night and there's Knuckles, passed out on his couch. He wakes up this morning and Blackie says, 'What the fuck you shoot your best friend for?' He says, 'I don't know.'" Logan shakes his head and chuckles. "He don't know. Fucken guy could barely remember he did it."

Danny felt nauseous. His chest tightened and the world began to swim and spin. Next thing he knew he was on his ass, propped against the wall of The Wolf and Benny Black was splashing a glass of water in his face. He looked up to see Terry, Blackie, and Logan, all hunched over him, staring down at him with concerned faces.

"Hey," Blackie said, slapping him. "You alright, bro?"

"Yeah," Danny said as everything came back into focus. "I'm okay. I just need a minute."

"I know. Some shit, huh," Blackie said. "Fucken Knuckles."

"Knuckles killed Cheddar?" Danny asked, one more time.

Blackie nodded gravely. "Yup, blew his fucken head off, the dumb fuck."

Danny was struggling to pull all the threads into place in his battered brain. His childhood friend was dead. And on top of that, he'd never thought to ask Cheddar about where he'd laid the wagers for the fight. Whatever money Cheddar had wagered was gone.

His childhood friend was gone, and Danny owed Hyman Goldstein three thousand dollars.

"Come on," said Logan. "We're goin' down to the Market Diner. Let me buy you some eggs."

23

Danny sat next to Terry Flannery in a window booth of the Market Diner across from Logan Coyle and Benny Black.

Cheddar's murder had done nothing to dull their appetites. The waitress brought eggs, bacon, home-fries, French fries, pancakes, waffles, and toast. There was barely enough room on the table for the ashtray. Terry had a cigarette going as he ate.

"Have some eggs, Danny," Logan prodded. "How're you not hungry after that fight?"

"You lifted that fuck right off his feet with that last right hook." Terry laughed. "That was some crazy shit. Almost sent him flying straight back to the Old Country with that one."

"He was lucky you had a bad wrist, Danny, you might have killed the poor fuck," Logan added, as he shoved a forkful of home-fries into his face. Danny couldn't tell if Logan was fishing to see if he'd faked the story about his sprained wrist. The only person who knew the truth, other than himself, had been Cheddar. There was no way Cheddar would have told any of these guys the truth. Not that it mattered. Cheddar was gone.

"He was one tough bastard," Danny said.

"He wasn't so tough when you were done with him." Terry laughed. "Bet you he ain't never been hit like that before."

"That's what you get for comin' into The Kitchen thinkin' you're some kinda tough guy. Fucken donkey," added Blackie. "There's Irish, and then there's Hell's Kitchen Irish. Am I right! Damn, I'm sorry I missed that one. You took him out in two minutes, huh?"

"Less than two," said Logan, chewing on some sausage. "A minute fifty and change. Gotta be a record."

If they'd lost money on him, and they'd definitely lost money on him, they didn't show it. All three of them seemed genuinely proud of his performance. He felt bad he'd cheated them. It wasn't right.

"They're gonna be lining up to challenge you now, Danny," Logan said, putting his fork down and leaning back with his coffee cup, draping his arm over the back of the booth.

"I'm done," Danny said.

"This fucken guy." Logan laughed. "Wha'd I tell you, Terry?"

"Every time." Terry nodded, shoveling more pancake into his face.

"Every goddamned time." Logan nodded. "If I got a dollar for every time you said you were done boxing, Danny, I'd be living in a fucken penthouse over on Park Avenue."

"I'm really done this time."

"Sure. Sure you are. Until the next time." Logan smiled.

"I can't believe Cheddar's gone," Danny said.

"Yeah. It's fucked up." Logan nodded. "It's a goddamn shame . . . but the kid was out of control. Him and Knuckles been high as a pair of kites for the last six months. You're all out of line. All a yis. I'm tellin' you, this shit's gotta stop. I gotta bunch a goddamned cowboys on my hands. Do you guys even know where we are standing right now? Look out that window. Whadda you see?"

The men all glanced out the window of the Market Diner. A yellow cab barreled up Eleventh Avenue, banging and rattling through ruts and pot holes. On the far side of the avenue a tired looking lady in bell bottom jeans and a pink t-shirt maneuvered a stroller around a stack of discarded wooden pallets. A guy wearing nothing but a pair of red satin shorts and white sneakers stood on the corner of Forty-third, waiting while his poodle took a dump.

Danny spotted Cockeye coming down the street with a young boxer he recognized from the gym. He hoped they didn't come inside. He could do without Cockeye seeing him at a table with Coyle and the crew this morning. To his relief, Cockeye crossed the avenue, and kept on going in the direction of The Ward.

"You wanna know what I see?" asked Logan, leaning forward, his elbows crossed on the table, regarding each of the men with an intense glare.

"I see a piece of ass I'd like to bang," said Blackie, nodding to a girl in denim shorts and headphones, headed downtown on a bicycle.

"See, this is what I'm talking about," snapped Logan. "I'm trying to say something here, and you guys are busy sitting around with your dicks in your hands thinking about your next piece of ass. Can you stop behaving like a goddamned child for five seconds while I talk?"

"Sorry, bro," Blackie said sheepishly.

"Let me tell you something . . . right now we are standing on the brink of a future you can't even imagine. Money. Power. Respect. You hear what I'm sayin! Look out there. Back in the thirties and forties this whole place was Owney Madden's. He ran the whole thing. Then Hughie Mulligan took over through the fifties and sixties, the docks, the loansharking, the unions, protection money, all of it—'til he handed it off to Mannion about ten years

116

ago. That greasy, no good, donkey fuck." Logan couldn't even say the name without having to clench his teeth. "Don't you see?"

None of the men spoke. They knew well what he was talking about. Logan wanted to be King of the West Side. He had the crown firmly locked in his sights.

A tired looking waitress stopped at the table with the coffee pot. She knew all the faces. Knew them since they were in high school. She didn't bother with any small talk. She filled the cups, dropped the check on the table, and moved on.

"In a few months they're gonna break ground over here on this new convention center. Right here. I mean . . . in our fucking neighborhood. Can't you guys see!"

"You do pretty good, Logan," said Terry.

"What! 'Cause I got a fucken shithole bar! I got a few lousy dollars out on the street!"

"You got a nice car. Nice house out in Jersey."

"Scraps. That's what I got. I got whatever scraps fall off Mannion's table. And Mannion's taking whatever scraps the guineas let him have. Well I'm done eating scraps. They can eat my scraps for a change. Why should I stand back and let those fucks tell me what I can and can't have. It's my fucken table," he said, slamming his fist on the table, making the plates jump and heads in the diner turn his way. "Ah, fuck this shit. Why am I even wasting my time!" Logan shoved out of the booth and stood up.

"Logan, sit down," Blackie said. "Logan, where you goin'?"

Logan dropped a twenty next to the check and stormed off. The three men watched him leave.

As he was passing beneath their window he looked up at them and raised his middle finger and grinned as he shook his head.

"Crazy motherfucker's gonna get us all killed sooner or later."

Blackie laughed, holding up his own middle finger to the window in response.

"You alright?" Terry asked, resting a hand on Danny's shoulder.

"Yeah. I'll be alright. It's just, Cheddar . . . you know."

"Yeah," Terry said. "Fucken Knuckles!"

"Bro, that dumb fuck better stay well away from Mack for a few days," said Blackie, shaking his head. "Mack loved that kid like a brother. I was Knuckles, I'd hit the bricks."

"Where would he go?"

"I dunno. The islands. Somewhere."

"Only island Knuckles knows is this one. He ain't goin' no wheres."

"Well he better find a corner and hide in it for a month or two is all I'm saying," continued Blackie. "My pad ain't the greatest hideaway if Mack is looking for him."

"He's stayin' with you?" Terry asked.

"Yeah, been crashing on my couch for the last couple of months. Get this, bro, I get in last night after my shift and there he is, on the couch, snoring like a goddamned train. He wakes up this morning, rubs his head, dumb fuck doesn't even know what day it is. I say, 'Bro, what the fuck you shoot your best friend for?' 'Huh, I don't know.' He says, 'I don't know.'" Blackie shook his head in disbelief. "I don't even think he even remembered he done it."

"Were the cops there?" asked Danny.

"Yeah, they came up. Took him down for some questions. He said it was self-defense. Cheddar pulled a piece on him. Everybody in the bar saw him do it. What're they gonna do! They don't give a fuck. He'll be fine."

"He's not gonna be fine," Danny said, standing to leave. "He just killed his best friend. He's not gonna to be okay."

118

"Jesus Christ! Now you're going," said Blackie. "Where the fuck's everybody goin'?"

"I got a headache. I gotta go to work."

"See you later," Terry said. "At the funeral home."

"What?"

"Cheddar. McManus funeral home, tonight. The wake."

Danny turned, and went out onto Eleventh Avenue. A light breeze came in off the Hudson. Fall was coming. It would be winter soon.

It would be winter soon.

24

As he entered The Ward he saw Cockeye sitting in his office behind his cluttered desk. Danny tried ducking past him but it was too late, Cockeye had seen him and waved him in.

"Whassup, Boss!"

"Close the door," Cockeye said.

Danny closed the door behind him.

"Let me see your knuckles."

Danny kept his arms by his sides.

"You ain't welcome in here no more."

"Boss . . ."

"Not enough you see one of your old pals laid out in a coffin two nights ago. Naw. That ain't enough. You sit at a table with his killers . . . eating pancakes. You have a nice lunch, Danny?"

So he did see him at the diner.

"They said Tommy jumped."

"Jumped! What about Cheddar? He jump, too?"

Danny kept his mouth shut. Kept his head down, staring at his feet.

"What they give you for your big fight? Two hundred? Three?"

Cockeye waited. Danny kept staring at his shoes.

"How many more kids they gotta throw off a roof 'fore you understand these guys are no good? Huh! How many more of your friends they gotta send to the morgue? You know that kid you hit last night's down in Saint Luke's getting his jaw wired!"

Danny looked up. Nobody'd said anything about the Irish guy being that badly injured.

"Least he's alive, right!"

"It was a fair fight . . ." Danny started, and regretted it the moment he spoke. Cockeye exploded out of his seat, sending papers flying as he tore around his desk to face Danny.

"Fair! Did you say fair!" He yelled. He grabbed Danny's fists in his and held them up to look at his bruised knuckles. "He was a kid. An amateur. He wasn't no match for you."

"He was tough."

"He was a street fighter. A punk. A dumb kid who didn't know no better. He got used. Same as you. What the fuck I been tryna tell you for ten years! You coulda been a real fighter, Danny. You still could . . . but you're too goddamn dumb." Cockeye smacked him on the side of his head. "You got rocks up there in ya head. Think you're some sort a wiseguy. Huh! That it! You're a punk. A no good punk like your pals. Ten years I give you a place to come in and do the right thing here. I took you in. I say, here, come in off the street . . . don't be like dose odda guys. Now look at you. Big shot. Sitting up there with Blackie and Coyle and Flannery like you're some kinda tough guy. Bunch of degenerate criminals. Well you ain't welcome in here no more."

"Boss . . ."

"We're done. I want you out of here."

"I fucked up a little bit . . ."

"I got kids in here looked up to you. Kids that need a place to come to get away from all that street shit. I'm in here tryna teach

121

'em some good, you're out there hanging out with a bunch of low-life criminals. Whaddya think happens when they see that, huh! See you sitting up there with Logan Coyle and Terry Flannery! You're out. I let you stay in here I'm no better than you and your sick friends. I want you to get your shit and get the fuck outta my gym."

"I'm sorry."

"Treated you like my own flesh and blood, I did . . ." Cockeye's voice cracked. He turned away but not quick enough. Danny saw the tears well up in his eyes.

"I packed your gloves and your stuff from your locker," Cockeye said, composing himself, his voice low and calm. He picked up a black gym bag from beside his desk and turned and handed it to Danny without meeting his eyes again. "Here. Go. You ain't welcome in here no more."

Danny stood for a moment, struggling for a word that could put this right. A word that would set the clock back a day or two. A word that could bring Tommy or Cheddar back. There wasn't one.

He took the bag and opened the office door.

There was silence in the gym. He knew all eyes were on him but he didn't turn his head to see them. He kept walking, out the door, down the stairs, and into the street.

On the corner of Forty-third he stopped. He opened the bag. Some musty shorts, a couple of t-shirts, and the worn red leather Everlast gloves Cockeye had bought for him for his first big fight.

He closed the bag, dropped it in a trashcan, and walked away from it.

Part 2

1

She had her arms wrapped around him when he woke. She was tucked in behind him. Her body warm. Her breath like summer on his neck. He turned to her and held her close. His mouth found hers in the half light and they made love again. He looked into her eyes and she into his and they understood without speaking every bruised corner of each other's soul. Here, in this hotel room, with the curtains drawn against the world, they had found an island of bliss.

There was a loud rap on the door.

They froze.

Danny hadn't told a soul he would be at the Skyline Motel.

"What was that?" Gabriela gasped.

"Did you let anyone know you'd be here?" Danny whispered, in reply.

"No."

"Nobody?"

She shook her head.

The banging came again. Louder this time.

"Let's go, Danny Boy." It was Benny Black. "Put it back in your pants. Let's go."

"Who is that?" Gabriela asked, pulling the sheet to her chin.

Danny got up, moved to the door, and cracked it a little.

"Let's go, Romeo." Blackie grinned.

"What?"

"Come on. Hop. We gotta bounce, bro."

"Where?"

"Fuck do you care! Get your pants on. Let's go. I don't got all day," Blackie said, turning away, making for the stairs, knowing Danny would follow.

Danny closed the door and began to get dressed.

"Where are you going?" Gabriela asked, deep concern now scrawled across her face where bliss had been written just moments earlier.

"I gotta go to work."

"On Sunday?"

He'd been seeing Gabriela for a few months now. She was under the impression he was working construction on a job up in Hunts Point. Which had been true, for a few weeks at least.

After Cheddar was killed, Danny was determined to distance himself from the neighborhood crew. He'd gotten himself a job as a laborer. He lifted blocks, mixed mortar, pushed a wheelbarrow, and tried to bite his tongue when the old Polish guy he was working for yelled at him to pick up the pace. His hands hurt. His back hurt. He made every effort to stick it out. Tried to do the right thing. Then one evening in The Wolf a few weeks back, Coyle offered him two hundred bucks to go with Blackie to collect a debt from a deadbeat gambler in the East Village. It had taken them less than an hour. The guy took one look at Danny standing behind Blackie and coughed up everything he had. The following morning on the site when Wictor yelled at him for more mortar Danny told him to get it himself.

"It's Wictor. There was a problem up on the job," Danny lied. "I gotta go. Stay long as you like. The room's good for another night."

"I don't want you to go."

"I'll see you later. Promise." He kissed her, and made for the door. "Make sure you lock this once I'm gone."

He pulled the door behind him, and made for the stairs.

"Holy shit. What's that stink?" Danny said, almost gagging as he slid into the passenger seat of the battered old Ford station wagon Blackie was sitting in outside the Skyline Motel. It smelled of fish, seaweed, and stale smoke.

"Probably your dick." Blackie laughed, inching out onto Tenth Avenue and heading north.

"Where'd you get this piece of shit?"

"Whadda you care! We're gonna steal a boat, we're gonna need a tow-hitch, right!"

"I think I'm gonna puke," Danny said, putting his hand to his face.

"Don't you fucken puke in this car. Put your hand down. The fuck are you doin'? I'm over here tryna look cool. You're gonna have the cops all over us."

"Sorry, Blackie. How'd you know I was in the Skyline?"

"I called the desk. Jerry told me you was holed up there with some Mexican piece of ass—"

"Peruvian."

"Whatever. We gotta make a quick stop first."

"Where?"

"Just up the street. Take five minutes."

"How do you know Jerry at the desk?"

"Jerry's Maureen's cousin."

127

"Jerry's Maureen's cousin?"

"Yeah."

"I didn't know that."

"What's to know!"

"I'm just sayin', I didn't know they was cousins is all."

"So now you know. Forget about it."

It had been nearly three months since Knuckles killed Cheddar. Three months since Danny'd shattered the Irishman's jaw in his last fight. Three months since Cockeye had kicked him out of the gym. Danny's mother was sicker than they first expected. There was an operation scheduled. She'd been pushing it off. She wasn't saying it, but Danny could see this was hard for her. To let them take a piece of her. She was in so much pain she couldn't make the stairs without help anymore. That left him the sole breadwinner in the house. So he'd been taking whatever work Logan threw his way. What was he gonna do!

Blackie pulled a left on Fifty-fifth and parked outside a red-brick apartment building.

"Let's go, cowboy," Blackie said, killing the engine. "Try to look mean."

Danny knew the drill. He followed him into the building and up four flights of stairs. Blackie knocked.

The door opened, revealing an elderly lady in a cheap blue frock. She looked about his mother's age.

"How you doin', Mrs. Kowalski," Blackie said, cheerily, shoving past her into the small apartment.

"I don't got it," she said.

"Sure you don't."

Danny followed him in and she closed the door behind them.

"Let me get you boys some coffee," she offered, shuffling toward the small galley kitchen.

"I look like I want your fucking coffee," Blackie snapped.

"Keep your voice down, please. The neighbors."

"I don't give a fuck about no neighbors. Where's my fucking money?"

"Tell him I need a few more days," she said. Her hands were shaking now.

"Where's your purse?"

"I, I . . ."

"Danny, go find her purse." Danny didn't move. He'd never made a collection from an old woman before. He wanted no part of this. The old lady eyed him with great concern. He was an imposing figure regardless of his intentions.

"I'll get it," she said, moving toward the bedroom.

"Oh no you don't," Blackie snapped, grabbing her by the arm and dragging her to the bedroom door. "Just show me where it is and I'll get it."

"It's right there, beside the bed," she said, her voice cracking.

Blackie went into the bedroom and came out with her purse.

"What's this?" he said, producing a handful of twenty dollar bills.

"That's my rent. It's all I got. Don't take that."

Blackie began counting it out. "Three hundred and eighty dollars. You're a hundred and sixty short."

"It's all I got," she pleaded. "Just leave me fifty bucks. How am I supposed to eat?"

"Don't eat. I'm doin you a favor, you fat fuck. Now you're on a diet. "

"Fuck you, you piece of shit," she spat, taking a wild swing at Blackie's head. Blackie ducked her arm and backhanded her, send-

129

ing her sprawling over the coffee table. Danny reflexively made a move to pick her up but Blackie blocked him.

"Hey. Don't touch her, bro. Let's go." Then to the lady, as she tried to gather herself off the floor: "You got a week to come up with the rest."

"I hope you die of ball cancer, you sick fuck," she yelled after them, as they went down the stairs.

"Nice. Nice mouth you got," Blackie yelled back.

Danny kept moving for the street.

"She's a feisty old broad." Blackie laughed, opening the car door.

"You shouldn't have hit her like that," Danny said, getting in.

"She had it comin'."

"You shouldn't push an old woman like that."

"What are you talkin' about! She swung at me first."

"You shoved her."

"So she slipped on a banana peel. Big deal. Here," Blackie said, handing Danny the wad of bills.

"I don't want it."

"It's for today. What . . . you think it's gonna look any different Logan hands it to you later. Take it. It's yours."

Danny took the money and shoved it in the pocket of his jeans.

"Now, let's go get this boat. And when we get up there maybe you just keep your trap shut. Better I do the talking."

"You sure this is gonna work?"

"How the fuck should I know!"

2

Coming around Columbus Circle to the entrance of the Coliseum, traffic was bumper to bumper. The National Boat Show was in full swing. Logan already had a buyer out in Long Island lined up for the boat. He'd made arrangements ahead of time with Jim Sullivan to have everything in place. Sullivan ran the Coliseum for Fat Joe Fallaci. There was five hundred apiece in it for Benny and Danny if they could get the boat out of there, and drop it out on the Island without getting pinched. Logan had assured them that the guard at the gate had been taken care of.

As they approached the entrance gate, Danny thought of the warehouse Wictor had been building up in Hunts Point. He'd been impressed with how hard that tough old Polish guy worked. Day after day. Block after block. The money wasn't great, but he had to admit it felt good. There was something about holding that four hundred bucks in his hand on a Friday evening, knowing he'd earned it fair and square. Knowing it was honest. Knowing he didn't need to look over his shoulder. He blocked it out of his mind. It wasn't enough. It just wasn't enough.

When they pulled up at the gate, a ruddy-faced guard leaned to the window.

"I help you guys?"

"We come for the boat?" Blackie said.

"What boat?"

"Logan Coyle sent us."

The guard stared stone-faced at Blackie, the angular pock-marked face, the sideburns, the handlebar mustache, the battered black leather blazer. Blackie didn't look like nobody was in the market for a new ocean liner. The guard leaned further and peered across at Danny. He glanced into the back seat and scanned the inside of the station wagon. Without saying anything more, he straightened himself and walked around to the rear of the car. Danny watched in the side view mirror as the man scribbled something on his clipboard then slipped a walkie-talkie off his belt and spoke into it.

"I don't like this," Danny whispered.

The guard appeared again at the window.

"Drive around the back, and just wait there."

Blackie didn't respond. He drove in back of the building where the very latest boats were lined up in the parking lot. He put the car in park and killed the motor.

"Maybe he went to get the cops," Danny said.

"Maybe," responded Blackie. "What's the story with this broad you're banging. She have any sisters?"

"No."

"Relax, bro. I'm only bustin' your balls." Blackie laughed. "I gotta tie a knot in my dick, thas what I gotta do."

"How many kids you have now?"

"Four. Four kids in a fucken two-bedroom apartment. I tell ya, every time I take my fucken shorts off that woman gets pregnant." Blackie sighed. "Take my advice, Danny Boy, don't have no kids. It's too much. Now I got this girlfriend . . . I tell ya, bro, the goddamn bills are killing me. I gotta hustle, day and night. I can't take a goddamn break. Can't even remember the last time we took a proper vacation, you know!"

"Maybe you need a little break."

"Yeah. I been lookin' at takin 'em down the shore next summer, you know! Rent a little place down by Asbury, Belmar, you know, little beach cabin. Nothin' fancy. Take 'em out fishin', lay on the beach all day. Somethin' nice, you know, with the little buckets and the shovels 'n' shit. They're good kids. Be real nice for 'em. You know what I mean?"

"Sounds real good, Benny. You should do that."

"Who am I kiddin', I can't even make the goddamn rent as it is. Look sharp. Here comes a suit."

Danny glanced up to see bull of a man in a dark suit barreling their way. He instinctively reached for the door handle. It wasn't too late to make a run for it.

"What're you doin'? Sit tight," snapped Blackie.

Danny froze.

The man leaned in the window.

"Who'd you say you were?"

"We're with Logan Coyle."

"Oh yeah! And who told you could come in here?"

"Listen, pal, all I know is, Logan Coyle sent me up here, said his old pal Jim Sullivan said we hadda pick up a boat or some shit."

The man scanned them for another beat or two.

"Okay. See that boat right there?" he said, pointing to a thirty-foot cruiser on a trailer about twenty feet away. "You back up real slow and I'll help you get it hooked."

In less than five minutes the trailer was locked on the towing hitch. No one so much as glanced in their direction.

The guy handed Blackie a slip of paper. "Hand this to the guy at the gate on the way out."

"That's it?"

The man didn't answer him. He simply walked away. Blackie and Danny got back in the car and started out. At the gate they encountered the same ruddy-faced guard. Blackie handed him the slip of paper.

"Have a nice day, fellas," he said. The gate opened and Blackie inched the car onto the traffic circle once more.

"Goddamn, that was easy."

"We're not there yet," said Danny, scanning the area for cops.

"I need somethin' to eat," Blackie said as he swung the rig south on Seventh Avenue. "You hungry?"

"Maybe we better just get this boat where it's going."

"I need a sandwich."

"I dunno, Benny . . ."

"Relax. I'm buyin'."

Ten minutes later Blackie pulled the car to a halt at a fire hydrant outside the Carnegie Deli.

"I'll be right back. You like pastrami?"

"Benny . . ."

"I'll get you pastrami."

Blackie was gone not more than a couple of minutes, when a cop on horseback rode up next to the car. He was eyeing, with some real curiosity, the shiny new boat hitched to this rust-bucket.

"Hey, buddy," the cop called.

Danny's heart was pounding as he looked up at the cop.

"Yeah."

"You gotta move this thing."

Danny glanced at the ignition. The keys were gone. Blackie had them in the store.

"Let's go, pal. Move it."

"I don't have the keys."

"I can have it towed for you if you like," the cop said, reaching for his walkie-talkie.

"Give me a second," Danny said, as he opened the passenger door slowly. "He just went in the deli. I'll go get him."

He was bracing himself to make a run for it. He was pretty sure he could lose this horse in traffic. There was no time to think about it. If he stayed a moment longer it would be too late. The moment that cop called in a tow truck, or put pen to paper to write a ticket, it was gonna be all over. It'd be too late. He'd be tied to the stolen boat. They'd have him. Three to six in the state pen.

He had one foot out of the car when Blackie reappeared with the sandwiches.

"Where da fuck you goin'?" Blackie yelled, seeing Danny with one foot out of the car.

"This your boat?" the cop called.

"Sure is," Blackie said, proudly. "Whassamatta? Dis guy givin' you trouble, officer? Dis fucken kid! I leave him two seconds . . ."

"You know you're parked at a hydrant here?" the cop said sternly.

"Where else was I s'posed to park it?" Blackie snapped.

"I dunno, pal. But you can't park here. It's illegal."

"Jesus Christ, guy stops for a fucken sandwich for two seconds . . ."

"Sir, you can't park a boat at a hydrant."

"So I'll move it."

"Just move the boat."

"Whadda you think, I'm gonna leave it here? This look like a good fishing spot to you, bro?"

The cop had to laugh at that one. So did Danny. Blackie was out of his fucking mind. Even angry he was funny.

"Just move the boat. And watch where you park it in future."

"You got it, pal. Have a great day." Blackie smiled as he climbed in the passenger seat and handed the brown paper bag to Danny. "You're gonna love this pastrami. Best in the five boroughs."

Danny took the sandwich bag and watched the cop turn his horse and saunter away, shaking his head, still smiling.

Later, back at The Wolf, Danny relayed the story of the cop on horseback to Logan, Flannery and Mack. It made for a great drinking story. It was classic Benny Black. The guy had balls of steel. Nothing rattled him. Everyone laughed. They were in high spirits. The boat was a sweet score.

"You did good today, Danny," Logan said, laying a hand on Danny's shoulder.

"Thanks, Logan."

"I got a couple of things coming up gonna put some real cash in your pocket. No more of this fucken chump change. We're gonna start earning some real money around here pretty soon. You stay close, okay?"

Danny nodded. Logan put his hand in his pocket and pulled out a roll of bills. He handed Blackie and Danny an extra two hundred apiece for the boat job and told them drinks were on the house. It was one of those nights in The Wolf when it felt good to be a part of a crew of guys who had your back. The drink flowed, the music played, and all seemed well with the world again.

Right up until Stevie Burke stumbled in the door around ten o'clock.

"You're not welcome in here, scumbag," Mack barked, seeing Knuckles stagger to the bar.

"I just want a drink."

"You don't drink here no more."

Knuckles pulled a gun out of his waistband and slapped it on the bar in front of Mack. "Here. Take it. Why don't you just put a bullet in my head."

Mack eyed Knuckles with contempt.

"Go ahead. Shoot me," Knuckles whined.

"Fuck you," Mack spat. "You ain't gettin' away that easy."

"Do it. End it for me. Can't be any worse than what I feel now." Knuckles began to sob. Logan nodded to Blackie. Blackie rose, and put his arm around Knuckles, and ushered him out the door. Danny went with them.

"Why can't I stay? Please, let me have a drink with you guys? I ain't got nobody no more," Knuckles pleaded.

"Are you fucken crazy, bro!" Blackie said, smacking Knuckles on the side of the head once they had him outside. "Fuck's wrong with you. You know how pissed Mack is with you? That boy was like a brother to him."

"I know, he was my friend, too. I said I'm sorry. I'm sorry, guys. I didn't mean it. I swear I didn't. I don't know what happened. I was drunk . . . Danny . . ."

"I know you didn't, Stevie. I know. It was an accident. But you gotta go home and sober up," Danny said. It broke his heart to see Knuckles like this. This was how it had been since the night Knuckles had shot Cheddar. Knuckles knew right away that he'd made a drunken mistake that cost him the only real friend he had in the world. He'd shown up at the funeral home and collapsed, sobbing, on the floor next to the open casket in front of the whole neighborhood.

"I miss him, Danny." Knuckles sobbed.

"I know you do, Stevie."

"What am I gonna do?"

"For starters you're gonna get the fuck outta here," snapped Blackie. "You got enough for a sandwich?"

Knuckles shook his head.

"Here." Blackie peeled off a couple of twenties. "Go get a bite to eat, okay. Try to sober up for ten minutes, for chrissakes. Go back up to the apartment. Get some sleep."

Three months after the killing, Knuckles was still sleeping on Blackie's couch. Blackie kept a flophouse a few blocks north of The Wolf. Blackie was the only one in the neighborhood who'd have him.

"I'm sorry, fellas." Knuckles sobbed.

"Fucken kid. Breaks my goddamn heart," Blackie said, as they watched him stagger away up Tenth Avenue.

3

As he sat in Saint Claire's, next to the bed the nuns had placed his mother in, Danny prayed for the first time in months. She was comfortable now. Asleep. And out of danger. They had her hooked up to a drip.

An elderly Irish nurse, in a nun's habit, appeared at his shoulder and led him into the hallway by the arm. She assured him that his mother would be fine after some rest and fluids. Then she took the time to scold him.

"Shame on you, leaving your poor mother alone while you're off galivanting. Where's your father in this mess?"

"I don't know, Sister," Danny replied, sheepishly. The majority of the nurses here at Saint Claire's wore the habit, and many of them were from the other side. Danny'd been raised in abject fear of the habit and the collar. He knew killers on the West Side of Manhattan who still trembled under the glare of an Irish nun with an accent.

"What do you mean, you don't know?" she spat. "I suppose he was in the bar next to you when your poor mother took a fall."

"No, Sister. I don't know, Sister."

139

"What do you mean, you don't know. Speak up when I'm talking to you."

"I don't know where he is. He was gone before I was old enough—"

"O' course he was, the tramp. He was an Irishman I'm supposin' by the thick ignorant head on ye?"

"I believe so, Sister."

"Aye. A fine army of drunks and degenerates we exported over here, alright. The worst of a bad bunch. And now your poor mother has to contend with you as well, does she!"

"I'm sorry, Sister."

"You can save your sorries for the good Lord above, I have no time for them meself."

"Sorry . . ."

"It's time for you to smarten up a wee bit, young man. Cut your shenanigans and grow up so that poor woman has at least one decent man in her life to rely on in her time of need."

She blessed herself, frowned, shook her head in disgust, and stormed off without another word, her hard shoes clipping the linoleum as she parted, leaving him to bear the extra layer of guilt she'd fastened to his soul.

It wasn't often he thought of his father anymore. He'd wasted years as a boy fantasizing that his old man would reappear again miraculously out of the blue. A tall, handsome man, with a strong jaw and a bright hundred-watt smile. At least, that's how Danny had envisioned him. He wasn't a drunk at all, not the way he'd pictured him. He was as successful as you please. He'd just been too busy off earning a fortune to stop by, but he'd be back . . . any minute . . . least that's how it had felt to Danny as a boy. He'd come strolling up Tenth Avenue, without a care in the world. He'd set down his suitcase, and hoist little Danny up in his arms. He had real strong arms. And a thick head of dark hair, and the kind of smile you only see in the movies. He was nicely dressed, too. Not flashy, like he was just putting it on for show, but real classy, low-key, like it was second nature to him. His white shirt would be open at the neck, his shoes polished to a high shine, and the ladies on the avenue would smile back at him over their shoulders, but he wouldn't so much as give them a second glance. He only had eyes for Ma, and boy had he'd missed her. She'd stand there for a minute, like she couldn't believe it was him, then they'd run into each other's arms and she'd throw her arms around his neck and he'd kiss her right there in the street for all to see, and he wouldn't give a damn who was looking on. Least, that's how Danny'd imagined it would be.

For years, he'd pictured it just so.

In truth, he didn't know the first thing about his old man. He'd never once been able to get his mother to reveal a single thing about him other than he was Irish. From the other side. She'd never even mentioned a name. By the time Danny was in his early twenties he'd given up entirely on the dream. He'd packed the image of his father away in a box along with Santa Claus and the Easter Bunny, where he belonged.

As he stared at his mother's face now in the hospital bed he wondered if she too had been able to pack him away.

"Danny," he heard a voice behind him and turned to see Gabriela there in the room.

"Gabriela," he said, taking her in his arms. "How'd you know I was here?"

"Stella downstairs in your building. She was in the store earlier. She saw them take your ma away in the ambulance. I just figured they'd take her here."

"I forget that everybody sees everything in The Kitchen."

"Until the cops show up," she said, smiling up at him. "Then nobody seen nuttin', am I right?"

"That's right, baby." Danny smiled.

"How is she?"

"She's gonna be okay," he said, leading Gabriela out into the hallway out of earshot of the bed. "They gave her some fluids, something to help her rest . . ."

"They going to run any tests?"

"I've got to get her out of that apartment. I have to get her out of the city."

"Out of the neighborhood?"

"No. I mean, out. Gone. Upstate. I mean I want to get her out of the city before it's too late." It was the first time he'd said anything to Gabriela about his thoughts of leaving the city. She studied him, looking to hear how this story ended, if she was still in it at the close.

"You never mentioned about wanting to move away."

"I know. But I'm thinking it."

"Oh."

"What would you think about something like that?"

"About you moving away?"

"Us."

"You and your mother?"

"No. Us. You too."

"You want me to move away from the city, with you and your mother?"

"Maybe."

"Where would we go?"

"I dunno. Upstate. Woodstock."

"Is that a town? How . . . I . . . You're serious about this?"

"Yes."

"When?"

"Soon as I can get the money together to buy a little house."

"I don't know. What about my job? My mother?"

"I don't know how I'd make it all work. I just know I gotta get her out. The stairs . . . this fucken neighborhood." He sighed, deeply.

"This is not just about getting your mother out of this neighborhood, is it?"

"Let's not talk about it right now." He could see the concern on Gabriela's face. He could see he'd spooked her. "I'm just worried about her, that's all. I see her in there in that bed and I think I should be doing more. I'm not doing enough to take care of her."

Gabriela tightened her grip on him and pressed her face into his chest.

"I'm here now," she said. "I'm not going anywhere. Where you go, I go."

He pulled her tightly to him. The warmth of her body against his. The feel of her hands on his back. The smell of peaches and lemon in her hair. He bent his head to kiss her.

His mother began to cough in the room.

"Where am I? Where am I? What's going on?" She'd awoken startled by her surroundings and she was attempting to climb out of the bed, and pulling at the tube in her arm.

"Ma, stop, it's okay," Danny called, bounding to her bedside.

"Where am I?" She gripped his arm, and glared up at him, like a terrified child.

"You're in Saint Claire's . . ."

"What for?"

"You fell. You passed out. It's okay, you were just low on fluids. They got you all fixed up now. You're gonna be okay, Ma."

143

"Don't leave me in here, Danny," she said, locking his arm in a death grip. "Don't leave me with these nuns."

"I'm not going to leave you, Ma. I'm right here. You just need to lay down . . ."

"Who's she?" she said, suddenly noticing Gabriela standing a few feet behind Danny by the door.

"That's Gabriela . . ."

"Is she one of them?"

"No. Ma, it's Gabriela, from Mazzella's . . ."

"Don't let her near me. Get her out of here. I don't trust them . . ."

"She's not a nurse, Ma—"

"I don't trust those Mexicans. Get her out."

Danny turned to see Gabriela's pained expression. "It's okay," she said, backing out the door. "Be with your mother. I'll see you later."

"What's she got to see you for?"

"Nothing, Ma. Nothing," Danny whispered, helping her back into the bed. She looked small and frail. Her skin was tighter somehow. Almost translucent. Her eyes were full of a bright confusion.

"You gotta get me out of here, Danny," she pleaded.

"I'm gonna get you out."

"Good boy. Good boy. Take me up to that little place in the country you talk about."

"Woodstock."

"That's it. We'll go up there. Me and you. We'll start over."

"I'm gonna take you there, Ma."

"Promise me."

"I promise, Ma," he said. "I promise."

4

"Hey, fellas. What are you doing here?" Blackie said, as he answered the door of his apartment wearing nothing but a towel wrapped around his waist.

"What! We need an invite to stop by and say hello?" Logan said, pushing his way into the apartment. Blackie knew better than to try and stop him. Danny and Mack followed Logan into the living room. Mack was carrying a six-pack of cans which he held up as evidence that they intended to stay for a spell.

"Guys! What are you doin'?" Blackie said, nervously. "I gotta get ready. I was just on my way out."

"Where's Knuckles?" Logan asked, calmly.

"I dunno, Logan. Kid's been drunk for a month."

"Where's he drinking?"

"Fuck should I know?"

"You know anything about where he's getting all this drinkin' money?" Logan said, slipping a revolver rigged with a silencer from underneath his jacket.

"Hey, Logan, I told you, I didn't have nuthin' to do with that," Blackie said, suddenly realizing the gravity of the situation.

Word on the street was, Knuckles had kidnapped a guy called

145

Dennis Williams, a local restaurant owner, and squeezed his family for a ransom. Problem was, Logan had ordered the same guy kidnapped only a month earlier and now Williams and his restaurant were under Logan's protection. Blackie had been the one Logan tasked with the original kidnapping and he'd taken Knuckles along on the score to help out.

Somewhere in Knuckles' booze-soaked brain he must have figured he could squeeze the guy's family for a few more bucks.

"You sure?" Logan asked, casually holding the gun with his finger on the trigger, the barrel still pointed at the floor.

"I'm sure, Logan. I swear on my kids."

"I told you Blackie didn't have nothin' to do with it," Mack chimed in. "It's this fucken Knuckles scumbag."

"Hey, fellas, I gotta hot date tonight," Blackie said. "I don't show up downstairs pretty soon, she's gonna come to this door."

"I know her?" Logan asked, as if he were pondering clipping her, too.

"She's just some broad."

"Okay, get your pants on. We're gonna hang around here for a bit, wait for Stevie. Have a little chat with him."

"Whatever you gotta do," Blackie said, hurrying to get dressed. "I'll be outta your hair in a minute."

Within seconds, Blackie was buttoning his shirt as he made for the door, keeping one wary eye on the gun Logan held in his hand.

"Hey, Benny," Logan called.

"Yeah."

"You didn't see us up here."

"Sure thing, Logan. No problem."

"I wouldn't want it getting back that you told Stevie to steer clear," Logan said, shifting the gun in his hand.

Blackie understood.

146

"Bro, I didn't see nobody."

"You might want to send him up here for something if you see him."

"I dunno if I'm gonna see him, Logan."

"Maybe you look for him. You tell him you left something up here for him. Okay?"

"No problem. I'll tell him," Blackie said, pulling the door behind him.

Danny dropped onto the couch and picked up an old newspaper from the coffee table. He didn't like that Logan had brought him along. But what was he gonna do. He was still into Hyman Goldstein for the three grand. He'd been chipping away at it but he was barely making the vig. Then there had been the hospital bills. And the rent was due again. And the birds still needed to be fed and cared for. And dinner with Gabriela every other night, and hotel rooms at the Skyline, and the nut seemed to grow and grow with each passing week.

He'd run into Liam in the neighborhood again the previous week and Liam had told him of a little cottage that was coming up for sale next to his own in Woodstock. Liam knew the owner. Said it needed some work, but assured Danny he could get it for a song. He'd just need to come up with a couple of grand for the deposit.

His mother was out of the hospital, but she was practically bedridden since that last stay. He couldn't take a nine-to-five even if he wanted to. A regular nine-to-five just wasn't going to cut it no more. Not to get his mother and Gabriela out of the neighborhood.

"Fucken Blackie." Mack laughed, after Benny had left the apartment. "That fucken guy is crazy. How many kids he got now?"

"Four," said Danny.

"Four kids and a wife at home and he's off banging some other broad!" Mack chuckled. "Fucken guy needs to tie a knot in it."

"Hey, Mack," Logan snapped. "You fucken guys keep it down! Knuckles hears you in here 'fore he opens that door we won't get a shot at him."

"Whaddya mean, shot?" Danny asked. "I thought you said we was just gonna rough him up a little bit."

"That's what I mean, Danny. I mean we got a shot at catching him. Now could you two retards just shut the fuck up and keep it quiet in here?"

Logan positioned himself by the bathroom door. He stood still as a statue, the gun hanging loosely by his side, his eyes fixed on the apartment door. Mack took a seat on the armchair across from Danny and opened a copy of *Hustler* magazine he found shoved down the side of the cushion. Danny put the newspaper down and sat on the couch with his hands folded in his lap.

It was almost an hour later when they heard footsteps in the hall outside the door. A set of keys jingled. Logan glanced at Mack and Danny, and put a finger to his lips to shush them, as they heard the key in the door. Knuckles was in the apartment with the door closing behind him before he noticed Danny sitting on the couch.

"Danny," he said with a broad smile, delighted to see him there. Then he noticed Mack in the other armchair, and before he could speak another word, Logan took one step toward him with the gun, raised it, and shot him right in the forehead.

The bullet cracked off his skull and ricocheted across the room, lodging itself in the wall just above Danny's head.

"Logan . . ." Knuckles said, raising his hand to his forehead. "What the . . ." The next shot went into his right eye and took out a large chunk of the back of his head. Knuckles crumpled to the floor. Logan stepped over him and put another one directly into the center of his face.

"What the fuck, Logan," Danny yelled, jumping off the couch. "What the fuck did you just do?"

"Did you see that first bullet?" Logan laughed. "Bounced right off his fucken head."

"Holy shit . . . that was fucken crazy," Mack said, stepping over next to Logan. He spat on Knuckles' lifeless body and started kicking him violently in the ribs. "How you feel now, you dumb fuck?"

Danny stood slowly, and approached the body lying by the door. He stared down at his old childhood pal, a pool of blood forming about his head.

Logan stepped quickly to the kitchen and returned with a towel, wiping the blood that had splattered on his face. "Grab me a knife," he ordered Mack.

Mack stepped into the kitchen and returned with a large butcher knife.

"Step aside. I got this," Mack said, lowering himself to one knee and plunging the knife into the center of Knuckles' chest repeatedly. "There, that'll do it. You gotta get the heart stopped, otherwise he'll keep pumping blood all over the place," he explained calmly, like it was a goddamn teaching moment.

"Let's get him in the tub," said Logan, shoving the revolver in the belt of his pants. "Danny, grab a leg."

"Guys," Danny said, staring down at Knuckles' lifeless body. "What the fuck! You just killed Stevie."

"No shit, Danny. Now grab his fucken leg," Logan barked.

"You said you were only gonna scare him," Danny said.

"Jesus Christ, Danny, what are we, in grade school here! He had it comin'. Guy's been pissing all over us for months. He shot your best friend, for chrissakes. Fuck him. Piece o' shit." Logan grabbed both legs by himself. Mack moved around and picked the body up by the shoulders. There was a loud sucking noise as the back of Knuckles' head came off the worn oak floor.

Danny ran to the kitchen sink and heaved repeatedly.

Logan and Mack carried Knuckles across the living room and dropped him in the bathtub which was right behind Danny in the kitchen.

"Crack me one of those beers," Logan said, nodding to the six-pack on the table next to Mack. Mack popped one and handed it to Logan.

"Hey, Danny, you want one?"

Danny heaved again.

"We gotta let him sit for a bit, let the blood congeal," Mack explained, to no one in particular. "Less of a mess when you cut 'em up."

"Cut who up?" Danny said, turning from the sink. "What are you talking about?"

"We gotta chop him up," said Mack, matter of factly. "Get rid of the body."

"No body, no crime," added Logan, nonchalantly.

"I gotta go," said Danny, moving toward the door.

"Wow!" Mack said, blocking his path. "Where the fuck do you think you're going?"

"I'm leaving," Danny said, eyeing Mack. The two men were about the same height and of a similar build, but both of them knew that Danny would take him apart if it came down to a fair fight. But nothing felt fair right now.

"I'm leaving," Danny repeated. "I don't want no part in this."

"Where you gonna go?" Mack asked.

"Hey, Mack, let him go. He doesn't want to stay, he doesn't have to stay," Logan said, stepping between the two men, and putting a hand on Mack's chest. "I don't want you to worry about this shit, Danny," Logan continued. "This didn't have nuthin' to do with you. You didn't do nuthin' wrong here, okay. But you gotta realize I can't let nobody fuck me like that. I'm tryna build somethin' here. For all of us. This is just business. Word gets out on the street I let this piece of shit fuck me in the ass then what respect do I get, huh! He was warned. I want you to go down The Wolf, have a drink, and forget this ever happened."

"Forget about it? You just shot Knuckles in the face. His fucken brains are all over the wall."

"Danny. It don't mean nuthin'. Sooner or later he was gonna put a gun to his own head. I heard you say so yourself. I did him a favor. I put him out of his misery."

"I'm just gonna go home, Logan."

"You're gonna go down to the bar, Danny. You're gonna sit down, and you're gonna have a beer, and you're gonna wait right there 'til we get done cleaning up here and we'll meet you there. Understand?"

Danny searched Logan's steely blue eyes. Danny thought of how casually he'd just shot Knuckles in the face. Logan wasn't asking Danny to go to the bar. He was telling him: *This is how it is.*

"Okay, Logan. I'll see you down there."

"Good boy, Danny," Logan said. "I want to talk to you about something. I been working on something special for you. I'm talkin' about a real opportunity here, Danny. A shot at the big time. You'll see. Now go on, get out of here. And remember, this never happened."

Danny opened the door behind him and went down the stairs as quietly as he could. He froze for a moment once he was out of the building. He had a strong sense that he'd left something behind him upstairs in the apartment. He checked his pockets. Keys.

Cash. Everything was there, but he couldn't shake the feeling that something crucial was missing.

He went across Tenth Avenue in a daze, and instead of turning south, past the Skyline Motel, he continued on down Fiftieth Street, across Eleventh Avenue, and under the rusty mess of the elevated Miller Highway, toward Pier 90. He turned south, with the sound of seagulls, and dark water lapping at the bulkheads, and out onto Pier 86, past the hulking mass of the *Intrepid*, in darkness. Past stacks of discarded wooden pallets and stinking piles of rat-infested fishing nets to the end of the pier.

Across the Hudson, the lights of Weehawken and Union City flickered in the icy fog. He could see lights on the Palisades as far north as the George Washington Bridge. A frigid gust of wind came off the river and stole into his bones. He and Cheddar and Knuckles and Terry Flannery and Tommy Ryan and Liam Kelly had spent many hot summer days down here as kids. Stripping to their underwear, and taking long running leaps off the pier into the cool murky water of the Hudson. They'd lain together, right here, flat on their backs, sunning themselves as their shorts dried, inventing stories out of clouds. "Hey, guys . . ." He heard Stevie's young voice call from the shadow of memory as they watched a plane pass high overhead in a clear blue sky, "One day when we're older let's save all our money and go away together on a big adventure."

"Where will we go, Stevie?"

"I dunno," Stevie said. "Anywhere . . . somewhere far away from here."

5

Two hours later Danny was walking into The Wolf when he saw Gabriela crossing the avenue toward him with that bright effortless smile of hers.

She came right up, and slipped her arms around his waist, and moved to kiss him.

He turned his head away.

"Don't."

"What?" She looked like she'd been slapped.

"I'm sorry. I can't talk right now."

"What's going on?" she said, trying once more to wrap her arms around him, to soften into him in that way that she did.

He put a hand on her shoulder and firmly pushed her away.

"I said, I can't talk right now."

She took a step back, and her eyes welled up instantly.

"Why are you talking to me like this?"

"I'm sorry. I just have something to do."

"Danny—"

"Can't you give me five fucking minutes?" he snapped. The moment he said it he wished he could take it back. Her eyes went wide. He'd scared her. He couldn't believe the words had come out of his mouth like that. But right now he felt nothing. He was numb. He didn't want her close to him after what he'd just witnessed up in that apartment. He didn't want any of that ugliness to wash off on her. He stood there, staring at her coldly, knowing there were no words to explain away what had just happened.

She turned slowly, and then hurried away up the street.

He let her go.

He remained there, frozen for a moment, watching her rush past his building and turn the corner onto Forty-fourth. The door to The Wolf opened behind him and two men he didn't recognize barged out. One of the men bumped into him. Without thinking, he hit the man a solid right hook. The man fell backward, his head narrowly missing the wall as he went down. The other man instinctively shoved Danny, and yelled, "What the—" but before he could finish his sentence Danny hit him, too. Both men were on the ground, stunned, struggling to get back on their feet. The door opened again, and Walter Hughes appeared. Hughes grinned at the sight of the two men on the sidewalk.

"Good man, Danny. Fucken assholes." Hughes spat. Then he ran over and kicked one of the men in the face, knocking him reeling into the street. He moved to the second man and began brutally kicking him, too, as the man tried to crawl away. "Piece of shit."

The two men moaned where they lay. Hughes booted the man nearest him once more, then he pulled a small handgun from the belt of his pants, and shoved it in the man's face. "I see you around here again I'll blow your fucken head off." Then he whacked the man in the skull with the butt of the gun.

A wide gash opened on the man's forehead and a trickle of blood ran into his right eye. "Go. Get the fuck outta here." The man scrambled hurriedly to his feet, grabbed his friend, and the two men took off hobbling as quickly as they could down the block.

Hughes turned to Danny as he shoved the gun underneath the rear of his jacket again.

"Let me buy you a drink."

When Danny entered The Wolf behind Walter, he was startled to see Trixie standing behind the bar, wearing a canary yellow boob tube. She had her hair up in ponytails and she was popping the cap off a bottle of beer, setting up a round of drinks for the whole crew.

The men seemed transfixed by her presence behind the stick. Like a honeypot in a bear's cave. Not one of them had turned their head toward Danny as he came in.

Danny had never seen a girl behind the bar in The Wolf. Ever. It just wasn't the kind of place any girl in her right mind would want to work. Not with this crowd of degenerates.

Trixie glanced toward the door and saw Danny standing there. She beamed a broad smile.

"What's she doing here?" Danny asked.

"You know this chick?" asked Walter.

"What's she doing here?"

"I don't know, but nobody's complaining." Walter grinned. "Hey, guys, Danny just knocked the shit out of those two scumbags outside."

A roar of approval and applause went up among the men.

"Looks like I owe you a beer." Trixie smiled, dipping into the icebox.

"What happened?" Danny asked.

"One of those scumbags pulled her top down," said Walter.

"What?"

"Yeah, just reached over the bar and, boom, ripped it right down."

Danny felt a surge of rage at the thought that Trixie'd been exposed in front of all of the guys at the bar. He reflexively spun around to go after the two men.

"Hey. Easy, pal." Walter chuckled, grabbing his arm. "Let it go. Fuck 'em. They're gone. We fuck 'em up any worse, the cops will be all over this place."

Danny thought of Logan and Mack up in Blackie's apartment with Knuckles' body in the bathtub. The last thing they needed right now were cops crawling all over The Wolf asking questions.

Trixie handed Danny a beer. "Thanks, champ."

Danny took the bottle and tipped it to his mouth. He didn't stop until it was all gone.

Trixie stood wide-eyed as he set the empty back on the bar.

"I guess you were thirsty," she said, and popped the cap off another cold one, and handed it to him.

"Yeah," he said, sheepishly, suddenly self-conscious under her gaze. "I guess I was."

"Hey, Danny," said Walter. "You seen Logan?"

"Naw. I ain't seen him."

"He said he'd be here."

"He's comin'."

"I thought you just said you hadn't seen him."

"He'll be here."

"Check this out," said Walter, extending his wrist, to show off a sparkling jewel-encrusted Rolex.

"That real?"

"Course it's fucken real. And I got four more just like it up in my pad if you wanna score one."

"Naw, thanks."

"I'll cut you a deal, man. Five yards. What do you say? Gotta be worth ten times that."

"I don't got it."

"I'll spot you."

Danny moved away from Walter and the rest of the crew. He took a stool at the far end of the bar by himself. He felt disoriented. Like he'd been shoved under water. It was hard to breathe.

Trixie followed him and stood directly in front of him with her back to the rest of the crew. She cocked her head to stare at him.

"You okay?" she asked, once he'd lifted his head to meet her gaze.

"Yeah," he lied.

"You're full of shit."

He just stared at her. The line of freckles across the top of her nose. That sweet knowing twinkle in her eyes. He had a strong urge to tell her everything. Somehow he knew she'd understand.

"You okay?" he asked.

"Sure." She grinned. "Just great."

"Those guys . . . from before . . ."

"Fuck those guys. You took care of 'em."

The door to the bar opened and Tony McElroy walked in.

"Looks like that's my shift's done," she said.

"How come you're working in here?"

"Logan reached out, asked me if I'd cover a shift 'til Tony turned up."

"You're a bartender?"

"You really think I need to know anything about bartending to stand back here and pop a few beers for this crowd?" There was that smile again.

McElroy made his way down the bar.

"Sorry I'm late, Trix," McElroy said, coming around the end of the bar. "Thanks for covering for me. You two know each other?"

"You didn't know," Trixie said, hopping over the bar and sliding down onto Danny's lap with her legs wrapped around his

157

waist. "Danny's my knight in shining armor." She draped her arms around his neck and kissed him softly on the lips. She looked directly into his eyes, and in that instant, he was in love with her. She smiled just then, still looking deep into his eyes, as if to say, "Gotcha." Then she hopped off his lap, adjusted her boob tube, tightened the elastic band on one of her ponytails, and said. "Okay, fella's, I gotta run." And before Danny could say another word, she was skipping off down the bar, past the line of guys, and they were all yelling at her.

"No."

"Please."

"No."

"Don't go."

"Trixie."

"Don't leave us here."

Trixie skipped on toward the door with that carefree smile of hers, waving as she went, and then she was gone.

"Don't even think of it, Danny Boy." McElroy grinned.

"What?"

"Don't."

"Who is she?"

"She's trouble. That's all you need to know. Trouble. Trouble. Trouble." McElroy laughed, shaking his head as he went off to serve the guys.

The door opened, and Benny Black walked in. He was alone. He must have ditched his date, Danny thought. Or perhaps he didn't have one and just used it as an excuse to get the hell out of that apartment before Knuckles showed up. He saw Danny, and made a beeline for him down the bar, ignoring the rest of the crew as he went.

"So, what happened?" Blackie whispered, when he was next to Danny. "Did he show up?"

Before Danny could respond, the door opened and Mack Cantor and Logan Coyle came strolling into the bar.

Mack was carrying a black garbage bag with something heavy in it.

Something about the size of a bowling ball.

6

"Give everyone a round on the house," ordered Logan, twirling a finger in the air, as he strutted the length of the bar with Mack in tow to where Blackie stood next to Danny. His eyes were wide and wild. Like he was coked out of his mind. But Danny knew Logan wasn't into drugs. This was some other kind of high.

"Hey, fellas," Blackie said, nervously. "What's in the bag?"

"Listen," Logan said, placing his hand on Blackie's shoulder. "I need you to do me a favor, okay."

"Sure, Logan. Whaddya need?"

"I left something in your refrigerator."

"In my refrigerator?"

"Yeah. I need you to go get it for me."

"Sure. What is it?"

"It's in a milk carton," Mack added.

"Milk carton?"

"Yeah," Logan continued. "I want you to go up to your apartment and bring me the milk carton in the refrigerator. You think you can do that for me, Benny?"

"Sure, Logan. I'll go get the milk carton. Whatever you say."

"Good man. Make sure you bring it right here, okay!"

"You got it, Logan," Blackie said.

As he walked away Mack set the black garbage bag on the bar next to Danny's drink.

"What's in the bag?" Danny asked.

"What do you think is in the bag?" Logan answered with a wry smile.

"I dunno."

"I'll give you a clue," Mack said with a grin. "It used to be on Stevie Burke's shoulders. Here, you can have that as a souvenir."

Mack slipped a bullet into Danny's hand.

"What is that?"

"That's the most beautiful bullet in Hell's Kitchen. That's the one bounced off Stevie's head. I dug it out of the wall."

"I don't want it," Danny said, shoving it back at him.

"Suit yourself," said Mack, slipping it into the pocket of his jeans.

"I got something special coming up for you, Danny Boy," Logan said, after knocking back a Jamesons and rapping his knuckles on the bar for a refill.

"I dunno, Logan, I might go back to construction . . ."

"Listen to this fucken guy. Fuck construction. Construction's for losers. Up at five every morning lugging concrete like some dumb Mick. You need that shit like a hole in the head. I'm gonna take care of you now, Danny. Proper. Okay! I just talked to an old pal of mine, Nicky Red. Got to know him in the can a while back. He's got some stuff going with a guy out of Bensonhurst called Sal DeCarlo. Ever hear that name?"

Danny shook his head.

"Guy's a big time hitter. The real deal. I tell ya, these fucken guineas got it made. Got their hands in every goddamn thing: porn, drugs, hookers, loan sharking, you name it, they can make

161

a buck off it. DeCarlo's got a whole crew of kids out swiping old Fords, Chryslers, Mercurys, anything with those big old velour seats 'cause they can ship 'em out to the Middle East and make a fortune on 'em. Know why? Get this . . . 'cause those fucken camel jockeys can't sit on anything made of leather. Somethin' to do with religion or some shit. This fucken guy's makin' money hand over fist. He's smart. That's what I'm talkin' about. These guys ain't wastin' their time knockin' over candy stores, Danny."

McElroy refilled Logan's glass and moved away. Danny was still staring at the black garbage bag sitting not two feet in front of him, trying to figure out if Logan and Mack were really that crazy that they'd cut off Stevie Burke's head and bring it into the bar. It was too ridiculous, too monstrous to consider.

"So Nicky Red tells me, he thinks he can talk to this guy DeCarlo about getting you in at The Garden," Logan continued.

Danny turned to Logan. "A fight?"

"Says these guys can get you in the ring at Madison Square Garden." Logan nodded.

"Against who?"

"I don't know all the details yet. But I told him you was the real deal. Told him we was interested. This could be big for you, Danny," Logan said, placing that hand on his shoulder again, and peering into his eyes. "This could be the shot."

"They'd put me in The Garden?"

"Told me he was gonna talk to DeCarlo. He couldn't guarantee it, but he was pretty sure he can set this thing up. Said we'd probably have to set up a trial fight. You know how it works. Something where they could come see you. Maybe put you in against one of their guys first. Somebody decent. A name. Smaller venue. So they see you in action, see you're worth the effort, then they can

162

make some noise, sell some tickets for The Garden. This could be it, Danny. A real shot."

Danny nodded. It wasn't how he wanted it to go down. But maybe this was it. This was what he'd always wanted. If he could get one good shot at something real. In The Garden. Some real press. He could turn it into something big. A career. Even if they had him on the undercard. He would show them. He'd just watched the Bayonne Bleeder, Chuck Wepner, go fifteen rounds with Ali back in March. He'd watched that fight on a small TV with Cockeye and a few of the crew, down at The Ward. Nobody figured Wepner would last two minutes with the Champ, but Wepner showed them. He'd even put Ali down in the ninth round. There'd been much debate among the crew at The Ward that night about whether it had been a real knock down or not. Some of the guys said Wepner had stood on Ali's foot and tripped him. But Cockeye was adamant. It was a knock down, fair and square. "If it was the other way around you think anybody would care if Ali stood on his toes? He don't get no special treatment in the ring just 'cause he's Ali. He got knocked down, he got knocked down. That's all there is to it."

Regardless of what you thought about the knock down, that one fight had made Wepner a superstar.

The ember of that fight still burned in Danny's heart.

Hope.

Danny also knew that if he got this right, this was a real shot at a decent purse. Not some chump change. This was the house in Woodstock. His debt cleared. It was his mother out of the neighborhood. A fresh start. But Logan didn't need to know anything about any of that. Not yet.

"Thanks, Logan," Danny said. "I'll do it."

"Good man, Danny." Logan locked his arm around Danny's

neck, pulled him close and kissed the top of his head. "I'm gonna take care of you, Danny. You're family to me."

"Thanks, Logan."

"In the meantime, I want you to go see a guy called Vinny Diamond over at a place called The Pink Paradise."

"The place on Forty-second?"

"That's it."

"The strip club?"

"That's not just some titty bar, Danny. That place is high-end. Nicky Red knows this guy, told me they needed somebody to stand out front, keep the riffraff out."

"I dunno about that, Logan."

"You dunno? What don't you know? Hundred a night! Plus tips! All you gotta do is stand there with your arms folded. Easiest goddamned money you'll ever make in your life. Plus you'd be doing Nicky Red a solid on this thing. He's gonna have to pull a lot of favors to get you this shot, Danny. We gotta take care of him on this one. You see what I mean! What! You gonna turn your nose up at a C-note a night, for standing around with your dick in your hand for a few hours?"

Danny reluctantly shook his head. Cockeye'd been paying him a third of that at The Ward. He'd only been making fifty bucks a day laboring for the Polish guy. A hundred a night to stand around and do nothing was more money than he'd ever made in his life. Plus, he really wanted that shot at The Garden. It would be temporary. It would take care of things at home. Keep his mother from having to stress about the bills; he'd finally be able to throw Goldstein a little something extra every week to get out from under the three large that was still hanging over his head.

"I'll do it."

Logan smiled, that broad, square-jawed smile of his, and his blue eyes sparkled like sun on a frozen lake.

"That's my boy."

The door opened just then, and Blackie walked in. Blackie's face looked ashen as he held a milk carton and approached Logan at the end of the bar.

"Here you go, Logan."

"Look at the face on him!" Logan laughed. "Whassamatta, Benny? You look like you saw a ghost."

"Yeah, a ghost's balls." Mack was doubled over.

"Here," Mack said, grabbing the carton. "Give me that fucken thing."

He grabbed it and held the carton up for all to see, and yelled, "Who wants a ball and a beer?"

A couple of the guys down the bar stared with puzzled expressions. Logan and Mack moved down the middle of the bar to where the crew were seated.

"I don't get it," said Walter Hughes. "What's in the carton?"

"Here," Mack said, handing Hughes the carton. "Why don't you have a look."

Hughes took the carton and peered in. He winced. "What the fuck is that?" he asked, as the others leaned in for a peek.

"Stevie Burke's dick," Blackie whispered, just loud enough for Danny to hear.

"What?"

"They cut him up, Danny. They fucking cut up Stevie Burke and put his balls and his dick in a milk carton. They laid his clothes out on the floor like he was still in them. The sick fucks."

"What?"

"His shirt and his jeans and his boots, they had it all laid out on the floor when I went in. Like in the shape of his body. I guess they thought they was being funny. There was blood all over the bathtub. What the fuck, Danny!"

Blackie followed Danny's eyes to the black garbage bag sitting in front of them on the bar. Mack walked back to where it sat, just then, and, with everyone watching, he casually reached into the bag and lifted Stevie Burke's severed head out by the hair. He held it aloft like some garish pagan offering, then, cupping it in his hand like a bowling ball, he sent it bouncing down the floor of the bar, where it stopped, resting on its side. Stevie's wide, lifeless eyes, stared up at the shocked faces of his childhood friends.

7

"Danny McCoy?" the cop said, as Danny stepped out of his building onto Tenth Avenue.

"Yeah."

"Joe Quinn, NYPD." The guy flashed a badge. He was tall. Irish-American. Nappy ginger hair. Wearing a beige tweed sports coat over a white shirt and tie, and brown slacks with a crease that could cut butter. Black shoes with a high military-grade shine. This was no ordinary beat cop. This guy was trouble.

Quinn flipped the badge wallet closed and slipped it into his rear pocket. Then he just stood there, staring at Danny, his fingers knitted casually in front of him. Like he was waiting for something. Like he had all the time in the world to just stand out here on Tenth Avenue and wait.

"I gotta go to work," Danny said, eventually.

"Course you do. Where you working these days?" Quinn asked.

Danny hesitated. He was on his way to meet Vinny Diamond at The Pink Paradise to see about that job as a bouncer. Danny decided the less he said to this guy about Vinny Diamond the better. So he just stood there and stared back.

Growing up in The Kitchen he had plenty of experience dealing

167

with Mick cops. Half the cops in this neighborhood were on Mannion's payroll all the way back to Hughie Mulligan. Maybe that's what this was: Mannion turning up the heat on Logan's crew.

A rat the size of a small dog darted out of a large pile of garbage on the sidewalk outside of the building. Both Quinn and Danny turned their heads to watch it. It grabbed a half-eaten slice of pizza and dragged it back across the sidewalk toward the pile of garbage bags.

"Place is starting to look like the South Bronx around here," Quinn said. "Look at this shit. It doesn't bother you, you gotta wade through this crap outside your door every day?"

Danny shrugged. The city's decline under the current mayor was front-page news every day. For weeks garbage had been piling up in the streets. The city's sanitation workers were refusing to come to work until somebody could figure out how to pay them. Cops were staying home or sitting down in the precinct twiddling their thumbs to pass the time. There was an air of chaos in the streets. The rats were growing bolder and fatter by the day. You couldn't walk a city block without hearing someone curse the name of Abe Beame.

"Whole city's turning into a sewer. Like the Wild West out here. Criminals starting to feel like they can get away with anything."

Danny shrugged again.

"I'm looking for Stevie Burke," Quinn said.

So there it was.

Danny folded his arms, sending an unspoken message that he wasn't going to be giving anything away.

"You know Stevie, right?"

"Yeah, I know him."

"His family's worried about him. Says he hasn't been home for a while."

Danny remained silent. He'd been hearing that a tall detective had been poking around the neighborhood asking questions. It wasn't unusual. They made the rounds after every murder on the West Side. But this was the first time one had come right to his door looking for him. And a detective at that.

"You're not worried about what might have happened to him?"

Danny shrugged again.

"You guys were friends, right."

"I knew him."

"Doesn't bother you that he's just . . . vanished?"

"I don't know. People go away."

"Where do they go, Danny? Huh! Lot of people just vanishing around here lately. Just up and disappearing. Doesn't seem strange to you?"

Danny shook his head.

"I think it's strange," Quinn continued. "I think it's very strange. Couple of months ago Stevie Burke shoots his best friend, in self defense of course, purely accidental, then, all of a sudden he just up and disappears! That seems weird to me. Almost feels like, the two events are . . . I dunno . . . connected, somehow. Doesn't feel that way to you?"

"I dunno."

"You fighting these days?"

Danny shrugged again.

"Saw you one time, few years back. You were up against some Mexican kid, what was his name, Ramon . . . damn, what was it . . . Ramon Quintera. That was a great fight. Guy was good. I didn't think you were gonna take him. But you put him down. You were a pretty good boxer. I really thought you had a shot."

Danny let it go. He knew better than to be seen yapping friendly to a detective in the middle of Tenth Avenue. He knew there were eyes on him right this second, watching his every move. You learned very early on in The Kitchen, you keep your mouth shut. Even if they took you down to the station and handcuffed you to a radiator and tried to beat it out of you. You kept your mouth shut. Even if they pulled you in front of a judge and threatened you with fifty years in the big house. You kept your goddamn mouth shut. Danny knew it. And he knew Quinn knew he knew it. This whole conversation was just a charade. It was Quinn's way of letting everybody know that he was on it. It was his way of saying that just because the city was falling apart at the seams, there was still someone out there watching. Someone who was going to do their goddamn job, pay or no pay.

"Have a nice day, Danny," Quinn said, slipping a stick of gum in his mouth. "I'll be seeing you around."

Danny watched Quinn make his way to a parked car where another plainclothes detective was waiting behind the wheel. Quinn continued to watch Danny as the car pulled out and went off up Tenth.

8

The Pink Paradise was not the high-end gentleman's club Logan had painted it to be. It was a narrow storefront sandwiched between an adult video store called Empire Porn and a dusty shopfront window displaying an assortment of hunting knives, blackjacks and subversive reading material, including one particular book that caught Danny's eye, titled, *How to Build a Bomb*.

Even the moldy neon sign hanging over the club's door was askew.

The inside was every bit as seedy as the exterior.

It was lunchtime when Danny walked in. A tired looking stripper was going through the motions for a small handful of construction workers gathered around a low, poorly-lit platform. The red carpet stuck to the soles of his feet as he walked up to the bar. It's possible it had been pink once upon a time, but there was nothing pink about the inside of this place anymore. This place was a dungeon.

"What can I get for you, pal?" asked a bartender with heavy bags under his eyes and a white shirt that looked like it hadn't seen an iron since the Kennedy era.

"I'm here to see Vinny."

The bartender's friendly smile disappeared as he took stock of Danny.

"He expecting you?"

"Nicky Red said I should come by and see him about a job at the door."

"You got a name?"

"Danny McCoy. I'm a friend of Logan Coyle's over at The Wolf on Tenth Avenue."

"Wait here. I'll go see if he's around."

Danny turned around to catch the aging stripper on all fours at the edge of the platform taking a dollar bill in her teeth from one of the workers. The guy grabbed her boob in his hand and gave it an ugly squeeze as she slipped her hand down into the front of his pants. The entire scene sickened and saddened him. This was not the sort of joint he wanted to be associated with. He'd turned to make for the door when the bartender suddenly reappeared.

"Follow me."

He paused for a moment. If he left without at least speaking to this Vinny Diamond guy, he'd have Logan on his ass for a month. He followed the bartender to the rear of the club, down a long, narrow, dimly lit hallway to a closed door at the end.

"Knock before you go in," the bartender said, nodding to the door before walking away.

Danny knocked.

"Yeah. Come in," came a voice.

Danny opened the door to a gaudy purple-colored office with bright yellow shag carpeting. Behind a large mahogany desk sat a man in an oversized tan leather swivel chair. He'd assumed Vinny was Italian, but this guy was South American. Maybe Mexican. He was wearing dark shades and a leopard print shirt open to his navel, revealing a thickly matted chest. Behind the man was a brightly lit fish tank that ran almost the full width of the wall. Every manner of brightly colored exotic fish seemed to live there.

"Come in. Come in," the man said, standing, and extending his hand across the desk. He was about five eight, thick black hair, fortyish. He had a square jaw and a set of teeth that seemed to glow when he smiled. "Vinny Diamond."

Danny took his hand. "Nice to meet you, Mr. Diamond—"

"Vinny. Sit down. Relax. Wow! You're a big guy. What are you, five ten, five eleven . . ."

"Something like that."

"Good shoulders. You're the fighter, right?"

"I fought some."

"Yeah, I hear you're good." Vinny smiled that white, luminous smile of his. He was wearing a ring on every finger. One more ludicrous than the next.

Danny let that go. It wasn't for him to say.

"I heard you're an absolute beast in the ring, am I right!"

Danny let that go, too. He didn't know how to respond to flattery. It made him uncomfortable. Put him on edge. Made him feel like he was being made a fool of. Or set up.

"You wanna get some decent fights. Am I right?" Vinny continued.

Logan hadn't mentioned anything about Vinny Diamond being involved in setting up the fight. It made sense now. That's why he was here. If he was going to get a leg up, he was going to have to play along with the hustle. He'd been foolish to believe it was free.

Logan never gave anything away for free.

"Listen, I don't wanna get involved in anything . . . anything that's not . . . you know . . ." Danny let it trail off.

"Not what? Legal? Above board? Danny! Baby! Like you need help! I mean, look at you! Whaddyou weigh?"

"Bout one seventy or so."

"Got a trainer?"

Danny shook his head.

"That won't be a problem. You were working with Cockeye Ward, am I right?"

Danny nodded. This guy had done his homework.

"I hear that guy was the real deal back in the day. Shame what happened to him. Shame. Poor bastard. Not to worry though, we got a guy of our own we can put you with."

"I don't need nobody."

"Course you don't. Course you don't. Let's not worry about that right now. We can talk about all that later. I gotta place up in the Catskills I can send you to train—"

Danny was shaking his head.

"—I can send a girl up there with you . . ."

"Thank you. I'm good."

"Of course you are. Of course you are. Okay. Yeah, I think I like this. I think I like this. I think we can do something with you." Vinny leaned back in his chair and nodded his head and rubbed his chin. "You got a name?"

"Danny."

"No, I mean, a name, like, Danny the Destroyer, or Danny the Gladiator, something we can put on a poster."

"Danny."

"Yeah, that's not gonna work. I'm thinking . . . we want something that says you're from here on the West Side, right! They love that shit. Make it local. Something like, Westside . . . slaughter? Maybe? No. Killer! Too much. Slayer! The Westside Slayer. Westside Slayer."

"I dunno."

"The Kitchen. Maybe it's something to do with Hell's Kitchen ... The Hell's Kitchen ... Hero, the Headliner ... no that's stupid ... the ... the ... The Hammer. What am I saying? It's Danny Boy. Danny Boy McCoy." Vinny burst into song. "*Oh Danny Boy* ... It's perfect." There was nothing original or new about the Danny Boy angle. Danny'd been hearing people sing that song to him since he was five years old. But he let Vinny run with his spiel. "*Oh Danny Boy, the pipes, the pipes are calling* ... I like it. Ooh yeah. That's good. I like it a lot. You like it, right."

"Whatever works, Mr. Diamond."

"Vinny. Call me Vinny. Yeah, this is good. We'll get you a cape, a long flowing white cape, silk, the very finest, with a shamrock on it. I'll have it specially made. Wow. I'm so good at this, I scare myself. It's my brain, it's like, you know ... Ideas! Ping! Yeah. I can see it now. A long flowing silk cape, with a huge emerald green shamrock. Gold trim on the lettering. Right! Matching shorts. Emerald and gold ... Green, white and gold! Hey, that's your flag, right? Green, white and gold. What did I just tell you? I'm so good at this shit. It's perfect. I'll have a few of my girls, the best we got, in green, white and gold bikinis, leading you into the ring—you will not believe these girls—we'll have them wearing those little tweed caps you guys wear ... and we'll have a hood on the cape, and when they lead you into the ring they'll slowly lower your hood ... Oh this is good. I like it. I like it a lot. Ladies and gentlemen, From Manhattan's Wild West Side, the one, the only, Danny Boy McCoy."

Vinny stretched out his arms, palms to the ceiling as if he were in the ring announcing Danny to a packed crowd at The Garden.

"I dunno, Mr. Diamond."

"Vinny. It's Vinny. Don't worry about it, Danny. You don't have to worry about a goddamn thing. Handsome guy like yourself.

They'll eat this shit up. You just worry about staying in shape. We want them to see your abs. You working out?"

"I been stayin' on my toes."

"Course you have. You're a professional. You guys are amazing. The dedication. I work out a little myself. You could probably tell."

Danny hadn't noticed. He still didn't.

"Benched one eighty last weekend. Not too shabby, huh!"

"Good for you."

"Yeah, I think you and I are going to get along real well, Danny. I can feel it. Can you feel that?"

Danny felt like this guy was a dick, so he let that go, too.

"I know some people might be able to set something up in January."

"A fight."

"You think you can be ready?"

"Against who?"

"Does it matter?"

"No. You could get something set up that fast?"

"Hey! I'm Vinny Diamond, baby, I can do whatever the fuck I want."

"Yes. I can be ready. Thank you, Mr. Diamond."

"Most of the staff here just call me Boss."

"Okay, Boss."

Vinny smiled. Danny could tell he liked hearing him call him Boss. "You handle this first fight properly. Put on a good show, put this sucker away, I can build from there. You know what I'm saying?"

"You got it, Boss. No problem. I got this."

"I know you do."

"Thank you," Danny said, sincerely. He hadn't had a real fight in some time. "I really appreciate this. I won't let you down."

"I know you won't, Danny baby. You're looking for a job in the meantime, am I right!"

"Logan mentioned you needed a guy on the door."

"Logan C. How is that crazy Irish bastard?"

"He's good."

"Fucken guy wants to be king, am I right!" Vinny seemed to be searching Danny's face for something more. Maybe dirt. Danny didn't trust this guy enough to start talking about Logan just yet so he let that slide. "Okay," Vinny continued. "Yeah. I need a guy at the door. You start tomorrow night?"

"Tomorrow night?"

"That too soon for you?"

"No."

"Good. I need a guy here for the night shift. Somebody big enough to keep these degenerates from getting out of line. They see a big guy like you at the door they think twice about getting too handsy with the girls. You know what I mean!"

"What time?"

"Six to two? Seventy bucks a shift sound good to you."

"I thought it was a hundred."

"A hundred." Vinny laughed. "Who the fuck said a hundred?"

"Logan."

"What is he, crazy! Fucken guy. I'll give you eighty. Eighty bucks a shift, and if you need your joint sucked, any one of the girls will take you in back and sort you out in a quick. Whaddya say?"

"I don't need a girl."

"Course you don't. Course you don't. You're a fucken stud. You don't need these whores. You're Danny Boy McCoy. Am I right!"

Vinny pulled open a drawer on the desk and produced a stack of hundred dollar bills. He peeled off a few and held it across the desk. "Here. Let's get you some threads."

"I can't take that. I haven't even done anything yet."

"Hey. You're working for Vinny Diamond now. You're my guy. You think I'm not gonna take care of you. Take this, and go get yourself a nice black suit, and a coat, so you don't freeze to death standing out there."

"I got a coat."

"Take it. Get something nice."

Danny took the money.

"There you go. Danny Boy McCoy, am I right? Huh. Am I right!" Vinny got out of his seat and stretched his hand across the desk, his glow-in-the-dark teeth on full display in a wide grin.

Danny got up and reluctantly took his hand.

"Listen, I got a little thing I gotta do, I'd like maybe you come along."

Vinny was still holding his hand firmly in his.

He wasn't asking. If Danny wanted the job, and the fight, he was going to be going along.

"Sure, Boss."

There was that smile again.

"Welcome to Paradise, my friend." Vinny grinned. "We're gonna get along great."

9

Vinny had Danny sit up front with his driver, Miguel.

"Where you from, Miguel?" Danny asked, as they made their way out over the Queensboro Bridge.

"Columbia."

So that was it. Columbia. Vinny was a Columbian who fancied himself an Italian.

Danny stared out the window at the East River and pretended not to notice Vinny in the backseat shaking a bump of white powder onto his fist and snort it clean.

It was a bright cold day. The car smelled like new leather and pine. He was going to be making money again. That was something. The rent. The groceries. He didn't want his mother stressing about those things. This was an actual job. He'd have steady money coming in every week. That was good. It was good.

Whatever else it was, he was going to find out pretty damned soon.

Miguel rolled the car to a stop on a quiet street of small row houses somewhere out in the borough and killed the engine.

They sat there for five minutes or so in silence.

Then Miguel said, "Hey, Boss, check it out."

Danny could see a long-haired guy in bell bottom pants, and a denim jacket with a fur collar up around his ears, about a block away. He had his head down and was smoking a cigarette. He opened a small gate leading to a house at the end of the block, skipped up the steps, and opened the front door.

"Let's give him a minute," Vinny said, slipping a handgun from inside his jacket, and removing the safety.

"Somebody want to tell me what this is?" asked Danny.

"Sure. This cocksucker took some product of mine. We're gonna have a little chat with him."

Danny wanted to say he didn't want any part of anything that was going to get physical, but it was pointless. He'd been in this position before plenty with Benny Black on pick-ups for Logan. There was no real way of knowing what a situation like this was going to be until you were actually in it.

The place to say "I'm not going" had been a half hour earlier back in Vinny's office.

But he hadn't said it.

He hadn't objected. He went along as he almost always did.

Now, here he was.

Whatever this was, he was in it.

The three men got out, and walked the length of the block, in silence. They didn't see another soul. The block was dead. This was a working-class neighborhood. Most people were at work. Kids at school.

When they reached the house, Miguel slipped quietly around the side of the house to cover the back. Danny stood behind Vinny as he knocked on the front door.

There was a sound of feet hurrying across linoleum, then silence, then a scuffle of some sort.

The door opened, and Miguel let them in. He had Longhair held in front of him, a hand clamped over the guy's mouth.

Once they were inside, Miguel let the guy go, and then punched him. Miguel could hit. The guy fell without a sound.

Miguel tied the guy's hands behind his back, and dragged him into the bathroom, propped him against the tub, and jammed a face cloth in his mouth.

Vinny filled a glass with water from the sink, and flung it in the guy's face to wake him up again.

"Go, put the kettle on," Vinny said, and Miguel went off to the kitchen. Danny could hear him run the faucet in the kitchen and the sound of the ignitor clicking under the gas burner.

Vinny leaned casually in the bathroom door, holding an eight-inch blade in his right hand, just letting the guy process for a bit.

Danny stood behind him.

"You know why we're here, Rusty?"

The guy's eyes were wide. Pleading. He was trying to speak but the cloth was jammed in there tight.

Danny didn't want to see any of this. He didn't know anything about this kid but he didn't need to know anything to feel sorry for him. He wanted to run. But it was too late for that now. He'd already seen too much to be allowed to walk away. If he made a move for the door that knife would be in his back. If he tried to stop it, he'd be in the tub next to the kid.

"Yes." Vinny nodded. "Yes, you do know why I'm here."

The guy started to cry.

"Aw, you sad, Rusty? You want your mammy to come get you?" Vinny chuckled. He reached into his pocket and pulled the vial of coke from his pocket and shook another bump onto his knuckle and snorted it.

"Danny, would you like some?" he said, offering the tiny brown glass bottle to Danny.

Danny shook his head.

"Suit yourself."

The guy was shaking his head. Mumbling. Tears streaming down his face.

"Lift him into the tub," Vinny said, motioning to Danny with the knife.

Danny slipped past Vinny and picked the kid up. He weighed nothing. Once he had him in his arms the kid looked up into his eyes. Pleading.

Danny avoided his eyes.

Placed him in the tub and stepped back out behind Vinny again.

He could hear the kettle whistling in the other room.

They all could.

Miguel came back with it in his hand. A trail of steam following him as he went.

He handed it to Vinny.

"Oh look, it's tea time." Vinny smiled as he popped the lid off the kettle and emptied the entire thing over the kid's head. The kid tried to leap out of the bathtub, his face red, and blistering from the burn.

Miguel stepped forward, and shoved the kid down again, his foot planted firmly on the kid's chest, holding him in the tub.

Danny turned away.

When he turned back again, Miguel was on top of the kid and Vinny was in there with the knife as the kid screamed and moaned and kicked his feet. But there was nowhere for him to go. He wasn't getting out of this one.

When Vinny stepped back, Danny could see that he'd cut open the kid's jaw and pushed his tongue down through it, so that it dangled on his neck.

The kid's eyes were wide in horror. He was trying to breathe but he was choking on his own blood.

"How you like your new necktie, Rusty," Vinny said, taking the kid by the hair. "That's what happens when you try to take Vinny's property. Nobody takes Vinny's property. You understand."

Danny was almost relieved when Vinny dragged the blade across the kid's throat and let him go to bleed out. At least the pain would end now. The horror.

On the drive back to the city, Miguel offered Danny a cigarette. He took it.

"I'm sorry you had to see that, Danny," Vinny said from the backseat, snorting another bump off his knuckle. But Danny knew that he did want him to see it. He wanted Danny to know exactly who he was, and what he was capable of. "But, that's business, you know. I let a guy like that steal from me, all the hyenas they come around, you know, they think Vinny Diamond's getting soft. Vinny Diamond's lost his edge. Next thing you know, I'm in a bathtub looking up . . . But that's not going to happen, Danny. You know what I mean!"

Danny understood perfectly what he meant.

This was the street.

He hated it.

But this was the world he was born into.

Lived in.

This, was The Kitchen.

10

Danny arranged the buttered toast, the tea, a bowl of fresh straw-
berries, and a glass of pure orange juice on a tray, and carried it
to his mother's bedroom. He placed the tray on the bedside table
next to her reading glasses and a chaotic assortment of pill bottles.

She opened one eye and squinted as he pulled back the curtains to crack the window.

"What are ye doin'," she groaned from the bed. It had been a
week since the operation. They sent her home, her chest wrapped
in a bandage, after only two days.

"Gotta get some fresh air in here, Ma."

"Is there not enough wrong with me already without freezing
me to death in me bed as well," she muttered, propping a pillow
behind her as she sat up.

"What's this carry-on?" she said, noticing the tray.

"I made you some breakfast."

"Why? What did you do?"

"Ma. The doctor said you have to eat."

"It's the Mexican, you've got her pregnant."

"No. Ma . . ."

"Well she better not think she's moving in here with me.

I've one child in this house to take care of already. I don't need another."

"She's not Mexican. She's not pregnant. And I'm not seeing her anymore."

"I knew it wouldn't last."

Danny bit his tongue. He hadn't seen Gabriela since the night she'd stormed off after he'd snapped at her outside The Wolf. The night Mack rolled Knuckles' head down the bar like a bowling ball. He never should have asked her out on a date in the first place. It was dumb. Now he had to avoid Mazzella's Fruit Market every time he left the house. Duck past with his head down like a goddamn criminal in case Gabriela, or her mother or, God forbid, Enzo, confronted him in the street.

He was a coward. He should have just gone to see her. Apologized. But he didn't. He'd put it off. He'd kept putting it off. A week had gone by. And another week. Then each time he thought he was ready . . . he thought of Trixie.

Trixie.

He knew she was trouble. Knew it.

But how he longed for her. How he wanted her.

He decided to keep his head down. Avoid both. Train for the fight. He needed to get in shape. He needed to take care of his mother, and his birds, and his debt to Hyman Goldstein.

The fight would put things right.

He pulled an envelope out of his pocket and handed it to his mother as she reached for her teacup.

"Who do I owe now?"

"Open it."

His mother took a sip of tea. Reached for her glasses. Opened the envelope and produced a few photographs.

"What's this?"

"That's the house I'm looking at."

"What house?"

"In Woodstock. Remember I told you Liam said a house was coming up for sale next to them."

"Wonder what's in it for him," she said, but she was still looking. Still flipping back and forward through the pictures, squinting, as she examined the cottage more closely.

"It's nice," Danny prodded.

"'Tis well for some."

"I can get it cheap?"

"We can barely pay the rent where we are."

"You'd move though. If I could get it."

"I don't know where anybody'd get that kind of money," she said, and she slipped the pictures back into the envelope and propped it between two medicine bottles on her bedside table.

"I want you to eat everything on that plate."

"What, are you my doctor now?"

"I want you strong. We're gonna get you get you good and strong again, and we're gonna get you out of here, Ma."

She lifted the cup to her lips with both hands and took a sip as she stared off out the window, a faraway look in her eyes. Then without looking at him she casually lifted a slice of the toast and took a bite.

11

He was holding the bird in his lap, slipping a tag around her leg when the door to the roof opened and Terry Flannery appeared.

Danny hadn't seen Terry in a couple of months. Terry'd been away. Upstate. A parole violation. They'd locked him up for consorting with criminals, which everyone at The Wolf thought was hilarious. How were you supposed to live in Hell's Kitchen and avoid consorting with criminals?

"Welcome home, Terry," Danny said with a smile. He was happy to see Terry back in the neighborhood.

"Hey, Danny," Terry said angrily, puffing on a smoke. "What's all this shit I'm hearing about Stevie Burke when I was away?"

"I don't know, man. I don't wanna say, you know."

"I know you don't wanna say but somebody better tell me something pretty fucken quick, Danny."

"I didn't have nuthin' to do with it, Terry."

"But you was there?"

Danny sighed deeply. "Yeah, I was there."

"And Coyle whacked him?"

Danny nodded.

"An' you just stood there an' didn't stop him?"

"What was I gonna do, Terry, wrestle Logan for the gun? I didn't know he was gonna shoot him. I thought we was just going up there to scare him a little. He didn't tell me nuthin'."

"Look at this fuck!" Terry said, suddenly, noticing Logan's Buick pull into a parking spot across from the building.

The two men leaned over the parapet and watched as Logan stepped out of his car and locked the door. He was wearing a sharp gray suit. White shirt, open at the neck. Dark glasses. His blond hair, neatly trimmed.

"You see this shit? Guy thinks he's Vito Corleone."

"Vito who?"

"*The Godfather*?"

Danny shook his head. He didn't get the reference.

"Movie about the mafia. I swear, ever since that damned movie came out I think it went to his head. I think Logan thinks he's one of them. Thinks he's the fucken Godfather."

Terry yelled down at Logan. "Hey!" It took Logan a moment to locate Terry on the roof of Danny's building.

"I wanna talk to you," Terry yelled.

Logan didn't look none too happy about Terry yelling at him off the roof of a building in broad daylight.

Danny and Terry watched him walk briskly across the street, and disappear into the building below them. In a moment he barged through the door.

"What the fuck, Terry!" Logan grinned, as he came toward them. "When'd you get out?"

"Did you kill Stevie Burke?" Terry spat, meeting Logan half-way and getting right up in his face. Logan was a good head taller than Terry but he was no match for Terry's rage.

"Terry . . ."

"Did you kill Knuckles?"

"Yes."

"Why?"

"Because he was a degenerate gambler."

"You killed one of our friends?"

"You gotta listen to me, Terry."

"Fuck is wrong with you?"

"Fuck is wrong with me? Who the fuck you think you're talking to here? I saw you kill a guy right down the block here 'cause he spilled a drink on you, for chrissakes. What are you, my fucken rabbi? Stevie was a degenerate scumbag and he deserved everything he got."

"He was one of us."

"He wasn't one of us, Terry. He killed your friend, Cheddar, shot him in the face. You know how much Mack loved that kid. Cheddar was like a brother to him."

"Mack was in on it?"

"Sure he was in on it."

"Why'd you have to cut him up?"

"What you want me to do? Lay him out on the avenue so they could send me up to the chair. You know that's not how it works. Listen, Terry, I know you liked him, we all did, but let's get something straight here, he was out of control. You know he was kidnapping people and using my name to collect the ransom?"

Terry glanced to Danny for confirmation. Danny nodded. That was the story he'd heard, too.

"Fucken guy was out of control. We tried warning him. Isn't that right, Danny? We warned him."

Danny nodded. He'd been warned. Not that it would have made a difference. Mack would have whacked him sooner or later anyway. But he'd been warned. Plenty.

"Prick was into me for a fortune, he's staggering around the neighborhood high as a kite for months, but he can't even pay the vig! Come on, Terry. You know you can't do that shit. I mean, what . . . I'm supposed to keep rolling over for this piece of shit and have the whole neighborhood see me take it in the ass! You know it don't work like that. He got warned, again and again. He didn't listen."

Terry put his head down. He obviously hadn't heard how bad Knuckles had gotten since he'd been away. Terry knew the rules of the street. You might be forgiven for fucking up once or twice, but you keep pushing your luck around here and somebody was gonna put a knife in your chest. That's just the way it was. Terry turned away from Logan and walked over to the parapet and stood there with his back to both men, staring off down Tenth Avenue.

"Whadda you call this one?" Logan said, turning his attention to the bird Danny still cupped in his hands.

"Cheddar," Danny said.

"No shit," Terry said, turning around. "You called him Cheddar?"

"Yeah. Cheddar was the first one to see him . . ." Danny let it trail off.

"Hey wait?" Logan said. "This is not the one belonging to, what's her name?"

"Bluey," Danny offered.

"Yeah, Bluey." Logan laughed. "And Henry, am I right?"

"Yeah, this is Bluey and Henry's boy."

"No shit," said Terry, stepping over to inspect the bird in Danny's lap. "Hey, Cheddar. Welcome to hell, little buddy."

"Can he fly?" Logan asked.

"Sure he can fly. I was just tagging him when you came up."

The two men leaned in as Danny held up Cheddar's leg to show them the blue band around her ankle.

Danny lifted the bird to his lips, and kissed its head, before tossing it out over the parapet. The three men watched the pigeon fall about fifteen feet before correcting itself into a long swoop south down the avenue, past The Wolf, before rising high, over the rusty tenement buildings, and banking off toward the Hudson.

12

Danny was at his post outside the Paradise Club when Trixie showed up. It was almost midnight. He had his collar up and his hands buried deep in his pockets in an attempt to shield himself from the icy-cold wind that ran like a blade across Forty-second Street, from the Hudson to the East River.

She had almost gone past him on her way into the club before she recognized him.

"Hey," she said, startled to see him standing there.

"Hey," he replied, equally as puzzled. He'd not been able to stop thinking about her since she'd slipped into his lap and kissed him at The Wolf the night Knuckles had been killed. That kiss was still on his lips. Nothing had ever hit him like that. It was like he'd stepped in the path of a subway car. He'd thought he was in love with Gabriela. He'd even told her as much. But it wasn't like this.

Nothing he'd ever experienced was like this.

"What are you doing standing here?" she asked with a look of real concern.

"I work here."

"Since when?"

"Since I saw you last."

"Jesus!" She seemed crestfallen at the news.

"What's the matter?"

"What are you doing here, Danny?"

"I told you, I work here now."

"For Vinny?"

"You know Vinny?"

Trixie shook her head, as if she couldn't believe Danny wasn't able to figure this out for himself.

"Oh, you work here," Danny said eventually, trying to sound like he'd be cool with that possibility.

"Nope. Not anymore," she said with an air of annoyance. "Try again, Einstein."

Then it hit him.

She was seeing Vinny Diamond.

His stomach dropped. He felt ill. That couldn't be it. There had to be another explanation. His head began to spin. He hadn't had an attack like this in a long while. He tried to fight it. He braced himself against the door frame as the world began to spin. His breath got short. Then he came to, propped against the wall outside the door of the club, with his ass on the sidewalk.

Trixie was there, hunkered in front of him like an apparition, like the very first time he saw her, over on Forty-fourth Street.

"What are we going to do with you?" she said, stroking his face with her hand.

"I'm good," Danny said as he tried to pull the world back into focus.

"Sure you are."

"You're going out with him?"

"Yup," she said, and he was pretty sure it pained her to say it. "I been seeing him."

There was so much he wanted to say.

Not Vinny. Not Vinny fucking Diamond.

"Come on," she said. "Let's get you up before he sees you out here like this."

She was right. He needed to get on his feet and shake this off. If Vinny saw him on his ass out here in front of the club, he'd be out of a job, but worse, he'd be out the fight.

He needed to pull it together. Trixie slipped her arms around him and helped him to his feet.

"Well I guess that's the first time somebody's literally fallen for me." She smiled sadly. "You okay?"

"Yeah. I'll be alright. It just happens sometimes."

"You go to a doctor about it?"

Danny shook his head.

"No. Course you didn't. Why would you?"

"I'm fine. It's nothing," Danny lied.

Two long-haired kids stepped up to the door just then, and went to move past him to enter the club. One of the guys eyed Trixie in her denim shorts and red leather boots. "Wow. You work here?" He slurred.

Trixie turned her head, and stared off down the block, ignoring him. "Hey, lady, I asked if you worked here," the guy asked a little more aggressively.

"Don't," Danny said, barely above a whisper.

"Wha'd you say?" the guy snapped.

"Leave the lady alone."

The guy took one look at Danny's expression and decided to drop it. The two men tried to move past him again to enter the club.

Danny stretched his arm across the door, blocking their path.

"Is there a problem?" said the taller of the two.

"Not tonight, guys."

"What do you mean?"

"You're not getting in here," Danny said, clenching his fists and taking a fast step toward the two men.

"What the fuck!"

"You and your friend have exactly two seconds to walk away before I stuff you both in a trash can."

The men froze. Danny began to count. "One . . ."

They turned, and briskly walked away.

"Vinny sees you chasing his customers away he's gonna get upset." Trixie laughed.

"Fuck Vinny."

"Listen, Danny, I don't want to see you get hurt, okay."

"How would I get hurt?"

"You know who Vinny is, right? Who he's with?"

Danny knew. Vinny was Columbian. So he wasn't a made man, but he might as well be. He was with Fat Joe and the Bensonhurst crowd. He'd been told Fat Joe owned a large stake in the Pink Paradise. And as long as Vinny was kicking up to Fat Joe, he was protected. Vinny was more dangerous than any made man because he didn't need nobody's permission to do what he needed to do.

"These guys don't scare me. Nobody's gonna hurt me. And nobody's gonna hurt you."

The door to the club opened and Vinny appeared.

"Babe," he yelled excitedly, eyeing Trixie up and down in her outfit. "Oh, wow, holeeee fuck . . . Oh yeah, baby. Look! At! You!"

He slipped his arm around her waist and pulled her to him and kissed her neck. "Goddamn, you look good! Look at this piece of ass! Doesn't she look hot?" Vinny said, turning to Danny, displaying Trixie like she was a new Rolex.

Danny clasped his hands in front of him and looked away down the street. It was too much. He had to shake this off. It was none of his business. Get it together, Danny.

"Wait?" Vinny asked, looking back and forth between the two of them, sensing the shift in energy. "You two know each other?"

"Sure. I know Danny." Trixie smiled, playfully, wrapping her arm around Vinny reassuringly. "I met him over at Logan's place when I was bartending there."

"You know, Danny's gonna be fighting for me pretty soon."

"For you?" Trixie asked.

"I didn't tell you! I'm gonna be managing our friend here. We're gonna go far, me and this kid." He slapped Danny's arm. Danny winced. "I'm gonna take this kid all the way to the top. Isn't that right, Danny?"

"That's right," Danny said, trying to control his breathing.

"You're damned right that's right," Vinny said, throwing a few playful punches at Danny's gut. "Listen. I need you to meet me here tomorrow, at noon. I got a little thing I want you to do for me."

Danny didn't respond. He hadn't signed up to be Vinny's errand boy. He was already angry that he'd allowed himself to be dragged into this position in the first place.

"Okay," he said.

Vinny's black Cadillac stopped in front of the club. Miguel got out and opened the rear door.

Danny watched Vinny lead Trixie to the car and give her ass a playful slap as she leaned into the backseat.

Vinny followed her in.

Miguel closed the door. Nodded to Danny. Got back in the car and drove away.

"Let it go, Danny," Danny whispered to himself, pulling the lapels of his coat up around his neck against the biting cold. "Let it fucken go, pal."

13

Christmas was a big deal in The Kitchen. The Irish in the neighborhood didn't care much for Thanksgiving. They still thought of it as a Protestant thing. Christmas was the real holiday here on the West Side.

From the roof of Danny's building he watched Mannion, standing in the back of a white box truck parked outside the Tavern, handing out turkeys. All the old ladies were lined up in their winter coats. Many of them with their own small offering for him in return. A loaf of bread wrapped in a tea towel. A freshly baked apple pie. An embroidered hankie. Gifts that cost no more than time, heart and effort. Gifts as valuable as any sack of gold.

Danny watched as Mannion patiently took time with each of the ladies to listen to what they wanted to say. It was an opportunity for many of them to whisper a favor in his ear. A greedy landlord that needed chatting to. A troubled son locked in the Tombs who needed a favorable mention to a judge so he could make it out in time for the Christmas pudding. A daughter selling herself down on the cobblestoned streets of the Fulton Fish Market for the price of a bag of dope, that needed rescuing. Or, an unemployed husband who needed a good word to get a job in one of the local unions. Mannion was priest, copper, and counselor to them all.

It was easy to see why he was so well liked. Mannion was more than a gangster. He'd become a politician. Which as far as Danny could tell, was really just a gangster who got better at public relations. With his movie-star looks and personable ways, it wasn't hard to imagine him behind the desk in the Oval Office. Kennedy had made that dream a reality for the Irish. A handsome, clean-cut Irish-American boy. The son of a bootlegger, who'd hustled his way to the Presidency. It represented hope. Possibility.

For now, Mannion could make do with being President of Hell's Kitchen, serving the community from the back of a box truck outside Mannion's Tavern on the corner of Forty-fifth and Tenth Avenue.

Logan Coyle was a different animal altogether, Danny thought. There was no box truck parked outside The Wolf a block to the south today, in this last week before Christmas. There wasn't so much as a string of lights to brighten The Wolf. There would be no tree. No puddings handed out to the crew. Coyle wasn't interested in serving the neighborhood. Coyle was interested in serving himself. And yet, he too was gifted with the same mystifying magnetism as Mannion. He kept them all strung along, with the promise of some other, brighter, more attractive future.

Coyle and Mannion. The twin harbingers of hope on Tenth Avenue.

Danny scattered some feed down inside the coop and whistled to his birds who had been out circling the neighborhood for an hour while he worked the bag. It was a bright, crisp morning in The Kitchen, and it felt good to be up on the roof working up a sweat, flogging the heavy bag, flushing some of the poison out of his system.

He never used to drink like this. He'd always prided himself on his discipline. But lately . . . there'd been nightmares.

Several times he'd awoken to Stevie Burke's severed head on the pillow next to him. His eyes wide. Knuckles whispering, "Danny. Hey, Danny. Why didn't you stop them, Danny?" Once or twice a week he awoke in a cold sweat and leapt from the bed to escape the horror.

Terrified to go back to sleep, he'd slip out the window onto the fire escape and creep up to the roof. Sit inside the coop with the birds to bathe in their innocence. Did the others awaken like this? Terry, Logan, Mack, or Blackie? He wanted to ask. But how? He thought of God. Sunday mornings at Sacred Heart on his knees for the eucharist as a boy. The Stations of the Cross. The Ten Commandments. He and Cheddar and Knuckles, teasing one another as they slipped into their vestments on a Sunday morning, secretly thrilled that they had been the ones chosen to serve as parish altar boys. He'd been raised with images of a bright airy heaven up above, and fiery eternal hell down below. The Kitchen strung somewhere between the two.

But lately, it felt the devil had a firmer grip on the rope.

So he'd been drinking more. It was the only thing that worked to stop the thoughts. And it did work. Momentarily. Those first three or four beers. A shot of whiskey if need be. It worked. Every single time. But there was never enough. More and more he found himself leaving The Wolf at dawn. At least at The Wolf he had the crew. Laughter. Music. They'd play "Rhinestone Cowboy" on the jukebox and serenade Cheddar and Knuckles like they were fallen comrades. Soldiers lost in war. Tears were shed. Hugs. Another shot of whiskey. He'd even taken to trying a little coke every now and again. Nothing crazy mind you. Just a little bump every now and again when things got blurry in the wee hours. He wasn't into it. Not really. But, you know . . . if it was there . . .

And then, there was Trixie.

Trixie.

He couldn't shake the longing. There wasn't an hour in the day he didn't see her face. Didn't ache to hold her in his arms. No amount of whiskey eased that pain. He ached so badly he'd turned to Gabriela for comfort on occasion. And then hated himself for it afterward. Gabriela was in love with him. She was good and proper and sweet and trustworthy. And he really did like her.

Gabriela always forgave him his trespasses.

And yet, somehow, through all of this, he was making money. More money than he ever had in his life.

He was working four or five nights a week at the Pink Paradise. He was good at his job. Someone crossed the line with one of the girls, he tossed them out. He felt protective of the girls. They weren't gonna get disrespected on his watch. Word got around that it wasn't that kind of place no more. The girls felt safer knowing Danny Boy McCoy was at the door to protect them. Suddenly there were more girls showing up to audition for a shift. Girls who would have never risked working the Paradise before. Then word got around that there were younger, classier strippers on stage. And with the high-class dancers came the money. Wiseguys. Cadillacs. Wall Street. Champagne money. Danny held the door for them. Showed them the respect they craved. Tens and twenties were slipped into his palm. Vinny raised the pay to a hundred a shift. Why wouldn't he? He was making a killing.

And then there was the coke. Everybody was doing it. The strippers. The customers. The bartenders. Even the goddamned cleaning ladies wanted a wrap. So Danny made sure they could get it. Blackie had a connection, hooked him up with as much as he could handle. Danny worked out a deal with Snake the bartender, and between them they kept the place flying high, and split the profits right down the middle.

It was easy money.

And it just kept coming.

For the first time since leaving Sacred Heart High, Danny had money in his pocket. He was caught up on the back rent. The bird feed and vet's bills were paid in full. He could afford Ma's medicines and groceries. He'd even gone out and bought her a real nice emerald-green, cashmere scarf for Christmas from Bergdorf's. Had them wrap it up in some of that high-end, classy wrapping paper, you see them with. The little silk bow. The whole bit.

She'd been doing much better in the last few weeks. The doctors told her the operation was a success. They were pretty sure they got it all. She was up and out of bed every morning. Dressing herself, making sure her hair was just right. She'd started cooking again. She'd put on some of the weight again. She was even talking about venturing out to morning Mass again pretty soon. One way or another, she assured him, she was going to be at midnight Mass at Sacred Heart on Christmas Eve, if it meant she had to crawl the seven blocks on her hands and knees to get there.

He had one more gift in store for her this year. He'd called Liam in Woodstock that very morning and told him he'd decided he was committing to buying the cottage. Liam was over the moon. Danny told him he'd be out there with a down payment the first week of January. But Liam insisted that he go next door right away and lock it in with a cash deposit out of his own pocket. He was pretty sure he could secure the deal for a couple of grand. Danny was reluctant at first to let Liam use his own money but there was little doubt in his mind he would be able to cover it in a matter of weeks. And he didn't want to risk losing the property by letting it sit a day longer. Besides, Ma was getting better again. It had been a rough year all around. What better Christmas present could he give her?

He told Liam to go ahead and lock it in.

He was finally making the push. This was the year. He was going to get Ma out of The Kitchen.

He should have been feeling over the moon. He was getting everything he dreamed of. Everything that is, except Trixie.

14

Mack had a rat in a cage in the back of The Wolf and he was working on it with a blowtorch and a ballpeen hammer.

"Watch this?" he said to Danny.

Danny had shown up looking for Logan but found the bar empty. He'd been walking out the door again when he'd heard the squealing coming from the storage room in the back. And then came Mack's twisted laughter.

Danny had inched the door open, terrified of what he might find on the other side.

And there was Mack, hunched over, in front of a small cage, a crazed look in his eyes.

Danny watched him lure the rat to the front of the cage with a scrap of bread then blast the rat in the face with a blowtorch. The rat's squeal sounded like a child's. It leapt to the rear of the cage, cowering, its face seared bald and pink, one eye roasted black, its scorched body trembling.

By all appearances Mack had been working on the rat for some time.

"You see that shit!" Mack laughed. "See how that fucker jumped."

The rat's tail slipped out of the rear of the cage and Mack whacked it with the hammer, severing about two inches off the end. The rat screamed louder, and hobbled to the center of the cage, as far away from the bars as it could get.

"What the fuck are you doing?" Danny asked, repulsed by the level of cruelty Mack was administering to this poor helpless animal.

"I fucken hate rats."

"Right. But you gotta torture it like that?"

"I'm solving our rat problem."

"What are you talking about?"

"Fucken filthy bastards are running rampant 'round here. Whadda you think the other rats will think when they hear this fucker screaming like this? You don't think that scares 'em! Guarantee there won't be a rat within a half mile of this place by the time I'm done with this fucker."

Mack leaned over a mirror where he'd chopped a few lines of coke, and snorted a fat rail.

"Want one?"

"It's ten o'clock in the morning, Mack."

"So?"

"It's Christmas Eve."

Mack seemed dazed by this information. He turned his head from side to side, like he'd heard some faraway part of him calling. A child's voice, hidden deep in the rubble. Then it was gone.

"Wanna beer?" he asked, moving for the door. "Let's have a drink."

They heard voices out front just then, and as they exited the storage room they saw Terry come in the front door with Darryl Hunt.

Darryl was one of those guys Danny knew from around the

neighborhood since he was a boy. He bounced around the bars on the West Side doing odd jobs for beer money. He had bad teeth and bad breath, so you didn't want to get up too close to him for a chat, but he was a likable sort, and people talked fondly of him when they mentioned his name. Darryl had an infectious, cracked smile for everyone he met.

"I want a small stage, or a platform built right over here in the corner we can put a band on it . . ." Terry was telling Darryl, when he noticed Danny and Mack emerge from the hallway that led to the storage room in the rear. "Hey, guys," Terry called, as he moved behind the bar to pull a few beers. "Darryl's gonna build us a stage. Finally convinced Logan to let us get some live entertainment in here."

Danny noticed Darryl freeze at the sight of Mack. A look of pure terror flashed in his eyes.

"I've been looking for you," Mack said, coldly. He marched directly up to Darryl, pulled a gun out of his pants, and shot Darryl in the middle of his chest.

"Jesus Christ!" Terry yelled as Darryl dropped to the floor.

Darryl groaned, and tried to sit upright as blood gurgled and spat out of his mouth, his eyes wide, a hand trying to stop the blood leaking out of his chest. Danny took a step forward, and then stopped again, seeing the crazed look in Mack's eyes.

Mack stood over Darryl, and shoved him back down with his foot. Darryl raised his arms and tried weakly to bat him away. But it was pointless. Mack lowered himself so that he straddled Darryl's waist, then he raised the hammer, and brought it down with a ferocious whack on Darryl's forehead.

Danny turned away and tried in vain to block the ugly cracking sounds of Darryl's skull coming apart. Mack swung the hammer, again and again.

"Take that, you rat fuck," Mack yelled, as blood and broken parts of Darryl's brain splattered around the bar with every swing of the hammer.

Danny and Terry remained frozen, unable to process the horror unfolding before them.

When he was done, Mack sat atop Darryl, panting heavily.

Terry was the first to speak. "What the fuck, Mack?"

"Lock the door," Mack said, calmly.

Danny carefully stepped around the mess, trying not to get any of Darryl's blood on his shoes, and bolted the entrance door.

"What the fuck, man!" Terry repeated, peering over the bar at the mess on the floor. "What the fuck did you just do?"

"He ratted me out to the cops."

"When?"

"Five years ago."

"Jesus, Mack. Are you sure it was Darryl?"

"I'm pretty sure," Mack said, as he stood. "Nobody rats on Mack Cantor. Throw me a couple of those garbage bags."

Terry obediently peeled a couple of large black trash bags off a roll on the shelf behind the bar and handed them to him.

Mack took them, and wrapped what was left of Darryl's head.

"Okay, give me a hand here," he said, slipping his hands under Darryl's shoulders.

"What are you going to do?"

"Fuck do you think I'm going to do? I gotta make him disappear. Grab him. We gotta get him in back."

Terry moved around the bar and grabbed one of Darryl's legs.

"You too," Mack barked at Danny, who was still standing near the door, hoping that he might be able to avoid any further involvement in this madness. "Danny. Grab a fucking leg."

207

Danny stepped forward, and reluctantly lifted Darryl's other leg, and the three of them carried him back, into the storage room, and laid his body on the floor.

As Terry straightened himself, he glanced at the rat huddled in the cage, which was still sitting on the counter next to the blowtorch. He glanced at Danny to see if he'd seen it too. Danny shook his head, as if to say, *Don't ask.*

Mack opened a drawer and produced a large serrated butcher knife, set it on the counter, and began stripping off his shirt.

"I'm not staying for this," Terry said, moving for the door.

"Nor me," said Danny, following Terry's lead.

"Where the fuck you two think you're going?" snapped Mack.

"Fuck you, Mack," Terry barked back. "This is your fucking mess. You clean it up. We're leaving. You wanna come lock the door behind us in case somebody walks in here, be my guest."

Mack paused for a moment as if contemplating a showdown with Terry Flannery. The room was cramped and the adrenaline was running high. There was a knife sitting an arm's length away from Mack's hand. Danny could see the possibilities flicker over Mack's crazed eyes, and then disappear again just as quickly. Mack let it go.

He followed the two men to the entrance door, opened it, peeked out to make sure the coast was clear, then held it while Terry and Danny stepped outside.

The door closed behind them and they heard the bolt snap shut.

Danny stood with Terry on the corner of Forty-third and Tenth. Terry pulled a pack of smokes out of his pocket, and shook a couple out of the pack. Danny took one, and lifted it to his mouth, and held it there, his hands shaking uncontrollably as Terry lit them both.

An icy cold breeze came up Forty-third off the river, and sliced right through them as they inhaled deeply.

It felt good to be outside.

Smoking.

Shivering.

Breathing.

15

Danny helped his mother up the steps into the church and kept her arm in his until he spotted a pew with enough room for them both. There was barely an empty seat left in the place. A lone female voice filled the air with a heavenly rendition of "Once in Royal David's City" as Danny ushered his mother into a booth about halfway up the church floor.

It was the first time she had been back at Mass since the operation and the joy was written on her face like a homecoming. This was her favorite night of the year. Midnight Mass. The Angel's Mass.

Hundreds of candles threw a warm orange glow on the faces of the parishioners and lit the gold stars in the sky-blue ceiling. As a boy, Danny imagined that this was exactly what it must have looked like in Bethlehem on the night Jesus was born. There was still magic and a communal sense of wonder to it all.

But that was many Christmases ago.

He slipped down in his seat until his knees found the hard wooden kneeler and he closed his eyes to pray.

It had been twelve hours since he watched Mack Cantor bludgeon Darryl Hunt to death with a hammer. The image of Darryl's face as he reached to defend himself seemed to be seared into Danny's brain now alongside the vision of Knuckle's severed head. There was no peace in Danny's heart tonight. No magic. No innocent sense of wonder. For Danny, this was a night of ghosts, not angels.

Perhaps the dizzy spells were early signs of cancer, he thought. Punishment. Tumors in his lungs and brain. Perhaps it really was true, what the priest had been saying all these years, about an all-seeing God. If God was all seeing then he had been witness to a lot of blood over these past few months in The Kitchen.

For the most part he'd been able to avoid thinking of such things, but here, on Christmas Eve, sitting next to his mother, in the Church of the Sacred Heart, there was no denying that his soul felt stained by everything that he'd witnessed of late.

He opened his eyes and scanned the crowd. Benny Black caught his eye, and nodded knowingly. Benny and his wife were seated just across the aisle from Danny, dressed in their Sunday best, bracketing four young children between them, neat as pins.

Three rows in front of the Blacks, he saw Gabriela seated next to her mother. He could only catch the side of her face, but she appeared sad from this angle. Her eyes closed. Her head bowed. She seemed deep in prayer.

All throughout the church, in every direction, he saw the familiar faces. The family members of his childhood friends. The Keenans, Burkes and Ryans. All families who'd lost a child this past year. He saw off to the right of where he sat, three or four of Terry Flannery's nine brothers and sisters. He didn't know them all by name. But he knew them well enough by sight. Logan's younger brother Henry was there, too. And Tony McElroy, who caught Danny's attention and crossed his eyes at him comically like he'd been doing in church since they were boys.

And even in that small act of familiar childish foolishness Danny'd sensed a trace of sadness in his old friend's eyes.

Here in the Church of the Sacred Heart it was clear how the fabric of the community had been torn and tattered over this past year by Coyle's crew.

Mack Cantor and Logan Coyle's fingerprints were all over this carnage.

Logan and Kate were nowhere to be seen tonight. Though Danny was pretty sure they too would be at Christmas Eve Mass tonight, back home, in New Jersey, with their own two small children in tow.

Danny wondered if death weighed on Logan's soul as heavily as it did on his this Christmas Eve.

He felt a hand on his shoulder and looked up into the smiling face of Pat Mannion.

"Danny. Mind if we squeeze past," Mannion whispered, motioning to a few empty seats in the center of the pew.

Danny stepped out of the pew to allow them in. Mannion, in a finely tailored gray tweed suit, was with Elaine and their three young children. Two boys and a little girl. The entire family cut fresh from a catalogue.

Seeing Danny's mother, Pat immediately reached for her hand.

"Missus McCoy, how wonderful to see you. So good to see you out and about again. We missed you at morning Mass this last while. You look great. You know Elaine, and Gerard and Toby and Deirdre," he said as he ushered his family past her into the pew.

"I do, of course, Pat. I do, of course." His mother smiled as they filed past her, each one of them excusing themselves politely as they went. "Ach. Aren't they beautiful wee children. 'Tis a credit to yourselves. A blessed Christmas to you all. Pat. Elaine."

"And to you, Missus McCoy," Mannion said, giving her hand

a final squeeze. "If there's anything you need," he said, solemnly, as he went on past to take his seat, "you know where to find me."

If there was darkness on Pat Mannion's soul, Danny saw not the least sign of it.

The organ started up again and the congregation rose to its feet just then as Father Connolly took to the altar.

"In the name of the Father, and the Son, and the Holy Ghost, Amen."

Danny bowed his head and prayed.

16

The sun-faded, red Chevy van had been sitting in the parking lot of the Market Diner since the beginning of January. Danny had been drawn to it on several occasions. He'd peered in the windows and checked the tires. It was perfect for what he needed. But the FOR SALE sign in the window was asking for just a little more than he had planned to spend.

The truth was, he was nervous about owning a vehicle of any kind. He was almost thirty years old and never owned a car. Sure, he could drive, just so long as you didn't put him in a stick shift. He'd just never needed a vehicle of his own before now. He'd have to get it insured. Keep it serviced.

He'd be responsible for it.

But maybe that wasn't the only thing that really scared him. It was more than that. The van meant he was getting out. It was a commitment. He didn't need a van to live in Hell's Kitchen. He needed a van to get out of Hell's Kitchen.

He called the number.

The guy who owned it was a short-order cook in the Market Diner. They haggled. Danny paid him cash, and drove it out of the parking lot.

*   *   *

A week later, Logan was strolling down Tenth Avenue with his kid brother, Henry, when he spotted Danny locking the van door.

"This yours?"

"Yeah. Bought it a few days ago."

"You bought a van!"

"Nice ride, Danny," Henry said. "I need to get me something like this?"

"Fuck do you need a van for?" Logan snapped at his brother.

"I dunno. Maybe I want to go for a drive. Whadda you care what I need it for?"

"You can't take a taxi?"

"You got a car."

"Yeah, I know I got a car, Henry, but I live in New Jersey. What am I gonna do, swim home!"

"So I can't get a car?"

"What the fuck do I care if you get a car?"

"You just said . . ."

"Jesus Christ, Henry, you wanna car, get a car . . . whad am I, your mother?"

"I'm freezin'," Henry said, walking off. "I'm goin' inside for a hot toddy. Come in and I'll buy you one."

"Maybe later," Danny called after him. It was a bitterly cold afternoon. A hot whiskey sounded inviting.

"Vinny must be payin' you pretty good over there," Logan said, still lingering by the van. Logan didn't seem to be in any hurry to get out of the cold. He was standing with his hands in his pockets, wearing only a light jacket and a shirt open at the collar.

"Yeah, it's alright. Thanks for hooking me up, Logan, I really appreciate it."

215

"I gotta get over there one of these nights when you're working. Got some real hot chicks working there now, I hear."

"Yeah, they're nice."

"You gettin' your joint sucked, or what?"

Danny shook his head.

"You're kiddin' me, right! All that tail, you ain't getting a taste! Don't tell me you're in love? Who, with that Spanish chick? What's her name? From the fruit market? You still bangin' that broad?"

"Gabriela." Danny shrugged. "I see her sometimes. I been tryin' to get in shape, you know . . ."

"Oh, that's right! The fight. I forgot. That's coming up pretty soon, right?"

"Two weeks."

"Two weeks!"

"What's the kid's name again?"

"Petkov."

"Petkov? What is that, Russian, or some shit."

"Bulgarian."

"Bulgarian. He any good?"

Danny shrugged.

"My money's on you, Danny. You hear me. You know that, right! All the way, champ. How you feel? You ready?"

"I'll be ready."

"It's out in Queens, right?"

"Some place in the Rockaways."

"I'm gonna bring the whole crew out there to cheer you on. Maybe we bring them in your van, huh!"

"Sure, Logan."

"What the fuck you need a van for anyhow?"

He still hadn't said a word to Logan about Woodstock. About

trying to get his mother out of the neighborhood. He didn't want him to know. He didn't want him standing in the way.

"I dunno, thought maybe I use it to start a little moving business, you know."

"Moving business?"

"Yeah, you know, somebody's gotta move some furniture you know. Couch, tables. You know. People gotta move."

"Yeah, I guess you're right. Good thinkin', Danny. Van like this could be useful. Wanna take me for a spin?"

"Sure."

"Great. Let's go," Logan said, and reached for the door handle.

"Now?" Danny didn't realize he meant this very minute.

"Yeah. Let's go."

Reluctantly he unlocked the door again, and Logan climbed in.

"You got a heater in this thing?"

"Yeah. It's got a heater."

Danny started the van and headed north on Tenth as Logan fiddled with the heating controls.

"Oh yeah. This is nice," Logan said, turning in his seat to check out the spacious interior. "Get a couch back here no problem. Make a right up here on Fifty-seventh."

"What's on Fifty-seventh?"

"I gotta see a guy."

"What guy?"

"Out on Ward's Island."

So that was it.

"Ward's Island?"

"Yeah. Nicky Red works out there at the sewage treatment plant. I gotta see him about a thing."

"How the hell we get out to Ward's Island?"

"Fuck should I know?"

"You have a map?"

"I look like I walk around with a fucken map in my pocket? Head up the FDR. It's up near the Triboro Bridge. It's a fucken island, for chrissakes. How hard can it be to find an island, Danny?"

17

The security guard at the main gate was leaning back in a chair with his feet up, watching a small TV on his desk. He seemed unconcerned with the two men in a red van stopped next to the booth, peering in at him through the grimy plexiglass window.

"Look at this fat fuck," said Logan, shaking his head in disgust. "That's our tax dollars hard at work right there."

"You pay taxes?"

"It's a figure of speech, Danny. Go in there and tell him we're here to see Nicky Red."

The guy was eating a slice of pizza when Danny entered. An open box with the remaining pie sat on the table next to the TV.

He barely more than glanced up when Danny entered the booth.

"Hey, buddy, we're supposed to see Nicky Red."

The guy raised his slice of pizza and pointed with it to the south side of the island. "Follow this around 'til you see the trailer by the water. He's in there." Then he shoved the slice back into his mouth again.

"Guy don't seem too concerned with us driving around in here," Danny said, once he was back in the van.

"Why should he? It's a shit processing plant. What the fuck we gonna steal?"

Danny followed the trail around the island past a series of low-lying concrete structures in darkness, and a enormous sand-colored building with bars on the windows, off to the right.

"Is that a prison?" Danny asked.

"Nut house," Logan replied.

"That's a big nut house."

"Lot of fucken nut jobs in this city. Gotta put 'em somewhere."

Nicky's trailer sat alone at the very southern tip of the island, almost directly beneath the Triboro Bridge. Danny recognized Nicky's beat-up Oldsmobile parked out front. Next to the Oldsmobile sat a shiny black Lincoln.

"Go over there and knock that door."

"I'm not knocking that door," said Danny. This place creeped him out. "That crazy fuck's liable to shoot somebody, they knock at that door."

"You really gotta relax a little bit, Danny," Logan said, climbing out. "Come on. Let's go."

Danny killed the engine and got out to follow Logan toward the rusty trailer perched on a bed of cinder blocks at the water's edge.

The moon was high and bright in a clear wintry sky. Traffic could be heard rumbling across the Triboro Bridge far above. Seagulls cried in the darkness. An icy wind coming off the East River burned his face and hands. A bare lightbulb hanging from a cord above the door illuminated the way.

Logan knocked.

"Who is it?" came a voice.

"It's me, you dumb fuck," Logan shouted.

The door opened. Nicky Red peered out.

"Logan, what the fuck, man." Nicky grinned. "Danny Boy. Good to see you. Come in."

The air inside the trailer was thick with the smell of paraffin and cigarette smoke. A burly guy with short dark hair and a white shirt open at the collar sat hunched over a small table shuffling a deck of playing cards.

"Logan, this is Sal DeCarlo," said Nicky.

"Hey, Sal," Logan said, extending his hand. "Heard a lot about you. This is my buddy, Danny McCoy."

"So this is the fighter!"

Danny nodded.

"You ready for this Bulgarian?"

Danny nodded again. He didn't like the look of DeCarlo. Whole thing out here gave him the creeps.

"How you two guys know each other again?" DeCarlo asked of Logan and Nicky.

"We were on a long vacation together a while back, upstate." Nicky laughed.

"Oh yeah, youse get a nice tan? Sit down. You Irish guys want a drink? Or is that a dumb question," DeCarlo said, nodding to the chairs around the small table.

Danny had hoped this would be a short visit, but seeing Logan removing his jacket and pulling up a chair across from DeCarlo, he knew they were in for the long haul. He had wanted to eat dinner with his mother. She'd told him she'd be cooking roast beef with gravy, carrots and mash potatoes. He'd also wanted to spend some time with his birds tonight. He'd made plans to drive his mother out to Woodstock in the morning to see the house. He'd arranged to meet Liam in the village square, so he could follow him out to the house. But he wasn't about to tell any of that to Logan.

Three hours later, when they all stepped outside the trailer to leave, Logan and DeCarlo were fast friends.

"You gotta come over and have a drink at my place," Logan was saying.

"I will," said DeCarlo, chewing on a fat cigar. "You gotta come out my way also."

"What's the name again?"

"The Capricorn Lounge. I'll tell the bartender to order in a keg of Jamesons—tell him the Micks are coming," said DeCarlo.

"I'll have my guy get a cappuccino machine installed, tell him the wops are coming," Logan responded.

"You fucking Micks." DeCarlo laughed.

"You fat guinea bastard," Logan responded. Both men laughed together.

"Hey, 'fore you go, check this out," DeCarlo said, opening the trunk of the Caddy and producing a silencer, which he proceeded to screw onto the barrel of a nine millimeter he had tucked in the waistband of his pants.

He handed the rig to Logan. "Go ahead. Blast off a few rounds."

Logan aimed the barrel of the gun into a large pile of dirt next the the trailer and fired off two rounds. There was barely a whisper, other than the dull thud of the rounds hitting clay.

"Jesus fucking Christ, Sal, that's incredible," Logan raved. "Where the hell do I get one of these?"

"Keep it," DeCarlo said, slamming closed the trunk of his car. "It's yours."

"Nah."

"A gift."

"Really."

"You need anymore, you let me know."

"I will. Thank you. This means a lot to me."

"I've a feeling we're gonna do a lot of business together, you and I, Logan."

"I'd like that, Sal."

Danny watched the two men shake hands.

Then DeCarlo climbed into his Cadillac, and they stood there watching him drive away.

"I knew you two would hit it off," said Nicky.

"You did good," said Logan. "You did real good." Then his eyesight drifted off toward the water and he began walking to the river's edge. Nicky and Danny followed him.

The three men peered down into the icy black river swirling below.

"Hell Gate," said Nicky absentmindedly.

Logan turned to him for explanation.

"That's what this stretch of the river is called," Nicky explained. "Hell Gate. Most dangerous currents around Manhattan. You fall in here, you're fucken gone, baby."

"Where?" asked Logan.

"Gone. This thing pulls you down and you're not getting back up 'til you're in the Atlantic."

"Hell Gate," Logan repeated.

"If you wanted to get rid of something, this would be a good place to throw it," said Nicky.

"Or some-body," added Logan, as he raised the gun again and emptied the chamber into the icy black water below.

18

A light snow began to fall before they were over the Tappan Zee Bridge. Huge flakes soft as feathers.

It was warm in the van, and the tires felt sure and solid on the road. He had the radio tuned into some station playing the oldies that his mother liked to listen to. Connie Francis, Patsy Cline, Johnny Mathis, Bobby Darin . . . Tony Bennett singing "I Left my Heart in San Fransisco."

He had never taken a drive with his mother, other than once or twice they'd shared a taxi to Calvary Cemetery in Queens for a funeral.

So the radio played, and they didn't bother to fill the air with pointless chatter. She seemed perfectly happy to sit quietly with her thoughts, as the countryside passed them by with the hypnotic softness of snow falling all about. There was something otherworldly about it all. Like moving through the world in a snowglobe.

He exited the thruway near Kingston and took Route 28 for a few miles into the hills, then made a right on 375, toward Woodstock. And as they emerged from a sea of snow-capped pine trees the landscape opened up again to the magnificent sight of Overlook Mountain directly up ahead.

She said, "Wow! Would you look at that! Isn't that lovely?"

It was lovely.

The village had a simple, easy feel to it. A general store. A gas station. A diner. All anchored around a steepled white church on the square.

It seemed almost impossible that people lived this way. Far removed from the chaos, the noise, the brutal life-or-death energy of the city.

Danny spotted Liam's Volkswagen van just as Liam stepped out to greet them with a wave.

"You made it. How was the drive?"

"Smooth sailing."

"Nice rig. This yours?"

"Sure is."

"You need to stop for anything or you wanna follow me out to the house? Ma has breakfast ready. You hungry?"

"Starving."

"Let's go."

Danny followed Liam on a series of winding roads, across a stone bridge, past a wide meadow, and more trees, and a narrow road that seemed to spiral up a mountain and then a dirt lane for a few hundred yards into a clearing where he slowed to a stop.

There, on a rise above a half-frozen pond, sat a small wooden cottage with a stone chimney and a wide screened-in porch.

"Is that . . ." His mother started to say, and then stopped herself, as if afraid she'd pop the bubble of this idyllic dream that had appeared before her amid the trees.

"That's it." Danny nodded, amazed that the house looked even more beautiful than it had appeared in the pictures. The photographs Liam had sent had not done it justice. It was fairy-book beautiful. What the pictures had failed to capture was the setting, and the old red barn sitting off to the right of a grassy yard. The majestic willow tree by the water's edge. The backdrop of the snowcapped mountain in the distance, behind the house.

Liam was out of his car and coming toward them with a broad smile.

"Well, what do you think?"

"It's beautiful," replied Danny's mother.

"Is it really for sale?" asked Danny.

Liam looked confused.

"What do you mean? This is yours."

"What do you mean, ours?" she said.

"Danny asked me to put a deposit on it. This is your house. The owners are gone. Moved the last of their stuff out a week ago."

"No!" she said, in disbelief.

Liam fished a set of keys out of his pocket and held them up.

"Wanna go inside?"

He reached inside the van and handed the keys to Danny's mother. She took them and stared down at them cupped in her hand in disbelief.

"I should park this somewhere," said Danny.

Liam laughed. "You're on your own property, Danny. You can leave it here."

"Where's your house?"

"It's about a half mile away, further out along the main road. I'll take you there afterwards."

"We're neighbors?" asked Danny's mother, seemingly unable to process it all.

"We're neighbors." Liam smiled. "We'll have to call it Hell's Kitchen North."

Even Danny was in disbelief. Yes, he'd told Liam to go ahead and secure the house with a downpayment. But somehow, he didn't believe he'd actually do it. He didn't think it could be this simple. It couldn't be this simple. No bank. No contract. No haggling over the price.

But here they were.

They walked up to the house and onto the wide wooden porch.

Danny watched as his mother turned the key in the door, and it opened easily with an inviting squeak, as if to say, *Come on in.*

There were three spacious bedrooms. Two bathrooms. A living room with a wide stone hearth. Plank floors throughout. A large bright kitchen with an enormous ceramic sink and a window facing off toward Overlook Mountain in the distance, over a breathtaking sea of snowcapped pine.

Danny opened the rear door off the kitchen and walked over to the old red barn and through the immense doors. The hard dirt floor was covered in loose straw. A few bales of hay were stacked in one corner, with chopped wood and an axe in the other. A workbench ran along one wall. Old rusty hammers, chisels, a bow saw, and an awl. A selection of garden tools, shovels, spades, and pruning shears. Birds flapped about overhead, drawing his eye up into a dusty cupola high above.

He turned and went out and followed the sound of running water down the long sloping lawn to a sparkling, crystal-clear river that washed easily along over a bed of smooth white rocks.

Liam joined him by the water's edge.

"Well! What do you think?" he asked as they both turned to see Danny's mother standing in the kitchen window, peering off at the view. "I think she likes it."

"I don't get it," Danny replied. "How much did you say it was?"

"I told you. Sixteen grand. I gave them the two grand deposit like we talked about. Then they figured three hundred a month in payments for the rest. If you can pay them more, pay them more."

"How is this possible?"

"I told you, Danny, Bill and Barb are like family. Really great people. Older couple. Hippies. They had this place rented to a cousin, old dude, Norman, cousin of hers. He passed away about a year ago. Been sittin' empty ever since. Believe me, they're just happy to have someone take it who didn't insist on getting lawyers and banks involved. You're saving them all the fees and the hassle. They don't want that shit. You gotta chill, man. This is not the city. People are just different up here. There's no hustle here."

"This is our house!"

"Sure is. It was more important to them that the house went to someone the neighbors approved of. They didn't want some asshole coming in here, tearing the place down or disrupting the whole place. Trust me, if you hadn't taken it I was gonna take it myself. It's a steal."

Danny felt a dizzy spell coming on.

"You okay?"

"I just need to sit down for a moment."

"Sorry, I should have taken you guys to get something to eat first. You're probably starving after your drive."

"That's probably it," Danny lied.

The truth is he'd gone back to Goldstein for the downpayment. He'd been so consistent with his payments over the past few months, as he chipped away at the initial three grand he'd borrowed, that Goldstein didn't even blink at giving him another couple of grand.

Only now, Goldstein was charging him the going rate, four points vig on the principle. The honeymoon was over.

Danny had convinced himself it was all doable.

It was doable.

So long as things didn't change.

He was making good money at the Pink Paradise.

Logan was still throwing him and Blackie a few bucks here and there for collections.

To hell with it, he thought. If not now, when?

He pulled the envelope of cash from his pocket and handed it to Liam.

"There's two grand."

"Good man, Danny," Liam said, looking relieved. "Trust me. You guys are going to love it up here. You're doing the right thing."

"I hope so."

Danny glanced back up at the house. His mother was standing in the open kitchen door with her hands clasped behind her back. Her face turned upward. Her eyes closed, and the corners of her lips upturned in a smile.

He could not remember the last time he'd seen her so supremely happy.

Maybe never.

She was home.

They were home. He'd find a way.

19

Danny sat on the wooden bench in the makeshift dressing room, listening to the announcer and the cheering crowd beyond the closed doors.

They were leading the Bulgarian in first.

He would have liked to have had this moment before the fight alone, but Vinny Diamond was there, with the dancers in their green, white and gold bikinis, and a handful of the Bensonhurst Italian crew. Guys Danny recognized from the Paradise Club.

Vinny brought Danny a burly cornerman for the fight. Danny had never met the guy before, but he seemed a solid sort. The guy was old-school. From out on the Island. A bent nose and a boxer's ear. Hank.

Hank laced him up, smeared a little Vaseline on his face, without so much as a word of advice.

"You good?" he asked when he was done.

"Yup."

"Good." Then he'd tapped Danny's gloves with his fists, and said, "You got this, kid."

What more was there to say before a fight? You got in the ring and you fought. You beat the guy or you didn't.

Danny closed his eyes to the chaos around him, and prayed. "Hail, Mary, full of grace . . ."

He blessed himself and opened his eyes. And there she was. Trixie.

Hunkered in front of him, staring up into his face with that smile of hers.

"I just wanted to wish you luck," she said, before placing her hands on his thighs and leaning forward to plant a quick kiss on his cheek. She stood and walked away from him before he had a chance to respond.

Vinny was busy prepping the strippers for the walk to the ring. Danny watched Trixie step over next to him and slip her arm around his waist. Vinny shoved her roughly and snapped, loud enough for everyone to hear: "Back it up. Can't you see I'm working here."

Danny felt his whole body go tense. His fists balled. It took everything he had not to spring out of his seat.

Trixie retreated to a corner with a weak smile, in an obvious attempt to make light of the humiliation.

"I want to see tits and teeth," Vinny continued, to his dancers. "You hear me, tits and teeth. You two, in front. One either side of him. And you two, right behind him. And when he gets up to the ring, everybody pause, you two in back, remove his cape. Make it big. Okay! Got it?"

The girls nodded. They looked excited to be out of the club for a change.

Danny put his head down and tried to let it go. They way he'd shoved Trixie.

She's not your girl, Danny.

Let it go.

Then came the deep baritone of the announcer's voice again.

"And now, ladies and gentlemen, making his way to the ring . . . give it up for, the one and only . . . the wide-eyed Irish warrior, from the wild West Side . . . Hell's Kitchen's very own . . . Danny, Boy, McCoy . . ."

Danny stood, and stretched his neck, as over the loudspeakers he could hear the beginning of his song begin to play.

"Oh Danny Boy, the pipes the pipes are calling,"

He pulled the hood of the silk cape over his head and the dancers assembled themselves around him.

"From glen to glen and down the mountainside,"

The double doors swung open, and he began the walk.

The crowd was on their feet already, many of them singing along to the song at the top of their lungs.

*"The summer's gone, and all the roses falling,
It's you, it's you must go, and I must bide."*

In the front row, he saw the familiar faces of The Wolf crew. Coyle, Flannery, Mack, Blackie, McElroy, Hughes, and Nicky Red, all there with their fists in the air, cheering and clapping him on.

*"But come ye back when summer's in the meadow,
Or when the valley's hushed and white with snow,
It's I'll be here, in sunshine or in shadow:
Oh Danny Boy, Oh Danny Boy, I love you so."*

The ring had been assembled in the middle of a huge ballroom of this grand old beach hotel. The place was packed, wall to wall.

Danny paused when he reached the ropes, and allowed the dancers to remove his cape. There were whistles and cheers of approval as the dancers raised their arms and smiled to the crowd.

A cameraman ringside leapt forth for the shot.

"But when he comes, and all the flowers are dying,
If I am dead, as dead I well may be,
Ye'll come and find the place where I am lying,
And kneel and say an Ave there for me."

He slipped through the ropes and turned to face the audience. He scanned the room 'til he found her face.

Trixie.

When he met her eyes she smiled.

He held her gaze.

This is for you.

"And I shall hear, though soft you thread above me,
And all my grave will warmer sweeter be,
For you will bend and tell me that you love me,
And I shall sleep in peace, until you come to me."

He turned away from her to face his opponent. The Bulgarian was dancing from foot to foot. He had fire in his eyes. Danny could see that this guy wanted this as bad as he did. This guy wasn't going to go down easy.

Danny let the room go silent around him. He stretched his neck and tapped his gloves together. He hadn't trained as much as he'd liked, but his body felt good. His mind felt calm and ready for battle.

He felt no fear.

Hank stood behind him and massaged his shoulders. It felt good. He was a good cornerman. He had big strong hands, and knew exactly how a muscle worked.

The referee signaled the two fighters to the center of the ring. Hank slapped Danny on the shoulder, turned and slipped out through the ropes.

The bell rang, and Danny went to the Bulgarian with his hands high, then, in a flash, unexpected even to himself, he dropped his right and caught Petkov with a punishing blow to the liver, easily dodging the powerful right that slipped over his left shoulder.

Petkov almost buckled.

Danny could see the pain register in his face. He could have finished him right there and then. But he paused. Stepped back. Let him recover.

He let the guy get a good look into his eyes. Let him read.

The guy was his height, similar build. Handsome. Beautiful even.

Danny stepped forward again and went to work on him.

Danny's mind felt about as clear as it had ever been in the ring. It happened sometimes. The magical synchronicity. An animal acuteness. A physician's clinical eye. He was anticipating every punch that came his way. It didn't matter how hard the Bulgarian hit him, nothing felt like it registered.

Danny hit him harder. Slammed punches into his shoulders and ribs. Brutal, bone breaking blows, but nothing that was intended to put him down for good.

He wanted this fight to last.

Back in the corner after three punishing rounds, Hank finally yelled at him.

"What the hell are you doing out there? You got him. Finish him off, for chrissakes, before he catches you with that right."

The Bulgarian did have a powerful right, and he wasn't wasting it. He was careful about letting it go. His ace in the hole. Danny had felt it go past his ear twice already and had been rocked by the sheer authority of it.

The bell rang again. They skipped toward one another in the fourth.

Danny had a sudden lust to feel the full power of that right hook.

He wanted to feel it on his face.

The thunder of it.

He wanted it to lift his head clean off his shoulders.

He fought the self-destructive urge to open himself up to it.

For the next two rounds they pounded each other with a solid barrage of blows that would have sent any normal man to an emergency room.

When the bell rang, at the end of the fifth, his shoulders burned, his ribs ached, and his face was swollen. He had a cut above his left eye. Hank worked some Vaseline into it and patched it with a butterfly stitch.

"Don't let him hit this again. Keep him off you. Watch that right."

Danny stepped into the sixth, and faced Petkov with his arms down, fists low in front of his chest, his chin held high and open. Petkov rushed in, then hesitated for just a moment, sensing it was some sort of a setup. A trap. A look of disbelief flickered across his eyes, and then it was as if he spotted the glimmer of suicide in Danny's eyes and he pulled back, and let him have that right with everything he had.

The glove caught Danny firmly on the left side of his jaw. It was everything he'd hoped it would be. Like getting hit with a concrete block. The thud snapped Danny's head a full one eighty.

His neck almost snapped.

A unified gasp of horror rippled through the auditorium.

The room flashed white.

That was it.

That was the punishment he deserved.

Without missing a beat, Danny came back with a right of his

own that went clear past the Bulgarian's left arm, and caught him firmly on the lower side of his jaw.

Danny could feel the power of the blow register across his entire back. He'd connected with everything he had. He could see Petkov's eyes spin in his head.

The Bulgarian seemed to freeze, and then his knees buckled as he crumpled to the canvas. Straight down, as if a piano had fallen out of a window and landed on his head.

The guy was still breathing, but he wasn't going to be getting back up again for a while.

The crowd went nuts.

Danny turned to see the Tenth Avenue crew screaming and punching the air with their fists. Logan was laughing and clapping and shaking his head in disbelief.

Danny stared down at his gloves.

Turned his hands over and saw where his wrists disappeared into the neck of the gloves.

He turned them back and studied the palms of the gloves.

Flexed his fingers inside and let his hands fall down by his side, half expecting them to fall to the floor.

He wondered, *Whose hands are these?*

20

He was driving across Forty-second Street in the rain when he spotted her hurrying along toward Seventh Avenue. It was night. She was in blue denim shorts and heels. She had her head down and her arms folded across her chest as if for protection. Every few feet she glanced back, over her shoulder, as if she were being stalked.

He slowed the van to a crawl. She hadn't seen him yet. It wasn't too late to drive on.

He could still drive away.

The smart thing to do was keep moving.

This was not his business.

But this ache he had for Trixie was like a cancer. It ate at him.

No amount of nights holed up in the Skyline Motel with Gabriela had done anything to satiate the longing.

It was a profound sickness of the heart.

"Don't do it, Danny. Don't do it. Keep driving . . . you fucken idiot," he whispered to himself, with his hands locked on the steering wheel in a death grip. "Don't you fucking do it, pal."

But he was already doing it. Even as he fought to convince himself otherwise. Even as he cursed himself. He was doing it.

237

He allowed the van to drift to the sidewalk next to a fire hydrant just up ahead of her.

He rolled down his window, and just as she was about to barrel past him, she glanced up and saw him there.

She froze. He saw at a glance that she'd been crying. The side of her face was freshly bruised. A cut had opened over her left eye. She put her head down again and tried to keep walking, but he was out of the van and caught her in his arms under the bright glare of a theatre marquee.

"Who did this?" he asked. But he didn't need to ask. She didn't need to tell him. He knew.

"Don't," she said, trying to pull away. "Don't." But he had wrapped his big arms around her, and gently, he pulled her to him. She turned then, knowing it was pointless, and buried her face in his chest and sobbed.

"It's okay. I've got you now," he said. "It's okay."

They drove in silence through the rain, toward the East Village. She had an apartment on Stanton Street.

He pulled in front of a bodega and parked.

They sat in silence, watching rain roll down the window, obscuring the world.

"He won't let me go."

"He doesn't own you."

She turned her face away from him and sighed deeply.

She didn't need to explain it further. Danny understood it perfectly. He'd spent months thinking of little else.

She was Vinny Diamond's girl, until Vinny Diamond said she wasn't.

She began to cry again. Softer this time.

"I don't know what to do." She sobbed.

He reached out and rested his hand on her shoulder. She didn't brush him away. He massaged her neck. He felt her hair on the back of his hand. She turned to him. Then he had his mouth on hers, gently at first. She was breathing heavily, and then they gave in to one another in a mad rush of want and abandon. They were reaching between each others legs, her tongue was on his, she was unbuttoning his jeans and pushing them down around his ankles as he was pulling her shorts off and then, she was on top of him, straddling him in the driver's seat, slipping herself down onto him as they stared into one another's eyes. He shoved her top up over her breasts and she arched her back as he took them in his mouth. She ground her pelvis down into his and he slipped his hands up her back and clamped them over her shoulders, pulling her down onto him, until she moaned, and they trembled together and he fought not to give out, fought to prolong this bliss, until he felt her whole body shudder and he released himself into her and they fought like crazed animals for each other's mouths, kissing, kissing, kissing, long after the shuddering subsided.

When it was over, they stayed like that, unable to let go. They clung to one another, and then she was slowly moving again in his lap and they stared wordlessly into each other's eyes as it began again.

After the second time, they went up to her small apartment and she lay on the bed as he undressed her in the sulfuric glow of a street lamp coming through the shades. They made love again, like it was the first time.

Afterward, she splayed on top of him. Their bodies were slick with sweat. And he held her. They still had said nothing. He was afraid to speak. Afraid that if he opened his mouth he would hear himself say, "I love you."

239

When they awoke sometime during the night they clung to one another and made love again.

Then as he lay on top of her, his arms resting either side of her head, his hands stroking her hair, looking down into her face, he could see a tiny river of tears flowing out of the corners of her eyes onto the pillow.

"What's the matter?" he asked softly. But she just continued to search his face. His eyes.

"What is it?" he asked again, caressing her face, leaning to each side of her face, to catch each salty tear on the tip of his tongue.

But she did not speak. She wrapped her arms around him and she held him tight.

He awakened to the sound of steam pipes clanging as the radiator cranked and rattled to life, and then, from beyond the bedroom, the sound of a pan on a stove.

A soft humming.

He found her in the kitchen, wearing his t-shirt. It hung almost to her knees. The neck was wide enough to reveal one thin bare shoulder.

"Can I keep it?" she asked as she lifted two eggs and bacon onto a plate.

"And what will I wear to get home?" he said, slipping up behind her, and pulling her to him, leaning to kiss her exposed neck, and feeling how her body tingled to his touch.

"I'll give you one of mine," she said, closing her eyes, as he continued to kiss her neck softly.

"I'll bring you another one," he said, reaching down and lifting it up over her head.

She turned to him as he cupped her in his hands and lifted her up unto the small kitchen table. She shifted herself to the edge of the table and wrapped her legs around him—

The buzzer on the wall next to the refrigerator sounded loudly, startling them both.

They stared at it, as if there was the remote possibility some-one had hit it by mistake.

Then it came again.

Vinny.

He released her, and she slipped quickly off the table.

"Shhhh," she said, putting a finger to her lips.

The buzzer sounded again.

"Fuck. I'm going to see if his car is outside," she whispered as she tiptoed out of the kitchen back toward the bedroom. He followed her, feeling suddenly vulnerable, standing there in his boxer shorts.

He sat on the bed and slipped into his jeans as she carefully peeked out through the shutters.

"It's him."

"What?"

"Shhh. He'll think I'm not home. He'll leave again."

"Is he alone?"

"No, Miguel's with him."

Danny remembered the van parked in the street. He didn't think either Vinny or Miguel had ever seen him in it. He'd parked it down the end of the block. They wouldn't be looking for it. Why would they look for his van? Images of the kid in the bathtub with his tongue pulled through his throat, flashed through his mind. Danny never thought he needed a gun of his own, until this very second.

"Does he have his own key?"

"I don't think so."

241

"You don't think so?"

"Not that I know of."

Danny pulled on his shoes and went back to the kitchen and pulled open a drawer. Nothing. Another drawer. He found a large butcher knife and reached for it. If they came through that door he'd go down fighting.

"They're gone," she said, reappearing in the doorway. She came to him and pressed her head against his broad chest and gripped him tightly. "What are we gonna do, Danny?"

"I don't know, yet," Danny said, laying the knife down on the counter, and caressing her hair. "I don't know."

First thing he wanted to do was go tell Gabriela that it was over, for good. A clean break. He would have to tell her to her face. He owed her that much. She was in love with him. He'd been pretty sure he was in love with her, too. But now that he'd been with Trixie he realized he'd never actually known love, until now.

He'd break it off with Gabriela.

Then he'd try and figure out what to do about Vinny Diamond.

21

He waited in the van down the block until he saw Gabriela leave the fruit market. He wanted to tell her right away. He wanted to do the right thing. Or, he thought, maybe he wanted to unburden himself of the guilt of last night's pleasure.

In the hour he sat in the van watching the front of the store for her to finish her shift, he'd almost managed to turn the whole thing around on her. What right had she to make him feel this way! It's not like he was really cheating. It's not like they were really going out anymore. Sure they were still spending a night together once in a while up at the Skyline, but they were adults. It was as much her fault as it was his. It's not like anybody was forcing her to go.

As she approached the van, with her head down, he thought she looked sad. All the bravado he'd built, crumbled.

He ached at the thought that he was about to break her heart.

She had done nothing to deserve this.

He decided he was not ready for this. He needed more time to think it through. It wasn't right to just throw this at her as she was ending a full shift. That was selfish of him.

Maybe she wouldn't see him.

Then she looked up, as if she had sensed him there, staring at her.

He intuitively smiled at her and she hurried around, and got in the passenger side.

She closed the door and sat bolt upright, staring straight ahead, with her hands balled into fists in her lap.

Had she found out already? It was impossible. How? His heart began to race as he retraced the last twenty-four hours. There was just no . . .

"I'm pregnant," she said.

Danny felt his face drain. He felt dizzy. He placed both hands on the steering wheel to brace himself. His ears began to sing. His chest felt cramped. Everything outside seemed to slip by in slow motion. A lady walking a dog passing by in front of the van, stopped and glanced at him as if she too had been frozen in her tracks by the news.

"Did you hear what I said?" Gabriela was saying.

A car went by and the lady with the dog continued on, across the avenue.

Danny tried to regulate his breathing. He reflexively rested one hand on his chest.

"Are you okay?"

He nodded. The words, *Are you sure it's mine?* hovered in his brain within speaking distance, but he fought back the urge to let them slip past his lips. Of course it was his. Of course it was. They'd never once used protection, opting instead for an unspoken approach of reckless abandon.

"Are you sure?" he managed to say, and even that question, he knew, was futile.

"Yes. I went to the doctor. I'm eight weeks."

He thought of Christmas Eve Mass. How she had appeared

that night. She must have known already. Maybe he did, too. It's not like it hadn't crossed his mind. They'd had the same conversation every month since they started sleeping together. *Did you get it yet?* It was just part of their routine. The answer had always been the same: *Yes.*

Except, they hadn't had the conversation in a couple of months now.

She had known. She had known, and carried the burden alone. That was Gabriela. Brave. Selfless.

"What are we going to do?" she asked, and in her voice he could hear the heartache. Her shoulders had slumped. She shook her head as if trying to dislodge the pain of his callowness. He had not shown the slightest excitement at the news. It occurred to him that she had probably hoped that he would have greeted the news with joy. And why wouldn't she? He had told her numerous times in the throes of abandon that he loved her.

Danny remained mute.

He didn't know where to begin with words. He'd spent the day preparing a speech about how he wanted to move on. He was already mapping his escape to the country with Trixie.

Trixie! Oh how he wished he were back in her arms this second. He should have stayed with her in her bed.

How was he going to support a child? How was he going to tell Gabriela that he was in love with someone else? That he no longer wanted to see her.

It was impossible.

"I'm sorry," he managed to say, not because he was sorry, but because he had no idea what else to say.

"What are you sorry for?"

"For not knowing what to do."

"I don't either."

She reached across the divide and took his hand in hers, lacing her fingers through his. "We'll figure it out," she said, regaining her composure.

He nodded and met her eyes for the first time since she'd gotten into the van.

"It's okay," she said, reassuringly. "People have babies all the time, right!"

This made him smile for some reason. A flicker of hope in a sea of darkness. She had a way of doing that to him. She was a strong woman. Strong and beautiful.

He squeezed her hand in his. He was going to have to figure out a way to deal with this. He owed her that much.

But how?

He had not mentioned Gabriela to Trixie. He didn't think he'd have to. Would she still feel the same way about him if she knew he was going to be a father?

22

"Great news, champ," Vinny yelled to Danny, as he stepped out of his Cadillac in front of the Pink Paradise.

Danny had decided that for now he needed to come to work. He needed the money, more than ever. The baby. The house in Woodstock. His mother. Hyman Goldstein. Trixie. How did it get like this? He'd been trying to do the right thing. Did his intention count for nothing!

He had dropped Gabriela at her home without any indication that he'd come by to see her to break it off. Worse, by reassuring her that he would be there for her throughout this ordeal, he'd inadvertently ignited her hopes that things were going to be okay between them after all. He'd even kissed her. What was he gonna do! She was beautiful. She was going to have his child. Their child. Is it possible he loved her too?

"Come with me," Vinny said, holding the door open for Danny.

"What is it?" Danny asked, unnerved at being asked to step inside the club with Vinny and Miguel.

"I got some good news for you." Vinny grinned, continuing to hold the door for Danny to lead the way. "Come on. I'm freezin' my balls off out here."

247

Danny considered making a run for it.

If Vinny knew he was sleeping with Trixie he was dead once he walked through that door.

He searched Vinny's luminous grin for some hint of treachery.

If Vinny knew, he wasn't showing it.

Danny turned and walked inside.

Vinny and Miguel followed him.

"Let's go back to my office."

Danny followed obediently through the crowded club. He barely registered the naked dancer twirling on the pole or the pounding music blasting from the overhead speakers.

He moved down the darkened hallway with a sense of resignation.

Once in the office, Vinny stepped around the desk, and slumped in his big seat. Miguel stayed a comfortable distance behind Danny, with his hands clasped in front of him, just inside the door.

"You look nervous, Danny," said Vinny, studying Danny's face. "What's up, *compadre*?"

"Nothing."

"Something bothering you?"

Danny shook his head. He looked up from Vinny's face and watched the colorful fish drifting about mindlessly behind the thick aquarium glass.

"I mean, if you've got something on your mind, you can tell me," Vinny continued. "Right, Miguel. He can tell us. We're all friends here."

"It's nothing . . ." Danny said, then without really meaning too, added, "My mother."

"What's the matter with your mother?"

"She's been sick."

"Whaddya mean, she's sick? The flu?"

"Cancer."

"You know about this, Miguel?"

"No, Boss, he never said nuttin' to me. Sorry to hear that, Danny. My mother passed a year ago. Same thing. I'll keep her in my prayers," Miguel said, blessing himself.

"Thanks, Miguel," Danny said, feeling pretty confident now that at least they hadn't taken him in here to whack him, but feeling guilty about bringing his mother's illness into it this way. Like a shield he was hiding behind.

"Man, it's always the good ones. Am I right!" said Vinny, pulling a small mirror from his desk drawer, and dusting it with some coke. "Listen, Danny, you need anything, anything at all, you let us know, okay. She ever needs a ride to the doctor, anything like that, you let us know. I'll send Miguel with the car. Right, Miguel?"

"Sure thing, Boss. Be happy to help."

"I appreciate that. Thank you," said Danny. Feeling even worse about things than if they'd stuck a gun in the back of his neck.

"I mean we gotta take care of 'em while they're still here, am I right?" said Vinny, before snorting a huge rail off the mirror, and offering the straw across the table to Danny.

Danny shook his head.

"So, Danny," Vinny said, reaching into a box on the desk to retrieve a fat cigar. "That was some fight the other night, huh!"

"That kid could fight."

"Yeah, but not like you."

"I got lucky."

"Lucky! Lucky! You hear this fucken guy? Luck. You nearly took his head off."

"A lucky shot."

"You know who was there?"

Danny shook his head.

"Davey Prince," Vinny said, taking a puff on his cigar, and blowing a line of smoke straight up in the air like an exclamation mark.

"The promoter?" Danny asked in disbelief. Davey Prince was the biggest fight promoter on the East Coast. The guy was a legend. Even if you weren't into boxing, you'd probably heard his name tossed around.

Danny hadn't seen him at the fight. Nobody at The Wolf had mentioned seeing him either. They would have said so.

"He owes me a favor. I asked him to come out and take a look at you. I didn't wanna tell you in case it threw you off your game. He slipped in at the first bell. Stayed in back 'til you put that kid out on the mat."

"Davey Prince watched me fight?"

"Sure did. Called me this afternoon to have a chat about it. He thinks you've got the stuff. You think you could be ready to go again in six weeks?"

"March."

"Saint Patrick's Day."

"Who?"

"Can you be ready?"

"With who?"

"Randy Taylor."

Danny felt a pang of terror. Randy Taylor was a tough son of a bitch. Danny'd watched Taylor fight Cleveland Parker less than a year earlier and it had been a blood bath. Parker was a beast in the ring, but Taylor had taken him apart like he was a child's toy.

Taylor was at the top of his game. He was in another league entirely.

"He thinks you guys could really pull a crowd."

"Where?"

"Not sure. He's thinking New Jersey. For Saint Patrick's Day."

"Is this a real fight, or just some show thing?" Danny asked. The fact that he was being asked to fight on Saint Patrick's Day set off alarm bells.

"Listen, Danny, not everything is about how good you can throw a punch. You know what I mean! It's show business. Look at you, you're a fucken stud. An Irish stud. On Saint Patrick's Day! Come on! The underdog from Hell's Kitchen, going up against the champ on Saint Patrick's Day—you know how easy that is to sell. It's a home run. Tickets are gonna go like that." Vinny snapped his fingers. "This is Davey Prince we're talking about here. You do this right for him, you know what's next. Right!"

He was right. If he could show Davey Prince that he could handle Taylor the way he handled the Bulgarian he could get a real shot. He could turn this into something.

"The purse?"

"Five grand. And that's if you lose."

"And if I win?"

"Do you really need to win this one?"

"Whaddaya mean?"

"I mean, how important is it to win every fight?"

"What!"

"Danny! Baby!"

"Vinny . . ."

"Relax. Danny!"

"What do you mean?"

"I mean . . . five grand? That's some nice change, no! Could really help with your mother . . . her not being well—that's all I'm saying."

"Are you asking me to take a dive for five grand?"

"Danny! A dive? Come on. Who said anything about a dive? You hear me say the word 'dive,' Miguel?"

Miguel shook his head. "I didn't hear you say nuthin' about takin' no dive, boss."

"I'm saying, we go out to New Jersey, we stay in a nice hotel, you go a few rounds, we get you a nice steak dinner, maybe a coupla broads . . . and you go home with five grand in your pocket, no questions asked. Listen, I owe Davey this one . . . we got something worked out. You wouldn't understand. You do the right thing for us on this one and he'll give us anything we need. You see what I'm saying."

He wanted to tell Vinny to go fuck himself. Storm out of the office. But. Five grand was a small fortune. It was a clean slate.

Five grand might be enough to put everything right.

Maybe he could talk to Gabriela. Come clean. Say he'd met somebody else. Let her know he'd be there for her. Work out some sort of weekly payment. He could come down to the city every other weekend. Take the kid out. Maybe even take the kid out to the country. That'd be nice. Set up a cot in the spare room. Paint it up real nice. Five grand. He could do all that. He could get out, get his mother out. Make a fresh start with Trixie. Leave all this darkness behind once and for all.

All of it. Even the fighting.

Nobody would need to know.

All he had to do was fall down.

23

He woke during the night with a start. He sat up. Someone was in the room with him. He felt a chill down his spine.

"Who is it? Who's in here?"

As his eyes adjusted to the darkness, he saw a figure sitting on a chair in the dark corner of the room.

"What are you doing in here?"

"I was talking to your friend," came the malevolent voice.

"Get out."

The figure clucked its tongue and stroked something in its lap.

"He said he missed you."

"Who?"

The figure laughed then, a low, callous laugh.

"Who? Who are you?"

"Here," the figure said, tossing the object he'd been holding.

Danny jumped from the bed as Stevie Burke's severed head landed on the sheets beside him. Stevie's eyes wide and staring in a sliver of moonlight.

*   *   *

When Danny woke, he could hear his mother in the kitchen. A pan banging on the stove. Daylight streamed mercifully through the slats of the blinds. There were no blood stains on the sheets. No chair in the corner of the room.

He fell to his knees. Blessed himself. And prayed silently.

He could not remember the last time he'd gotten on his knees to pray. Maybe Christmas Eve! He'd been brought up with daily prayer. He'd been brought up with a deep sense of guilt if he did not pray. A feeling that he would be punished for his sins. The guilt had been marinated into his very bones. He'd grown to resent the guilt. Grown angry at God. Grown angry that God could see everything. Could see every single thing he did.

Now, as he prayed, he questioned the very existence of God. And yet, he prayed . . . fervently . . . begged for forgiveness . . . for protection.

"Who were you wrestling with last night?" his mother asked when he joined her in the kitchen. She had a pan of sausages and eggs going on the stove. The window was cracked to release the greasy steam.

Danny let it go.

"Thought you'd brought the whole bar home, the racket comin' out of that room."

Danny poured himself a cup of hot tea, relieved by the clean feel of the cup in his hands. By the familiar sight of his mother standing by the stove, a fist on her hip as she prodded and poked at the sausages with a fork.

"How'd yesterday go?" he asked, changing the subject. She'd gone to see the doctor for the follow-up exam.

"I'm talkin' no more about it," she said.

"What did they say, Ma?"

"That's me done with doctors. They've seen the last of me down there, I can tell you that."

"What happened?"

"They're well able to take your money. They have no problem doing that."

"Did they find something else?"

"What happens now's between me and the good Lord. Should never have gone down there in the first place. Once they get you in there . . ." She let it trail off.

Danny's heart sank. Of course, they'd found something else.

"We'll get you out to Woodstock soon," Danny said. "Country air will do you good."

"Wouldn't hurt I s'pose. Who knows what poison comes in that window the last fifty years."

"I'll get us out," Danny said.

"How many?" she asked, lifting the first sausage onto his plate.

"Two's plenty."

"Have three," she said. "Boy your size."

24

He was sitting in a booth across from Trixie in the back of a diner on Delancey a few blocks from her apartment. He'd taken her here to come clean with her about Gabriela. He'd been just about to get to that, when he saw Detective Quinn stroll through the door.

Trixie turned to see who he'd recognized, just as Quinn slipped into the booth beside her, positioning himself directly across from Danny.

"Cold out there," Quinn said, rubbing his hands together, blowing into them to warm them. "Hey, Danny. How's the breakfast here?" Quinn said, leaning over to examine Danny's plate.

Danny set his fork down and sat back.

The waitress stepped over to the table and placed a hand on Quinn's shoulder.

"You joining us for breakfast, hon?" she asked.

"No, I think I'll just have a coffee for now, thanks, love."

"You got it, handsome," she said, patting his shoulder and moving away.

"This is nice," Quinn said. "Isn't this nice?"

"You mind telling me who the fuck you are?" Trixie scowled.

"Oh, hi, Theresa," Quinn said, as if he were only just noticing her there next to him.

Trixie recoiled as if Quinn had just thrown a picture of a corpse on the table. Danny had never heard the name until now. He'd always assumed Trixie was her given name. "I'm sorry. Should have introduced myself? Detective Joe Quinn."

"Do I know you?" she asked. But the bravado was gone, replaced by a flicker of dread in her eyes.

"Naw. You probably don't remember me. Saw you dance someplace a couple of times. Good dancer."

The waitress was back with the coffee. "You sure that's all, hon?"

"This will do for now, thanks."

"You got it."

"Love these old diners. Mmm, coffee's not bad here."

"What do you want?" Danny asked.

"Now why does everybody always have to assume I want something! That really hurts my feelings. Can't a guy just show up and have a cup of coffee with old friends? Man, you really know how to hurt a guy, Danny. Hey, I see you got a big fight coming up, Saint Patrick's Day. Randy Taylor! Now, that's gonna be some fight. That guy's no joke. You ready for him?"

Danny shrugged.

"You're looking good. You been working out. Doesn't he look good?" He nudged Trixie with his elbow. She moved farther away from him toward the wall. "I'm gonna put my money on you, Danny. That's gonna be some night. Can't wait. Could really be something for you, this one, huh. Get you a real shot. Me and all the boys are all rooting for you. I mean that. You must have got yourself some new management to pull that off, huh . . . oh, that's right . . ." Quinn said, tapping his forehead. "You're with that guy now . . .

what's his name ... Vinny ... Vinny Diamond, right! Hey, hold on, isn't that where I saw you dance? The Pink Paradise! That's right, you were dancing at the Paradise Club for Vinny Diamond. I remember now. Gee, that's a small world. Isn't that crazy!"

Danny tried to catch Trixie's eyes but she kept her head down, staring at her knees like she'd been slapped.

"Listen ... we didn't ask you to sit down," Danny said, moving to put an end to this painful charade.

"No, no, course you didn't but that's okay. I'm used to it. How's your mother? She okay? Used to see her at Mass up at Sacred Heart. Haven't seen her for a while."

"You don't go to Sacred Heart."

"Says who? I go to Mass wherever I can find it. I like to think of myself as a complicated Catholic. You a religious man?"

Danny shrugged.

"You believe in heaven and hell? Right and wrong?"

The conversation made Danny feel uneasy. He said nothing in the hopes that Quinn would drop it and move on.

"'Do not fear those who kill the body but cannot kill the soul. Rather, fear him who can destroy both soul and body in hell,'" Quinn said. "Oof. That one packs a punch. Right! Matthew 10:28. Who do you fear, Danny?"

"I'm not afraid."

Quinn smiled then. A thin, knowing smile.

"We both know that's not true. What about you, Theresa? You scared?" Trixie kept her head down. "Yeah, I know. You're scared. I wouldn't blame you, kid. Surrounded by fools. Fools who are gonna use you up and spit you out like a wad of gum that's lost its taste."

Danny felt like a child sitting there. A helpless boy. He wanted to lash out at Quinn. Smack him. Knock his teeth in the back of his head.

"Anyway. That's enough outta me. I'll leave you two lovebirds to figure it out," Quinn said, lifting his cup and draining the last of it, then sliding out of the booth and patting his pockets like he was searching for a missing wallet. "You mind getting that for me?"

Danny shook his head.

"Aw, thanks, Danny. You're the best. Nice to see you, Theresa. Oh, Charlotte wanted me to let you know that Bella sends her love. Says she misses you real bad."

Danny watched as Trixie's body practically slumped onto the table. She kept her head down and said nothing.

"Oh, one last thing, Danny . . . I've been looking for another guy from the neighborhood. Darryl Hunt. You knew Darryl, right? About yay high. Kinda scruffy. I believe he was a handyman or, an odd-job guy, something like that. Nice guy from what I hear. Bad teeth. Big heart. Been missing for a few weeks now. Just up and vanished—like your old buddy, Stevie Burke. You hear anything about that?"

Danny shook his head.

"Gettin' like the goddamned Bermuda Triangle up there these days," Quinn said, scratching the back of his head. "Hey, maybe that's what happened to Hoffa! Stopped in The Kitchen for a quiet beer one night and just—" Quinn snapped his fingers for effect, "disappeared. Well, anyway, thanks for the coffee. I owe you one. And listen, both of you, and I'm being serious here, if I can do anything to help you kids, you let me know, okay? I can help. Do you hear me, Theresa . . . I can help. It's not too late. Good luck with the fight, Danny."

Quinn turned and walked away, calling out to the waitress as

259

he made for the door: "Thanks for the coffee, love. I'll be seeing you around."

"Anytime, hon." She smiled as she watched him go.

Trixie began to sob quietly.

"Are you okay?"

"Fucken asshole."

"Who's Bella?" Danny asked.

"My daughter," Trixie said, lifting her face.

Danny sighed.

"How old?"

"She's three." And then she broke down and cried. Danny moved around the table, slipped into the booth next to her, and held her while she sobbed.

"It's okay," he said, trying to soothe her. "It's okay."

She was shaking her head against his chest. "It's not okay." She sniffled.

"It's okay. We're gonna figure it out."

"We can't. He's never going to let me go."

"Who?"

"Her father."

"Who's her father?"

She looked up at him then, her eyes swollen and red. "Vinny."

"Vinny Diamond is Bella's father?"

Trixie dropped her head again in defeat.

"You're not seeing him anymore, right!"

"It's complicated, Danny."

He held her to him. A fresh wave of fear washed over him. The quickened pulse of blood. A sense that he was drowning. No. That he was being crushed. Buried beneath a mountain of dead bodies.

25

He was coming out of Central Park onto Seventh Avenue at a solid clip when he heard Logan Coyle calling his name.

He'd been putting in a few miles every morning. Up Seventh, into the park, around past the ice rink and the zoo, all the way up the east side to a Hundred and Tenth, then cut west, around the reservoir, and back down again, past the fountain, the great lawn, and back out onto Central Park South at Seventh Avenue again. The running cleared his head. Helped him think.

He still hadn't told either Trixie or Gabriela about the other just yet, but he was planning to sort all that out.

Soon.

When the time was right.

The five grand from this fight would help with all that.

He'd finally get his mother up to the house in Woodstock. Before it was too late. He felt she was running out of time. Fast. It had to be soon.

He'd ask Trixie to come with him. He'd ask her to bring her kid along. He'd take care of them both. He could do this thing. He was ready.

Then he'd break the news to Gabriela. He'd come clean. Tell

her that he'd met someone else. He'd give her a chunk of the money as a jump start to take care of the kid. He'd do his bit. He'd be there.

Maybe he'd get a job out there in Woodstock. Liam had mentioned a contractor who might need a guy. He was looking forward to getting back to some honest work.

He could do this thing.

He was pretty sure he could do it.

He looked around, following Logan's voice, until he saw him waving to him from a parked car on the southwest corner of the block.

He jogged across the avenue, intending to say a quick hello, and continue on his run.

As he got closer, he noticed Terry Flannery was in the passenger seat, staring somberly out the window. Mack Cantor was seated in the back, sporting an angry scowl.

"Hey, guys," Danny said.

"Get in," Logan snapped.

"Naw, it's okay, I just gotta finish out this run."

"Get in the fucken car, Danny," Logan said, fixing him with that all too familiar, steely blue gaze.

Danny opened the rear door and slipped in next to Mack.

He nodded to Mack, but Mack didn't respond.

Terry was peering out the window. He didn't turn around.

Logan did.

"Tell me you are not banging Vinny Diamond's girl," Logan demanded. "Please tell me you are not that fucking dumb, Danny."

Danny sighed deeply, and dropped his head on his chest. This was not good. If Logan knew, other people knew. If Vinny Diamond knew, it was only a matter of time 'til he'd be wearing his tongue for a necktie.

"What I fucken tell you!" Mack said, shaking his head. Grinding a balled fist into his other hand.

"Ah, Jesus Christ, Danny! What the fuck!" said Logan. "You decide you're just tired of living, is that it?"

"I love her."

Even Terry was shaking his head in disbelief now.

"Ah Christ," Logan said, rubbing his forehead.

"This is not good, Danny," Terry said quietly, still peering off out the window.

"What am I supposed to do, guys?"

"Keep it in your fucking pants!" spat Logan. "Say, sorry, honey, you're cute but I'd really like to keep breathing for another little while. I don't know . . . anything. Literally any other fucking thing, Danny."

Logan seemed at a loss. He turned again, and sighed deeply.

"Do you have any idea what that fucken animal is gonna do to you when he finds out?"

"He doesn't know?"

"I know he doesn't know, Einstein. If he knew, you think you'd be sitting here in the car with us?" Logan barked. "You'd be strung up on a meat hook in a warehouse in Brooklyn somewhere right now, with a car battery hooked up to your nuts and some fucken psycho going to work on you with a carving knife—and she'd be hanging next to you. This is Vinny Diamond we're talkin' about here, Danny! I mean, this fucken guy's . . . he's got the Columbians, the Italians, the drugs, the porn . . . guy's practically got his own goddamned army. Man . . ." Logan said, turning back in his seat to stare blankly out the window. "You sure know how to pick 'em, you dumb fuck."

"She must give some head." Mack laughed.

Danny clenched his fists. He wanted to punch the smile right off Mack's face.

Logan started the car and began to drive south.

"She's not his girl," Danny said.

"She's his girl 'til he says she's not. She's the mother to his kid, for chrissakes. Did you know about the kid?" Logan asked, glancing at Danny in the rearview mirror as he turned right toward the Hudson.

"Yes."

"And you thought he'd just roll over and let you fuck her behind his back?"

"How did you find out?"

"We got a guy in Midtown North."

"A cop?"

"He does some favors for me, keeps an eye on things, let's me know when I need a heads-up. You got some guy Quinn following you around?"

Logan glanced back to see Danny nodding.

"When were you gonna let me know about that, huh? Some fucken detective following you around asking you questions and you don't let me know! What the fuck, Danny!"

"I'm sorry, Logan," Danny said, realizing that this was much deeper than the Vinny Diamond situation. He'd put himself in a precarious position getting in the car with these three.

"Where we going?"

"What did this cop want with you?"

"I dunno. He's just some detective, wants to know if I knew anything about Knuckles, or Darryl Hunt—"

"And?"

"I didn't tell him nuthin', Logan. You know me. I ain't stupid."

"You sure 'bout that?" Mack asked.

"Fuck you," Danny snapped.

"Guys ... guys ... easy back there," Logan said. "It's okay. I believe you, Danny. But you gotta realize you're in a whole world of shit right now. I mean, maybe you just let this ... what's her name ..."

"Trixie."

"Trixie, right, maybe you cut her loose. You know what I mean. You don't need that broad. That's a fucken death sentence. You're a good lookin' guy, you get tail left, right and center. You win this next fight against Taylor, you're gonna have more pussy than you can shake a stick at. Am I right!"

Danny stared off out the window. They went down Eleventh in silence for a bit. Then Logan pulled the car over a block north of The Ward.

"What are we doing here?" Danny asked, after a minute of silence.

"You remember I was telling you about the new convention center they're gonna build down here."

"Yeah."

"Well this is where it's happening. Right down here." Logan signified with a wave of his hand, taking in the whole west side of the avenue. The abandoned train tracks. The empty lots running all the way down the highway. "They wanna clear the last of these old buildings that side of the street, and the stubborn prick that owns this one don't wanna sell," he said, nodding toward the corner lot that included the garage, and the two-story building that housed The Ward.

"So, they gotta to build around it?" Danny said, still not getting what this was about.

"No, Danny, they ain't gonna build around it. It's gotta go."

"Yeah, but if the guy don't wanna sell—"

"I got the contract to make this problem go away."

"How you gonna do that?"

"We're gonna burn it."

"Logan—" Danny started, but Logan cut him off.

"I don't wanna hear it, Danny. We don't do it, they give the contract to somebody else. One way or another it goes. But I don't want nobody else doing it, see. This is our neighborhood and we gotta do what we gotta do."

"I can't burn The Ward."

"The Ward! It's a fucken closet, Danny. One stinkin' room. They can set that shit up anywhere. This whole building's gotta go, okay, it's the last hold out, and I'm gonna give you three guys a grand apiece just to light a fucking match."

"Alright then." Mack nodded, rubbing his hands together excitedly.

"I could sure use a grand right about now," added Terry. "Hey, Danny doesn't wanna go I'll take his share."

"You mean we can split it," said Mack.

"No," Logan snapped. "That's not the deal. I want this thing done right, and I want you three to do it together. Friday night."

"That's the sixteenth."

"So!"

"I got the fight Saturday, Saint Patrick's Day."

"So, it's not like I'm asking you to do it Saturday night. You're working over at the club Friday night, right!"

Danny nodded.

"That's when this thing happens."

Danny could see it was pointless arguing. Logan wasn't asking. He was telling him how it was going to go down. The whole spiel he'd given him about Vinny Diamond and the detective was just Logan's way of saying, you do this, or else . . .

"One in the morning, you slip away from your job, Danny, just stroll up the block. You'll be gone twenty minutes, tops, that way anybody asks you where you was, you was working, they say they didn't see you on the door, you tell 'em you went up the block for a slice of pizza. You two clowns get the gas cans organized. Have them ready. Two gallons should do it. All three of you meet at Danny's van. You put the gas cans in the back of the van. Then the three of you drive over here, real casual. Like you're in no big hurry. Don't attract no attention. You can park over here, Danny . . . this side of the street, right here, so you can see anything coming up or down the avenue. You hear me? You keep the van running, lights off. There'll be nobody around. This place is like a fucking ghost town over here after ten o'clock. You two guys go over there real easy, and youse douse the place. Douse it real good. You drop a match, and, boom. You stroll back over here real smooth. Don't run. You get back in the van. You keep the lights off, Danny, and make a left here. Once you're down the block, you pop the lights back on, and just cruise back up Tenth, park the van, and everybody split up. You go right back to work, Danny. You don't even have to lose your shift. Easiest goddamn grand you ever made in your life."

"I don't wanna do it, Logan."

"I'm not asking, Danny," Logan snapped, turning to him again. "I'm telling you. This is how it is. I need to know you're one of us, Danny. I look out for you on this whole Vinny Diamond mess. I keep an ear out for this detective . . ."

"Cockeye built this thing for the kids."

"He'll build them another one."

"He don't have no money."

"This Friday night. One o'clock. You understand? What you

think happens to that girl of yours if Vinny finds out she's been sitting on your dick? Huh!"

Danny let it go. He didn't have a choice. If he didn't go along, Logan would make damn sure Vinny found out about Trixie. And if Vinny found out about Trixie . . .

"What about the garage?" Terry asked.

"Everything. The whole corner lot. Burn that fucker to the ground."

"Hey, Danny . . ." Logan said, reaching back to pat Danny's leg. "You gotta start believing I got a plan for us, okay. We're talking about the future here, okay. We're all in this together. We just gotta get rid of the old to make way for the new. You'll see, another year or so they come in here and start building this thing, we're gonna have more money than you ever dreamed of. You'll be able to build a brand new boxing gym for all the kids in the neighborhood and hand Cockeye the keys as a gift."

Logan leaned over and opened the glove compartment and pulled out a revolver. He slipped it between the seats.

"Take this."

"Me!" Danny said, startled at the sight of the gun.

"Yeah, you."

"I don't want it."

"Take it."

Danny took it. He'd never owned a gun. Never even wanted one.

"I want you to keep it in your pocket. Anything goes wrong Friday night—"

"Like what?"

"Like, I don't know . . . but this way you're not sitting over here with your dick in your hand if the shit hits the fan."

Danny didn't want the gun. But now that he was holding it in his hand, he liked the way it felt. The solid weight of the thing. The worn wooden grip in his palm. He really didn't want it. But he felt a quickening of the pulse. An unexpected surge of power. He felt stronger with it in his hand.

"Just be careful with that thing, okay. Don't go waving it around."

"How do I use it?"

"You point it at the bad guys and pull the trigger."

"That's it?"

"That's it."

Danny was aware of all three of the men staring at him now. The energy in the car had shifted now that he had a gun in his hand. Like they were on equal footing now.

He didn't feel as anxious as he had just a few moments earlier. He didn't feel as vulnerable.

He had a sudden impulse to shoot all three of them . . . *bam, bam, bam.* Just for the hell of it.

It was insane to think that he held their very lives in the palm of his hand.

He liked the feeling.

Like he had control over something.

26

Standing at the door, tapping his feet, and rubbing his hands to keep warm, Danny kept a troubled eye on the time. The Paradise had been like a graveyard for most of the night, then at ten-thirty they started to pour in. A rowdy bridge-and-tunnel crowd in Rangers jerseys.

He hated nights like this. Girls were gonna get manhandled. Tempers were gonna flare. Glass was gonna get broken. And sooner or later, blood would spill. It always did after big games at The Garden.

Word had gotten around to the sports crowd that the Paradise Club was where it was at. The girls were hot, the drinks were cheap, the VIP rooms were off the charts, and you could buy first rate blow right at the bar.

It was an explosive formula.

By midnight, Danny had tossed three guys into the street who couldn't keep their hands to themselves. He'd had to drag one particularly vicious little prick into the alley next to the club and slap him unconscious. Ten minutes later he'd watched the kid stagger out of the alley, dazed and befuddled, and wander off down Forty-second Street toward Times Square.

At twelve forty-five, he simply walked away from his post at the door. He strolled the three blocks west to where he had the van parked outside of Flannery's building on Forty-third and Tenth.

Mack and Terry were already in the van waiting for him when he got there.

He could smell the gasoline as soon as he opened the door to get in.

"Jesus Christ, get this thing started," said Terry, his teeth practically chattering. "I'm fucken freezin' my nuts off here."

Mack was seated on the floor behind Terry's seat with his back against the wall of the van, his legs outstretched before him, his arm resting on the two red gas cans.

Danny started the van, and drove.

West of Tenth Avenue was like a ghost town this time of night. The only traffic you were liable to encounter were the Johns, with New Jersey and Connecticut plates, cruising south on Eleventh Avenue looking for a little last minute action before heading home to their idyllic family lives in the suburbs. But it was so cold tonight even the hookers had stayed home.

Danny felt off. He'd been feeling off for days. He had not been sleeping well. His bedroom had become a playpen of demons and phantoms. Nightmarish faces whispered from every shadow. He wondered if he was losing his mind.

On the nights where the terror was unbearable he would slip out the door, pulling it quietly behind, so as not to wake his mother. Down the stairs, and down to the corner of the block to see if any of the guys were hanging around The Wolf for a little company. There was always someone to have a drink with at The Wolf, no matter what the night. No matter what the time.

But lately the booze only made it worse. The more he drank the more he craved Trixie. Then he'd get in the van and drive to the

Lower East Side, praying she was home. On the nights she wasn't, he worked himself into a frenzy, conjured images of Vinny forcing her into every form of degradation. And then, out of rage, jealousy, and desperation he'd gone to Gabriela instead. Oh how he hated himself for that. Waking with her in his arms in the Skyline motel, knowing that he'd thrown his frenzied rage at her . . . knowing he'd cried in her arms afterward, knowing that she'd comforted him . . . knowing that he'd caressed her belly, held his lips to his unborn child and tearfully whispered, "I am your daddy, I will take care of you . . ." knowing that he'd wrapped Gabriela in his arms, and whispered, "I love you. I love you . . ." again . . . those words. He wanted to take a blade and carve out his tongue at the base, throw it off the pier into the dark waters of the Hudson, so he could never utter those words again. Never inflict them on another living soul.

Dawn would bring him home, to his birds. And they would save him. At least in part. At least momentarily. And he would run. And he would punch. And as long as the sun shone he could regain some mastery over his demons. He could see the path clear again. There was a path through all this madness. He believed that. He was close. Real close. The fight with Taylor was only a day away. He would take that purse and start to put some of this right again.

He could have his mother out of The Kitchen in less than a week.

Then he'd come back, and tell Gabriela the truth. Come clean. Tell her that he was in love with someone else and that he was moving away. Make sure she understood that he was still going to be there for her. Still going to take care of her and the baby. His responsibilities.

Then he'd take Trixie out to see the house. Show her the future, and what it could be like for them in Woodstock. Tell her that she could go get her daughter now. That he would take care of them both. That they could be a family out there where no one could ever touch them.

To hell with the boxing.

Fight this one last fight.

Take the dive.

Collect the money.

And get out of The Kitchen.

"Pull in here," Terry said, pointing to a spot, a block north on the east side of Eleventh, within eyesight of The Ward. "Don't fucken move. And don't kill that engine."

Danny killed the lights but kept the motor idling.

Terry got out and opened the rear sliding door. Mack handed him one of the gas cans, banging it off the passenger seat. The gas sloshed and pungent vapor filled the inside of the van.

"Jesus. Be careful with that shit," whispered Terry.

Mack pulled the door closed, leaving it open just a crack for easy access on the way back, and the two men walked off side by side.

In the darkness their silhouettes appeared like the shadows of two businessmen casually strolling home together with briefcases after a long day at the office.

In the time it took them to walk the block, not another car or person passed on the avenue.

Danny followed the two dark figures scurrying around the garage and the adjoining building. There was an office on the ground floor of the building where The Ward was housed. He heard a crash of glass as one of them flung a gas canister through the large front window.

An instant later, an explosion sent a mess of glass and metal shooting across the street.

Danny scanned the street 'til he saw the two figures sprinting back toward the van.

By the time they were in the van again, flames were curling out of the window and racing up the façade of the building. A dumpster against the wall of the garage threw flames twenty feet into the air, where they curled and crawled along the flat tar roof in the wind.

"Go. Go. Get out of here," Mack yelled, as he threw himself into the back of the van and pulled the side door closed behind him. Terry was already in his seat, staring in awe at how quickly the entire building had been engulfed.

"Holy shit. I didn't expect that." Terry laughed, his eyes wide, as Danny swung the van east on Fortieth, making sure to keep the lights off until they were almost all the way to the other end of the deserted block.

"You guys see that shit?"

"Holy crap, we blew that place to pieces."

"Must have ignited the gas line."

"Damn. Glad we weren't inside. We never would have made it out."

Danny drove in silence. He pictured the old posters of all his favorite fighters curling to ash on the walls of The Ward. The heavy bags melting off their chains. The canvas ring collapsing in on itself. Paint melting on the faces of the old metal lockers. The carved wooden sign nailed over Cockeye's desk that read, FIGHT THE GOOD FIGHT, being eaten by flame.

This too, he tried to convince himself, along with all the other broken things in his life, he would put right again.

27

After dropping the van off on Forty-third, Danny was back in front of the Paradise Club by one-fifteen. If anyone had missed him they didn't show up to say so.

No sooner had he resumed his post than he heard a ruckus inside the club. He entered to a brawl. A couple of guys wearing Los Angeles Kings jerseys must have slipped in while he was gone. The Rangers crew were pounding the West Coast crowd to a pulp. Glasses were smashed. Shirts torn. Insults hurled. Innocent bystanders were punched in the fray. It was over again as quickly as it had begun. By one-thirty the Kings fans had been ejected, and the Paradise was back to business as usual.

Stationed at the door again, Danny could hear the roar of distant sirens.

At about two o'clock Miguel pulled up to drop Vinny off outside.

Before Vinny even began to speak, Danny could see that he was wired. His eyes wide and his lower jaw sawing back and forth like he was viciously chewing a chunk of charred steak.

He carried a brown leather satchel and he was glancing up and down the block like a man who didn't want anyone knowing what was inside it.

"Oh Danny Boy, the pipes the pipes are calling," he sang, as he approached the door. "You ready for your big fight?"

"I'm ready."

"Listen." Vinny leaned in close, there was a smell of whiskey on his breath. "A lot of people have bet big on you to go down in this thing tomorrow night. *Capisce!* Fourth round. No more Danny Boy. You got it?"

"I got it."

"You got it!"

"I got it, Boss."

"Good boy. Don't let me down."

"I won't."

"Listen, once you get everybody out of here, come back to see me in my office. I got some people coming by a little later. We're gonna go to a little private party, if you know what I mean," Vinny said, holding up the satchel. "You wanna come with me out to the Island. Going to be wild."

"I dunno, Boss. I gotta get my sleep. I gotta big fight tomorrow."

"You don't need to be in shape to fall down." Vinny laughed. "Come back when you're done."

"I'll come back and see you."

"Good boy, Danny," Vinny said, patting Danny's shoulder and disappearing inside.

Danny was leading the last of the stragglers out the door, getting ready to close up shop, when Trixie showed up.

"What are you doing here?" Danny asked, shocked to see her at the club. He didn't want her anywhere near this place.

"Vinny told me to come by. Something about a job."

"What job? You shouldn't be here."

"What am I supposed to do? I gotta play along for now, Danny. You know that, right. I got a kid involved in this mess."

"Fuck him. I'll take care of you."

"You don't get it, Danny. He finds out about you and me he's gonna kill us both. This is not a game. You don't know him like I do."

"I don't want you with him."

"You gotta trust me. Okay!" Trixie said, giving his hand a quick squeeze before pushing on past him and on to Vinny's office in the rear.

Danny bit his tongue. This was not the time or place to get into a big fight with Trixie over Vinny Diamond. He had to keep his cool for now.

He did a quick walk-through of the club to make sure there was nobody passed out in any of the bathroom stalls. Checked the girls' changing rooms one last time to make sure all the girls were gone. Then Snake slipped Danny a few twenties, and Danny saw him out, and locked the door behind him.

He hated being in the club after closing. Once the dancers were gone, and the music stopped, the place reeked of despair. There were ghosts in this place. The ghosts of painful childhoods, and long ruined dreams.

As he made his way back to Vinny's office he could hear yelling from behind the closed door.

He thought he heard a slap, and he quickened his pace.

When he flung open the door, Vinny had Trixie pinned to the wall, and he was screaming at her.

"Who is it? Who are you fucking behind my back? Huh?" He raised his hand to strike her but Danny reached out and caught his wrist. He held it firmly in his big hand and stared down into Vinny's crazed, bloodshot eyes.

"I think you should go on home now, Trixie," Danny said, calmly.

"Get your fucken hands off me," Vinny yelled, yanking his hand free. Danny let him yank it free, but he didn't back away. "You got some balls, grabbing me, motherfucker."

"Trixie," Danny continued calmly. "Come with me. I'm going to let you out."

"The fuck you are," Vinny said, pulling a gun from inside his jacket. "She's not going anywhere. Trixie belongs to me, and she is coming to Long Island to dance for my friends."

"I really don't think that's a good idea, Vinny," Danny said, keeping his voice at a low register, in an effort to deflate the energy in the room, while Vinny was waving the gun around. Danny could feel the weight of his own gun in his coat pocket.

"You gonna try and tell me what to do," Vinny spat.

"Vinny, I'm not telling you anything. Just please, lower the gun, and let's all take it easy, okay. I'll come to the party with you. You and I are going to this party. But Trixie just told me outside she's not feeling well. She's got the flu. Did you tell him?" Danny asked, looking to Trixie to go along with the charade. Trixie shook her head. "You don't want her going out there getting everyone sick. That's no good."

Vinny took a step toward Trixie and pushed the muzzle of the gun up under her chin.

"You tell him you're sick?"

She nodded.

"Why didn't you tell me?"

She shrugged helplessly.

"If I find out you're fucking somebody behind my back I'm gonna put a bullet in that pretty little head of yours, you understand. You hear me?"

She nodded as much as she could against the barrel of the gun pressed up under her jaw.

"Go, get her out of here," Vinny said, dropping the gun to his side. "You, come back. I wanna talk to you."

Vinny laid the gun on the desk and pulled open the zipper on the brown satchel.

Danny walked Trixie to the service door in the rear of the club that lead to the alley. "I'll call you in a few days," he said.

"Be careful with him. I've seen him like this before. He's liable to do anything."

"Don't worry about him. I got it."

"He's dangerous, Danny."

"Go home and get some rest," Danny said.

Trixie give him a quick kiss and hurried away. Danny watched her navigate the garbage cans, the dumpsters and the shadows down the long dark alley, until he could see her exit out onto Forty-first Street.

Then he closed the door and locked it.

28

Back in the office, Vinny had removed six bricks of brown powder wrapped in clear cellophane out of the satchel and set them on his desk.

"You ever seen this much shit?" He grinned, still wild-eyed.

Danny shook his head.

Heroin.

"You know how much that's worth?"

Danny had a pretty good idea. A lot.

Vinny pulled a small mirror from the desk drawer. He produced a baggie of white powder from the inside pocket of his jacket. Shook a small mound of it onto the mirror, and began chopping at it with the edge of a credit card.

"I want you to keep an eye on that whore," he said, before bending to the mirror and sniffing a careless rail. "Oh Jesus, that's good."

"Don't call her that," Danny said, almost in a whisper. His pulse was hot. He was struggling to keep his breath regulated. He had a fight coming up in less than twenty-four hours. A fight that Vinny Diamond had organized for him. A fight that could change his life. Change his mother's life. He also had this job, which had worked out real well for him over these past few months. It was the first time he'd had real money in his pocket. He'd been able to get a handle on things. Pay his bills. Stay ahead of the wolf. He'd grown to like that feeling. Truth be told, he also liked the feeling he had when he stood outside at that door. When he was at that door, this was his fucken club.

"What? Are you, serious?" Vinny said, wiping his nose.

"I'm just sayin', Trixie's a nice girl."

"Nice?"

"Yeah. She's a good girl."

"Yeah, good on her fucken knees." Vinny laughed as he bent over the mirror again and sniffed another fat rail. "Goddamn, that is good shit. You sure you don't want a blast?"

"No."

"Come on, man, lighten up. Let's party. Forget that whore."

"Don't . . . call her a whore."

Vinny straightened himself and rubbed at his nose and regarded Danny with an air of confusion. He was staring at him and blinking one eye, as if he couldn't quite locate the area of his brain responsible for logic. Then he burst out laughing. A loud, disingenuous laugh. He leaned on the back of the chair to steady himself. Slapped the palm of his hand on the desk.

"Oh, Jesus Christ, you fucken Irish guys, always with the big bleeding heart. Danny Danny Danny. Don't be fooled by these tramps. They're whores. All of them. Trust me, baby, okay, I know. It's my business to know. If you hadn't walked in here she'd be under this desk right now sucking my dick."

"Please, Vinny," Danny said, really trying to control the rage he felt building in his chest. "Don't talk about her like that."

"Danny. Danny Boy! What are you doing here? What is this? I can't even tell if you're serious. Can you just chill the fuck out!

Come on! Let's go up into the bar and have a drink. My friends are coming by in a few, we're going to deliver this shit out to Long Island. Let's have a good time, huh. Don't worry about that little whore—"

"I told you . . ."

"Sorry . . . You, 'told me'!"

"I told you." Danny nodded.

"Danny. Listen, I'll admit I'm a little high right now, but . . ."

"I'm with Trixie," Danny heard himself say.

Vinny gave his head a comical shake as if he were trying to shake some of the high off of him.

"What did you say?"

"I said, I'm with Trixie. Trixie's with me now."

"Oh, wow! Okay! You're freaking me out here. I hope this is a joke, Danny. It's a joke, right!" Vinny said, eyeing Danny with real concern, his eyes reflexively darting to the gun sitting on the table between them.

"It's no joke. I'm in love with her."

"Ah. Okay. Fine. So . . . you're in love with her! Great! She's yours. You happy now?" Vinny giggled nervously. "Danny and Trixie sitting in a tree . . . whoop, de, fucking, doo. Whatever, man! I don't give a shit. Take her. You can have her. Can we go have a drink now?"

"And if I see you raise your hand to her or hear you call her a whore again, I'll kill you."

Vinny froze. A rolled bill in one hand, his other clutching the armrest of his chair, his eyes wide, as if he were gearing himself to spring forward for the gun.

They were both startled by the sound of the buzzer.

"Ah. That'll be my Italian friends," Vinny said, calmly. "You should go let them in."

Danny looked into Vinny's eyes and realized he'd just signed his own death warrant. Vinny was never going to let him walk out of the club alive.

Danny shook his head slowly from side to side.

The buzzer sounded again.

"What are you doing? Danny. Go answer the door," Vinny tried with a little more authority.

Danny didn't move. He'd been in this position a thousand times in the ring. Sooner or later someone was going to take a swing. It was all going to come down to who had the fastest reflexes. Sometimes you landed the punch. Sometimes you landed on the canvas.

Intense banging increased on the outside door.

Muffled yelling.

Vinny lunged for the gun.

Danny was across the table before Vinny could reach it, and had him by the throat. He clamped his other hand over Vinny's mouth to keep him from screaming out for help. The buzzer sounded again. Vinny kicked and struggled for all he was worth. He was strong, but he was no match for Danny, sober, and so much stronger.

The phone on the desk began to ring. Still, Danny held tight. He had Vinny pinned underneath him. Vinny kicked and wrestled but he couldn't even get a swing at Danny. Danny had his arms pinned. Eventually Vinny just gave in. Stopped fighting.

Danny held on tight.

After what seemed like an eternity, the banging stopped.

The buzzer rang for the last time.

Danny waited, until he was fairly confident that whoever was out there had given up and gone away.

He cautiously released his grip on Vinny's throat.

Vinny did not struggle. Instead, he stared up at Danny. His eyes frozen in a look of disbelief.

Danny slapped him. But it was over. Vinny was dead.

Danny sat back on the edge of the desk and stared at Vinny's lifeless body slumped in the chair before him.

This was not what he had intended to do.

The colorful array of fish continued swimming about behind the thick glass, unperturbed by it all.

Danny looked down at his fists.

He had just strangled a man to death.

He had only wanted to keep him quiet.

It was an accident.

Right!

He'd had no choice. It was self-defense. If he hadn't shut him up then it would have been him. He'd be dead.

These were the rules of the jungle—the rules of The Kitchen. Kill, or be killed.

There was no time to think about it right now. He had to act. And fast.

Vinny was connected. Which meant he was protected. He was protected because he was a guy who made a lot of money for a lot of the right people. Danny'd seen the Italians who showed up at the club to shake his hand. These were not the type of guys who were going to let him explain his way out murdering their business associate.

And then there were the drugs. The smack. The Columbians.

He doubted that anybody was going to shed a tear over Vinny Diamond, but there were going to be a lot of angry people asking questions about who the hell just turned off the faucet to all the easy money Vinny generated. Easy money and easy girls.

If the Italians or the Columbians traced this back to Danny, they'd take turns working on him for a month. Then they'd come for his mother. And for Trixie too.

He had to get Vinny out of the club before the early morning cleaning crew showed up.

He packed the bricks of dope back into the brown leather bag. He lifted Vinny's knife, his gun, and his credit card, and threw them all into the satchel with the drugs. He lifted the mirror and set it in the top drawer of Vinny's desk where he would have placed it if he were going to leave the office out of his own free will.

Everything had to look like that is what had happened here. Vinny had left the club, with the satchel of drugs, alive.

He threw the bag over his left shoulder and lifted Vinny's lifeless body over his right. Vinny was not an easy lift. But Danny could handle him. He was in the best shape he'd been in in ten years. For just a brief moment, he wondered what would happen now with the Saint Patrick's Day fight tomorrow night. But there was no time to think about any of that right now. He'd deal with that later. Right now he needed to stay focused if he was going to stay alive.

He stopped in the door of Vinny's office one last time and scanned the room for any sign of a struggle. Anything that looked out of place.

Everything appeared exactly as it had been before. He switched out the light, and carried Vinny through the club, to the rear service exit.

He opened the door, and peered cautiously into the alley. It was empty, and dark, as it had been before. He slipped out and closed the door behind him, checking to make sure it locked. Then he carried Vinny's body halfway down the alley, and set it down next to a dumpster.

As quietly, and as quickly as he could, he emptied two large black garbage bags he found in the dumpster. He took the bags and slipped one over Vinny's head, pulling it down, concealing the upper half of his body, and pulled the second one up over his legs until the two bags were overlapped at his waist, concealing him entirely. He laid the body down next to the dumpster along the wall, set the satchel next to it, and covered the lot with a few more full garbage bags from the dumpster.

Then he pulled up the collar of his coat and exited the alley out onto Forty-first Street. It took him less than ten minutes to reach the van and drive back again to park next to the alley.

The block was as desolate as when he left it.

He slipped into the alley and retrieved the body and the satchel. He carried the body out and laid it down in the back of the van still wrapped in the black trash bags. He shoved the satchel between the two front seats.

He closed the door, and scanned the block one last time. Every storefront was shuttered. Only one or two of the street lights were working the entire length of the block. There wasn't a sinner in sight who could tell what had happened here.

He climbed back in the driver's seat. Turned the engine.

He froze as he heard something move, in the dark, behind his seat. A rustle of plastic. The hair on the back of his neck stood up. He flung open the door and leapt out of the van.

The plastic had rustled. What the fuck! He was sure he'd killed him. Vinny was definitely not breathing when he'd carried him out.

Had he checked for a pulse?

No.

But, there was no way he was still breathing. He was sure of it. Or at least he had been sure of it. Until now. He should have checked his heart. He should have made absolutely sure.

He reached for the gun in his coat pocket. If Vinny was still alive in there, he would have to finish him off.

Goddamn it, Danny, why didn't you check his goddamn pulse!

Danny braced himself, gun in hand, as he reached for the handle of the sliding side door.

He realized he hadn't even checked Vinny for a gun before moving him. What if he opened the door and Vinny had a gun leveled at him? Well then it would be down to who got lucky. Who was blessed with the fastest finger.

He flung open the door, and rammed the gun into the darkness.

At a glance, the body seemed exactly as he had left it. He pointed the gun into the dark corners of the van. The bag moved again. The plastic rustled loudly, and before he could react, a large greasy rat burst out of the opening of the bag and leapt right at his face, its teeth bared, like some crazed demon sprung from the bowels of hell.

He jumped back, but not quick enough. It hit him squarely in the chest, and before he could swat it away, it locked its claws into the front of his coat and clambered its way up his chest as if intent on latching onto his throat. He jerked his head to the side and it went out over his left shoulder, leaving a trail of wet slime on his neck as it passed.

Danny yelled out instinctively. Cursed the fleeing rodent, and quickly tried to regain his composure. He reflexively put his hand to his neck and swiped, half expecting to see blood. It wasn't blood. It was oil, or sweat, or grime, or whatever it was rats collected from crawling around through sewers and dumpsters of rotting food.

The rat must have slipped into the bag when it was lying next to the dumpster. Had it already begun to feast on Vinny? He wasn't about to open the bag to find out. He pulled a discarded broom handle from a nearby pile of trash and poked the body several times to make sure that was the only vicious hitchhiker he'd picked up back there.

Satisfied that it was only the one rat, and that Vinny was indeed dead, he closed the door again.

For a moment he considered taking the body directly to The Wolf, asking Mack, or Logan to help him make it disappear, but his gut told him, *No. Don't do it.*

He needed to deal with this one by himself.

If anyone else found out he killed Vinny Diamond then it would be one more person he'd have to worry about. Right now, his was the only mouth who could tell what happened here. He needed to keep it that way.

In a matter of minutes he was out on the West Side Highway, traveling north, under the lights of the George Washington Bridge, and an incredulous moon.

He knew exactly where he needed to bury this body, and where he could find a shovel to dig the hole.

He heard the muffled voice of Cockeye Ward whispering up at him from the brown leather satchel sitting on the floor between the two front seats.

"Get rid of it."

"Shut up," Danny barked, aloud.

But the whisper came again. More defined this time.

"You know, this shit is destroying the neighborhood."

"Please, shut the fuck up."

"Alright, Danny, on your soul be it," he heard Cockeye's voice whisper.

Danny was halfway across the Tappan Zee Bridge.

He slammed the brakes. Grabbed the satchel. Stepped from the van, and flung it off over the guardrail into the darkness high over the Hudson River.

"Are you fucking happy now?" he yelled after it.

29

Danny woke to the sound of his mother playing the latest Chieftains' album. She was blasting it loud enough to shake him out of bed. He glanced at the clock. It was almost ten o'clock.

Damn.

It was Saint Patrick's Day.

The parade started in an hour. He had to hustle. He had to get her over there. He'd only managed to get an hour of sleep. He glanced down at his hands, blistered from digging. His shoulders ached. The ground had been hard and rocky. He'd managed to get the body covered. But barely. He would have to go back and take the time to bury him properly when the ground thawed fully. He hoped a bear didn't dig him out in the meantime and drop his skull on somebody's lawn.

But there was no time to think about all that now. He had to get his ma to Fifth Avenue for the parade.

Sure, Christmas was a big deal, but there was no day of the year more important to his mother than Saint Patrick's Day.

He leapt from the bed and got dressed, hurriedly dragging on the one Aran knit wool sweater he owned for the occasion and a gray tweed cap she'd bought him a few years back.

By the time he entered the kitchen she had bacon sizzling on the pan and a freshly baked loaf of soda bread sliding out of the oven.

"You decided to join us for a while then," she said, as he reached for a mug.

"Go . . ." she said, taking the cup from his hand. "Sit yourself down there and I'll get it for you."

It had been a long time since he'd seen her in such high spirits. She looked stronger than she had in a while. She had her hair pinned up, and she was wearing her green tartan dress and her polished black walking shoes. She flitted about the kitchen like a woman half her age. It was the first time in months he felt hope . . . that she might actually pull out of this thing.

"Would you listen to that song," she said, holding up a finger to silence him for the Chieftains.

"That's lovely, Ma. What's it called?"

"*Tabhair dom do Lámh* . . ." she said, in the original Gaelic, slipping a plate heaped with eggs, sausage, bacon, beans and mushrooms, potato bread and soda bread under his nose. "Give me your hand."

He lifted his hand to her.

"No." She smiled, slapping his hand away. "That's the name of the song, ya knucklehead: 'Give Me Your Hand.'"

He listened to the tune as he wolfed the meal into him. He hadn't realized how hungry he was. This would be the last big meal he would allow himself today. He couldn't comprehend that he was going to be in a boxing ring in just under twelve hours.

He'd considered ditching the fight entirely, but that would only create more suspicion. He had to play along with the storyline that Vinny Diamond had just gone missing. It's doubtful anyone was really looking for him yet. He was pretty sure that anyone who

291

knew him would just assume Vinny was off getting laid somewhere. It might be days before a real enquiry would begin.

As he and his mother walked the ten blocks to Saint Patrick's
Cathedral they encountered the usual trail of New Yorkers from
the West Side making the annual pilgrimage to Fifth Avenue. It
was a cloudless day, temperature hovering in the upper fifties. A
perfect day for the parade.

As they passed O'Grady's, four red-faced bagpipers spilled out
of the bar in kilts and ghillie brogues and hurried along in front of
them leading the way.

A block out, they could hear the rattle and snap of drums as
the first marching band broke the line to a great cheer.

He looked to his mother and her face was as bright and thrilled
as a child's.

"Ach, do you hear that!" she said. "Isn't it great to be Irish?"
She reached over and actually took his hand in hers just then, and
squeezed it like he was still her darling boy. And for a moment he
felt like he still was.

Afterward, on the way back, they stopped into Connolly's. It was
part of her tradition. The one day of the year she'd step into a public house to raise a glass of Jamesons.

Danny shouldered himself in at the crowded bar, making way
for his mother and himself.

A large, round-faced Irishman planted on a stool next to his
mother, recognized him.

"By Jaysus, if it's not Danny Boy McCoy. Sean Mulrine, big
fan."

"Sean. Nice to meet you."

"Here," he said, sliding off his stool. "A stool for the lady."

"Thank you. This is my mother."

"A pleasure to meet you, Missus McCoy. A fine cub you've raised. He's a credit to us all."

Danny could tell his mother was loving the recognition. She had a smile playing at the corners of her mouth. The smile of a woman who was trying hard not to smile.

Sean insisted on paying for the drinks.

His mother raised her glass and said, "Shall we toast Saint Patrick!"

"With all due respect, ma'am," said Sean, "I've an awful aversion to toasting an Englishman. It gives me terrible indigestion."

His mother laughed at this. It wasn't just what he said. It was the way he said it. He was one of those Irishmen that had the gift. He was funny, even when he wasn't being funny.

"Sure, Saint Patrick's not English," his mother admonished him, happy to go along with the craic. "That's a terrible blasphemy altogether."

Danny sipped his pint of Guinness, delighted to watch his mother bantering with the Irishman. She had a way of reverting to a more primal Irish version of herself when she was around other Irish people, people from the other side. It wasn't a side of her he saw very often.

"Blasphemy!" Sean spat, in exaggerated contempt. "As English as roast beef, he was. I'm only surprised he didn't land over in a bowler hat."

His mother giggled at that.

"No, let's toast a great Irishman, Missus McCoy—"

"Peggy," she corrected him.

"Peggy."

"Who do you have in mind?"

"The man who discovered this great country we're standing on this very minute."

"Christopher Columbus?" asked his mother, knowing she was willingly stepping into another setup.

"Columbus, me hole. Pardon my French ma'am—Peggy— didn't Saint Brendan himself paddle hes canoe over here a thousand years earlier."

"A canoe?"

"A canoe."

"Across the Atlantic, in a canoe!" she exclaimed. "That's some canoe."

"Oh, only the very besht," said he. "Irish made. The finest ash and goat you ever seen."

"Goat?"

"The way it was, you see, he'd have wrapped the ash stick frame, in the goat skin—"

"Goat skin?"

"Oh aye, 'tis very waterproof the goat skin," Sean continued, sincerely, taking a measured sip of his pint before continuing. "You'll never see a goat complaining about the rain, I can tell you that."

His mother tipped her head back and laughed aloud at this. Even Danny had to laugh. Irish guys like Sean amazed him. There really was an ocean of difference between the Irish and the Irish-American. Something about the humor that hadn't quite survived the crossing of the Atlantic. There was no one on earth more absurd, more preposterous, more gifted at telling a humorous story than a big bellied Irishman with a brogue.

It was good to see his mother laugh. He hadn't seen her wipe a happy tear from her eye in years.

He made sure the bartender had Sean backed up for the next one before they made for the door.

His mother snickered the whole way home.

"A goat!" she'd say, and she'd start again. "Complaining about the rain!"

30

Danny made his way to the fight with the crew from The Wolf. They piled into the back of his van like sardines: Flannery, Blackie, Mack, McElroy, and a few others who just happened to be in the bar when the van was leaving.

Most of this crew had been on the piss for half the week celebrating Saint Patrick's Day.

Like they needed an excuse to get loaded.

Like they gave a single goddamn about Saint Patrick.

Danny drove, Terry rode shotgun, and Mack sat between them on an upturned five-gallon drum, working on a pint of vodka.

Danny had planned to drive alone, but Terry had been out front of The Wolf smoking a joint, and had spotted him as he opened the van door to leave. He'd asked Danny for a ride, then said he just needed to dash back inside to use the bathroom real quick before they hit the road. The entire crew had followed him out, Blackie locking the door behind him as they left.

One by one they'd piled into the back of his van.

What was he gonna do!

He just wanted to get this fight over and done with.

He'd been struggling with it all afternoon. After he'd left his mother back home following the parade, he'd spent the rest of the day on the roof with his birds, trying to get his head straight.

He let the birds out and waved them around with the flag for an hour or so. Then he spent some time on the heavy bag working off the Irish breakfast. He felt strong. As strong as he had in a long time.

But he felt unsure.

The Italians had big money riding on him to hit the canvas in the fourth.

They were going to be asking questions about Vinny.

Maybe they'd be glad Vinny had disappeared.

What he wanted more than anything was to get his mother out of The Kitchen. Seeing her smile today had renewed his determination to make that happen.

As long as he kept going through the motions today there was no way anyone would suspect him of having killed Vinny the night before. Certainly none of the neighborhood crew would suspect him.

"You alright there, Danny?" Terry asked as they went out over the George Washington Bridge toward the turnpike.

"I'm good."

"Don't worry about it," Mack said. "They'll build another one."

"Another what?"

Mack checked over his shoulder before leaning in to whisper in Danny's ear. "The gym. They'll build another one."

Danny had been so preoccupied with everything else that had happened in the last twenty-four hours he'd totally forgotten that they'd burned The Ward to the ground. He'd betrayed one of the only people who'd ever been really good to him.

He'd betrayed Cockeye.

When they got out of the van, he pulled Blackie aside.

"I want you to be my cornerman tonight."

"What!"

"I need you in my corner."

"Me?"

"Yeah."

"Not for nuttin', Danny, but I don't know shit about boxing."

"You don't need to know. They got a guy, Hank, he'll do the work."

"Fuck do you need me for then?"

"Maybe I just wanna have somebody I know, with me, in my corner."

Blackie nodded. "Okay, Danny, you want me in there, I'm there, pal."

"Thanks, Benny."

Miguel was the first one to ask him if he'd seen Vinny.

They were in the changing room before the fight. Some place in Bayonne. The floor practically vibrated every time the crowd cheered. Danny figured there had to be at least a few thousand in attendance, by all the noise.

"Naw. I thought he'd be here," Danny said.

"He was in the club last night?" Miguel asked.

"Yeah, came in about one-thirty when you dropped him off."

"You see him?"

"Yeah, I just told you, I saw him."

"You saw him inside the club?"

"Yeah."

"Then what?"

"I dunno. I said goodnight and I went home."

"You saw him at the end of the night?"

"Yeah."

"Where?"

"He was up in the bar, having a drink."

"By himself?"

"Yeah."

"There was nobody else there?"

Danny shook his head.

"Where was he in the bar?"

"What the fuck. He was behind the bar, pouring himself a drink, I figured he was checking the take. He had me check the bathrooms. Then I said, I gotta go, and he said, okay see ya tomorrow at the fight."

"And that's it?"

"Yeah. That's it. What's the problem?"

"He didn't say nuthin' about going nowhere?"

"He didn't say nuthin' to me."

"Funny, he's not here," Miguel said, and he seemed to search Danny's eyes for some clue.

"He better be fucken here, with my money," Danny said.

"Don't worry about your money. You just do what you gotta do," Miguel said, leveling him in his gaze. "You understand what you gotta do tonight, right!"

Yeah. Danny understood. Fourth round. Hug the canvas.

"I'm sure he'll be here," Miguel concluded. "Must've gone off with some broad. Probably on his way over here right now. Can't imagine he'd miss this."

Miguel moved on to talk to the dancers, assuming Vinny's role for the event, making sure everyone in Danny's corner knew what the hell they were supposed to do.

"What's that asshole's problem?" Blackie asked, stepping over next to Danny.

"Nuthin'."

Danny noticed one of the Italians approach Miguel and whisper in his ear. Danny'd seen the guy around the club over the last few months, Guiseppi or Giacomo or some shit. Guy didn't look none too happy. He glanced over at Danny with a frown, and caught Danny staring back at him. The guy whispered something else to Miguel. Miguel glanced back at Danny and shook his head.

There was a loud commotion in the hallway outside the dressing rooms just then, and everyone turned to see Chuck Wepner enter the changing rooms and approach Danny. Danny couldn't believe his eyes. This was the guy who went the full fifteen rounds with Ali. The guy was a legend. And here he was. In Danny's dressing room!

"Hey, there he is." Wepner grinned, approaching Danny with an outstretched hand. "Danny Boy McCoy. Hearing great things about you, kid. Wanted to come by and shake your hand."

"Wow! I really appreciate it, Mr. Wepner," Danny said, taking Wepner's big hand between his two gloves.

"What! You think I'm gonna let you come to my hometown, not come out to pay my respects! How you feeling?"

"Strong."

"That's what I like to hear. Got a lot of drunk Irishmen out there in that crowd tonight. Sound pretty excited to see you fight. You better not let them down."

"I won't."

A wiry looking reporter in a porkpie hat shoved a microphone between the two men.

"Danny Boy McCoy, Chip Johnson, *New Jersey Tribune*. How does it feel to be the underdog on tonight's card?"

"Ready to bite," Danny responded.

Wepner placed a hand on Danny's shoulder, and nodded. "Ready to bite. That's the spirit, kid."

A cameraman stepped in and a flash went off.

Wepner went off again without another word.

The reporter continued: "So, Danny, you nervous at all? Taylor's looking strong out there."

Danny shook his head. He was done talking.

Blackie, picking up on it, grabbed the reporter by an arm and ushered him out the door. "Go on. We're done here. You got your shot."

"I've just one more question," the reporter protested.

"Scram, 'fore I kick your ass," Blackie snapped.

Danny was glad he'd brought Blackie along. Blackie was rough around the edges but he was one of the few people in the world Danny still felt he could trust.

The announcer's voice boomed over the loudspeakers. The crowd cheered as he started his introduction of Randy Taylor to the ring.

Danny closed his eyes to the chaos around him, and he prayed.

Hail, Mary, full of grace . . .

He'd killed a man.

The Lord is with thee . . .

What could he do? He had to do it.

Blessed art thou amongst women . . .

It was kill or be killed.

And blessed is the fruit of thy womb, Jesus.

Vinny would have killed him in a flash if he'd beaten him to that gun.

Holy Mary, Mother of God . . .

Vinny was abusive to the girl he loved.

Pray for us sinners . . .

301

He was a murdering, drug-dealing, low-life, scumbag, piece of shit.

Now . . .

He deserved to die.

And at the hour of our death . . .

He'd done the world a favor.

Amen.

Danny blessed himself, as the first bars of "Danny Boy" began to play over the loud speakers.

Hank placed his hand on Danny's shoulder.

"You ready, kid?"

Danny nodded. He was ready.

Danny went down into the ring flanked by the dancers. His head down. The thundering roar of the crowd sent a vibration up through the soles of his feet.

Hank parted the ropes for him, and Danny climbed up into his corner, followed by Blackie, who'd thrown a towel over his shoulder. If nothing else, he certainly looked the part.

Danny backed into his corner and rested his gloves on the ropes.

He locked eyes with his opponent. Taylor nodded at him like they were old pals.

Danny didn't nod back.

He couldn't even remember hearing the bell.

Taylor came dancing at him with the cockiness of a man who knew the fight was in the bag.

Seeing the arrogance in his eyes sparked something in Danny. Rage.

Danny snapped a fast right and landed one on his jaw that caught him off guard. Taylor was taken aback. Like he wasn't expecting that at all. Like he hadn't expected a fight.

He shook it off and continued to dance in close again, threw a loose left, and a right, but Danny blocked him again without much effort at all, and buried a thunderous right hook into Taylor's rib cage. He could feel the bottom ribs crack.

Taylor buckled.

Gasped for air.

The disbelief was written in his eyes.

This is not how this was supposed to go down.

He held his elbow over his side for protection as Danny went to work on him like a shark with a whiff of blood.

The next punch opened Taylor's eyebrow, sending an arc of blood high over the ropes into the front row.

Danny took two steps back and dropped his fists to his side until he was sure he had Taylor's full attention. Once he was sure Taylor was focused on him, he skipped back in again, and delivered the *coup de grâce*. Taylor could do nothing to stop it. He'd obviously strolled into the ring thinking he was coming here to pick up a check. He'd taken Danny for a sucker. For a loser and a cheat.

Danny pulled back and let loose with his right.

It happened so fast Taylor had no time to block it.

It caught him so squarely on the jaw that for a second Danny was afraid he might have killed him.

Taylor swayed for a second. Blinked. Then crumpled to the canvas.

The whole thing was over in less than ninety seconds.

Danny stood over his opponent as the referee counted him out. Taylor's eyes flickered up at the lights in disbelief.

Danny lifted his head and glanced into the front row. Logan, Flannery, Mack and the crew were on their feet screaming, clambering to get into the ring. Behind them stood a row of stone-faced Italians.

Giovanni—that was his name. Danny remembered it now, the Italian guy from the changing room, lifted his hand, and, staring directly at Danny, dragged a finger across his throat.

Danny smiled back.

Blackie rushed in and wrapped his arms around Danny from behind and picked him up in the air, as The Wolf crew rushed in to hoist him onto their shoulders.

He was a hero.

Or a corpse.

Maybe he was both.

Part 3

1

There was a naked man hog-tied to a light pole on the corner of Forty-fifth and Tenth, outside Mannion's Tavern. Danny felt compelled to cross the street for a closer look.

Whoever had stripped and tied the man had used a black marker to scrawl the words, DO NOT REMOVE, across his chest.

The man looked to Danny with desperate, pleading eyes. "Hey, buddy, do me a favor. Cut me down."

Danny didn't recognize the guy. White. Mid thirties. Beer paunch. His dick shriveled into a thick bed of dark pubes in the cold March air.

"Please," the guy begged.

Danny turned and went back across the street with his hands in his pockets to keep them warm. This was The Kitchen. If somebody had taken the trouble to strip a guy and tie him to a pole, odds are, he deserved it.

It was best to leave such things alone.

The guy yelled after him: "Hey, fuck you, you piece of shit."

Danny went on down to The Wolf and ordered a beer.

It was two days since the fight. McElroy was behind the stick. Terry Flannery, Blackie, Mack, and the rest of the crew were still there wearing the same clothes they'd been wearing on Saint Patrick's Day.

They'd spent the previous days celebrating Danny's win.

Apart from the few hours he'd been at home to check on his mother, get a few hours sleep, and feed his birds, Danny'd spent most of the time since the fight in the bar with them.

He'd been tempted to go see Trixie, and he was tempted to go see Gabriela. But he fought the urge to see either. Right now he just wanted to be with the guys. He wanted to stay drunk and not think about what was coming. He was pretty sure that whatever was coming was not going to be good.

The Wolf felt like the safest place in the world to be right now.

"Anybody know why there's a naked guy tied to a post up the street?" he asked, slipping onto the same stool he'd left a couple of hours earlier.

"Scumbag thought he could get away with stiffing me." McElroy grinned, popping the cap off a beer for Danny. "Owes me two large, and thinks he can still slip into the neighborhood for a blow job. Manny the Cuban tipped me he was over there this morning with one of his girls. You believe that shit? Can't afford to make the vig but he's got fifty clams to drop on some fucken gash. I sent Kevin and Kenny to tell him I said hello," he said nodding to the two guys at the end of the bar.

Kevin and Kenny raised their beers to Danny at the mention of their names. The boys seemed proud of their work.

"You didn't cut him down, did you?" McElroy asked.

"Nope. He's still there," replied Danny, lifting his beer for a sip. "Nice touch tying him outside Mannion's place."

"That was Kev's idea." Kenny laughed.

"Mannion's gonna love that," said Danny.

The door opened, letting a shaft of sunlight into the dim room and Logan strolled in holding a newspaper aloft.

"Danny Boy McCoy Takes a Bite Out of Taylor," Logan proclaimed, holding up the copy of the *New Jersey Tribune* he'd brought in with him from across the river. "You guys see this. I'm framing this one for the bar. What a fight! Man, you really showed that asshole," he said, slapping Danny on the shoulder. "Give these clowns a round on me. Please tell me you guys have been home since Saint Patrick's Day."

"I don't think any of these guys have been further than the bathroom in three days." McElroy grinned.

Logan shook his head. "Smells like it. Need to open a window in here or fumigate this fucken place." Logan stood in stark contrast to the rest of this crew. He was clean-shaven. Hair freshly trimmed. A tweed sports coat over a crisp white shirt. Freshly pressed black pants. He looked like a guy who'd gotten a solid eight hours of sleep and eaten a healthy breakfast. He looked like a businessman.

The door to the bar opened and Pat Mannion walked in, flanked by his two top men: Dillon and The Greek.

"Well would you look at this shit!" Logan said, his hand still resting on Danny's shoulder.

All heads turned as Mannion strolled up to Logan, leaving his henchmen standing either side of the front door to watch his back.

"I'd like to talk," Mannion said to Logan.

"Nobody's stoppin' you."

"In private."

"Fuck private. I've got nuthin' to hide from these guys. You wanna say something to me you say it."

"I'd rather we sit down, like gentlemen—"

"Who the fuck you think you're talkin' to? You ain't no gentleman. Nor am I. You have somethin' to say to me, you say it right here and then get the fuck out of my bar."

"Okay, Logan. That's the way you want it. There's a naked guy tied to a pole outside my bar this morning."

"A what?"

"Some of your guys stripped a guy and tied him outside my bar."

Logan looked like he was suppressing a sly smile. He glanced around for confirmation of this claim. McElroy shrugged as if to say. *Yeah, we stripped the guy.* Logan turned back to Mannion.

"So, what's the problem," Logan said calmly, taking a step toward Mannion, closing the space between the two men, until their chests almost touched. Mannion was about a half head taller than Logan, but Logan stared up at him with those cold blue eyes, leveling any height distance between them.

"It doesn't have to go down like this, Logan," Mannion said, never taking his eyes from Logan's. "There's plenty of room in this neighborhood for everybody."

"Oh, I don't think that's true at all," Logan replied. "In fact, it's feeling pretty crowded, you ask me."

"You sure this is how you want it?"

Danny was sitting not two feet from both men, he could see Logan was staring straight through Mannion, all the way back to the puddle of piss Mannion made his father sit in twenty years earlier.

Mannion could see it, too. He casually turned and walked back toward the door. He nodded to Mack as if he were asking him if he were sure this is where he wanted to be. Mack had been one of Mannion's loyal soldiers for years. He'd tended bar at the Tavern, and worked as an enforcer for Mannion's numbers racket alongside the two men standing by the door right now, Tommy

Dillon and The Greek. By not getting up to follow his old pals out the door Mack was making it crystal clear where his allegiance now lay.

Mack was with Logan Coyle.

No one else spoke as Mannion made his way to the door and all three men quietly stepped outside again.

"Prick," Logan said under his breath, still staring at the door with a cold murderous gaze.

It had just gone midnight when the Italian walked in.

Danny'd been expecting it. Someone was going to come asking questions about Vinny Diamond, sooner or later. And here it was. They'd sent Giovanni.

The TV above the bar was playing the *Tonight Show*. McLean Stevenson was filling in for Carson. He was interviewing Bea Arthur. But the sound was off, and Flannery had just put "Money" by Pink Floyd on the jukebox for about the third or fourth time that night.

There were only four of the crew left in the bar: Flannery, Mack, Logan and Danny.

Logan had stayed and gotten as drunk as the rest. The Mannion thing had set him off. The humiliation his father had suffered at the hands of Mannion still festered in him like an untreated wound. Just before the Italian had walked into the bar, Logan had been leaned in close to Danny whispering to him about how his mother had cheated on his father not long after Mannion had kidnapped him. He connected the two events. The way he saw it, his mother was punishing his father for being weak, for allowing himself to be humiliated by Mannion like that. It was humiliation heaped on top of humiliation. In Logan's obsessed mind Mannion was responsible for it all. Far as Logan was concerned, Mannion may as well have stepped into his parents' bedroom and murdered them both with an axe. It was crystal clear Logan would never rest until he orchestrated his brutal revenge.

Unlike Mannion, the Italian, Giovanni, had strolled in alone. In fact he moved very much like a man who did not feel like he needed to fear anyone or anything.

He walked like a man who understood he represented the full weight of the Fallaci family.

He came straight up to Danny and, ignoring Logan entirely, said, "Me and you gotta talk. In private." He nodded for Danny to get off his stool and join him in the back of the bar.

"Wow, wow, wow! Who the fuck is this guy?" Logan said, stunned that this guy had the balls to come strolling into his bar and interrupt him with such profound arrogance.

"Let's go," the guy said to Danny, continuing to ignore Logan like he wasn't even there.

Danny moved to leave his stool, resigned to go deal with the Italian, but Logan reached out his arm and placed it on Danny's shoulder, stopping him.

"Hey, Danny. Sit."

Giovanni turned to Logan. "Listen, pal, maybe you just wanna go back to sipping your drink. This doesn't concern you."

"Oh. I think it does concern me."

"Naw, I really don't think it does. You know who I am?"

"Do I know who *you* are?" Logan asked. Danny could see he had that crazed twinkle in his eye again.

"Listen, Logan—it's Logan, right?"

Logan looked surprised that the guy knew his name. Flattered even.

"Yeah, I know who you are, but I don't give a fuck. I'm here to ask this dumb fuck what the hell happened to my associate, Vinny Diamond."

"Vinny Diamond?"

"Yeah, your pal here was the last person to see him at the club, and I got a few questions for him. You got a problem with that?"

"Yeah. I got a problem with that. How about I ask him? Hey, Danny, you know where Vinny Diamond is?"

Danny shook his head.

"There, see, he doesn't know nuthin'. Now, why don't you turn around and take your fat, spaghetti-eating ass out of my fucken bar 'fore I get upset."

Giovanni reached under his jacket but before he could reach his gun Logan slammed a beer bottle over his head. The bottle shattered, opening a wide gash over his left eye. Without pause Logan jammed the broken neck of the bottle into his jugular. Giovanni clamped his hand to his throat but Logan just kept right on ramming the glass into his neck and face. The Italian stumbled backward, flailing his arms in a powerless attempt to stop Logan's vicious onslaught. He tripped on his heels and went down. Logan went down on top of him. Danny turned away as Mack ran to lock the door and secure the blinds.

Eventually the Italian's legs stopped kicking. And Logan sat astride him, panting, holding the bloody bottle in his hand.

"You got any more questions you wanna ask, you dumb guinea fuck?" Logan yelled into the dying man's face. "I'm sorry, what's that, I can't hear you. You'll have to speak up a little."

Logan stood over the man with a hellish blood-spattered grin as the last desperate gurgles issued from Giovanni's mangled throat.

"Somebody grab me a knife," Logan said, calmly. But Mack was already on it. He knew what had to be done. He had returned from the kitchen carrying a gleaming butcher knife. He knelt casually, as if in preparation for prayer, raised the knife in both hands, and buried the blade deep into Giovanni's chest.

"There. That'll stop it," he said.

Danny sat in a booth with his back to the action as they went to work on Giovanni. Terry sat with him, getting up every once in a while to play Pink Floyd on the jukebox again to block out the sound of flesh being sawed and bones being cracked.

When it was done, and Giovanni had been parsed out into several black trash bags, Logan sent Danny for his van, and as Danny sat with the motor idling, they loaded Giovanni's mutilated corpse in through the side door.

Mack made a quip about Danny's van being "The Meat Wagon," and they all laughed.

All but Danny.

They went out over the Queensboro Bridge, and drove until they found an empty lot in the midst of some derelict industrial buildings, where he was able to back the van up next to the water, and then they threw the body into the East River. Logan didn't want to take this one out to Ward's Island. Too many questions. He didn't want Nicky Red, or DeCarlo, to know he'd whacked one of theirs.

Then they drove back to The Wolf and entered the bar before dawn.

Mack got behind the stick and poured a round of whiskeys to toast the night. Terry rolled another joint, and went back to playing Pink Floyd, and Logan handed Danny a twenty and sent him to the deli up the street for some bacon, egg, and cheese breakfast sandwiches for everyone.

As he stepped out of The Wolf, squinting in the cruel glare of the morning sun, Gabriela was there waiting for him.

It was the first time he had seen her in weeks.

2

"Can we go somewhere to talk?" Gabriela asked. She was wearing a blue knee-length overcoat, with a red wool scarf tucked in around her neck. Danny tried to interpret her expression but she revealed nothing of anger, disappointment . . . or love.

"What is it?" He reacted with the impatience of a child. If she was going to berate him he wanted to hear it now.

"Can we just sit in your van for a moment?" she said, nodding to the red Chevy parked outside The Wolf.

He didn't want her in the van after they'd just used it to ferry Giovanni's dismembered body to its final resting place in the East River, but he did want to get her away from the front of The Wolf and he wanted desperately to hear what she had to say, no matter how painful it might be.

"It really smells in here," she said, once they were seated in the van.

"I can open a window . . ."

"No. It doesn't matter. Let me just say what I need to say and . . ." She paused here, folded her gloved hands neatly in her lap and closed her eyes as if in silent prayer. She opened her eyes,

316

sighed deeply, and stared straight ahead. "I'm going to talk and I just want you to let me talk, okay."

Danny nodded, and braced himself.

"I think I've been in love with you since I was ten years old." She stopped, and swallowed hard. A single tear ran down her cheek. Danny was tempted to reach out and wipe it away, but he knew that he was going to have to hear what she had to say now without interruption.

"Damn it. This is hard," she said, composing herself to continue. "I'd see you come into the store and my heart would skip a beat. I'd try to place myself in your way so you'd have to say hello to me. You were so big and strong. You were different than all the other boys in the neighborhood. Just the way young boys would look up at you . . . like they wanted to be you . . . Danny McCoy. I knew you could be anything you wanted to be . . . a movie star, even. I knew it." She stopped and smiled at this. "Then you asked me out." And here she lifted her hands and joined them together under her chin as if in prayer. "You asked me out and I thought my heart would explode. Yes. My knight in shining armor. That was the happiest day of my life. Yes. And I gave myself to you . . . all of me . . . because I thought you'd protect me. I thought you'd love me . . . I thought I could trust you."

"I . . ."

"Don't. Please," she said, dismissing him again with a shake of her head. "Let me finish. I thought I'd feel safe. And then . . ."

She shook her head and sighed again before continuing.

"I knew you were seeing someone else."

There it was.

"I didn't want to believe it at first. I was too much in love. I didn't want anything to pierce that bubble, our precious, precious bubble. So I followed you. I know, I'm embarrassed to say it. But I did. I had to know. I had to see it for myself. And even after I found out, even after I knew you were sleeping in someone else's bed, I stayed with you. Slept with you. Loved you. I thought I could win you back from her. But I was wrong."

"I'm sorry."

"I know."

"I didn't want for it to happen."

"I know."

"I want you to know I'll take care of you and the baby—"

"There is no baby."

"What!"

"There was. But there's not anymore."

"How?"

"I don't want to talk about it."

"I do."

"It's gone. I needed you and you weren't there. You weren't there, Danny."

Danny was crushed. He was angry. Confused.

"What do you mean, it's gone? You have to tell me what happened to it."

"No. I don't. I'm going to keep that part to myself. That's mine. It's my pain. You don't get to have it."

Her hands had curled into fists in her lap and he thought for a second she might reach out and punch him. Slap him. Scratch his face. He would have welcomed it. Anything. Anything other than this.

"I want to say something else to you before I go," she said, composing herself again. "And then I'm going to leave you alone. You were a good person. I really believe that. I think deep down you still are. You were special. You had a job."

"It was a shit job."

"It was real. You gave people hope. What do these other guys do? Your friends? Steal? Drink? Do drugs? They take. They take and they take and they take."

"I'm not like them."

"You *weren't* like them. The man I fell in love with wasn't like them. But don't kid yourself, Danny . . ." she said, turning to him now so he could see the full weight of the hurt he'd caused her. "You're just like them now."

"I'm sorry," he said, but she brushed it aside like it was dust.

"I have about a year left before I finish my law degree. I'd really appreciate it if you just left me alone now, okay! Don't come in the store. Don't call me. Don't talk to me if you see me on the street. Just let me be. I don't want your darkness in my life. I'm not like you. And I don't want to be. Goodbye, Danny."

She reached for the door handle and got out and walked away.

He watched her walk the full length of the block until she turned east on Forty-fourth Street.

She did not look back.

3

Without the purse from the fight, or the door job at the Paradise Club, he was in trouble. Danny had taken the weekly envelope he'd been receiving from Vinny for granted. Within days of the fight he was broke. Worse than broke. He owed Goldstein. He owed the monthly payment on the Woodstock house. The rent on the apartment was due. The electric bill. His mother's meds and doctors visits. Insurance payment for the van. Gas. Food. Bird feed. Not to mention the bar bill he was racking up at The Wolf.

Even Hank, his cornerman, had come looking for him at The Wolf. Hank had gone to the Paradise to see Vinny about payment for working the fight, but he'd found the place shuttered. He thought Danny might be able to help him out. Danny told him the truth. With Vinny gone it was unlikely anybody would pay him for the fight. He certainly didn't expect to see any of it. It wasn't like he could go to the Italians to see if they would straighten him out. Not after he'd killed Vinny and helped toss Giovanni's body in the East River.

He hadn't been to see Trixie since he'd seen her out of the club the night before the fight. He'd assured her he would take care of her and her kid. And now, by killing Vinny, he'd eliminated her only source of financial support. He wasn't sure how she'd react if she found out he'd killed the father of her child. He couldn't be sure she wouldn't hate him for it. So he decided she would never know.

He did the only thing he could think of to make some fast money. He turned to Logan. Logan was more than happy to put him to work.

Logan had been growing his loan shark operation steadily over the past year or so. Danny had heard it through Blackie that Logan had gone to Hyman Goldstein for the extra capital he needed to expand the business. He had tens of thousands out on the street. Maybe as much as a hundred and fifty grand in total.

"I want you to pair up with Blackie," Logan told him. They were seated in the Market Diner. Logan, Blackie, Terry and Danny. "I got a handful of deadbeats I want you guys to go see. I just want you to scare 'em, okay. Don't be goin' crazy. I don't want nobody whacked. They ain't much good to me dead. Dead men can't make the vig."

"Sure thing, we'll just slap 'em around a little bit," Blackie said, crunching on a stick of bacon.

"No. I don't want you smacking 'em around. Not right out of the gate. I want you to tell 'em this is their last chance to pay up without getting hurt. You tell 'em next person they're gonna see walking through the door is Terry."

Terry smiled. Danny had noticed that Terry was beginning to enjoy seeing the fear he instilled in people. Terry's reputation as a psychopathic murderer was becoming something you heard whispered all over The Kitchen. You paired that with the whispers of Logan and Mack chopping up anyone who got in their way, and there were very few people who were going to risk pissing off any of the crew from The Wolf.

"I had a visitor yesterday," Logan said, casually sipping his coffee. Nobody spoke. But he had their attention. "Two Italian guys waiting for me by my car as I was about to head home. Wanted to know if I'd seen their old pal Giovanni."

"Whaddya tell em?" Blackie asked.

"Fuck you think I said: 'Giovanni who? I don't know no Giovanni. Never heard of 'em.' Then they wanted to know if I'd seen Vinny Diamond."

"Vinny Diamond?" asked Terry. "What's the story with that guy?"

"I don't know," Logan said, setting his cup down and fixing Danny with those steely blue eyes. "Where's Vinny, Danny?"

All eyes were fixed on Danny.

"Fuck would I know?"

"You do know he's missing though, right!"

"Yeah. I heard."

"And you don't know nuthin' about it?"

Danny shook his head. Logan smiled. He smiled like he didn't believe a word Danny was saying.

"They said you was the last one to see him."

"So!"

"So. Nuthin'. I'm just telling you what they told me. They also said he had a large shipment of smack—in a brown leather bag. They said, Miguel swears he dropped him off with the bag and that you opened the door to let him in. And they say that's the last time anybody spoke to him. Not even the bartender remembers seeing him. You know how they know Miguel was telling the truth?"

Danny continued to say nothing. Logan was going to tell him.

"Because the Columbians who are looking for their missing shipment of smack, tied Miguel to a chair and went to work on him with a chainsaw."

Danny felt his hands start to shake. He moved them to his lap.

"So they're pretty sure Miguel told them whatever they needed to know."

Logan continued to stare at Danny as if he were hoping the horror of what had happened to Miguel might shake him into revealing something of the truth. Danny fought any urge he had to come clean. Logan continued.

"See the Italians hadn't paid for the drugs. Vinny, your dickhead boss, had taken it from the Columbians to sell to the Italians. But he never got around to selling it to the Italians. They never received the product. And now, the Columbians are the ones who are missing about a million dollars of their product. You see why they might be a little bit upset. Right! You could see why they'd want me to check with you to see if you knew anything about it."

The image of the brown leather satchel sailing off the side of the Tappan Zee Bridge into the darkness flashed in Danny's brain. Now he was going to have to fit Miguel's body into that hole he'd dug in his heart for everyone else.

"The bartender, Snake, told them Trixie was also in the club when he left."

"Did they kill Snake, too?" Danny asked.

"I dunno. Maybe. They say he's disappeared."

"What about me?"

"I gave them my word you had nuthin' to do with it."

"Thanks, Logan."

"But they wanna talk to Trixie."

"Who does?"

"The Columbians."

"Jesus Christ, Danny, you got yourself in some pile of shit now," Terry said, shaking his head.

"Fucken Columbians don't mess around, kid," Blackie added.

"You still bangin' that broad?" Logan asked.

"I haven't seen her in a few days."

"Since when?"

"The night before the fight."

"The night Vinny went missing?"

Danny nodded.

"At the club?"

"Yeah." Danny nodded.

"Ain't that a fucken coincidence."

"Are they gonna kill her?"

"Probably, if they can find her. The bartender was able to tell them where she lived. They went by to pay her a visit. She's gone. Place is cleaned out. You know anything about that?"

Danny breathed his first sigh of relief. He shook his head.

"Are you fucken sure, Danny? Look at me," Logan said, forcing Danny to look in his eyes. "You tell me. Do you know where she is?"

"I don't know, Logan. I swear on my mother."

It was true. He didn't know. And he was relieved that he didn't.

"Maybe Vinny took the drugs and ran off with this fucken broad," Blackie concluded. "She was a sweet little piece of ass, I can tell you that. Man, you take that to an island somewhere, big bag of drugs, nothin' to do but sun your balls, and fuck that little peach all day. I'd go." He laughed. "Fucken bang that shit all day long. Sign me the fuck up."

Danny restrained himself from reacting to Blackie's remarks.

"That's pretty much how the Columbians see it right now," said Logan. "Vinny was in the hole. He owed the Italians and the Columbians. Big time. They reckon he knew they were going to punch his clock so he set them up on the deal. Took the drugs and disappeared with the broad. Fucken guy has any brains he'll never show his face around here again, I can tell you that. Same for that fucken broad."

"What about me?" Danny asked.

"Looks like you dodged a bullet on this one, Danny. Long as you're with me. You stay close. They gave me their word they won't touch you."

"Thanks, Logan."

"No thanks needed," Logan said. "You just owe me."

Danny nodded. He did owe him.

He owed Logan his life.

4

He found her collapsed behind the bathroom door. A bundle of bones and skin so fragile he thought for sure he must be missing parts of her when he lifted her in his arms.

She'd convinced him that she was done with treatment and that she was on her way to a full recovery. And seeing her out and about on Saint Patrick's Day he'd had no reason to doubt her. But the doctor who took him aside outside of her hospital room made it clear it had all been an act. His mother was dying, and she had known as much for months. She wasn't on treatment because none had been offered.

"So what can we do for her?" Danny had asked.

"We've made her comfortable for now," the doctor said, placing a hand on Danny's arm.

"Can I take her home?"

The doctor rubbed his arm and shook his head. "Why don't you go take this moment to be with your mother."

Danny understood.

The doctor turned, and Danny watched him walk away down the corridor.

"Well, what did he have to say for himself?" His mother scowled sleepily when he re-entered the hospital room.

"He said you're as fit as a fiddle." Danny smiled. If this is how she wanted it played, he'd play along. He owed her that.

"I knew it," she said, dryly.

"He asked me if I could try talking you out of running the marathon this year."

"You'll have to hide my running shoes." She smiled, taking his hand as he sat up on the bed next to her with his back against her pillow. He pushed close to her and draped his arm around her shoulder, pulling her close so she could rest her head on his shoulder.

"He said the bowling's gotta go too."

"I suppose they'll try telling me I'm not allowed to play football next."

She moved closer to him, cautiously, like a dog that hadn't been petted in a long time, settling her head on his chest. They hadn't been this close since he was a child. And he regretted that now.

"When you get out," he said, brushing her silvery hair softly with his hand, "I was thinking we could take a trip to Ireland."

"Oh yes. That's a great idea," she said, patting the front of his shirt with her free hand. "I'll have to get some new walking shoes."

"Oh, me too."

"We'll want to be looking our best."

"I'll rent a nice car."

"Good boy," she said, her voice almost a whisper now. "That's good."

"And we'll just drive, we'll take off without a map."

"That's it. That's my good boy." Her voice softer now. Almost inaudible.

"Maybe we'll head south first, go all the way around the coast. We'll stop whenever we feel like it. We'll see a place that looks nice and we'll just stay for a day or two. All the best hotels of course. We'll go to all the little fishing villages you talked about. We'll eat lamb stew and shepherd's pie. We'll take our shoes off and go for a long walk through wet grass in green fields . . . and we'll go on to Donegal . . . your home place . . ."

He felt her sigh, and release a deep breath. A long peaceful exhale that seemed to go on and on like a breeze over a wide green field.

5

The entire neighborhood filed through the McManus Funeral Home to pay their respects to Ma McCoy. Logan Coyle stepped in and took care of all the arrangements. Told Danny not to worry about any of that for now. Danny was grateful for the help. He hadn't the first clue how such things worked. Logan seemed to know intuitively. Logan had always been like that. The adult in the room. Logan helped him pick a casket. Made arrangements for flowers and a hearse. He even organized a burial plot up in Valhalla at the Kensico Cemetery. A cemetery with so many Irish buried there, they called it the thirty-third county.

In a daze, Danny stood near the casket and shook hands. He'd had them lay her out in the outfit she'd worn for Saint Patrick's Day. They'd folded her wooden rosary beads into her hands. She looked annoyed. He was pretty sure she'd be rolling her eyes, if she could open them, at most of this crowd. Most people had that effect on her. She would have had little patience for the disingenuous piety of Terry Flannery, Mack Cantor and Benny Black peering down at her in repose. He imagined her straining to turn her head away from their gaze as they prayed over her.

He half expected her to sit up and tell them to take a hike.

She would have been pleased to see Pat Mannion and his wife Elaine. She'd have taken great pride that they took the time.

Mannion took Danny's hand and said, "The neighborhood has lost a great woman. It will never be the same. If there's anything you need. Anything at all." And Danny believed it. Mannion was like that. There was a decency to him. There was no angle here.

Enzo Mazzella came in alone. Danny winced as he approached. He sensed Enzo had trouble taking his hand. He would have been upset with him about the Gabriela situation. Of course he wasn't going to say it here. But Enzo wasn't there because he wanted to comfort Danny. He was there to pay his respects. He was there because he had known and cared about his mother for half a lifetime. She was one of his ladies. Danny watched him wipe a tear from his face as he stood in prayer next to the casket. Maybe the only genuine tear of the day.

He wanted to go after him. Apologize for how he had treated Gabriela. Thank him for being kind to his mother. For making sure she never went hungry—that she didn't have to let her son go hungry—even when he knew she didn't have the money to pay him. Enzo Mazzella had probably given him more sustenance freely than any other man in his lifetime. And he'd rewarded him by breaking Gabriela's heart.

It was toward the end of the night Gabriela came in.

She was alone. She was wearing a knee-length black coat. Her long black hair was tied back in a ponytail.

She wrapped her arms around him and hugged him wordlessly.

"I'm sorry," he whispered into her ear. She smelled like honey and lavender, and she was all warmth and goodness and he wanted to hold on to her, fold her into him forever. To own some of that goodness. But she pulled away, gently, respectfully, and bowed her head as she moved away from him, to bless herself at his mother's casket. She left without uttering a single word. She kept her head up as she passed through the door. Virtuous. Dignified. Principled. Everything he had failed to be for her.

The last person to show was Cockeye Ward.

Everyone else was gone.

The room was empty, but for Danny, alone, seated in the front row, taking this last quiet moment to be with his mother.

Cockeye nodded to him and went on to the casket, kneeled, and prayed silently for a few moments. Blessed himself, and then came to sit next to Danny.

"I'm sorry for your loss."

"Thanks, Boss."

"She was a good woman."

Danny nodded. He'd heard it a thousand times in the past few hours. And it was true, every single time.

"You gonna be okay by yourself up there?"

"I'm good."

"What about that girl, the pretty one you brought by The Ward that time . . ."

"Gabriela."

"That's the one. She still around."

Danny shook his head.

"You lost her? You always was a dumb fuck."

Danny grunted a laugh. It was the first time he'd laughed in days. It was a welcome reprieve from the grief.

"I read about your fight with Taylor," Cockeye said, nodding his head. "He's good that guy."

Danny was surprised to hear him bring up the fight. Though he shouldn't have been. Cockeye had always believed in him.

"So, what are you gonna do now?"

"I dunno. Take care of my birds. Try to figure shit out."

"I know this might not be the time, or the place. But I think it's time for you to take a shot."

"How?"

"That Taylor fight has people talking. Got a lot of press. National. Nobody expected you to take him. You made a real name for yourself there. We work this thing proper, you could take this all the way."

"We?"

"Yeah, we. If you're up for it, I can get you a real shot."

"Against who?"

"Carlos Cabrerra."

Danny turned his head to look at Cockeye. That got his attention. Carlos Cabrerra was ranked one of the top in the country.

"Cabrerra's people are looking for something big for him. Somebody help them pack The Garden."

"Madison Square Garden!"

"You go up against Cabrerra, and you beat him, you'll get a shot at the belt."

"World title?"

"If you beat Cabrerra."

"The Garden?"

"This is your big shot, kid."

"Why are you doing this?"

"I been around this game a long time. Shot like this comes around maybe once in a lifetime. You don't reach out and grab it, it's gone, and you ain't gettin' another one."

"I dunno, Boss."

"You don't know!" Cockeye spat angrily. "What don't you know!"

"I just . . . I don't know."

"The hell you don't know? I'm handing you the dream, kid."

"Whose dream?"

"Mine . . ." Cockeye said, and then catching himself, stopped short, paused, then continued on again, as if it was too late to stop this propulsion of words. Of truth. "Yes . . . mine, goddamn it, sure, it's my dream, and yours. Yours and mine and every other young kid in this whole screwed-up neighborhood. Every kid who never stood a chance, every kid who ever looked up to Danny Boy McCoy and thought, 'Hey, my life ain't worth shit, but maybe I could do that one day . . . maybe I could make somethin' outta myself with nothing but these two goddamn hands and the will to go out and fight for it.' That's who . . . every little kid from a broken home and not a nickel in his pocket to do a goddamn thing about it other than rob, cheat or steal . . . that's who . . . that's whose dream it is. You think this is just yours? Well you're wrong. It ain't." Cockeye stood. His fists balled in anger. "It ain't your dream. It's ours."

Danny bowed his head.

"Listen. I can't make you fight. But I can train ya. If you're willing to put in the work I can get you ready for this guy."

"You'd train me?" Danny said, looking up.

"Yeah . . . I'll train ya . . . but you gotta be ready to put in the work, kid. This is the big leagues. This ain't some goon in a warehouse down on the docks. We get in that ring with Cabrerra you better be ready."

Danny nodded.

"Meet me downtown. Monday morning. Tierney's."

"Tierney's?"

"Spud Tierney's gym, he lets me use the place since—" Cockeye stopped himself. "Since the fire."

"I heard about that."

Danny pictured the flames ripping through The Ward.

333

"Everything I ever had that meant something to me was in that place."

Danny closed his eyes.

"Every ounce of sweat for twenty years . . ." He let it trail off. "First pair of boxing gloves my dad ever gave me. I should never have left them there. I'm a goddamned dummy."

Danny kept his head down. He couldn't bring himself to meet Cockeye's gaze, afraid Cockeye would see the flicker of flame in there, The Ward still burning, bright as hell in the corner of Danny's eyes.

6

Cockeye was training another fighter when Danny entered Tierney's Gym with Blackie. Blackie stepped over to a heavy bag and threw a few punches at it.

"Bam bam bam. Hey look at me. Fucken Ragin' Bull over here," Blackie yelled to Danny.

"What's he doing' here?" Cockeye asked, sidling over to Danny.

"I want him in my corner."

"Are you crazy?"

"I want him with me."

"For what? What the fuck does he know about boxing?"

Blackie had picked up a skipping rope and was trying desperately to get his feet off the ground as he spun it around.

"Nothing."

"So why the fuck would I let him in my corner."

"It ain't your corner. It's mine."

"Yours?"

"He was with me for the Taylor fight. He helped me."

"Doing what?"

"I want him there."

"He's a clown."

335

"I need him."

"Get him out of here."

"Damn it, Boss. He goes, I go."

"Fine," Cockeye said, throwing his hands up, walking away, shaking his head. "Fine. Long as he stays the hell outta my way."

Danny watched as Blackie tripped himself with the rope, stood up and tossed it aside.

"Wha'd he say?"

"He said, okay."

"Really?"

"Yeah."

"You sure? I don't wanna step on his toes none."

"I want you there."

"Okay, Danny Boy. That's what you want."

Danny watched Blackie follow Cockeye to the other side of the gym. Blackie got his attention and offered him his hand and Cockeye took it.

They spoke for a minute or two and then Cockeye yelled to Danny, "Don't just stand there. Get your gloves on."

Cockeye wasted no time working him into a sweat. Danny felt like there was punishment in it for putting him on the spot by bringing Blackie into the gym. He'd only thought he was in shape before Cockeye got to work on him. Cockeye was pushing him way beyond where he had pushed himself. Danny was about to throw in the towel and ask for a break when Cockeye tapped him on the shoulder and nodded toward the door as a man in a brown fedora entered the gym.

Danny recognized the guy immediately as *New York Gazette* reporter, Murray O'Connell. Murray was something of a legend about town. He wasn't specifically a sportswriter but he didn't need to be. Everybody who picked up a copy of the *Gazette* read his daily column, "Murray's Message." Hell, most people only bought the paper to see what Murray had to say next. He was a hard-boiled Irish-American story man. He didn't just cover crime, he turned crime into entertainment. Same for sports, politics, or celebrity gossip. Murray could put a twist on a cat getting stuck in a tree.

He'd come in chewing on a Danish, carrying a cardboard cup of coffee, and took a seat by the window where he had a full view of the gym.

Murray moved like a half-cocked Bowery bum. That was his disguise in a city littered with trash. He wore a rumpled, ill-fitting tweed suit, a wrinkled white shirt, a tie hung carelessly about his neck, and a tired scowl on his saggy jowls. He had the perpetual look of a man who'd just staggered out of a three-day bender. It was all an act, of course. He was a man who didn't want to be thought of as someone who liked all the attention he was obviously bringing to himself. But Murray made damn sure he was seen, make no mistake about that. His real signature was the brown felt fedora he wore everywhere, perched askew on his big meaty head. A side profile silhouette of that hat atop his rotund noggin and his prominent bulbous beer nose was as recognizable to any New Yorker as Hitchcock's.

Murray was an unassuming slob with an eagle's ponderous eye for a detail. He gave Cockeye a tired nod of his head as if he hadn't the slightest interest in what was going on. But he was watching.

Murray O'Connell didn't miss a goddamn thing.

7

Goldstein's goon had grown accustomed to seeing Danny show up at the club to make payment, every single week. Even when he couldn't afford to make the vig, Danny still made the trek to Seventy-sixth and Broadway to show face, and pay what he could. He'd learned enough about working the collection end of the business for Logan to know that you didn't bother a guy who was showing up and making an honest effort to chip away at the vig. The guys who got hurt were the ones who thought they could outrun the debt. They learned the hard way. It's not easy to run with a broken leg. Or a pair of concrete boots.

"Hey, Danny Boy McCoy," Lou called excitedly when Danny walked in. He'd grown to like Lou. Lou was a sports fan and a pretty likable guy, when he wasn't sending guys to the city morgue. He and Danny had the collection end of the business in common and they'd share stories about deadbeat hustlers and what they had to do to keep them in line. He also liked to chew on Danny's ear for a bit on boxers and fights that were being whispered about.

The whisper of a fight was one thing. A fight was a whole other kettle of fish altogether.

Boxers were a fickle bunch. There was no such thing as a *sure thing* in the fight world. A card might change five or six times on the run-up to a big fight. Then a fighter might just decide not to show on the night. Maybe he realizes he hasn't put in enough time training and he doesn't want to get his ass handed to him in front of a live audience. Maybe he got a cold, or a hangover, or a pulled muscle, or maybe he worked out all his pent-up rage in the sack with some broad the night before a fight and realized he didn't save enough juice for the ring. There were a million reasons a fight might not happen. The real miracle was that any of them happened at all.

Lou was excited because he had just heard that Danny was going to fight Carlos "The Thing" Cabrerra.

"You think you can take him?" Lou asked.

"I better. Ring's no place for a guy thinks he's gonna get beat."

"So I can put everything I have on you."

"You do what you're gonna do, Lou, and I'll do what I gotta do."

Danny wasn't going to bet on himself this time around. He was done betting. He was doing this one for Cockeye. He was partly responsible for destroying everything Cockeye had ever owned in The Ward, and he wanted to make some attempt to level the karmic scales on that front. He was also doing it for the kids in the neighborhood. Cockeye was right: this wasn't just his shot, it was theirs too, damn it.

"I need to see Hyman. He around?" Danny asked.

"Sure. Let me make sure he's free." Lou turned and nodded to the goon at the end of the bar to go check. The goon set his paper down and went on into the back.

Danny was already in debt up to his balls, but he needed more. Liam had called looking for him at The Wolf a few days earlier. When Danny called him back, Liam told him the owners were getting nervous that he wasn't making his payments on time. He'd managed to send an envelope up the first few months, but he just couldn't manage to get out from under the mountain of bills that kept accumulating. Sometimes it felt that he'd been cursed to poverty. Maybe money only happened to other people. He'd been banking on the purse from the Saint Patrick's Day fight to settle everything across the board but with Vinny gone and the Italians ready to string him up for refusing to take the dive, he'd never seen a penny of it. And now he was stuck with a house in Woodstock he didn't even know he wanted. Now that his mother was gone, what was the point! But Vinny's body was buried there. And as long as Vinny's body was there, he had to make damn sure he kept the place. He had to keep it or get Vinny's body out of there and let it go. He'd never even made the drive back out there to make sure Vinny's body got buried properly. For all he knew, Vinny's bones had been dragged off all over the mountains by an army of hungry wolves. He hoped that was the case. But he knew in his heart that Vinny Diamond was exactly where he had left him in a shallow grave behind the barn.

"Danny, my boy." Hyman smiled as Danny entered the office and took a seat across from him in the sparse office. "It's good to see you. How is your mother?"

"She passed a little while back."

"Oh no, I am sorry to hear that. How terrible to lose one's mother."

"And you? How are you feeling?"

"Me?" Hyman said, releasing a coarse unhealthy laugh. "They open me up, they clean the pipes, they stitch me back together again. I am like Frankenstein. Hyman Frankenstein."

They both smiled at this.

"How is our friend Mr. Coyle these days?"

Danny wasn't sure how to answer this query. Logan had so

many hustles going on at any one time these days it was best to play dumb.

"He's good. You know! Logan."

Goldstein nodded.

"He's stepping on some toes I hear."

This was slippery territory. The last thing Danny needed right now was Logan hearing he was up here talking to Hyman Goldstein about him behind his back.

"I've been doing business in the neighborhood for many years now with Mr. Mannion. You know . . . there's an order to things. I do some business with your Mr. Coyle, too, of course, but . . . well, there's an order, you understand!"

Danny nodded. He was here to borrow more money from Goldstein. He could have gone to Logan for it, but he didn't want Logan knowing exactly how much of a hole he was in financially. He was already indebted to Logan for way more than he wanted to be.

"You know the name Joe Fallaci?" Goldstein asked.

Danny nodded.

"So these people, they have an arrangement with Mr. Mannion on the West Side. They do their thing, he does his, I do mine, we all co-exist . . . you follow? We take care of business." And here Goldstein rubbed his hands together quickly like he was spinning a stick to light a fire. "Together . . . Irish. Italians. Jews. We all make a little something to survive. This is New York. This is how it is done, you understand."

Danny nodded.

"Next time you speak to your friend, maybe you tell him, that we all work together. I try to talk to him but I don't think he hears me. It's better we all get along . . . these people, Danny . . . they don't like nobody to upset their business. You follow?"

Danny was following. Goldstein was trying to let him know that if Logan didn't stop stepping on everybody's toes they'd put him in a new pair of shoes. Made of concrete.

But Danny understood something Goldstein didn't: Logan Coyle didn't give a flying fuck about Pat Mannion. Danny was tempted to tell Hyman the story about Mannion tying Logan's father to a chair and humiliating him, but he let it go. It wasn't his place. He was also tempted to tell Goldstein that Logan was sick of the Italians thinking they could come into Hell's Kitchen and swagger around like they owned the place. He blamed Mannion for that, too. He certainly wasn't going to tell Goldstein that by the time they broke ground on the new convention center over on Eleventh Avenue, Logan intended to be running the whole West Side by himself.

Danny kept his mouth shut. It was better that way. He just needed a loan. He just needed to keep his nose clean and pay his debts.

He'd been training again with Cockeye four or five times a week down at Tierney's Gym. Cockeye was trying to keep him on a tight regime. And for the most part Danny was sticking to it. But it had been a lot harder to stay out of The Wolf since his mother had died, and Trixie was gone. The apartment had grown cold. Ghosts lived there. Most nights he wound up falling asleep on the couch. He thought of how Tommy Ryan's place had looked on the day they'd nailed his hand to the table. The filthy kitchen, the half-eaten Chinese containers, clothes strewn everywhere, a smell of death in the air. He felt himself slipping in that direction and it scared him.

"Anyway . . ." Goldstein said, finally. "You didn't come to chat about my health, or Logan Coyle."

"I need to borrow a little more."

Goldstein opened his black notebook and quietly studied Danny's account.

"Mmm. I see you're already struggling quite a bit."

"I know, but I've been showing up, I been doing a pretty good job of making the vig."

Goldstein nodded. Danny knew that as long as he made the vig Goldstein would keep this going for a lifetime.

"I'm training for a big fight."

"I've been hearing about it. Madison Square Garden." Goldstein nodded. He looked pleased with himself. Danny could see he was not immune to the association of Danny's fame. "I'm looking forward to it."

"I'll get you a couple of decent seats."

"You don't need to do that?"

"It's no problem."

"I'm flattered. Thank you, Danny. You gonna beat this sucker?"

"I'm gonna beat him so bad his own mother ain't gonna know who he is."

Goldstein laughed.

"How much you need today?"

8

Danny was coming out of Goldstein's club when Murray O'Connell practically tripped over him on the sidewalk outside.

"Ah jees, sorry, pal," Murray muttered, and then turning, as if in shock. "Hey, you're Danny Boy McCoy."

Danny was taken aback. He had been expecting Murray to approach him at the gym. He'd even suspected Murray might casually slip onto a barstool next to him in The Wolf for the initial chat. Danny knew it was coming. But he'd never expected to see him here. Not outside Goldstein's place.

It unnerved him.

Had Murray been following him?

"How funny is that, huh! Me running into you all the way up here. Hey, isn't this—" Murray said, pointing to the sign over the door of the club. "Oh, jees . . . what's-his-name's place? Jewish guy! It's on the tip of my tongue. Mafia. Loan shark, guy?"

"Goldstein."

"Yeah, that's it, Hyman Goldstein, that's the guy. He's a big hitter, that guy. I didn't know you and Hyman was pals. Ain't that somethin'!"

It was something. And no doubt, Murray was thinking of making it even more of a something. Danny moved to walk on past him. He had a feeling this was press he could do without in the run-up to the biggest fight of his career.

"I guess I shouldn't be surprised, right! You up here visiting Hyman. He's down your neck of the woods all the time right, probably met him at that place you drink, what is it, The Wolf, or was it up at Mannion's place? Anyway. Nice to see you, Danny. How's that right arm feeling?"

Danny walked on. It didn't sound like Murray had any real concrete dirt to spin on him just yet. But the bloodhound was sniffing. That was for damned sure.

Danny shoved it aside. The mid-July heat made it nearly impossible to think straight.

He stopped at the post office to mail Liam the monthly payment for the house in Woodstock. Then he went on to his building and out onto the roof to spend time with his birds. He'd been spending a lot more time with the birds since his mother died. It was another way to avoid sitting in the apartment.

The birds were lethargic from the heat.

He jerry-rigged a small fan in the coop and stirred powdered glucose into their drinking water. Then he dragged out a hose and sprayed both them and himself.

The more he saw of people lately, the better he liked spending time with his birds.

9

"So get this, you're not gonna believe this shit," Blackie said excitedly, hopping into Danny's van, the Meat Wagon, outside of Danny's building. "Dillon just got whacked."

"Tommy?"

"Yeah, Mannion's guy. Tommy Dillon. He's just been fucken whacked!"

"When?"

"Couple hours ago. He was down at this funeral home on Lexington . . . one of his old pals, dead of cancer or some shit, and him and a couple of his old buddies step across the street to Donovan's for a drink. He's not in there five minutes, and this fucken guy gets up from the bar, real casual, guy's waving goodbye to the bartender like he knows him, and just as he's passing by Dillon when he pulls out a snubnosed thirty-eight, puts it to the side of his head and pulls the trigger. Boom. Splatters bits of Dillon's brain all over his buddys' faces. They can't fucken believe this shit, right, they're just talkin' to the guy, havin' a laugh, next thing, boom, they're pickin' his brains outta their teeth. Guy walks out the door cool as you please and gone, disappears, just like that."

"Tommy Dillon's dead?"

"Yeah, knucklehead, I just told you. Dillon's toast. Somebody fucken whacked Tommy Dillon."

Danny and Blackie were in the van on their way to do a pick up from Manny the Cuban's whorehouse over on Forty-fifth. Manny was one of the business owners in the neighborhood who'd settled on Logan Coyle for protection. Every business in the area was paying somebody or other for protection these days. For most of them it had been Mannion, but lately Logan had been expanding his own security business in The Kitchen.

The racket went something like this: Logan showed up with Terry, Mack, Blackie and Danny in tow, and offered to protect the business for a couple of hundred a month. The guy says "I don't need it," so they show up the next night and throw a brick through his window. That doesn't work, maybe the guy suffers an accident. A baseball bat falls on his ankle on his way home one night. Or a lead pipe drops on his head accidentally as he's opening his car door. Pretty soon the guy feels like maybe he needs some protection. Couple of hundred dollars in an envelope for Logan and he don't suffer no more mishaps.

Sooner or later everybody paid.

Or, they disappeared.

"How'd you hear this?" Danny asked, staring north on Tenth at Mannion's place.

Danny was having trouble processing the news. Dillon was a tough son of a bitch.

"Mack," said Blackie, lighting a smoke. "He heard it from Mannion this morning. He's pretty shook."

"Mack?"

"Yeah. I think this one really rattled the crazy bastard."

"They were friends?"

"Friends! Those two was thick as thieves. Mack and Dillon

come up together. They was Mannion's top guys for years before Mack started hanging around The Wolf with Coyle. Those guys go all the way back."

"Who did it?"

"Fuck should I know! Maybe he pissed off the wrong guy."

"Doesn't make you nervous?"

"Fuck I have to be nervous about?" Blackie said as they were pulling up in front of Manny's building.

Blackie produced a pistol from inside his jacket and checked the chamber. "You packing?"

Danny nodded.

He'd taken to carrying the gun with him at all times. He hoped he never had to pull it on anybody, but he decided he was safer with it than without it the way things were going lately.

"Anybody comes for me gonna get a taste of this." Blackie laughed, holding the gun up recklessly. "Bam bam bam."

Manny's whorehouse was on the second floor above a fabric shop. Manny owned the whole building. A drab three-story affair. Fabric store on the ground floor to give the place an air of legitimacy. Manny's whorehouse on the second floor, and Manny's apartment, or lair, as Blackie called it, up on the top floor.

Manny was an old-school pimp. He had a harem of loyal ladies who worked for him, and in return he took care of them. Protected them. Gave them a place to stay. They had their own apartment in the back on the first floor. Seven or eight of them. They got out of order, he smacked them around a little bit. They got caught stealing from him or too far into the junk, he threw them out on the street.

From what Danny'd heard, the ladies seemed to like the setup. But Danny didn't like Manny one little bit. Manny made his skin crawl. He wore shades all day long, even when he was inside, so you could never really get an honest read on the guy. When he did smile, he revealed a bright row of gold teeth on top.

He was seated at the small bar in the second-floor lounge, sipping on a Bloody Mary when they were buzzed in.

Three of his ladies were sitting around in lingerie, reading fashion magazines.

"Hey, it's my Irish *compañero*." Manny grinned, waving them to sit with him at the bar. "Pinkie, get the boys a drink."

Pinkie, a long-legged beauty with waist-length, peroxide-blonde hair, set her copy of *Vogue* on the glass-topped coffee table, and sashayed behind the bar.

"What can I get for you boys?"

"I know what I'd like?" Blackie grinned.

"This fucken guy. Always with his tongue out." Manny sneered. "Have a drink first, my friend. You can have that when you're done."

"Damn, Manny, I want your life," Blackie said.

"You don't want my life, you just want the pussy and the beer. Believe me, man, you don't want my hardships."

"What fucken hardships? You wanna see hardships! I'll swap you my life for a week."

Pinkie set two beers on the counter and went back to lounging.

"Jesus Christ, how do you do it?" Blackie said, watching her go.

"Pinkie," Manny said, "Take this fucking guy in the back, for chrissakes. Guy can't even think straight."

Pinkie stood and smiled politely as she nodded to Blackie to follow her down the corridor to one of the rooms.

"Goddamn you're the best," Blackie said, almost sprinting after her.

"What about you, Danny Boy? You want to take one of the girls for a little stroll?"

Danny shook his head.

"Not Danny." Manny grinned. "Never Danny."

"I'm training."

"Oh yeah, you got that big fight."

Danny nodded.

He had no desire for any chitchat with Manny. He wanted to get out of this place. Fast as possible.

"I guess I give this envelope to you," Manny said, reaching behind the counter and retrieving an envelope and sliding it across to Danny. Danny was just about to lift it when Manny stopped it, pinning it to the bar with the tip of his finger. "I hear your manager has disappeared?"

Danny gave the envelope a quick yank and shoved it in his pocket.

"Interesting guy, Vinny Diamond. I knew him a little bit."

"That's nice."

"Funny how he just disappeared."

Danny turned his back to the bar and leaned against it. He could feel the gun shoved in his belt press against the small of his back.

"Least they found the girl though, right!" Manny said, lifting his Bloody Mary, and sipping it through a straw. He seemed to be watching Danny for his reaction. But it was impossible to tell with the shades.

"Who?"

"The girl."

Danny shrugged, like he didn't know what Manny was talking about.

"Trixie."

Just hearing her name made his knees almost buckle. It had

been four months since she'd disappeared. The night before the Saint Patrick's Day fight.

"You knew her, right?"

"Not sure."

"Sure you did. Trixie. Vinny's girl."

"Was that her name?"

Manny seemed to have a smile playing at the corners of his mouth.

Danny had to be careful how he played this. Logan Coyle wasn't the only one making money out of this place. Manny was connected with the Italians same way Vinny was. If he said the wrong thing here he might never make it out of this club alive.

He felt a bead of sweat run down his back and hit the handle of the gun. What if this was a setup? This wasn't a pick up Danny was normally sent on. What if Blackie was already dead back there? In the room, with his throat cut. Or, what if Blackie was in on it? Danny shifted his right hand to his waist. He wondered if he would be quick enough to get the gun out of his pants and pull the trigger before Manny had a knife in his chest.

"Cute as a little button," Manny whispered under his breath.

"What?"

"Trixie. Such a sweet little piece of ass."

A door banged, startling Danny, he spun around to see Blackie emerge from the dark corridor, pulling up his zipper.

"Jesus Christ almighty, girl's got a mouth like a goddamn silk glove."

"Maybe you be able to relax and have your drink now." Manny grinned.

"If my fucken legs stop shakin'. My old lady smoked pipe like that I'd never leave the damned house."

"We gotta go," Danny said, before Blackie could settle in.

"Sure thing. After this beer."

"We gotta go now," Danny said, more forcefully.

"What's your big hurry?"

"Yeah, Danny, what's the rush?" asked Manny.

"I'm supposed to be at the gym twenty minutes ago."

"Relax, Irish. Have another drink." Manny sneered.

"I'm going," Danny said, and made for the door, half expecting a bullet between his shoulder blades.

"Guess we're going then." Blackie scowled.

"Hey, Danny," Manny called.

Danny turned.

"I'm just fucking wit you."

Danny looked confused.

"They didn't find her."

Danny stared coldly at Manny.

Manny winked.

Danny wanted to take the gun out and put one in Manny's face.

"They're searching though." Manny smiled, a sick, sadistic smile breaking on his face. "And when they do . . ." Manny opened his mouth and flicked his tongue back and forth.

Danny turned and went on down the stairs.

"Don't let that fucker get to you," Blackie said as they reached the street. "He just likes to get your goat up, is all. Fuck him."

But it was more than that. Manny had wanted to see what Danny's reaction would be. He was sure of it. Manny was fishing.

He had to find Trixie before they did.

10

For the next month Danny kept his head down and trained hard. When he wasn't in the gym he spent most of his time with Blackie. Logan kept them busy chasing envelopes around the neighborhood. Most of the deadbeats they confronted were keen to make some sort of payment right away. Word was getting around that you didn't keep Logan Coyle waiting. They'd even started making weekly pickups at a couple of theatres along Forty-sixth street. Broadway was Mannion's turf, but Logan had somehow managed to muscle his way in and get a few local girls on staff. The girls got a cushy job and were more than happy to kick up to Logan every week. Everybody was happy.

Then there was the Theatrical Local 817. These guys were responsible for delivering props and equipment to practically every film set in Manhattan. It was unchartered territory. Logan and Terry had managed to muscle their way in there, too.

It was easy pickings.

Everybody needed protection.

And yet, even with all the running around, it was still a struggle to survive. It wasn't just Blackie and Danny. Terry, Mack, and McElroy were all struggling to make ends meet. Mack was work-

353

ing back to back bartending shifts between The Wolf and The Sunbrite. Terry was selling nickel bags of weed up in Hell's Kitchen Park just so he could take his new girlfriend out to dinner. By the time Danny and Blackie kicked up to Logan they had barely enough left over to stay afloat.

Meanwhile, Logan was driving a new Cadillac, and was having a new house built over in Fort Lee, New Jersey.

Still. No one complained to Logan. He'd just point to the beer sitting in front of them at the bar and say, "Maybe if you stopped drinking so much of this shit you could afford a new pair of shoes."

And he was right, to a certain extent. Logan had always been smarter about how he managed his money than the rest of the crew.

So, Blackie came up with a few scams of his own to keep them afloat.

"You know how much I pay for a pack of these fucken things?" Blackie said, holding up a cigarette as they rolled uptown in Danny's van on their way back from Tierney's Gym.

Danny shook his head.

"Sixty fucken cents. You know how much they're selling them for in North Carolina?"

Danny still hadn't a clue.

Blackie stared at Danny, as if he were waiting for Danny to do the math. But Danny wasn't doing any math. He wasn't really listening. He was lost thinking about Trixie.

Hearing Manny the Cuban say, "They found her," had thrown him into a spin.

No matter how hard he trained, how fast he ran, or how much he drank, he hadn't been able to shake Trixie from his head.

He'd even thought of going to Detective Quinn for help. But he knew that would be suicide. If Logan found out he'd gone to a cop for help finding Trixie he'd be in the bottom of the East River in about six different pieces.

There was another possibility, of course. One he didn't want to believe was possible. Maybe Trixie didn't want to be found. It was possible she didn't want to see him. Didn't love him. It was possible she figured out he was the one who got rid of Vinny Diamond and hated him for it.

He hoped that was the case. Prayed that was case. He could handle her hate.

What he couldn't handle was what she might be enduring at the hands of the Columbians or the Italians if they thought she had something to do with Vinny's disappearance. A girl like Trixie was dispensable to these animals. Who was gonna come looking for her?

"Twenty-nine cents."

"What's twenty-nine cents?"

"The cigarettes, you fucken knucklehead. A packet of cigarettes costs twenty-nine cents in North Carolina. Are you listening to me?"

"I'm listening."

"So!"

"So what?"

"So, we take a drive down to North Carolina, we fill the back of this fucken wagon of yours with cartons of cigarettes and we come back and sell 'em to every bar, every smoke shop, every old granny in the neighborhood. Man, we could make a killing."

"What about my birds?"

"What about your birds? You wanna take 'em with us?"

"I can't be away. I gotta feed them."

"We'll leave 'em a couple of cheeseburgers. Can you get your head out of your ass! We split the driving. We get down there in time for breakfast. We hit a handful of liquor stores, grab as many smokes as we can in a couple of hours, then we grab a couple of coffees for the road, and boom, we come straight back. Trust me, you'll be back in time to read 'em a fucken bedtime story and tuck 'em into their beds."

Like most things involving Blackie, Danny went willingly along. Blackie was a born hustler. He had a way of making a fast buck and he didn't mind putting in the hours to get it. He wasn't like the others. Violence was not his thing. Blackie treated the hustle like it was a legitimate gig. He got up every day and he went to work. Most of the other guys Danny knew spent most of their time hanging around The Wolf getting stoned. They bet the horses, rolled the occasional drunk tourist over on the Deuce, sold pills or a little weed, to get by. Lately a few of them had even stumbled into moving some H. Up until a few years ago heroin was something you only heard about north of a Hundred and tenth. But lately H was everywhere. Rumor was they were bringing it back from 'Nam in the coffins of dead soldiers. Danny'd been shocked when he'd visited Goldstein up at his club, to see junkies sprawled all over Sherman Square, on Broadway, just north of Seventy-second Street. "Needle Park," Lou at the club called it. Smack was no longer a Harlem thing. Smack was on the Upper West Side.

"When?" Danny asked.

"Let's go now."

"You want to leave right now?"

"No, I was thinking maybe we might pack a little picnic basket and some suntan oil, go up 'n' sunbathe in the park for a few hours? Yeah, Danny, now."

"I . . ."

"Fucken guy. Go feed your birds. I'll grab us a couple of heroes for the road. Whaddyou want? Chicken parm? I'll get two chicken parm, and a coupla cokes," Blackie said, as he jumped out of the van, closing the door behind him without waiting for a reply.

Danny smiled. Maybe he liked Blackie so much because he was a distraction. Just being around him was an adventure. The more time he spent hanging around with Blackie the less time he spent obsessing over Trixie. He cared too much.

Maybe he needed to be more like Blackie, and less like Danny Boy McCoy.

11

"Holy sweet fuck! What's this shit? Pull in here," Blackie yelled, as they pulled up in front of the Sunbrite Saloon on Tenth Avenue.

It had taken them a little over thirty hours to make the trip to North Carolina and back. Danny had hoped to park the van and go straight home to feed the birds. He was in need of a long shower, and a good night's sleep.

But all that was going to have to wait for a little bit longer it seemed.

There were emergency trucks all over Tenth Avenue. Flashing lights. A small army of cops. And a horde of spectators huddled on the corner of the block.

"We can't park here," Danny said, nodding to the cops. "The cigarettes."

"What the fuck they care what we got in the van," Blackie snapped. "Pull in here."

Danny pulled the van over in a spot in front of the Skyline Motor Inn.

"There's Terry," Blackie said, rolling down the window and yelling to him. "Hey, Terry."

Terry Flannery lurched across the avenue, puffing on a smoke.

358

Blackie opened the passenger door to let him squeeze in beside him on the front seat.

"What the fuck!"

"They got Mack."

"Who got Mack?"

"I dunno, man, but they sprayed his brains all over the bar an hour ago."

"What the fuck!"

"He's dead, man."

"No."

"Mack's dead?"

"You see it?"

"I showed up two minutes after it happened. Oh, man . . . this is bad."

"It was a hit?"

"First Dillon, now Mack, the fuck do you think?"

"I think we better go see Logan."

"What's all this shit?" Terry asked, peering into the back of the van as Danny navigated the van out of the parking spot.

"We took a trip south?"

"South of what?"

"North Carolina. Two fifty a carton."

"Get the fuck! I'll take a couple."

"See. Wha'd I tell ya, Danny. Makin' money off of 'em already," Blackie said, reaching back to grab a couple of cartons and handing them to Terry.

"Okay, if I pay you later," said, Terry.

"Jesus fucken Christ! You hear this shit! Not back in the fucken Kitchen two seconds 'til we're getting ripped off again."

*   *   *

There were two detectives in The Wolf, chatting to Logan, by the time Danny, Blackie and Flannery strolled in ten minutes later.

"Like I told you," Logan was saying. "He works for me, from time to time, behind the bar here. But I barely knew the guy."

"Really!" the larger of the two cops droned. They looked like a pair of narrow-backs. Second generation Paddys. Pair of them sporting big fat mustaches, just in case anyone might mistake them for a couple of Catholic schoolgirls.

"I thought you and him were real tight," the smaller one squeaked.

"Listen, I know the guy's name. I see him in here sometimes when he works the bar, but we ain't tight. Maybe we ate breakfast together once or twice."

"Ate breakfast together." The cop laughed.

"Yeah, I think he had ... What the fuck did he have ... it was a while ago. Oh yeah ... pancakes. Blueberry pancakes. That's it. You might wanna write that down."

Flannery, Blackie, and Danny took three empty stools, and without having to be asked, McElroy set them up a few beers. Practically the whole crew was seated at the bar. Everybody obviously had the same idea they had: get to The Wolf, see what Logan had to say, and tie one on. Mack getting whacked was exciting stuff.

"Pancakes!" The detective nodded. "That's all you got?"

"No ... I remember now, he had a side of bacon also ... and eggs. Two."

"You rather we drag you down to the station to continue this chat?"

"Listen, he worked as a bartender for Mannion more than he did here. Why the fuck you not up there asking him these questions?"

" 'Cause we're here asking you."

"Maybe I need to go ask Mannion who he's paying to keep all you guys away from his door."

"Don't push it, Coyle."

The detectives were talking loud enough for everyone in the bar to hear. They knew they weren't going to get anything out of Logan. Or anybody else in The Wolf. Or in The Kitchen for that matter. They just wanted it on everybody's radar that they were ticking the boxes. That they were making the rounds. Acting like cops are supposed to act. These guys didn't give a flying fuck Mack got whacked. Probably figured he got what was coming to him.

"So I don't suppose you know nuthin' about any murders he might have committed?"

"Murders?" Logan responded with an exaggerated look of shock. "Mack wouldn't hurt a fly. Guy was a teddy bear."

The large cop turned to eyeball everyone at the bar.

"Regular bunch of choir boys we got in here."

Walter Hughes let out a laugh.

The big cop walked down to stand next to his stool. Hughes stared up at him with a big shit-eating grin.

The cop slapped the bottle out of Hughes' hand, sending it smashing against the far wall.

"Ah, jeez," he said. "Looks like you spilled your drink, Hughes."

Hughes kept his mouth shut after that.

Danny kept his head down. As did the rest of the crew. This guy was two seconds away from knocking Hughes off his stool and booking the whole bar for resisting arrest.

Danny didn't want to spend the night in the Tombs. He was tired. He wanted to get home to feed his birds.

After a tense moment the cop managed to restrain himself. He patted Hughes on the shoulder and smiled. "Well, it's been real nice seeing everybody. I'm sure we'll be seeing all you maggots again real soon. Enjoy the rest of your day, fellas."

Once the door closed, Logan screamed at Hughes. "Fuck's the matta wit you? Next time you see a cop in my bar you keep your fucken mouth shut and let me do that talking."

"Sorry, Logan."

Petey Ryan, who was drunk, on the stool next to Hughes, smacked him on the back of the head. "Yeah, shut the fuck up, Walt." Hughes spun around, and punched him in the face. The two men tore into one another. Stools clattered to the floor. A bottle smashed. Logan jumped between them. He grabbed Ryan by the shirt and slapped him hard. Then he dragged him toward the door and shoved him out on the street, kicking him as he went.

"Get the fuck out."

Then, turning to the remaining crew, yelled, "Jesus fucking Christ. This is what I gotta deal with. You guys don't think we got enough shit to deal with right now? This place is crawling with cops. Mack's brains are all over the Sunbrite Bar. And you lot behaving like a bunch of goddamn retards."

"Sorry, Logan," Hughes said, sheepishly.

"I should throw you out, too. Next man causes trouble in here today I'll fucking bury him. You understand."

Everybody understood.

"Terry, Danny, Blackie, come with me."

The three men obediently followed Logan to a booth in the back of the bar. The rest of the men went back to talking among themselves.

"What have you guys heard?" Logan asked.

"I was just up there," said Terry. "I just missed it go down."

"You get a look at the guy?"

"Naw, he was gone when I walked in."

"This was before the cops got there?"

"Yeah, I went up to see Mack, and I walk in and there's a bunch of screaming. Some chick had blood on her face. Mack's on the floor . . ." Terry shook his head blankly.

"What?"

"His brains were out the side of his head."

"Did anybody see it happen?"

"Yeah, everybody was in the bar. They said this guy walked in the door, walked over to Mack and just real casual put a gun to his ear and pulled the trigger."

"So he knew who Mack was?"

"Sounded just like what happened to Dillon."

Logan sat still as a rock for a moment.

"Somebody's sending Mannion a big message? Or me?"

"Who knows, maybe they ain't connected," added Blackie. "Fucken Mack's crazy. Who knows who he pissed off. How many married broads he bangin'?"

"Naw, that ain't it," said Logan. "Somebody's making a play."

"The Italians?"

"Maybe. Everybody's gotta stay on their toes. If this is a play, it could be me next."

"Or Mannion?" Terry offered.

"Yeah, or any of us," added Blackie.

"I don't want any part of this anymore," Danny said.

"Part of what?" Logan scowled.

"It's not right."

"What's not right?

"Every week it's somebody else. I mean . . . what the fuck . . . this is nuts. Aren't you guys afraid that maybe we're bringing all this on ourselves?"

"On ourselves?" Logan frowned.

363

"Yeah. You know . . . God?"

"God?" snarled Logan.

"Yeah. God."

"Listen, Danny, this ain't no time for your Catholic-school bullshit here . . . praying ain't gonna put Mack's brains back in his skull right now. And it ain't gonna stop whatever maniac is out there coming for me next—or you. Right now we gotta be smart. Okay. We gotta stay tight. Anybody hears anything—I mean any-fucking-thing—you come right here and you tell me. You got it! I'm at home in New Jersey . . . you call me. Okay?"

Each of the men nodded.

"We gonna hit the mattresses?" asked Blackie.

"What mattresses?" Logan frowned.

"Like in the movies, you know . . . we get the mattresses out and lay 'em on the floor."

"This is not a fucken movie, Blackie. You understand! This is real life. What the fuck is this shit? Prayers! Mattresses! Our fucken pal's up the street with his brains all over the floor. Can you guys get your heads out of your ass for five seconds?"

"Sorry, Logan," Blackie said, somberly. "Let's drink a toast to Mack."

All four men lifted their glasses.

"To Mack," Logan said. "May God have mercy on his soul."

They tapped their glasses.

"To Mack," Blackie added, and then shaking his head, "Cheap bastard, owed me twenty bucks."

"Well I guess he managed to duck that one," said Terry.

12

Any doubts they had about a hitman stalking the neighborhood were dispelled when they got word that The Greek, Pat Mannion's top enforcer, was gunned down leaving his building on Thirty-third Street.

According to the report Logan picked up from a local cop, the hitman came strolling down the block, walking a small dog. The Greek was out front of his building waiting for his driver, as he did every morning at the same time. Guy walks up wearing a pair of dark sweatpants and a hoodie and pops him in broad daylight.

Danny understood that logically he should be afraid. But he felt nothing upon hearing this latest news. The murders felt a step removed from him somehow. Like he was not a part of it. Like it was happening in a parallel universe. It didn't seem real. Dillon, Mack, and The Greek, all whacked in broad daylight by some crazed hitman. It couldn't be real.

He spent a lot of time questioning this lack of emotional distress. For the longest time he had been suffering from dizzy spells. Blackouts. And then suddenly the attacks had just stopped. He wondered if some core emotional connection to the world had gotten mangled by all this horror he'd witnessed of late. He'd expected to feel deep anguish over the death of Vinny Diamond. But it never came. He'd murdered a man with his bare hands. And yet, he felt no guilt. It felt justified. If there was a God, surely he would understand that Vinny Diamond was a bad motherfucker, and that he deserved to die.

Not that he was completely immune from anguish. He thought of Cheddar and Knuckles plenty. He missed them both. Their deaths haunted him. Sure they were fuckups. But they were his childhood friends. In a way they had been like the brothers he never had. They were that close. He couldn't help thinking about all the things that had been cut short for them. All the possibilities. The adventures they had pictured together as kids. They'd never even managed to take that flight together that they'd talked about so often. That would have been something. He wondered about that now. Why the three of them hadn't just gone away together on vacation. It's not like they didn't talk about it. Down to Florida. Or even down the Jersey Shore together for a few weeks in the summer, for chrissakes. They'd talked about it plenty. Promised they would. Next year. It was always, next year. It broke his heart to think that his old pals had left the world without so much as building a goddamned sandcastle. This wasn't how it was supposed to be.

He missed his mother too. But it wasn't heartache he felt with her. That was more like an emptiness in his life now. A vacuum. A space that had been occupied by her that he knew would never quite fill again. It wasn't so much a ghost she left behind, as it was a void. At least he'd been there with her when she passed. He hadn't managed to get her out of The Kitchen. But at least she'd lived long enough to see him try.

The one that really haunted him, though, was Trixie. He hadn't been able to save Cheddar, Knuckles, Tommy Ryan, or his mother, but maybe there was still some slim possibility that he could save Trixie. Maybe, if he could find her, there was still a chance he could get her out to the house in Woodstock. Trixie, and her kid. That's if the Italians or the Columbians hadn't already ended that dream.

Danny was out for his morning run when Detective Quinn casually brushed by him outside Saint Patrick's Cathedral. Danny might have continued on had Quinn not said his name.

"Sorry, Danny."

He turned to see Quinn already climbing the steps toward the towering bronze doors.

Danny reflexively glanced all around. A few office workers made their way toward Rockefeller Center. There wasn't a familiar face in sight. He was tempted to keep running. It wasn't like Quinn had asked him to follow him inside. But Quinn was the only one who might know where she might be.

Danny found him in a pew off to the left about halfway down the church. He genuflected. Blessed himself and slid onto the bench next to him.

Quinn had his head tipped back, staring up at the vaulted ceiling of the cathedral.

"Really somethin', isn't it."

Danny tipped his head back and looked up too.

"Most people think it's marble," Quinn said, lifting a finger to point upward. "But it's not. Not the ceiling. Was supposed to be, but money got tight during the Civil War and they had to make do with plaster. You believe that? Plastered it and painted it to look like marble. Blows my mind. You can't tell the difference. Look at that craftsmanship. This was our people built this place, you know. Our ancestors. Yours and mine." Quinn nudged him with his elbow. "You know that?"

Danny didn't respond. But he was curious.

"Ever hear of the Potato Famine? Course you did. Back in the old days, you see, the original Saint Patrick's Church was way down on Mulberry Street . . . You know it?"

Danny didn't respond. He knew it.

"Great church, served the community for many many years. New York City was smaller back then, not much more than a village really. You know. That's why they call it The Village down there. And then, the Irish famine happened . . . and half the population of the country landed over here, over the space of just a few years, about a million of them, landed right here. Imagine that! Small little village . . . a million Irish people just rolled into town. And they were hungry . . . and they were scared . . . you gotta realize, most of these people hadn't planned on getting on a boat and risking life and limb to cross the Atlantic Ocean back then . . . but these people were running for their lives . . . it was that or die of starvation . . . so they came . . . in droves . . . and most of them were still very religious you see . . . and this little church, Saint Patrick's Church down on Mulberry Street, well it just wasn't cutting it no more, as you can imagine . . . just wasn't big enough . . . all these Catholics . . . and these people needed somewhere they could go to Mass on a Sunday . . . somewheres they could ask God to help them find some work and food. So the archbishop at the time, guy called Hughes, he said, 'Let's build the biggest cathedral in the country.' People thought he was mad, 'Hughes' Folly' they called it. This was farm country up here you understand. And they came up here and they built this thing. You ever think about that? How the heck did they do this? Come up here and build this thing in the middle of a damn field. Bunch of uneducated, half-starved immigrants. With their bare hands."

Danny scanned the majestic vaulted ceiling, the great marble columns, the enormous stained glass windows. The perfection of it all. The detail. The scale. He couldn't even begin to imagine how this might have been built by hand, over a hundred years ago. Its very existence seemed to suggest the possibility of the impossible. Of miracles. Of the divine. His life felt small and pointless in comparison to all this grandeur, all this honest blood, sweat and tears.

"I wonder what our ancestors would have thought of you Irish boys over here in Hell's Kitchen today, huh," Quinn said, dropping his head and sighing deeply. "You heard about The Greek, I'm sure."

Danny glanced nervously over his shoulder to see who else was in the church. Only a smattering of people on their knees. No one he recognized. No one who seemed to be looking their way. He didn't want to be caught talking to Quinn. Who knew what old grandmother from The Kitchen might be in here this very minute fingering her rosary beads, sneaking furtive glances in their direction.

"If I had to take a guess," Quinn went on. "I'd say it's the Italians, Fallaci's crew, making a play for Mannion's territory. You thought about what that might mean for Coyle? Or for you?"

Danny kept his mouth shut and let him go on. He'd spotted a black crow high in the cathedral. He wondered if it was finding enough food and water to survive in here. There were the holy water fonts of course. It would find those. Food might be harder to come by. Lots of tourists. But who eats food in a church? The bird's hunger bothered him.

"Whatever psycho they have on this is good. Make no mistake, Danny Boy, this is a professional hitman we got on our hands. He's methodical. Clean. He's in, he's out, not so much as a fingerprint. That's Dillon, Mack, and The Greek. And from what I'm hearing, those guys were heavy hitters in their own right. It's not like they weren't on the lookout for a guy like that showing up. I mean, The Greek was sixty-two years old. This was a guy who survived that life for half a century. Old school. Hard as nails. Sharp as a jailhouse cat. And this guy got him right outside his own building. Boom. Coroner told me he hit him with a hollow point. Ever see what one of those can do to a man? I mean, what chance does that leave the rest of you clowns? How do you fancy your odds against a guy like that?"

"I'm looking for Trixie," Danny said.

"What do you mean you're looking for her? Is she missing?"

He was surprised to hear Quinn didn't know anything about her disappearance. Surprised and disappointed. He knew he was getting into tricky territory here asking a cop for help. But Quinn was good at tracking stuff down. He'd found out Trixie's real name. That she had a kid. He knew exactly where Danny would be this morning on his run. Maybe if he put Trixie on his radar he'd be able to track her down, too.

"How long's she been gone?"

"Around Saint Patrick's Day."

"About the same time Vinny Diamond disappeared?"

Danny nodded.

"Those two things connected?"

Danny shook his head.

"And you don't know nothing about where Vinny went right?"

Danny shook his head again.

"You sure about that?"

Danny made to leave, but Quinn caught his arm. He sat again.

"I'll tell you what: I'll dig around, see if I can find out where the girl's at, but you gotta start giving me something here, Danny."

There it was. The slippery slope.

"Find Trixie for me."

"I'll look. That's the best I can do." Quinn reached into his pocket and produced a card. He handed it to Danny. "Take this. You hear anything. About her. Anything. You let me know."

Danny took the card and stood to leave.

"Do you have any food in your pockets?"

"You hungry? I got some peanuts," Quinn said, pulling a creased brown paper bag from the pocket of his jacket.

"Can I have them?"

"Sure. Take the bag."

Danny took the bag and dumped them onto the bench.

"What are you doing!"

"For him," Danny said, nodding up at the crow perched high on an outcrop of one of the great marble pillars.

Danny genuflected in the aisle. Blessed himself. And walked back toward the bronze doors, feeling the chill of his sweat-drenched shirt, and Quinn's eyes, on his back.

13

Mannion came to see him on his roof. Alone.

Danny was shocked to see him. He looked out of place up here. He looked smaller somehow. Human-sized.

"Hey, Danny," Mannion said, offering his hand.

"Pat."

"I tried your apartment. Your neighbor told me I'd find you up here. These yours?" he said, gesturing toward the coop.

Danny nodded.

"How many?"

"Hundred and sixty-four."

"A hundred and sixty-four pigeons?"

"I lost a few recently. They flew off. I think they're upset with me. I ain't been spending as much time with them as I used to."

"How long you been doing it?"

"Forever."

"You like it that much, huh!"

Danny was surprised to hear Mannion ask about his birds. Under normal circumstances he would have been wary. He'd have been looking for the play. The angle. But there was something about Mannion. About his tone, that felt . . . broken. He could see it in the way the birds reacted to him. Like they sensed it in him, too. A vulnerability he'd never seen in Pat Mannion before. Like the guy's shell had been peeled away.

"Yeah. I like coming up here," Danny said. "It's peaceful. You know!"

"Maybe I'll get myself some pigeons once we get settled in out there."

"Out where?"

Mannion turned to Danny. "I'm getting out, Danny."

"Out of the neighborhood?" Danny couldn't believe what he was hearing. This was Pat Mannion's neighborhood. Mannion was the king of the West Side since as far back as Danny could remember. Hell's Kitchen was Pat Mannion's kingdom.

"I don't want this anymore," Mannion said, somberly. "I got three young kids, Danny. I figure I get Elaine and the kids out of here. I don't know, maybe I'll get a job somewhere."

"You're selling the Tavern?"

"I want you to tell Coyle. I'm letting it all go. Will you do that?" Danny nodded.

"I don't care. I don't want any of it anymore. Tell Coyle he can have it. I don't want no more trouble. I'm forty-three, Danny. I just wanna go live my life in peace, you know. Just go be a dad. Live long enough to see them grow up."

Mannion looked shaken. It was the first time Danny noticed gray in his hair. His skin looked ashen. There was fear in his eyes.

"I'll tell him," Danny said.

"I just feel like I'm being stalked. You know! I can't walk out my door without looking over my shoulder. I mean . . . Dillon, The Greek, Mack . . . those guys, you know, we worked together, but they were my friends, too. You know! I knew those guys. This shit isn't worth people getting killed. This isn't how this was supposed to be. Sure it was always a tough business. But not like this. There's no sense to it anymore. No . . . logic. I don't want whatever this is now. I don't want no part of it."

"I'm getting out too," Danny said, surprised to hear himself offering anything personal to Mannion. He hadn't even told his own crew about the house in Woodstock.

"Good for you, Danny," Mannion said, putting a hand on Danny's shoulder. He seemed genuinely pleased. Moved, even.

"I just gotta do this one last fight, and then I'll have enough to get out."

"I been reading about that fight. That's gonna be a big deal. Good for you, Danny. I'll be there cheering you on, you can be sure of that. Maybe I'll bring the boys."

"I could see about getting you tickets."

"Naw. You don't need to do that. Where are you going?"

"I got a little place out in Woodstock."

"Wow. Good for you. I heard it's real nice out there in the mountains?"

"Yeah. It's real peaceful."

"Maybe I'll come out and see you when you get settled. Bring the boys up. Teach 'em how to ski."

"You need a place to stay, I got room."

Mannion smiled. Danny was pretty sure they'd never see each other again. But they were offering something of themselves here. Comfort? Support?

Decency.

"You bringing the birds?"

"I'm gonna try. Where are you guys going?"

"We got a little apartment out in Queens. It's not much. But it's enough. A place to make a fresh start. There's a good public school around the corner, we got the kids signed up in there. It seems like a real nice neighborhood. You know. Like what this place used to be. Somewhere the kids will be safe. And Elaine . . . and me. You'll tell Logan, right! I'm out. I know he'll believe it if it comes from you."

"I'll tell him."

"You're a good kid, Danny."

Mannion offered his hand again. Danny took it.

"You take good care of yourself," Mannion said. "I'll see you at the fight."

"I'll see you there."

"Can you believe we're actually getting out of The Kitchen?"

"Not yet, I don't," Danny said.

"Yeah, me either," Mannion said, turning to leave.

14

Blackie tapped Vinny Diamond's body with the tip of his shovel.

"Bro, you sure you didn't leave some of them drugs wrapped up in there wit him?"

"I told you. I threw them over the bridge," Danny said.

"You couldn't keep one little fucken kilo!"

"I don't want nuthin' to do with drugs."

"You know how much that shit is worth?"

"You see what it's done to the neighborhood."

"Can't believe you whacked Vinny Diamond."

"I didn't whack him."

"He looks pretty whacked to me, bro."

Danny had done the thing he told himself he would never do. He told another human about killing Vinny Diamond. Truth is, he couldn't even remember doing it. He'd been drunk. It was late. He was in The Wolf. He'd just spent the previous afternoon listening to Logan rave on about the recent murders, about Mannion leaving the neighborhood. Logan didn't believe for a second Mannion was really walking away from it all. He was convinced it was a play.

It was like he didn't want to believe it. Like Mannion had been his adversary for so long he wasn't going to be able to exist without him right there, up the block, to rage against.

Danny listened. And he drank.

He must have blacked out at some point. When he came to, he was stretched out in the back of the van and Blackie was driving. The sun was coming up and they were way up the thruway near the Kingston exit.

Apparently he'd gotten so drunk, he told Blackie about killing Vinny Diamond, and about how he'd buried him in a shallow grave behind the barn, and Blackie had insisted they got right away and bury him properly.

That was Blackie. If something had to be done, he didn't fuck around, he was gonna go and get it done.

It was a relief to have Blackie in on it. "A problem shared is a problem halved," Danny's ma used to say.

Blackie hunched over and grabbed Vinny by the legs. Vinny was still wrapped in the black plastic bags he'd been buried in, but the smell, now that they were moving him, was overpowering. Danny reached to grab Vinny under the shoulders and felt the flesh give like the skin of a rotting pumpkin. He heaved, and turned to puke.

Blackie laughed. "Can you stop fucking around?"

They lifted the body out of the hole, and set it aside. Then they dug the hole six feet deep, and Blackie shoved Vinny back in again.

"Wanna say a prayer?" Blackie asked, after they'd packed the dirt back in again and covered it with dead leaves and some branches.

"You serious?" Danny asked.

"Sure. Go ahead. Couldn't hurt. Maybe the big guy up there hears you, he'll knock a few years off your bid, know what I mean!"

"God bless, Vinny. Sorry I had to kill you."

"There you go. It's done. You leave this shit behind you. Sick fuck deserved everything he got." Blackie spat on the grave. Kicked some of the leaves. "Fuck you, you piece of shit scumbag. Have a nice dirt nap, motherfucker. Come on, I'm goin' for a swim."

"Now?"

"Yeah now. I wanna wash this stinky fuck off me, then I wanna see inside this fucken house of yours, and then I wanna go into town and get some eggs and bacon. I'm fucken starvin', bro."

Danny watched Blackie stride down the garden toward the river, casting off his clothes as he went. The sun was well up and it was hot already. One of the first hot days of the year.

Blackie was buck naked by the time he reached the water's edge. He went right in, squealing like a kid.

"Holy fuck that's cold. I think my balls just disappeared. Danny, you gotta get in here."

Danny sat on a rock as Blackie splashed around in the river. The grass, trees and bushes had bloomed since he was here last. Wild daffodils and lilacs threw splashes of color all over the lawn. He wished his mother had lived long enough to see the place in all its glory. Witnessing it now, like this, renewed his desire to fight for this place. He had to keep making the payments. It was still possible to get out of The Kitchen. Still possible he could find Trixie and convince her to come with him to start a new life.

He had to believe there was still hope. Without hope, he had nothing.

"Hey, Danny, look!" Blackie whispered, pointing off into the trees. There, in a clearing not fifty feet away, stood a family of deer, grazing. There were five of them. Two adults and three others that were much smaller. The shortest was no taller than knee-high. Its coat a bright coppery brown marked with a smattering of white dots, still unsteady on its twig legs.

"This place is fucken paradise, bro," Blackie said shaking his head.

It was, Danny thought . . . or would be, if it weren't for the body they'd just buried in back of the barn at the top of the garden.

They were sitting in a cafe on the village square an hour later polishing off a hearty breakfast of eggs, bacon and sausage.

"I could get used to this," Blackie said, shoving the last piece of toast in his face.

"You'll always have a place to stay long as I'm able to hold onto the house," Danny said.

"Maybe I'll bring Bridie and the kids out 'fore the end of the summer."

"Do it."

"You'd be alright with that?"

"Bring them up."

"Oh man, the kids would love it . . . swimming in that river every day! Little bit of nature. All the birds, and the deer 'n' shit. You mean it?"

"Yeah. Come up. Stay. Long as you like."

"Aw, thanks, Danny. I'm gonna take you up on that. This is awesome. You got a dime on you? I gotta call the club, make sure Bridie's not over there right now lookin' for me." Danny fished some change out of his pocket. "Don't worry, I ain't gonna tell nobody 'bout your little place out here. Longer you keep this place a secret the better. Fuck those other guys."

Danny watched Blackie go to the phone in the back by the

bathrooms. There were a handful of locals sitting around casually shooting the breeze over their coffee and eggs. A Bob Dylan
song was playing on the radio. Outside on the square, a lad with
dreadlocks was sitting on an orange blanket, strumming an acous-
tic guitar. A girl in a long flowing tie-dye dress and a large flop-
py hat sailed by the picture window. She caught Danny's eye and
smiled a wide dreamy smile. He smiled back. He wished he hadn't
killed Vinny Diamond. There was something of himself buried
back there by the barn. He had a sudden urge to race back to the
barn and rip away the dirt. Drag Vinny's rotting corpse into the
village square for all to see. Say, "Look. I did this." Just get it out
in the open and deal with it.

He turned to see Blackie come back to the table again. Blackie
looked stunned.

"Oh man," he said as he took his seat.

"What?"

"Fucken Hughes is dead."

"Walter? How?"

"I'm not sure. He got into some sort of a row with some guy
outside the bar. Far as I can tell he pulled a gun on him."

"Who did?"

"Hughes pulled a gun on the guy. And that fucken cop was
there—"

"What cop?"

"Remember that hard-on who smashed the bottle out of his
hand the day Mack got whacked. Somehow this cop was there . . .
he got involved . . . I don't know if he was walking by . . . or what . . .
but he winds up popping Hughes in the chest. Fucken killed him.
Walt's fucken dead, man! You believe that shit! Walter Hughes.
Ain't that a bitch?"

"It just never stops," Danny said blankly, staring off out the window.

"It's fucken crazy." Blackie chuckled. "Logan is pissed, I can tell you that. Flannery's ready to go after this cop, says it's the cop's fault."

"You ever think we're all at fault?"

"How the fuck's it my fault?" snapped Blackie. "I'm up here wit you, communin' with nature 'n' shit."

"I mean . . . like it's all connected. You know! All of it."

The waitress, a pretty girl in a crop top and a pair of faded denim shorts that hung lopsided on her angular pelvis, came to lift their plates.

"Get anything else for you two?"

"Yeah, your phone number." Blackie smiled. She smiled back. "I ain't kiddin' . . . hear me out . . . how about I take you out for a nice dinner . . . you and me . . . somewhere nice . . . maybe a little wine, a little dessert . . . whatever you want . . . then maybe I take you out in the woods, we go look at some rabbits 'n' shit."

She laughed. She had a bright wholesome smile.

"Rabbits?" she said.

"Yeah, like the little bunny rabbits. My pal here, just bought a little house over here, it's got the river, and the trees, and the animals . . ."

"Animals?" She was grinning ear to ear. It was impossible not to grin at Blackie.

"Yeah, he's got everything over there, you wouldn't believe it . . . he's got the deer, he's got the birds . . ." Blackie was counting off the animals on his fingers. "He's got the rabbits."

The waitress was loving it. Danny guessed she didn't get too many like Blackie rolling through here. "What else you got over there, Danny?"

"Mice."

"He's got the mice . . ."

"Mice!" She laughed.

"Yeah . . . you know, he's got the little mice . . . maybe we have a barbecue . . . and we watch the little mice runnin' all around. Whaddya say?"

"You're funny."

"And you are very sweet." Blackie smiled. "The breakfast was absolutely first rate. My compliments to the chef."

"I'll let him know."

"And you can give him the check," he said pointing at Danny.

The girl smiled, and walked off carrying their plates. Blackie watched her go. "I like it out here," he said to no one in particular. "I like it out here a lot."

"I can't believe Walter Hughes is dead!"

"Yeah," Blackie said, absentmindedly. "Ain't that a bitch. I guess he had it comin', the dumb fuck."

"We all got it comin'," Danny said. "Doesn't scare you?"

"What?"

"Dying."

"How the fuck could I be scared! I'd be dead."

"I mean now. Before."

"What I gotta be scared about. I'm gonna die when I'm gonna die."

"What about what happens after?"

"You think too much. That's your problem, Danny Boy. You need to stop thinkin' so much. You know what I mean! You need to think less. Like me."

Danny chuckled.

"I know where I'd like to be buried right now though, I can tell you that." Danny followed Blackie's eye-line to their waitress, bent over, casually wiping a table. "Somethin' happens to me, I want you to bury me with those shorts she's wearing, okay."

"Okay." Danny laughed. It was pointless with Blackie. He envied Blackie his complete oblivion.

"I'm serious, bro. You gotta come up here and you find her and you say 'Hey, Sweets. Blackie's gone. We're gonna need those shorts you're wearing, for the funeral.'"

Danny laughed.

"You gotta promise."

"I promise."

"Ya lyin' fuck." Blackie grinned.

15

"We've got Trixie," the older guy in the backseat said calmly.

There were three of them in the car. Italian. The two in the front were younger. Broad shoulders. Wide necks. They didn't turn around. They didn't have to. These guys weren't like Coyle's crew. Or even Mannion's crew. These guys were the real deal. Professionals. Polished. Clean shaven. Not a hair out of place. A hint of high-end aftershave in the air, instead of stale beer and cigarette smoke.

The old guy in the back seat next to him was from another time. Black felt fedora. Dark brown suit. White shirt. Silk tie, knotted just so. Dark shades. Diamond pinkie ring the size of a shot glass. Skin like bronzed leather.

Danny didn't put up a fight when the old guy held open the rear door and told him to get in. He knew at a glance that if these guys wanted him dead he'd be dead already. If they wanted to break his legs he'd never see them coming.

They'd waited down the block from the gym. God knows how long they'd been sitting here. If they were in the least bit frustrated, they didn't show it.

It was cool in the car. And quiet. Nothing but the faint rumble of the motor and the low hum of the air conditioner.

"Is she okay?" Danny asked, eventually.

"She's okay. For now."

Danny felt an explosive surge of rage. He wanted to punch the old guy in the face. Catch him by the throat and strangle him into telling him where she was. He was pretty sure he could hurt all three of them before they could get a bullet in his head. But these guys knew he wasn't about to do that. They'd kill him, and then they'd kill her, and then they'd go out for a plate of linguini and clam sauce, and that would be the end of it.

This wasn't a personal visit for these guys. It was just business.

"You got the fight coming up at The Garden in two weeks. You're gonna take a dive."

"I can't."

"I know. But you will. We want you to make it look good. We don't want nobody saying you threw it. You understand! Fifth round. Nice and clean. You go down."

Danny didn't need to ask them *or what*. He knew the what of it. They'd kill Trixie. And then they'd probably kill him, too.

"You do this nice and we'll take real good care of you. We let Trixie go, and everybody goes home happy."

"How do I know you have her?"

The guy in the passenger seat reached inside his jacket and produced a Polaroid. He handed it back over his shoulder to Danny without turning around.

Danny took it. Looked like a hotel room. A bed. Two bedside tables. Lamps. An ashtray. Unmade bed.

Trixie.

They'd made her hold up a piece of cardboard. They'd written HI DANNY on it in black marker.

She looked tired. A defiant gleam in her eye. Beautiful as ever. Just seeing her filled him with hope. She was alive.

"You hang on to that. Anytime you think about maybe not doing what I'm telling you to do . . . you just take a good long look at that pretty girl."

"How do I know you'll let her go?"

"Because we're not like you Irish guys. We're not animals. We're businessmen. We say, this is what we're gonna do, this is what we're gonna do."

Danny knew there were no guarantees. He might take a dive and they still might kill her. But he knew if he didn't take the dive, she was dead. For sure.

"You guys makin' quite the name for yourselves up there in The Kitchen. You tell your boy Logan Coyle, he better stay in his lane. He doesn't, he's liable to get himself in an accident. Like his pal, Mack."

So it was the Italians.

"We got business interests in the neighborhood. You understand!"

Danny understood the business interests. Hyman Goldstein was the biggest loan shark on the West Side, maybe the biggest on the entire east coast, and everybody knew Hyman was their guy. Hyman took care of the Italians and they took damned good care of him. Mannion had been happy to let them have it. Danny didn't blame him. It was an arrangement that had kept the peace between the Italians and the Irish in The Kitchen for years.

"All this cowboy shit. It ain't no good for business. Now you got this new convention center coming up. We got some interest in that, too, you understand. You tell Mr. Coyle, no more of this cowboys and Indians stuff. You look at his old friend Pat Mannion. Pat did the right thing. He's a smart man. He got out. He makes a nice life for himself with his family. You tell Coyle. Go on home. Back to his nice house in New Jersey. Make a nice life for himself with Kate and the kids. It's better this way."

Danny could imagine how Logan was going to react to a suggestion like that. That the guy had used his wife's name. That they knew where he lived.

"We're doing' you a favor here, Danny."

"Sure you are."

"Vinny Diamond," the old guy said, turning a blank stare to Danny.

Danny said nothing. The guy was fishing. Only two people on planet Earth really knew what happened to Vinny Diamond.

"Columbians think it was Miguel," the old guy went on. Continuing to stare at Danny for any reaction.

Danny gave him nothing.

"They asked about you. The girl too. I told them you had nothing to do with it. I told them, maybe they was in it together . . . Miguel and Vinny. Couple of fanooks." He brushed his chin with the tips of his fingers.

"Maybe when we get the club up and running again we give you your old job back at the door. You see how I take care of you!"

He put his hand out and rested it on Danny's shoulder.

"You're a good kid, Danny. Do the right thing. Everybody goes home happy. Fifth round. *Capisce!*"

Danny stood on the sidewalk and watched them drive away. He took the Polaroid from his pocket and kissed it.

There was still a chance.

16

"He said what!" Logan snapped. He was with Danny in the Meat Wagon. Even Danny had started calling it that. Why not? There'd been two bodies transported in the back of this thing already. One of them in pieces. What else would you call it! "These scumbags come near my family or my home I'll kill every motherfucken one of them," Logan continued.

It was early afternoon. They were sitting on Pier 86 in the shadow of the *Intrepid*. Danny'd picked Logan up outside The Wolf. He wanted Logan to hear about the Italian threat without every ear in the bar listening in. He knew Logan would blow a fuse.

Danny didn't mention Trixie. And he sure as hell wasn't about to let Logan know he'd just been to see Quinn to give him the Polaroid the Italians had given him. Quinn had taken it. Scratched his head, and slipped it in his pocket.

It was best to leave Trixie out of it completely with Logan.

"You see what's happening here, right!" Logan said, after hearing it all. He was staring off blankly over the Hudson. They had the windows down to let a breeze run through. The air conditioner was running but it was just about shot. Something else that needed fixing. Something else Danny was gonna need money to pay for real soon.

"It's all come down to this. Mannion's gone. He's out of the neighborhood. But is he really gone? Is he really giving up control? Or is this just a move? I don't know." Danny didn't interrupt him. Logan wasn't talking to him as much as he was just trying to draw a mental map of the situation they were all in. "His three top guys got whacked so you gotta believe that's got him rattled. Sure, Mack was with us, but the Italians don't know that, right! Far as they're concerned Mack was still with Mannion. Mack was with Mannion for years . . . So they lump him in with Dillon and The Greek. They take 'em all out. Mannion's entire crew. And then Mannion packs up and moves to Queens. He's out. Now they see me as the last guy standing between them and the whole neighborhood. The convention center. They want it all, Danny. They got their guy Hyman Goldstein in here. Everybody in the neighborhood's into that guy. I mean, I'm into him for nearly a hundred large myself. Half the guys we know are into him for thousands. He's like the central bank of Hell's Kitchen. Can you imagine the fucken vig alone on that shit. Every bookie. Every bar owner, grandmother and construction worker. You ever think about that?"

Danny'd thought about it plenty. When you owe a guy like Goldstein money you can't help but run the numbers in your head. It becomes part of your daily routine. He was into Goldstein for nearly five grand now himself. A debt he hoped to settle with his next fight. But he wasn't about to let Logan know about that either.

"That little black book he carries around is the fucken holy grail," Logan went on. "You get rid of that book you collapse the bank. Or . . . you own it. But you touch that bank you better be ready for war. You touch a hair on Hyman Goldstein's head you better be ready to take on the Italians, because they'll come for us then alright."

Logan paused. As if the next thought on the tip of his tongue was too scary to even contemplate.

"Unless . . ." He stopped. He couldn't bring himself to say it.

He smiled then. If Danny had to guess, he'd say Logan had just come to an understanding of himself just then. A realization of where he stood in the grand scheme of things. An awakening of who he had become.

"'Uneasy lies the head that wears a crown,'" he said, after a brief pause.

The sound of a jackhammer rattling into action on the pier just to the north of where they sat caught their attention and they turned to look. A crew of guys in orange vests and hard hats were rising from their lunch break, grabbing sledge hammers, pickaxes and wheelbarrows in the blazing mid-day heat.

"There's a shift coming, Danny. The future is knocking at our door. Might be here already. We're probably standing right in the middle of it. Right now, on this pier. One foot in the past and one in the future."

Logan took a long pause as they watched the men work.

"Maybe we never really had a choice in any of it. You know what I mean! You think of our ancestors getting off the ships, right here, just over a hundred years ago. Right here on this pier. Trudging down the gangplank with every goddamned thing they owned crammed into an old beat-up cardboard suitcase. You imagine that! Must have been insane. And what did they do? They went down to The Village to look for a place to sleep, or they stayed right in here in shacks, right along the wharf here, where the work was at. Immigrants. Most of 'em Irish, and Italian. Right fucken here. This shit's been going down for a hundred years. They're tired. They got no money. They gotta hustle to get a bite to eat. A bed to sleep in. Who gets the jobs? Who gets the power? Who gets to feed his family? Keep them safe. Make no mistake, Danny, you don't protect what you got, somebody else is gonna take it away from you. Human nature. Owney Madden. Hughie Mulligan. Pat Mannion. You think they had a choice? You think they chose the life they had, or did they just find themselves, one day, pushed up to the front of the scrum. The guy with the balls to do what everybody else was afraid to do. The guy everybody else could stand behind to feel safe. There's always gotta be somebody in front. Somebody willing to do the ugly work. Maybe it's just my turn. Maybe it's my turn to stand in front. And maybe I never had a choice."

Logan paused again. As if he were seeing it all now. His place in it. And what was about to unfold.

"You know what happens if I don't do it, right! If I don't stand up! What happens to what's left of this Irish neighborhood of ours here! We lose it. That's what happens. And the Italians step in and run it for us. They're doing it already with Goldstein here. Bank of Goddamned Irish America. Fat Joe getting fatter by the day off our backs. Make no mistake, Danny, they got their eyes on that new convention center. Money. Power. Politics. Control. This ain't no different than what they're doing down there in Washington, it's the same goddamned thing, rules are exactly the same, eat or be eaten, only here in the street, we don't got the luxury of keeping the blood off our hands. Here in The Kitchen the guy with the most smarts, and the most balls, to do what's gotta be done. That's who wins. That's who wears the crown."

"What are you gonna do?" Danny asked. He could see that Logan had already decided. It was obvious in the way he let his breath go.

Acceptance.

"I'm gonna accept the crown, Danny. It is what it is. It's my time to stand in front. Can I trust you to be with me."

"Sure, Logan," Danny said. "I'm with you."

In truth Danny wasn't quite sure what he just agreed to. But he could feel the power and the truth of what Logan had just said. To hell with it. Maybe it was time to give in and go with it all. Let the inevitable tide roll in.

Maybe it was true what Logan had said. Maybe they never really had a choice.

"I want you to do me a favor. Be at The Wolf tomorrow morning at eleven o'clock," Logan said.

"I got the fight tomorrow night."

"I know. Don't worry. You'll still make the fight. I'll get Terry and Blackie sorted to be there. And I'll bring Nicky Red."

"Nicky Red?" Danny was surprised to hear Logan mention Red like he was part of the crew. Red had been spending a lot of time at The Wolf since he and Logan had gone to visit him at Ward's Island. But still. Nicky Red was Italian. But maybe that was the point.

"He's gotta be there. Trust me. This is how it's gotta go down. Just be at the bar in the morning with the guys. Eleven o'clock. Keep the door locked 'til I get there. Anybody else shows up, tell 'em we're closed for the day."

Danny didn't ask what was going to happen. Whatever it was Logan had planned he was going to go with it. Logan had been good to him. Taken care of him when he needed it. For better of worse, now that his mother was gone, The Wolf crew were about as close to family as he had left in the world.

17

"Hey, Danny. Danny Boy McCoy." It was a group of kids sitting on the stoop of the building next to his own. A gaggle of them. Street urchins. They'd watched him park the Meat Wagon and yelled as he went to pass them by. They were a ragtag bunch. Wild. Feral as street cats. Hair every which way but straight. Scuffed sneakers. Bent teeth. Pants torn at the knees. Danny knew them all to see but didn't know their names. One kid, not older than twelve or thirteen, was puffing awkwardly on a cigarette. Another popped some bubblegum. "Hey, Danny Boy, you gonna fight tomorrow night?"

"Yeah."

"You gonna beat his ass?"

"I'm gonna try."

"Try! You're gonna whup his ass. You're Danny Boy McCoy."

"We'll see."

"Hey, Danny, you think I could be a boxer?"

"Sure. Let's see what you got."

It was the shortest of the bunch. The kid with the cigarette dangling out of the corner of his mouth. He stood and put up his fists. Danny grabbed his fists and positioned them. "Like this. You

393

gotta protect your face. Get that back leg back. That's it. Brace yourself." He threw a few light punches and pretty soon the rest of them were off the stoop, all trying to get a shot in. Danny bopped and shoved them playfully, easily keeping them all at bay. Then he let them get him, dropping to his knees, taking a soft one to the chin, before keeling over on the sidewalk.

"I got him. I beat Danny Boy McCoy," the boy yelled. "I'm the champ."

"No. I'm the champ," another yelled.

Danny gathered himself.

"One d-d-d-day, I'm gonna be just like you Mr. Mc-C-C-Coy," a tall gangly kid, about twelve years old, stammered nervously.

Danny stood and ruffled the kid's hair. "You just keep punching, okay. And you kids lay off those cigarettes. They'll stunt your growth."

"No they won't," one kid said. "That's a big load o' bologna."

"Oh yeah! What do you think happened this guy," Danny said, pointing to the short kid with the smoke.

The rest of the kids laughed at this and took the opportunity to gang up and poke fun at their pal, shouting: "What's up Tiny Tim." "Tim's a short-ass."

"Hey, fuck you, I ain't short." the kid spat, throwing away what was left of his smoke.

Danny left them at it.

"Hey, Danny," one of the kids yelled as he walked away. "Can we see the belt when you win tomorrow night?"

"If I win," Danny said.

"If you win! You're gonna beat him easy," the boy yelled. "You're Danny Boy McCoy."

All the boys cheered and whooped in unison.

"Danny Boy McCoy. Danny Boy McCoy."

"You're the champ of Hell's Kitchen."

"Go, Danny."

Danny was pushing open the door to his building when he heard someone clap behind him.

He turned to see the familiar face of Murray O'Connell, of the *New York Gazette*, leaning against the front fender of a parked car.

"That's quite the fan club you got there, kid."

Danny wasn't in the mood for Murray. He turned to continue on into his building.

"I'm writing a little piece on the fight. Couple of minutes of your time. That's all."

Danny turned reluctantly. The kids had gathered themselves off the stoop and were sauntering off down Tenth Avenue, shoving and punching one another playfully.

"You're a big deal in this neighborhood. All these little kids. They look up to you. That's real nice. How you feel about that responsibility?"

"They're not my responsibility."

"You might like to think they're not, but those kids are looking up to you for something. Something they don't get to see around here very much."

"Oh yeah. What's that?"

"Hope."

Danny hung his head, hearing the words of the Italian whisper in his ears: *Fifth round. Nice and clean. You go down.*

Trixie.

"What's the matter, champ? You think this guy's got the hop on you?"

"I can take him."

"You sure about that? You know, at least two guys who fought this guy threw in the towel on their boxing careers after they went a few rounds with this animal. You know that?"

Danny hadn't heard. He knew the guy was tough but he'd been deliberately avoiding digging around to find out anything more about the guy ahead of the fight. It was hard enough to get in a ring. He didn't want to know a guy's whole story. He just didn't want to know.

"One guy hasn't been right in the head since. Hector Ramirez . . . ever hear of him? Was a real contender until he stepped in a ring with this guy two years ago. I stopped out to see him a couple of days ago. He's cleaning toilets at a gas station in Far Rockaway. Speech is all fucked up. One eye bent so far out of shape the guy could practically read you the tag on the back of his own shirt. You ready for that kind of action tomorrow night?"

"I gotta go now. Gotta get to the gym."

"Sure, sure, I don't want to hold you up—just one last thing though, for this piece I'm working on, if you wouldn't mind." Murray paused here. Danny got the sense that he'd just been teed up for the real query. "This crew you're running with now. Coyle, Flannery, Black, McElroy . . . and the rest of that gang down there at The Wolf. You don't think they got anything to do with all these murders happening lately, do you?"

"I don't know nothin' about that stuff."

"Sure. Or Pat Mannion picking up his family and skeddadlin' all the way out to Queens. That don't seem a little bit weird to you?"

"How?"

"Naw, I'm just saying . . . you know . . . rumors . . . a guy says something here, 'nother guy says somethin' over there . . . pretty soon you get the feeling these things, you know . . . maybe they're all connected."

"I dunno, isn't that up to the cops . . ."

"Yeah . . . and journalists, I guess. What would you call your gang if you had to put a name on it?"

"Gang?"

"Yeah, that's what this is, isn't it? A gang of some sorts."

"I'm not a part of no gang."

"How about The West Side Boys?"

Danny laughed uneasily.

"Or, I heard some of the guys down at the precinct refer to you guys as West Side Story."

"I'll be seeing you around, Murray."

"Sure, kid. I'll see you at the fight."

Danny opened the door to his building and was stepping inside when Murray called to him again.

"Hey."

Danny turned.

"Knock this son of a bitch on his ass tomorrow night. Okay! Do it for the kids," Murray said, then he turned and shuffled off up the block.

The sun was going down as he parked the Meat Wagon in the parking lot of Valhalla Cemetery, the Thirty-third County, and made his way through the headstones to his mother's resting place.

"Hey, Ma," he said, resting on his knees next to the temporary wooden cross bearing her name. "I brought you some flowers. They didn't have none of the orange roses that you like but these looked real nice."

He laid the bunch of daffodils under the wooden cross.

The last of the evening sun shone blood-orange, low, through the trees. Birds whistled cheerfully in a great oak that sat not thirty feet away.

"This is real nice up here. We got you a real nice spot," he said, glancing all around at the manicured expanse of the graveyard. "They keep this place real tidy. And don't you worry, Ma, I'm gonna come visit you all the time. You don't got to worry about that. I'm right here. And when it comes my time, I'm gonna have them put me right here next to you, okay? That's a promise. You ain't never gotta be alone."

He leaned to pick a few errant weeds.

"I'm gonna get a real nice headstone for you too. Marble. The very best. You'll see. With your name on it, real nice."

He paused. Scanned the graveyard to make sure no one could hear him talk, before continuing.

"I got a little favor, Ma. You gotta help me out. For tomorrow night. This fight. I don't gotta tell you what's happenin'. You can see. They got me in a real tight situation here with this thing. I don't see no way out."

He paused again as if there were a possibility she'd offer him some response.

Nothing. Not from his mother. Not from the birds, or the sun, or the freshly trimmed grass.

He blessed himself and lay down beside her grave, closed his eyes, and folded his hands across his chest.

"But maybe I don't got a choice. Maybe none of us really got a choice," he said, echoing the line he'd heard Logan use. "Maybe there ain't no stopping what we got comin'. I just want you to know, I'm tryin', Ma. I really tried to do the right thing here." He paused, letting the train of thought run its course. "But maybe, there just ain't no point, you know what I mean . . . maybe I just gotta go with what comes. Let it all fall down."

18

Thin slats of light filtered through the filthy shuttered blinds, sending bars of light in a slow dusty march across the threadbare floor. Terry Flannery sat at a small table by the door, nervously nursing a beer. Blackie was seated at the bar, hunched over a glass of whiskey, chain-smoking Marlboro Reds. Tony McElroy was behind the stick, absentmindedly polishing glasses with a rag. Nicky Red stayed in the back room. Out of sight.

Danny sat in a booth, watching the door. He still didn't know what was coming next.

Logan hadn't told him. Hadn't told any of them. He'd decided it didn't really matter. Whatever was gonna go down was gonna go down. And he was going to stand with them. These were his friends. What was he gonna do!

It was nearly noon when McElroy moved to the jukebox to play a little music to crack the silence.

"Play something cheery this time, you depressing fuck," Blackie called to him.

"How about this?" McElroy smiled, turning from the jukebox as the familiar sound of Bruce Springsteen's "Jungleland" began to play.

Terry Flannery clapped his hands just then to get everyone's attention. Someone was coming.

Terry lifted a newspaper and buried his head in it just as Logan walked through the door followed by Hyman Goldstein.

"What you having to drink?" Logan called loudly. Too loudly.

Goldstein paused, not three feet inside the door, startled by something in Logan's tone. Danny heard it too. Why was Logan shouting? And why was Goldstein here?

"I think, I left something in the car," Goldstein said, nervously patting his jacket pockets as he glanced around the room and saw the uneasy faces of the handful of men seated in the bar. Something was wrong. Something was off.

He spotted Danny just then, and for an instant he smiled, as if he believed he'd be safe now with him there.

"Relax, take a seat. Let's have a drink," Logan insisted. "Sit."

But before Goldstein could take another step Nicky Red came barging out of the back room with a thirty-two and went straight past Danny with the gun raised.

"No. Stop," Goldstein managed to yell just before the first shot hit him in the middle of the forehead.

Danny watched in shock as Goldstein crumpled to the floor.

Nicky Red stood over him and calmly put another one into his face.

Hyman Goldstein was dead.

"The door," Logan yelled. "Lock it. Nobody gets in."

Terry stood and bolted the door.

Then he walked back to where Goldstein lay, face up, on the floor of the bar, and stared down at him.

"Give me that," Logan said, reaching for the gun. Nicky Red obediently handed it to him. Logan pointed the gun at Goldstein's chest and pumped another one into him.

"Get over here," he said, motioning to McElroy who was still frozen mid-stride on his way back from the jukebox.

McElroy stepped forward as Logan held out the gun to him. McElroy took it.

"Put one in him," Logan said.

"But he's dead already."

"Pull the trigger, Tony."

Tony popped off another round into Goldstein's lifeless body.

"You too," he said to Blackie, taking the pistol from McElroy's hand and passing it on.

Blackie took the gun and put one in Goldstein's chest.

"Terry."

Terry took the gun and followed suit.

"Danny," Logan called. "Get over here."

Danny didn't argue. He stood and approached the circle of men.

"This is it," Logan said, offering him the gun. "There's no going back now."

Danny took the gun and aimed it down at Hyman Goldstein's bullet-riddled corpse and pulled the trigger.

Logan seemed overcome with emotion. Danny and the others watched as he grabbed Nicky Red in a bear hug and the two men, an Irishman and an Italian, embraced over the bullet-riddled corpse of the most powerful loan shark on the east coast of America.

"Let's get him in back," Logan said, slipping off his jacket, draping it over a barstool and rolling up the sleeves of this shirt. "Two on each end."

Danny and Blackie picked up his legs. Logan and Terry took him by the arms.

"Get the door," Logan ordered McElroy, as they carted him back toward the kitchen.

Once they had him laid out on the linoleum kitchen floor, Logan continued to undress. He stripped down to his underwear.

Then he began undressing Goldstein, casually giving orders as he went.

"Hold his arm."

"Good. Lift this leg."

"That's right. Get a garbage bag for these clothes."

"Well look at this," Logan said, producing a small black book from inside Goldstein's back pocket. He flicked through it. "This, ladies and gentlemen is the holy grail. This is the key to the kingdom." He was shaking his head as he scanned through the names and figures jotted in meticulous penmanship. "Hey, look, it's you, Danny. This is you."

Danny froze. He'd never told Logan just how much he was into Goldstein for.

"Wow! You're into him for quite the bundle. What you need all this for?"

Logan, naked but for his underwear, his arms bloodied to the elbows, fixed Danny with his steely blue eyes.

"For Ma. The doctors," Danny managed to say.

Logan nodded.

"Don't worry, Danny. We'll work something out," Logan said. Danny noticed he didn't say "forget it." Logan was the new official bank of Hell's Kitchen. Danny was pretty sure everyone in that black book was going to pay every red cent owed.

"Hand me my knives," Logan said.

Nicky Red opened a drawer and produced three large knives. He and Logan had obviously gone through the planning of this procedure in advance.

Nicky handed Logan a large serrated kitchen knife.

"I'm gonna sit out front," Danny said, feeling nauseous at the sight of Goldstein's pale, mangled corpse on the floor at his feet.

"Not yet, Danny. I want you here for this next part," Logan said, as he knelt next to Goldstein's body, and began sawing into his throat with the knife. Danny closed his eyes but he could not block out the sound of a rough knife sawing through skin and flesh. There was an eerie silence as Logan worked through sinews, muscle and bone. Then, Logan stood and lifted the bloody head by a fistful of gray hair.

"Feel how heavy that is," he said, offering it to Danny.

Danny shook his head. He couldn't do it. He couldn't hold the head of a man he'd grown to like.

"That's alright," Logan said. "Why don't you take off, Danny. You got the fight tonight. You don't need to be here for the rest of this. Just leave me the keys to the Meat Wagon so we can get him out of here when we're done."

Danny nodded. Logan wasn't asking for the keys, he was telling him he was taking the keys.

"Hey, Danny, I better come with you," Blackie said.

"Where the fuck are you going?" Logan scowled.

"I'm in his fucken corner, that's where. This is a big deal, Logan. You know that. We gotta get this guy ready."

Logan seemed to weigh it all for a beat.

"Fine. Go. The two of you. Get out of here."

Danny handed Logan the keys to the van.

"Hey, Danny. Blackie," Logan said. "We did good here today. This is it now. No turning back. Okay!"

"We're with you, Logan," Blackie said.

"Good. Go. We'll see you there tonight. Let's take that belt home, okay, Danny. We're gonna hang that thing right up behind the bar for everybody to see. Danny Boy McCoy. Champ of Hell's

Kitchen," Logan said sincerely, as he stood in his underwear, arms bloodied to the elbows, a large serrated knife in one hand, the severed head of Hyman Goldstein dangling by the hair in his other.

Danny and Blackie were back up in Danny's apartment before either of them spoke.

"Jesus fucken Christ, he's insane," Blackie said eventually, peering out the window onto Tenth Avenue. "Did you see that shit! The fucken guy's an animal. You know what this means?"

Danny sat at the small kitchen table. He knew Logan was on the verge of something big, but he'd never suspected he'd whack Hyman Goldstein.

"He's gonna get us all killed, the crazy fuck," Blackie went on. "You understand! Logan Coyle just hit the Italians."

"But Nicky Red? Nicky's Italian," Danny said, still trying to make sense of it all.

"Don't you see? Nicky Red's the messenger. Logan wanted him there to see the whole damn thing. You get it! He wants Nicky to go back and tell them exactly what happened. He's not trying to hide it. He's saying, 'Yeah, I killed your guy. What the fuck you gonna do about it!' The crazy fuck."

Blackie actually laughed aloud.

"You gotta give it to the crazy Mick bastard, he's got some balls, I'll tell ya that. He's got some fucken balls. I need some tea. Let's have some tea. Your mother got any of that good Irish stuff around here?"

"Top cabinet, on the left."

"There it is," Blackie said, taking down a box of his mother's Irish teabags. "Love this shit. You wanna cup?" He was already filling the kettle like he'd lived there his whole life.

"Yeah," Danny said. Not knowing if he wanted a cup or not. Blackie continued rattling on.

"Logan Coyle just took out the Italians' top earner in the whole neighborhood. Not just that, he fucken swipes the guy's entire business from under their noses with that little black book. It's fucken genius."

"He's crazy."

"Crazy genius, bro. Think about it! If he didn't move they probably gonna whack him anyway. Probably would have whacked us all. Come on! He's gotta have been next on their list. Right! So what's he do, he fucken shoots first. Motherfucker! Now they're thinkin', *This guy's fucken crazy.* They're gonna think twice about sending some guy after him now. They don't know what to do with his ass."

"They'll kill us all."

"Maybe. Maybe not. They might just respect us a little bit more from here on out."

"Yeah. If they don't kill us all."

"If they don't kill us all," Blackie conceded, dropping a Barry's teabag in his mother's china teacup.

19

Cockeye brought about ten young kids from the neighborhood to escort Danny to the ring. Kids he'd been training over at The Ward before it had burned to the ground. Danny recognized a handful of them. They were huddled in a corner of the changing room, excitedly chatting among themselves.

Danny had dreamed of this moment for most of his life. A fight at Madison Square Garden. But now that he was here he felt caged.

The changing room felt small. Claustrophobic.

The muffled thunder of the crowd, signaling the end of the undercard bout, sent a pulse up through the soles of his feet. He was taped and gloved. The hood of his green, white and gold silk cape hung about his head.

Go down in the fifth or Trixie dies.

He closed his eyes and he prayed.

When he opened his eyes again Cockeye was there checking his laces.

"How you doin'? You ready for this?"

Danny nodded.

"You see all those kids over there?" Cockeye said, motioning to the kids standing in a pack by the dressing room door. "You're giving them a story they'll take with them to their graves. Fifty years from now they'll be telling their grandkids about the night they escorted Danny Boy McCoy to the ring in Madison Square Garden. One of their own, from Hell's Kitchen."

Cockeye was talking but Danny could only partially hear what he was saying over the chorus of voices and images at war in his head ... Trixie, on some dingy motel-room bed right now being watched over by a couple of thugs who were going to be let loose on her if he didn't throw this fight.

Fifth round. Nice and clean. You go down.

"Hope," Cockeye said. "Most powerful word in the English language. That's what you're giving them Danny."

Anytime you think about maybe not doing what I'm telling you to do, the Italian had said, *you just take a good long look at that pretty girl.*

"You stay sharp out there," Cockeye was saying. "And watch out for that right. Don't let it near you. Stay on the outside. Pace yourself. Wear him out. Wait for your shot. You hear me?"

We're not animals.

"Danny," Cockeye snapped, slapping him on the side of the head. "Are you with me here? Where the fuck are you at?"

"I'm here."

"Are you sure? Because if you're not here you're in for a serious ass whupping out there. Come on. Wake up. Get your head in the game."

The lone voice of a young girl came over the loud speakers. The entire stadium fell into a hush at the angelic sound of her singing.

> *"Oh, Danny boy, the pipes, the pipes are calling,*
> *From glen to glen, and down the mountain side."*

"I know you were there," Cockeye said calmly, almost in a

whisper, as he looked deep into Danny's eyes. Danny looked back and he knew that any attempt to lie was futile. Cockeye knew he'd helped burn his gym to the ground.

"The summer's gone, and all the roses falling,
It's you, it's you must go and I must bide."

"I'm sorry," Danny said. "I'm sorry. I didn't . . ."

"But come ye back when summer's in the meadow,
Or when the valley's hushed and white with snow,"

"I know Danny. I know. I just want you to do one fucking thing for me, okay."

"Anything."

Cockeye wrapped his arms around Danny and hugged him tightly.

"Go out there and win this fight."

"It's I'll be here in sunshine or in shadow,
Oh, Danny boy, oh Danny boy, I love you so!"

"Let's go, lovers," Blackie called, loudly clapping his hands to get Danny and Cockeye's attention. "Let's make this thing happen." He had arranged the ten young fighters in formation to follow Danny to the ring.

"Let's do this thing," Cockeye said, releasing Danny and slapping him on the shoulder.

Danny stepped to the front of the crew and made the long walk down through the crowd. There wasn't a whisper in the stadium other than the soaring voice of the young girl.

Blackie stepped up and parted the ropes for Danny to climb into the ring as the young girl sang the last bar of the song.

"For you will bend and tell me that you love me,
And I shall sleep in peace until you come to me!"

Danny moved to the corner of the ring and let them lift the cape from about his shoulders.

There, in the corner facing him was a man who knew nothing about the inner turmoil of his opponent. Danny felt neither fear nor fight. The man across from him had two arms, two legs, and was stretching his neck to and fro and smashing his gloves together in a manner meant to intimidate, but Danny felt none of that. He was a big man. Two inches on Danny at least. Solidly built. Broad powerful shoulders and eyes clear as glass.

They met and tapped gloves. The referee raised a hand and dropped it at the ring of the bell and it was happening.

Danny felt detached from it all. The man came at him with a brutal onslaught and caught him with a right that almost put him on the mat in the first seconds of the fight. Danny moved and danced and punched back but he felt removed from it all. Numb. Uncertain of why he was there or what was expected of him now.

There was no way forward that saved everyone.

Trixie.

Cockeye.

Italians.

Irish.

Logan Coyle holding the severed head of Hyman Goldstein.

He was aware of the crowd cheering but he heard nothing of it.

He caught one in the liver and it almost buckled him.

The bell went.

Back in the corner, Blackie and Cockeye rubbed his shoulders, dabbed a cut over his eyes, yelled at him, and then the bell rang again.

It went like that for the next three rounds.

The bell rang at the bottom of the fourth round and he sat on the stool as they threw water on him. Cockeye was screaming at him: "Are you trying to get killed out there. Wake up. What are you doing?"

Go down in the fifth or Trixie dies.

The bell rang again and somehow he was on his feet again and the man moved toward him with a smirk as if he knew that Danny had given up and he caught him with a right that spun Danny's head around, knocking his mouth guard onto the canvas.

Danny flopped back, and slammed onto the canvas.

The crowd went nuts, screaming.

Their voices were coming to him now.

He could hear them for the first time.

"Get up, Danny."

"Get up."

"Come on, McCoy."

The referee was above him flinging fingers in the air as he counted him down.

Danny rolled his head to the side and caught the face of a young boy who had escorted him to the ring. And next to him, the others. All ten of them. Young boys from the neighborhood. And not one of them was screaming. They looked heartbroken. Devastated. He saw in their faces the faces of his childhood friends: Cheddar, Knuckles, Tommy Ryan. He saw the future being ripped from their eyes with each new finger the referee threw in his face.

One boy looked right at him and mouthed the word, *Please.*

The boy was begging.

Danny closed his eyes and saw Trixie's face. Smiling.

He opened them again, and the boy had tears in his eyes, and he was shaking his head like his whole life's dream was dying on the canvas, right in front of him.

Danny heard the voice of Logan Coyle.

"Maybe none of us really got a choice. Maybe there ain't no stopping what we got comin'."

Danny mustered everything he had.

He rolled over, and pushed himself to his feet again, just before the referee hit the ten count.

The crowd went insane.

But Danny wasn't listening to them anymore.

Danny stared down at the young boy.

The boy screamed and put his fists in the air. Tears in his eyes. Hope.

Then Carlos "The Thing" Cabrerra came at him to finish him off. This time, Danny turned to him, and started pushing back. Cabrerra seemed to sense the shift and he came at Danny with everything he had left. He was connecting too, solid crushing blows, but Danny pushed him on back against the ropes with a storm of bone smashing blows of his own. His arms were like two powerful pistons blinding Cabrerra every which way he turned. *Bam. Bam. Bam. Bam.* He was hitting Cabrerra so fast and from so many different angles Cabrerra couldn't move fast enough to shield himself from them all. It was impossible. Like walking into the propellors of a prop plane.

The ribs.

The jaw.

The liver.

His eyes.

His ears.

Up until now, Cabrerra had been bludgeoning an opponent who'd barely thrown a punch to defend himself. He'd worn himself thin on Danny for four and a half rounds, thinking that the next punch would surely put him away. He was exhausted and unprepared for the warrior who came at him now. Danny unleashed all of it. He let loose. This was the Danny Boy McCoy the entire neighborhood had turned up to see.

Hope.

Danny swung hard and low and caught Cabrerra in the liver and as Cabrerra dropped his elbow reflexively to block the pain, Danny's right caught him full and square on the jaw. A punch so profound and sure of its target it felt like a shockwave across the width of his back. Across the whole entire West Side of Manhattan.

Cabrerra stumbled, and managed to drape an arm over the top rail, saving himself from the canvas, but only for a second, before he spilled over, tumbling into darkness.

The crowd went ballistic.

They leapt to their feet in such triumph that for an instant the entire audience seemed to levitate.

Hope.

A mad, primordial, triumphant wail filled the stadium.

Cockeye was in the ring, holding Danny in his arms. Blackie was in the ring also, with his fists in the air taking the victory lap for him, screaming at the top of his lungs.

Danny locked eyes with Cockeye and yelled through the din: "Take the purse and open a new gym for them." He pointed to the kids screaming ringside. "It's for them."

Cockeye was nodding his head. He had tears in his eyes.

"I'm sorry, Boss," Danny said. "I'm sorry."

Cockeye threw his arms around Danny and held him, crushed him to his chest, kissed him, like he was his own sweet boy, come home to him at last.

20

Danny pulled his hood up over his head and slipped quietly out of The Garden, past reporters, and screaming fans. He wanted to get home. As he always did after a fight. To be alone with his pain.

With his memories of Trixie.

He'd failed her.

The Italians would come for him now.

And if they didn't, he'd go looking for them.

They'd pay for what they did to her.

All up Ninth Avenue the bars were filling from the spillover from The Garden. It was an electrified crowd. He heard his name zip by in snippets of street conversation all the way back to Tenth Avenue.

He entered the building and climbed the stairs to the roof.

He was on the last flight when he noticed a feather. Then another. He bounded the last few steps and flung the door open.

He moved from one bird to another. Touching each one for signs of life. They'd put up a fight. Fresh feathers were scattered everywhere. They lay on the floor and in their nests where they'd been tossed, their wings cocked this way and that, their heads limp. Dorothy, Rubin, Rocky, Wilbur . . . Cheddar. He stroked each one of them, apologizing as he went.

"I'm sorry," he said, again and again and again. "I'm so sorry."

The Italians had gotten there before he could.

On the back wall of the coop they'd scrawled the number five in bird's blood.

He didn't hear the roof door open. Or the footsteps behind him.

He jumped when he heard Detective Quinn's voice. Half expected to see the flash of a muzzle in his face.

"Aw, Danny. Aw no. Not your birds. Ah jees. I'm sorry, kid," Quinn said, surveying the carnage.

Danny turned his back on him so Quinn could not see his tears.

He moved to the edge of the roof.

A soft summer breeze drifted up Tenth Avenue and over the parapet. He closed his eyes to let it wash over him and heard a soft voice next to him.

"Hey, Danny."

He opened his eyes.

There she was. Standing next to him. Her tired, pained eyes staring up at him.

Trixie.

Danny wrapped his arms around her and began to sob. She slipped her arms around him and buried her head in his chest. They swayed gently together for a long time, letting the tears come.

Neither of them spoke.

It was Quinn who broke the silence.

"That picture you gave me. I gave it to a buddy of mine in the Bureau. He had it examined. The dumb fucks left the stationary on the bedside table. Corona Motor Court Inn. We hit the place during the fight."

"Do you have them?"

"One of 'em. One of 'em must a thought he was in a gangster movie, made a dive for his gun. He ain't with us no more."

"Thank you."

"I wouldn't stay here though. These guys are gonna come for you, sure as shit. And her. You got somewhere you two could go for a little while?"

"Yeah," Danny said. "I got somewhere."

"Can you get out tonight?"

Danny nodded. He looked down at Trixie.

"That okay with you?"

She nodded.

A pigeon dropped out of the darkness and rested on the parapet.

"Bluey," Danny said, offering the bird his hand.

Bluey stepped up onto his wrist and he caressed her. Her heart beating wildly.

"It's okay, girl. I got you. I got you."

Danny stared up into the darkness, scanning the moonless night over Hell's Kitchen for other survivors.

None came.

Colin Broderick, originally from County Tyrone, Ireland, has published five books, including the novel, *Church End*.

He has also written and directed a few feature movies, most notably *Emerald City* and *A Bend in the River*, both of which are available on VOD. He lives on the Jersey Shore with his wife and three kids and Charlie, the dog.

Author's Note

Dear reader:

I really do rely on you to spread the word.

If you have enjoyed this book, please do me a huge favor:

1. Post about it on social media. Tag me directly. Or use hashtag #OnceUponATimeinHellsKitchen.

2. Give it a rating, or a review, on Amazon, Goodreads, or elsewhere.

3. Pass it along to a friend, or, better still, buy them a copy, as a gift.

4. Tell a friend about it. Tell all your friends about it.

Every little nudge really helps. And I really do appreciate all of it.

If you'd like to find out more about my books or movies, or, you'd like to buy a signed copy, or, contact me directly, please visit my website:

www.colinbroderick.com

Thank you.
Colin

Acknowledgements

First off, I'd like to thank Director Phil Joanou, who yelled at me when as a young Irishman, fresh in New York City, working construction, I accidentally drove a work van smack-dab into the middle of the raid scene, during the shooting of his movie, *State of Grace*, outside Fanelli's Cafe, in 1989. I think somehow winding up in the middle of that scene, and seeing the camera and the director, yelling, and the actors Sean Penn and Gary Oldman alongside the van laughing at me sitting directly between them and the camera, left a real deep-seated imprint on my soul. It was my first time on a movie set. I have been fascinated with this particular story ever since. Mr. Joanou, if you're reading this, I'd love to see the outtakes if you still have them.

I'd like to thank author T.J. English for his exhaustive research on his book *The Westies*. There's really no way to understand the full extent of that particular chapter of Irish-American crime history, without hearing what T.J. has said on the matter.

I'd also like to thank my old friend, Carl Mazzella, who gave me a place to stay above his Fruit Market on 48th and 9th Ave, at the end of my last big drinking binge in 2006. Even when after I had lost all control, and couldn't pay the rent, he never once lost his patience with me. I'll never forget your kindness or our many nights sitting out front drinking brandy and chatting. Rest easy, my old friend.

I'd like to thank you: The reader. Without you, this whole exercise wouldn't be nearly as rewarding. I really do appreciate you. Thank you for your continued belief and support along the way.

I'd like to thank the handful of early readers of this novel, who gave me encouragement and advice, most notably, my friends: Josh Brolin, Tom McCaffrey, Joe and Diane Andrusaitis, Diana Anderson, John Duddy, and Cameron Crosby. Thank you.

I'd like the thank the two artists who worked on development of this cover: Moses, and, Adeel, and to cover artist, Cheakina, who nailed the final look.

Thank you, Jaye Manus, for your editorial touch, and for formatting this book. I really appreciate your patience and your talent. You really knocked it out of the park.

And lastly, but most importantly, my wife Rachel, who has endured, and supported me, and encouraged me, through every single step of this process. Thank you, my love. I love what we have.